Praise for *Never Meant to Meet You*

"As these neighboring families blend, the authors do a good job exploring the common ground between African American and Jewish experiences: the characters feel like real people with racial and religious identities that inform their worldviews, but don't define them . . . It's an impressive feat sure to move romance fans and women's fiction readers alike."

—*Publishers Weekly*, starred review

"[A] sparkling story of unlikely friendship."

—*Booklist*

"Friendship and romance go hand in hand in this warm, engaging story that should appeal to readers who enjoy novels by Susan Wiggs and Debbie Macomber."

—*Library Journal*

Praise for *Tiny Imperfections*

"Frank and Youmans pack their debut with drama . . . The glitzy, high-stakes world and gossipy narrative voice will put readers in mind of *Crazy Rich Asians*."

—*Publishers Weekly*

"Frank and Youmans' humorous and touching debut novel explores how being a Black woman affects their protagonist's personal and professional experiences in a tale that will resonate with readers of all demographic backgrounds."

—*Booklist*

"Offers a delightful view inside the cutthroat world of private school admissions that is hilarious, cringeworthy, and all too relevant in today's ultracompetitive educational landscape. I ate this book up like a box of candy; you will too."

—Tara Conklin, author of *The Last Romantics*

"*Tiny Imperfections* is a funny, heartwarming take on finding love in a most unexpected place."

—Anissa Gray, author of
The Care and Feeding of Ravenously Hungry Girls

"Parents and anyone who's ever been to school will love this peek into the turbulent world of private school, from two women who have worked in it for more than twenty years. Get to know three generations of Black women in San Francisco as they navigate that universe, along with their relationships, motivations, and a heaping helping of drama."

—*Good Housekeeping*

"Youmans and Frank manage to tackle a woman's journey through work, race, and motherhood beautifully in their debut. *Tiny Imperfections* is laugh-out-loud funny and full of heart. I can't wait to see what they bring us next!"

—Alexa Martin, author of *Fumbled*

"Overeager parents are just one of the many things heroine Josie Bordelon has to deal with as head of admissions for a tawny private school in San Francisco. These two authors are brave enough to expose the insanity and hilarity that happen during application season . . . A really funny read."

—Laurie Gelman, author of *Class Mom*

"Humor, charm, and intriguing drama combine in this novel—written by a best friend author duo—about the competitive world of private education."

—*Woman's World*

"Youmans and Frank's deep dive into private school culture sets the stage for a dishy, charming story of West Coast elitism and parenting at its pushiest. But it's the characters, especially the marvelous Bordelon women, who give this delightful novel its heart and humor—and who make you long to be part of the family even after the last page."

—Amy Poeppel, author of *Small Admissions* and *Limelight*

"Perfectly captures the absurdist bubble of San Francisco's tech upper class. A rollicking good read that reminds us that money, power, and influence will never be enough to make someone truly happy."

—Jo Piazza, author of *Charlotte Walsh Likes to Win*

The
Better
Half

The Better Half

a Novel

Alli Frank & Asha Youmans

MINDY'S BOOK STUDIO

Text copyright © 2023 by Alli and Asha Productions
All rights reserved.

No part of this book may be reproduced, or stored in a retrieval system, or transmitted in any form or by any means, electronic, mechanical, photocopying, recording, or otherwise, without express written permission of the publisher.

Published by Mindy's Book Studio, New York

www.apub.com

Amazon, the Amazon logo, and Mindy's Book Studio are trademarks of Amazon.com, Inc., or its affiliates.

ISBN-13: 9781662512339 (hardcover)
ISBN-13: 9781542034166 (paperback)
ISBN-13: 9781542034173 (digital)

Cover design by Sarah Congdon

Printed in the United States of America

First edition

For Scott and Jeff.
We got it right the first time.

A NOTE FROM MINDY KALING

When was the last time you laughed out loud while reading a novel?

Alli Frank and Asha Youmans's novel *The Better Half* had me LOLing throughout. I was charmed by the story of Nina Morgan Clarke, a woman who is on the cusp of everything she has worked toward for years, and the one-night stand with a man named Leo West that may derail everything . . . in the best possible way.

Nina is just about to start her first year as head of school at a ritzy private school, and she is prepared. As a Black woman, she's confident, cool under pressure, and accustomed to the type of BS that bubbles up in privileged academic spaces. But her life outside school—Leo, and the emotions he reawakens in her—is a new kind of challenge, a new kind of opportunity.

With every surprise thrown Nina's way, I connected with her a little more. With every interaction between Nina and her BFF, Marisol, I wished I could step into the pages and hang out with these two amazing ladies. With every gesture Leo made to win Nina's heart, I melted just a little bit more.

Charming, hilarious, and honest, *The Better Half* celebrates the absurdity and joy in life and does so with grace and heart. I'm so proud to bring Alli Frank and Asha Youmans's dynamic story to Mindy's Book Studio, and to share it with you all.

FIRST TRIMESTER

ONE

I need some sleep, Marisol. I don't care if it's in a bed, on a massage table, or by the pool. Just lay me down and leave me there. You know what I'm saying?" I plead. I'm trying as hard as I can to shed my buttoned-up exterior and loosen up for summer, but it feels like something's stuck in my gears.

"I got you, Nina, I got you! Chilling only, promise. Check my bag, I even brought a book." Marisol, my Mexican sister from another mister, nods to her purse on the passenger floor by my feet. Now I know she's lying.

I dig through this season's got-to-have-it handbag with custom clip-on strap. "Four back issues of *People* magazine do not make a book," I tease.

"It does if you include the *Vanity Fair* that's in my suitcase. Those articles are hella long." Marisol lays her foot heavy on the gas, taking advantage of a rare stretch of light traffic on Highway 101 heading north toward Santa Barbara. The rule follower in me wants to point out that she's pushing eighty miles per hour, but I bite my tongue. Wind sneaks in from the edges of Marisol's drop-top sports car, a fortieth birthday present to herself. My box braids are barely tousled, and it's a good thing too; I spent six hours in the salon chair to have my hair handled for the entire weekend. I can't wait to curl up by the pool and pleasure read with a stack of real novels I've been dying to devour. I know I'll be the one up at 6:30 a.m. laying down towels and sunhats to claim a prime poolside spot. Marisol's more rise and shine by nine.

I reach out to add some tunes to the ride. Marisol spares no expense when it comes to her car's system. She's got sound that bumps.

I turn the bass up and select The Notorious B.I.G.'s "Going Back to Cali." The catchy hook on this West Coast tribute track takes me there, and I sneak a peek at Marisol to see what she thinks of my selection.

"You are *so* weird. You're the only grown woman I know who makes heading to a bougie resort in a printed kaftan, blasting gangsta rap, look normal," Marisol says, shaking her head no but smiling yes. "But heyyy! This is my song!"

"You mind if I close my eyes? I just need to catch a minute of sleep." Not waiting for an answer, I recline my seat back as far as it will go, then slip my feet out of my sandals and put them up on the dashboard, my toes enjoying the cool of the windshield. These are my last days of personal freedom before my life's consumed by my first year running the show at the Royal-Hawkins School.

Two years ago, Allister Nevins, the thirteenth headmaster of the Royal-Hawkins School, announced that after nineteen years at the helm, he would finish the twenty-four months left on his contract and then retire to his beloved English countryside. I knew my moment had arrived. I had kept my head down, worked hard, focused, and played my academic and professional cards right my whole life. Reputable colleges, check. Distinguished high school science teacher position and department chair, check, check. Upper school academic deanship riding teenage procrastinators right into top universities. Check, check, check. And most recently, seven years as assistant head of the Royal-Hawkins School, otherwise known as the on-campus punching bag for all personnel and parents. One big fat check.

No doubt, after Headmaster Nevins's retirement announcement, my calculated hustle would land me squarely where I wanted to be: a viable candidate for the head of school position. Or so I thought.

After a few days of immense encouragement and enthusiasm from individual members, the board informed me that I had little chance among the field of applicants they were expecting unless I earned a doctorate immediately. They wanted the trifecta (a woman, a first-generation American, and a person of color) with a trifecta. Which meant that on top of my BA from Wellesley and MA from Columbia Teachers College, I now had to earn my doctorate in education. I suspected that if I made it to the final round interview, and the board of trustees chose me, they'd want all qualifications among candidates to be equal. No tokenism here! I get it. It's called covering their corporate ass.

What followed the board's mandate was two years of me pulling hundred-hour workweeks. As assistant head, I ran Royal-Hawkins while Headmaster Nevins spent his last days focused on his farewell tour and mansplaining the school's alarm system to me, which I've been successfully arming for years. Professionally, I had my administrative duties to tend to plus taking on my final degree at UCLA in the evenings and on the weekends. Personally, I was busy raising my daughter, Xandra, and prepping her to apply to Pemberley, the boarding school outside New York City her father had attended, for her freshman year of high school. I was spent. For those two years my entire world was consumed by Google Docs. And then a week ago, after what seemed like a lifetime of going and doing and stressing, it all came to an end. In one day, I had picked Xandra up from LAX at the end of her freshman year, moved my Bruins tassel from the right to the left, wheeled boxes into my new office, and sent out my first *Message from the Head of School* to families and alumni of Royal-Hawkins. I expertly hid my woes of middle-age exhaustion and feelings of impostor syndrome from the school community. Now it is time to celebrate my accomplishments with Marisol. Despite our close bond, we tend to differ in our definitions of *revelry*. I know Marisol's packing pot gummies in her purse, whereas I have chewable melatonin.

"Wake me up a few minutes before we get there. I don't want the valet to catch me drooling on myself." I lick the corners of my mouth to start clean.

"Oh, I see how it is. You're worried what other folks think, but you're okay looking all raggedy for me. I've been waiting for this girls' weekend for forever, so you better be ready to turn it out!" Marisol nudges my knee and blows me a kiss with her pouty, apple-red glossed lips. I know she's excited to have me all to herself for the next couple of days after an extensive girls' night out drought, other than our monthly afternoon spa dates. Buried in life or not, we both agree: after forty, we have to do the work necessary to keep ourselves pulled together given our public-facing jobs.

I doze in and out, and when salty air tickles my nose I can tell we're nearing the Pacific Ocean. Marisol pats my arm and announces, "Freshen up, girlfriend. We're five minutes away."

"I can't wait to check out the hotel's room service menu. You think they have wedge salad?" I ask, bringing the seat back upright.

"I thought you wanted to go pure monastic this weekend. All sprouts, lean proteins, and not talking to anybody but me."

"I believe salad *is* comfort spa food. Iceberg lettuce slathered in blue cheese and bacon . . . yum. But you're right, my plan for the rest of the evening is straight to the room, robe on, full Buddhist. Dinner in bed cooked by somebody other than me and surfing free streaming options is my idea of enlightenment."

"I don't think Buddhists eat meat."

"Hey, don't eff up my plan with a technicality."

"You better have brought something sexy to wear. You know, just in case we decide to leave the room," Marisol tosses out, looking for our turn so she doesn't have to make eye contact with me. "I didn't use a weekend hall pass from Jaime and my monsters to play backgammon in bed with you all night."

Damn, I knew it. And I know her. Marisol avoiding eye contact is my hint that my best friend has plans of her own, and there will be no fondling the remote in my future. I suppose I can start to correct the damage done to my circadian rhythm from all my degree gathering when I get home.

We unload our bags at the hotel, and Marisol decides we're going to get cute and hit the lounge before the evening rush. Within thirty minutes of our arrival, a crowd has already formed a human fence around the bar, so we choose a table close to the retractable wall of windows open to the ocean. Settled and in need of cocktails, we resort to a tried-and-true method of choosing who will wade into the fray for drinks.

"One. Two. Three. Shoot. One. Two. Three. Shoot. Paper covers rock twice, you lose!" Marisol howls triumphantly while I stifle a yawn. You'd think I'd be better at this game. It's how Xandra and I determine who gets to decide takeout on weekends.

Marisol stretches her bare chestnut arms up in victory, a joyous smile radiating across her face. She projects her voice above the hum of the bar so I'm sure to hear her order correctly. "Margarita, blended, light salt, twist of lime, half straw." I feel like a Starbucks barista. "Thank YOU! Now go, go, go, *Mami's* looking good and feeling parched!"

I wish I could say Marisol's a gracious winner, but I have thirty-five years of evidence to the contrary. We first met when she schooled me at double Dutch on the asphalt strip between our apartment buildings in Queens but then felt so bad for gloating that she shared her TWIX bar. She's a competitive bitch with a conscience.

"Aren't we supposed to be celebrating me this weekend? You should be hustling the drinks," I declare, standing up and smoothing down my sleeveless turquoise wrap dress. Peering across the bar, I see I'll have to fight my way through an unexpected cross section of a wedding party catching a buzz the night before the nuptials and a conference group undoubtedly drinking heavily to forget a blistering day spent listening to PowerPoint presentations.

"I probably should but . . . nah! You lost fair and square." Marisol waves me onward to chart my solo course to Margaritaville.

"Sorry. Sorry. So sorry." I excuse my way through the millennials sporting bandage dresses to reach the lounge bar at the Biltmore. I spy a sliver of space in between two men ignoring one another, both fixated on getting the lone bartender's attention.

"Excuse me. 'Scuse me. Sorry. Sorry. Just. Trying. To get. In here." I suck in my breath, wedge myself between the two men, and smile sheepishly at the guy on my left when my boobs graze against his upper arm. Sensing a new competitor has entered the fray, he eyes me up and down. I can't hold it in any longer, I blow out my breath in his face. "Sorry." I wince.

"No problem." Leering guy laughs. "But I have to warn you that your effort to get here and snag a spot may not have been worth it. I've been waiting for the bartender for ten minutes. Last round took me twenty to get drinks. Maybe with you here I'll have better luck."

I nod, not wanting to be rude, but also hoping to avoid chitchat. I have a full school year of that coming up in two months. I'm here to get in, order cocktails, and get out. Fingers crossed I can coax Marisol into taking this margarita to go . . . to our room. Making small talk with a random White dude in a spiffy suit is not on my evening's agenda.

"If you can get in your order and mine in the next three minutes, I'll buy for the both of us. I'm failing miserably here. So's he." The slick suit nods to the guy on my other side, who I can only assume is a groomsman given the back-and-forth bro banter with a posse of dressed-up surfers hovering behind him.

"You don't have to do that," I say, hoping he'll take the hint that I prefer to mind my own business and buy my own drinks. I look over my shoulder in an attempt to catch Marisol's eye and get her over here to save me. She's busy chatting up a mother of the bride type sitting erect, wrapped in a pastel shawl, at the cocktail table next to ours. In thirty seconds or less, Marisol will have slipped this woman her Clean Slate business card and gotten her to crack a smile. She can spot a woman with an expensive beauty regimen anywhere.

"Please let me, that way I won't feel like such an ass for standing here this long just to order a club soda and lime." The suit laughs and runs his hand along his slightly stubbled jawline, and I find myself appreciating his strong chin. After initially avoiding eye contact, I now notice that conference guy's hazelnut-hued eyes and absurdly long dark lashes are pretty fantastic. So's his honesty.

"Don't you drink?" I can't help but ask. Not that I really care about his alcohol habits, but why anyone over the age of thirty would be sober in this sardine-packed bar does pique my interest a little.

"Someone has to remain standing to take care of the first-year associates while they puke in the azalea bushes at midnight. I pulled the short partner stick." I was right, total conference guy. "Plus, I drank too much last night, myself. I'm still recovering, so be gentle with me."

"That's awfully responsible of you." My eager bar buddy subtly tips his head and delivers a half smile in acknowledgment of the middle-age compliment. Smooth. "The taking care of your associates part, not the nursing a raging hangover at your age part." I want him to know I'm not that easily impressed.

"Understood." We both laugh, and I rack my brain trying to remember the last time I even semiflirted in a bar. It had to be pre-Graham. Since our divorce, the few dates I've had have been fix ups through friends; the bar scene is alien to me. "The offer still stands. You help out a recovering man no longer in his boozing prime but still in the throes of last night's regret, and I'll buy the drinks."

I'm not sure if it's the dim of the bar, his easy banter, or the past few years when the only men I encountered were professors, fathers, or colleagues that prompts me to lighten up. I give my sober companion the same obvious once-over he gave me minutes before. He moves from leaning over the bar to standing up straight, aware of exactly what I'm doing. He even does a tight turn in our small space, so I get a glimpse from all angles. Confident. I like it.

"My name's Nina, and you're too old to have regrets," I offer in a mock scolding. So schoolmarm of me. The bartender finally moves toward us, taking away my new friend's attention. I hope I'm not left awkwardly hanging with half an introduction. We're passed over for the brosman ordering multiple shots of something that will surely light his insides on fire.

We both chuckle at our invisibility. Twenties trumping forties. "Nice to meet you, Nina. I'm Leo. And while I regret waiting this long for overpriced water, I don't regret meeting you."

Swipe.
Swipe.
Swipe.
Swipe.

"Look at you, having a *homent*," Marisol accuses, opening our room door looking smug, catching me in the five-star hotel walk of shame. "Struggling with your hand-eye coordination this morning?" She looks rested and is wearing the plush hotel robe I had been dreaming of, the smell of maple smoked sausage encasing her like a breakfast angel. I, on the other hand, look delirious and am wearing the scent of a one-night stand with a total stranger. "You gonna share where you've been with . . ."

"Leo. His name's Leo." I giggle into my hand like a fifteen-year-old whose crush just walked by her locker. I'm eager to get out of these clothes, brush my teeth, and chug the carafe of coffee I spy over Marisol's shoulder, but she's blocking the door to our room.

"Leo. And are we going to have to play twenty questions and end up late for our facials, or are you going to give it up easily to me this morning just like you did last night with Leo? You know I'll be pissed if I get shortchanged on my HydraFacial waiting on you to spill it."

"You get one question. The rest of the deets by the pool after our treatments, *if* I have the strength to relive all the work me and Leo put in!" I smile and hug myself by the elbows, squirming in my clothes as I recall the feel of Leo's hands rubbing all over me last night. And this morning. "I have to shower before we head to the spa. I don't need some judgy aesthetician deciding she smells marathon sex sweating out my pores."

"Seriously? Only one question now?" Marisol fake whines and places a hand on her hip in defiance of my boundaries.

"One question, so make it a good one." I stand frozen, waiting for whatever lecherous detail Marisol is going to ask for in the hallway of this reputable hotel.

"I wanna know just how high that vanilla cone stacked up after a lifetime of chocolate."

I'm sitting by the pool, sipping a tall iced tea, trying to read my book. Too distracted with memories from last night to focus, I instead sneak a voice mail check-in at school before Marisol shows up and calls me on our "no phones weekend" pact. July 1 is technically my first official day as head of school, and I don't want to blow it out of the gate by missing an important communication.

Whew, only one voice mail, and not surprisingly, it's from Courtney Dunn. Every year, without fail, before she and her family trek off to the trendiest exotic locale according to *Travel + Leisure*, she lets me know the exact lineup of teachers she wants for her daughter, Daisy, and her stepson, Ben. And every year, I politely refer her to page 46 of the parent handbook containing the school's policy on requesting teachers. It's a not-so-fun annual game of control freak cat and uptight mouse we play. This year, however, Courtney has added a new twist. In addition to ranking her faculty favorites, she's also asking to join the Royal-Hawkins board of trustees. I take a moment to consider it. That would be a no. I know I'll hear from Courtney the minute the Dunns return stateside, so I'm not going to waste my precious pool time worrying about her. I cheers my self-restraint with a last chug of iced tea and flag down the pool boy making his rounds.

Ding.

I look left and right to see if Marisol's glowing face is strutting toward our chaise longues before I check my texts. Xandra knows phone warden Marisol put me on a tech diet, so I'm not sure who it could be.

261 252 8600 12:20 PM

> Are you having as hard a time concentrating today as I am?

Who is this? I don't recognize the number on the caller ID. I start to write back *wrong number*, then stop myself. Wait, did I give Leo my info last night? Or this morning? I don't remember doing it, but a few new things happened in the last twenty-four hours, so today anything's possible. I was channeling a version of myself I hadn't seen in quite some time. Maybe one of my other personalities sleeps with White guys and gives away her digits.

Nina 12:20 PM

Is this Leo?

261 252 8600 12:21 PM

It is.

Nina 12:21 PM

How'd you get my number?

. . .

Ugh, the dreaded three dots. Waiting for a text response is the worst, particularly when the response could be a humiliating one.

261 252 8600 12:22 PM

> I ran into your friend Marisol in the lobby. She chewed me out for ruining her girls' weekend. Then she yanked the pen out of my shirt pocket and wrote your number on my hand.

Of course she did.

Nina 12:23 PM

> You carry pens in your pocket? That's not sexy.

Whoosh.

AHHHH. Get it back, get it back. I want that text back! Why'd I call him out for not being sexy?! Damn trigger finger.

261 252 8600 12:23 PM

> That's not what you said last night. Besides, I'm a corporate lawyer at an employment conference. Something's bound to be unsexy about me. But you . . . you look incredible in that off-the-shoulder yellow swimsuit. I think the pool boy tripped over his hormones on his way to refill your iced tea.

I drop my phone and survey every inch of the pool patio. I don't see Leo. Or I don't recognize him. God, I hope my thighs are looking more J. Lo than Jell-O. Please let me maintain my self-respect and spot the man I let crawl all over me within hours of meeting.

Nina 12:25 PM

> How do you know I'm wearing a yellow swimsuit?

261 252 8600 12:25 PM

How do you not see me? I'm the one looking ridiculously overdressed in a blazer and slacks standing by the towel station. Or do you not recognize me?

I look directly behind me toward the towel stand. Leo gives me a warm smile and a thumbs-up.

261 252 8600 12:26 PM

Nice job, Sherlock.

Nina 12:26 PM

Come over here, pressed button-down and all. I'll buy you a drink this time.

261 252 8600 12:26 PM

Can't. I have to head back for my 12:30 session on updates in wage and hour law. But before I go, one question for you. What are you doing next weekend?

Nina 12:27 PM

Depends on how good the offer is.

261 252 8600 12:27 PM

Want to go to Yosemite with me?

Shit. This guy thinks Black people camp.

Nina 12:28 PM

For safety reasons, I should probably know your last name and have you buy me dinner before I willingly follow you into the woods.

261 252 8600 12:28 PM

West.

Nina 12:29 PM

Don't you want to know mine?

261 252 8600 12:30 PM

I already do Nina Morgan Clarke.

TWO

This is not how this was supposed to go. I pull into the only parking spot I can find after circling the block four times. My back bumper hangs a foot into Leo's neighbor's driveway—the Silver Lake equivalent of felony trespassing. The day before school starts is predictably crazy, but I got to my office at 6:00 a.m. thinking if I arrived early, I could sneak away in the middle of the day while the teachers were working in their classrooms. Mimi, my assistant, said she'd have my back if anyone came looking for me. After ten years working under Headmaster Nevins, whose trademark communication style was reserved and efficient at best, she's enjoying a shift in main office atmosphere. Mimi's consistently ten steps ahead of where I have no idea I need to be, and my gratitude for her is endless. Every morning, I show up with two piping-hot lattes. I need to keep Mimi motivated on the ass-saving front through my first year as head of school. Second year I'm in charge, she can hang me out to dry for not knowing better. But this afternoon the fire chief showed up unexpectedly to test our sprinkler system, and even Mimi couldn't get me out the door.

"I'm sorry, I'm sorry, I'm so sorry." My relationship with Leo started with me apologizing at the Biltmore eight weeks ago. Now it's the end of August, and our summer affair is headed for a similar fate as I hurry over to Leo and his mix of suitcases and duffel bags littering the sidewalk. I'm late and attempting to look suitably apologetic, while his mound of luggage reminds me just how long he'll be gone. A charley horse from too little water during back-to-back meetings seizes my left leg. "Ow, ow, ow . . ." I grab my hamstring midgallop, and my gait turns into an awkward limp. I hope my apology and my pain will elicit some sort of forgiveness on Leo's part. Given the folded arms across his chiseled pecs and the look on his face, I'm not giving myself winning odds.

Today's the day Leo told me about two weeks ago, after we had spent more of our summer nights together than apart. Following work I would rush home, strip out of my master of the universe outfit that was some version of a sundress that stopped below my knees but bared my shoulders in the Pasadena summer heat, and throw on shorts, a tank top, and strappy sandals. Leo and I would meet in central LA so my father, Fitzroy, or Xandra wouldn't discover us. And so we were closer to Leo's house when the warm evenings and the giddiness from a couple of glasses of wine sent us tumbling into Leo's bed. I was always sure to make it home before Xandra's curfew.

That evening in mid-August, while I was perusing the menu to determine if we were still hungry enough to order a second round of sushi, I asked a question every woman should be cautious of when in the midst of a new relationship. "So, what are you thinking?" I was hoping Leo was going to say he was thinking about ordering more *hamachi toro*. Instead, he closed his menu.

"I'm thinking I have to tell you something," Leo admitted, fiddling with his chopsticks. I knew right then the something had nothing to do with sushi, and my appetite sank. "I've had an amazing time with you this summer but . . ."

Jesus, not the *but*. At forty-three I'm too old for the *but*. The *but* is a young woman's game. I'm supposed to be past the long, drawn-out explanation that always circles back around to the universal, *it's not you, it's me*. Or worse, there is a wife waiting in the wings. I didn't want to hear Leo's lengthy explanation in an effort to spare my feelings. I prayed he would end it quickly so I could at least walk out of the restaurant with enough dignity to fit into my clutch.

As I looked around the dining room, I was thankful we were eating in Brentwood and not Pasadena where a Royal-Hawkins family might witness their spanking-new head of school being publicly dumped. Tears do not elicit confidence. And then there was the matter of my lucky star necklace on Leo's nightstand. Xandra gave it to me. How was I going to get it back?

Leo canted his head left to grab my attention and my eyes. "At the end of this month I'm moving to Singapore to open an office for Smith, Bodie, and Strong. It's been in the works for about eighteen months."

So, it's not me, exactly. Hooray! Sort of. I took a long drink of ice-cold water to buy myself a moment to think. What I probably should have done was a shot of sake. "And you're telling me this now rather than, say, before the camping trip when you made me sleep on dirt and eat dehydrated noodles because?" While my body was in the conversation, my brain was busy catching on that this was simply another way of saying Leo was leaving, and we were done. I had my phone in my lap, ready to call Marisol so she could meet me at my house and let me cry all over her. If she and I had ordered room service at the Biltmore like I'd wanted, I wouldn't be here, being broken up with right before school started.

"Because this"—Leo pointed back and forth between the two of us—"or I should say because these past six weeks have been so much fun, Nina. And so, so . . ."

"Poorly timed?"

"I was going to say wonderful. Truly wonderful. I never expected it," Leo said endearingly.

It's true. My first summer concert ever at the Hollywood Bowl, we sat fourth row center. And wine tasting in Ojai for the weekend was delicious in every way imaginable. But it was weeks later while walking down the street, Leo assuredly holding my hand, that I took notice for the first time that being with him felt comfortable, even natural. I assumed he would want to be more inconspicuous, to avoid potential judgmental stares. Instead, he seemed not to notice or care what people thought about us being together. In fact, one of the things that deepened my attraction to Leo was that he so boldly inhabited his space, and with him, so did I.

"I'm conflicted here, Nina. I've been on this project to open an office in the Asian Pacific since it was barely an idea years ago. And I've been focused on bringing it to completion no matter what. While all my friends have been busy raising their kids, this has kind of been like my kid." Interesting, I'd never heard Leo talk about kids other than to humor me when I shared story after story about Xandra.

"Sure, I thought I would bump into problems with my visa or renting an apartment overseas, but I never imagined it might be a woman getting in my way of crossing the ocean. But it's not forever, Nina, just four or so months." Leo laid it all out there like the time would pass in the blink of an eye rather than acknowledging that he would be gone twice as long as we had been together.

I didn't want to admit it, but I understood Leo's commitment to his career. He had been working tirelessly to make his professional dream come true just as I had been meticulously laying the groundwork for years so I could someday be right where I was, head of school.

As I stared at Leo across the table, taking in this change in our trajectory, I worked to convince myself that his leaving and giving us both an easy out was probably a good move overall. The past months our visible differences in ethnicity and background were pushed aside, or, more accurately, ignored because of how hot we kept it in the bedroom. Having cheated on my personal self with my professional self the past two years, I told Marisol I was in it for the sex, plus, I would never actually date a White guy. I had never dated one before, nor did the idea take up any space on my bucket list. But then Leo gave me an incredible midlife summer of love, and our budding affair along with my new job were positive signs, so I thought that maybe the second half of my life would be the best half of my life. Now, facing our realities,

I could see Leo's profession would always come first, a male tale I was all too familiar with.

"I want to have a memorable last two weeks with you and, if you're up for it, we could make a go of it long distance. You're the best thing to happen to me in a long time, Nina. I want to see how this goes."

I remember smiling at Leo, touched by his naivete at how difficult this would be, but agreeing to try, not wanting to crush his optimism. My cynical side gave it three weeks.

His days would be my nights, and I love my sleep. An ocean away, Leo would be buried in opening a law office, and at home I would be buried in opening a school year. Leo would always be White. And I would always be Black. Add that to a host of other differences between us, and the distance seemed insurmountable. Right there, over soy-soaked wasabi, I was positive we'd fizzle out sooner rather than later.

Being late to take him to the airport today was not part of my plan to send Leo off to Singapore with an unforgettable goodbye. Reaching his side slightly sweaty, out of breath, and muttering "Sorry" is next-level tragic. Leo looks like he might dump me by takeoff.

"Nina, I told you if you couldn't take me to the airport today, it's no big deal, I'd grab an Uber. I've called you five times, and you didn't even pick up your phone." Leo's jaw is clenched, and he's pointing at the time on his watch. Late to get Leo, I ran out of Royal-Hawkins so fast I left my phone on my desk. This is not how I wanted our last hour together to be.

"You're twenty minutes late, and you know how I feel about being rushed for the airport. Especially flying international." To be fair to me, Leo and I have not flown together, so I've yet to see his type A travel habits in action. We'd only talked about the possibility of going somewhere someday.

Leo opens his hand, palm up, in a signal to hand over the key fob. He pops the trunk and in eight swift moves loads his luggage. Instead of giving me the keys so I can drive him to the airport and wish him bon voyage with a rom-com-worthy kiss, I'm met with, "Get in. I'll drive."

In the passenger seat, I don't know what to do with my hands. Leo grips the steering wheel in a way that doesn't look like he wants to hold one of them. Minutes tick by without us exchanging a word.

"Let's call Marisol, I want to say goodbye to her," Leo says, softening a bit, and points to his cell phone on the center console. Marisol's always my best asset.

"I'm pretty sure she's in meetings all afternoon, but I know she'd love a voice mail from you," I offer.

"Never mind. I'll shoot her a text from the airport. This morning she texted and bet me twenty dollars you'd be late picking me up. I told her no way; you'd want every last moment you could possibly squeeze out of me."

Jeez, is Leo not going to let this one go before he gets on a plane and leaves me?

"So, you need to pay her twenty bucks. I'm not forking over cash for your bad habits," he teases. The sides of Leo's mouth turn up slightly, and I sense him relaxing.

"Funny, you don't call my lateness a bad habit when I'm tardy to work so we can get in a morning quickie," I throw out, hoping a little humor from my end will be well received. Leo booms out a hearty laugh, and just like that I'm done with driver's detention.

"You know we're going to have to get creative with me in Singapore and you in Pasadena, right?" Leo winks at me as he accelerates through the last yellow light to make it to the freeway on-ramp.

"I don't know how creative I can be in my office. When you'll be getting home in the evenings, I'll be arriving at work. I can't get freaky in the main office; Mimi has impeccable hearing."

"I said creative, not loud," Leo informs, reaching over to unbutton the top of my blouse for a peek at my lacy lavender bra. "I want to see these lovelies on screen." Clumsily, Leo fondles my boobs from the driver's seat with his right hand. The guy's left-handed.

"You focus and drive right, and maybe you can get a last peep show in short-term parking." The fact that in twenty minutes he'll be gone is beginning to sting my eyes and cause a catch in my throat.

As we exit for Los Angeles International Airport, Leo's hands are back on the steering wheel to maneuver the lanes. "No time to park. I'm going to pull right up to the terminal. You wait with the car while I run and grab a cart. If any of those airport parking hounds gives you trouble, tell them to sit tight, I'll be right back." Clearly, Leo doesn't know Black folks don't mess with people in uniform.

"Okay," I mumble. Leo's gone into operational mode whiplash fast. I need a bit more physical connection with him, I'm already missing being curled up in bed playing with his thick dark hair. But the moment has passed. Or at least, it's passed for Leo.

Chucking me the keys, Leo hops out of the car like a kid starting the first day of a new school year full of possibilities. I slowly get out, pop the trunk, and struggle to pull even the smallest of Leo's bags out it's so stinking heavy. It feels like he's moving away for forever.

Running back with a cart, Leo rides it the last fifty feet like the excited man-child he's transformed into before my eyes. I hold the cart while he loads the luggage. Leo unearthed the woman in me that had been laying low since my divorce five years ago, and for that I'm grateful. Right now, that woman sure would like to continue getting some action from this tall, toned, self-possessed man swinging luggage in front of her, but I tell myself how lucky I was to have the past couple of months. I had an unexpected summer surprise that I should be thankful for rather than resentful that it's ending because now, with Leo gone, I can put all my focus on the students and families at Royal-Hawkins. And that's a good thing. Really.

Too soon, the bags are loaded, and there's nothing left to do but say our goodbyes. I tug at a rogue thread on Leo's cuff, not sure who should be the first to say whatever needs to be said to try to make this grim moment less painful.

Leo adjusts the top duffel, making sure it's secure. His hands are calloused for a lawyer, one of the first things I noticed as he deftly undid the tie on my turquoise dress in his room at the Biltmore. I'm going to miss those hands something awful. Leo turns to me, hooking his arms around my waist, pulling me close. "Nina Morgan Clarke, it's been one hell of a summer." I nod my head in agreement. The only way I can keep my composure is if I don't speak. "We are two smart people insanely attracted to one another," Leo says, planting a lingering kiss on my lips. "We can make up our own rules on how to do us." I'm pretty sure the rules of long-distance mean talking on average three point five times a week, and even then, the probability of us lasting is nil. "Anything's possible for us, Nina."

I clear my throat and unhook Leo's arms from around my waist. I need the moment to end, this is already too hard. I have a school to get back to running and a daughter to parent. The real world is calling me back to claim my place.

"You're right," I say, kissing Leo on the cheek. I whisper into his ear, "It's been a hell of a summer." I take one last look at Leo, turn, and head back to school.

THREE

FROM: Courtney Dunn
DATE: August 30
SUBJECT: new year, new start for all
TO: Nina Morgan Clarke

Dear Nina,

I left you a voice mail at the end of the school year, but never heard back. Writing today to say I hope your summer was as invigorating and purpose-driven as the Dunns'! I'm sure you know, last year in first grade Daisy showed a real passion for oceanography. Serendipitously, the children's piano teacher, Adia, was going to Costa Rica to help her sister who was having a baby. So, I decided we would all fly there, and Daisy, Geoff, and I would submerge ourselves in some global volunteerism while Adia helped her sister with the newborn (sadly my stepson, Benjamin, couldn't join us, he was in Provence with his mother). The envirotainment program our travel consultant found housed us in a dreamy beachfront villa and came with a chef who made us incredible plantains morning, noon, and night. The whole experience really connected us to the dire need for ocean conservation. And bonus, Adia was close by so she could babysit in the evenings, and Geoff and I got to go out and have some fun *pura vida* style!

A little bird told me you scored big and hired the number-one draft choice for the middle school history teacher and basketball coach. We can't wait to meet him. Benjamin is over the moon about his new coach, and trust me, at 12, he's not over the moon about much.

Summer catch-up aside, I'm writing to tell you Geoff and I are beyond thrilled Daisy is attending Royal-Hawkins under the leadership of its first Black head of school. Being a sixth Latina myself, diversity is so important to us. I now feel Daisy will have a stronger voice in her school community, and I know all the parents of color feel as I do; comforted their children have a head of school who will prioritize their well-being.

As I mentioned in my June voice mail, I'm excited to join Royal-Hawkins's board of trustees and provide some much-needed diversity to the group. With the Dunn family's leadership level of giving and my experience running a robust life coaching practice, I know I can bring great insight and strategic direction to the school.

Jai,
Courtney

This has to be a head of school record, I think to myself as I rest my forehead on my keyboard, chin dangling off the desk. The cool of the space bar soothes my skin. My left hand feels around for the wastebasket under my desk. Located, I draw it directly into my sight line. I might need it before my first board of trustees meeting in ninety minutes and counting. You would think I'd have an ironclad immune system after twenty years working with teenagers, but damn if I didn't make a rookie mistake last week by shaking hands with every incoming middle school student on the first day of orientation. Germy tweens. I couldn't help myself, though. I love this age of firsts—first pimple, first pube, first period. I've always been partial to kids who are old enough to pack their own lunch and can write a solid five-paragraph essay.

Without looking up, I use my right hand to search the desktop for my cell phone. I can text for reinforcements without moving my head.

Nina 4:26 PM

Sol, happy first day of school. I'm sick.

I can't believe I had to start my first day of school at the helm sick. From 8:00 a.m. to 4:00 p.m. I duct-taped myself together with iron will and desperation and feigned great excitement for the fresh start that every school year brings. I think I sold my fake enthusiasm well. Since 4:22 p.m., though, I've been sequestered in my office staring down the barrel of a metal trash can. My whole career, hell my whole childhood, has been leading to this exact day, and all I have to show for it is a growing fever and nausea. Maybe I'm lovesick.

My brother, Clive, is two years older than me, and the morning my mother, my father, and I took him to his first day of kindergarten was one of the worst days of my life. I still remember it clearly because when I was a kid, my father only took a handful of days off work, and two of them were for my brother's first day of school and for mine. I thought my mother had borrowed the itchy plaid wool dress I wore that day so I, too, could go to school. After all, I matched Clive's crisp white button-down, blue V-neck sweater, and miniature tie my parents made him wear despite the eighty-degree weather. Turns out there's no such thing as a summer and winter uniform when your immigrant parents are busting their behinds to make ends meet. Clive and I simply wore my mother's version of dressing on a dime.

At the new kindergarten family coffee on Clive's first day of school, my parents stood in the corner of the classroom, also dressed in their Sunday best. The way they tell it, the year before they had been in church when a handsome young man, fresh from his graduation from Princeton and brimming with potential, was invited to the pulpit to speak. He was just like us, from Queens with working-class parents from Jamaica who also had big plans for their children's futures. When he spoke, my mother took notes on the back of a grocery list she had fished out of her pocketbook. In large block letters, underlined, she wrote down COLLEGIATE SCHOOL. From that day on, in her mind, there was no other education option for Clive. My folks had no clue how difficult it was for the privileged sons of New York to get into Collegiate, and even less of an idea who Clive was competing against. Mom just believed she wanted it more than any other mother out there. Getting her son into a good school was nothing compared to her efforts to get herself and my father into America.

That first day of school, Mom and Dad were more relieved to have found a path for their son into such a storied institution than intimidated by the foreign culture of New York's Upper West Side. Clive was the one stuck in it for the next thirteen years. In the brief time they had been in America, my parents felt luck had been on their side. They applied my brother to private school with that same optimism, never considering Clive might not fit in or excel. In our home there was one thing my immigrant parents were convinced of: that their children were capable of high achievement.

The ancient director of admissions had reluctantly shared during an early tour of Collegiate that the board of trustees was encouraging a little more color in the school's sea of white. Naturally, our parents threw Clive right into the deep. Clive was the only brown-skinned boy in his kindergarten class. Even with best intentions at play in the early eighties, schools across the country had yet to figure out that perhaps their lone Black student might need a few peers to pal around with and maybe an adult or two to have his back on campus.

At the time, I don't think my parents were worried about Clive and his lack of familiar playmates. For a couple of Jamaicans who only had the opportunity to complete their primary education, they believed they had managed the American dream successfully. The childhood Clive and I had, compared to how our parents grew up, made it difficult for them to sympathize with the challenges of race and poverty in America. They figured the hopes they had for their son were sure to come true if Clive worked as hard as they did.

While my folks dreamed of Clive's future life as an engineer or doctor, I, too, felt like I was in a dream. When my brother ran off to join some other boys on the playfield, unimpressed with any academic offerings indoors, I walked around the classroom touching every pencil, running my fingers along the spine of every book on the low shelves, deciding my favorite color on the circle rug where I would sit when the teacher rang the bell.

When it was time for families to leave, the expectation was that a few skittish students would melt down. The teacher was experienced at tactics to overcome separation anxiety and stood at the ready for attempted escapees who sprinted after their parents. What no one expected—particularly my parents, for whom appearance and propriety were everything—was the little sister, me, becoming an unmovable force because I did not get to stay. When I realized the purpose of my dress was so I would look presentable dropping my brother off and that the three of us were leaving, I was inconsolable.

Even at age three, I knew I had found my place: school. It was where I would most fit in, where I would spend the rest of my life, first as a student, then as a teacher, and finally as an administrator. I loved school before I was even allowed to attend. It was a long two-year stretch, spent teaching my dolls how to read and coercing neighborhood kids to sit in straight rows to recite the alphabet in call and response, before my parents pulled off a second education feat. I got to start kindergarten at the Spence School for girls on the polished streets of the Upper East Side of Manhattan. In the quarter century my parents lived in the United States, they had faced down plenty of adversity AND gotten two kids into the most coveted private schools in New York City, followed by top colleges and graduate programs. You couldn't tell Fitzroy and Celia Morgan they didn't make it in America.

Forty years after my tantrum on the kindergarten rug, my love for schools endures. At this moment, however, given my crushed heart and fluish symptoms, my social and emotional bandwidths are limited to people under eighteen years old. Parents like Courtney Dunn grate on my nerves. I need a minute to talk to Marisol, so I don't end up calling Courtney back and leaving a voice mail with something like . . .

Courtney, just because you made tasty nachos at last year's Cuisine of Many Cultures night does not make you any more Latina than my killer Moscow mules make me Russian.

God, I'd love to do it, but what if she actually picks up?

I check my phone to see if Marisol's responded yet. Apparently, my text isn't interesting enough for her to bother lifting a thumb. Waiting for Marisol to hit me back, I start and delete several texts to Leo to find out if I infected him for his first day of work. I give it a second thought because other than texting *landed,* Leo hasn't reached out, and complaining about being sick is so not hot. I'm already missing our easy banter, but I don't have it in me to be clever about feeling crappy, so instead I put out a second siren call to Marisol.

Nina 4:48 PM

> Just like Tag Team, Whoomp There It Is! Told you!! Courtney named me the FIRST BLACK. I knew it was only a matter of time before she emailed. Call me, ASAP. No wait . . . read email from Courtney first then holla so we can rip it . . . I mean her apart.

Being sick gives me a nasty attitude.

Any opportunity for a poetic performance or a musical reference and I'll take it. My dad, a novice patois poet, instilled in me a love of colorful wordplay that I enjoy weaving into my daily life. I forward Courtney's predictable email to Marisol and rest my head back on my desk. Mimi has gone home for the day, so if this is truly my end, it's unclear who will find me before morning and who'll be the unlucky one to share the bad news with Xandra at Pemberley.

My cell phone buzzes across my desk. Goody, a lifeline.

"You knew it was a matter of time, right? Everyone's probably saying it behind your back, but leave it to Courtney, the matron of the hashtag-speak-your-truth movement, to say it to your face. And are you sure you're sick, not just feeling sorry for yourself over Leo? Or nervous for tonight? Maybe looking for an out after you signed away your life on the head of school contract. Why you want that job remains a mystery to me." On top of my malaise, Marisol's line of questioning is feeding my first-year insecurities.

"I've told you why a million times," I whine into the phone.

"I know, I know. So those rich kids can see some leaders of color blah, blah, blah. By the way, I think half of Paco's eighth grade class is going to flunk out of school and head straight for the thug life. And I'm talking about the White kids." Marisol knows why I work in private schools. A question, given the color of my skin, I'm asked about a hundred times a year. I'm pretty sure Allister Nevins was never asked that question.

"I'm not nervous, I think I've got an early season case of the crud," I low moan on top of my whine.

"Uh-oh. Sorry, Sweets. You tell that to Leo yet?"

I don't want to admit to Marisol I haven't talked to him and he's already been in Singapore twenty-two hours. "No. I figure if he's feeling crappy, maybe he'll blame jet lag instead of me. Starting off a long-distance relationship being judged for spreading germs is not cute. That's why I'm on the phone moaning to you instead."

"Legit rationale for not telling the truth. Take three Advil with a Red Bull chaser and pretend it's a hangover. You need to rise to the occasion tonight, Headmistress Clarke." Now that's some quality advice I can use. Marisol's always been one of the smartest Royal-Hawkins moms as well as my personal favorite. I know where Roan Dawson, my director of admissions, hides the energy drinks he slams before school tours, and I'm pretty sure Mimi has stocked my ibuprofen stash.

"I don't know what I'm more bothered by, Courtney congratulating me for being the first Black head of school, her throwing down her questionable Latina roots, or chasing clout to be on the Royal-Hawkins board. Can you even be a sixth anything? As a science teacher, I don't believe the genetics or the math pans out on that one."

"Sounds like an ancestory.com question," Marisol says with little interest. I can hear her filing her fingers, keeping her stiletto nails on point.

"Or a question for the puberty lady. Her first trip to the sixth-grade suite to talk tampons and testosterone with the kids is next week." Lucille Paulson is our high school music teacher with a penchant for animal print scarves and grapefruit-scented body spray who moonlights as the Royal-Hawkins sexpert. Over the years, Marisol and I have speculated about Luscious Lucy's sex life, since Marisol's sons and Xandra have both gone through her sex ed class.

"Did you notice how Courtney signed off on her email? *Jai?* What does that even mean? Speak English, Courtney. I'm not bilingual, despite Pablo's best efforts."

"I'm sure as shit *jai* isn't Spanish. I don't even think it's Spanglish. And you haven't let poor Pablo off the hook tutoring you yet? That man's a saint for working with you and that accent. You sound like Chula Vista Barbie when you speak Spanish." Marisol's on the other end clucking at me through her teeth. "My offer still stands to be your teacher if you want to give Pablo a break."

"No, thanks. Last time you gave me a Spanish lesson, you only focused on the naughty words," I lob back. "And by the way, we were discussing Courtney, not my abysmal accent."

"Hold on, googling now . . . HA!" Marisol snorts. "*Jai* means victory in Hindi. If that isn't some subtle mind fuck, I don't know what is. That woman is angling HARD for a board seat. Are you sure you don't know why? Do you think she was with Winn Hawkins back in the day? Maybe she has some unresolved feelings she wants to work out between passing next year's budget and running a capital campaign." Marisol's lost in writing Courtney and Winn's imagined love tryst. "You know, the one that got away, her one true love, or just some straight-up stalker woman scorned sort of thing. Girl, you know private schools are like Japan. Proper on the outside, deviant behind closed doors." After Marisol's ten-day trip to Japan this summer with her younger, unmarried sister-in-law, she learned more about the sex fetish phenomena of Tokyo than about samurai warriors, tea ceremonies, and pagodas combined. Now she's convinced kinky lurks behind every ramen joint in California.

The image of Courtney and Winn knocking boots is more than I can handle on an already queasy stomach, so I bypass Marisol's speculation altogether. "I swear I feel like I'm having a bonding moment with President Obama right now. Is it a good or bad thing being called the first Black president of the United States? Or the first Black head of school? Or the first Black anything?! I don't know. Yeah, it's the truth, but does it matter? Do I care? Or do I only care because Courtney's the one always saying out loud what most people are thinking?" I need to remember to read up on how Obama responded to folks when he was referred to as the first Black president versus plain ol' president. Or how FLOTUS dealt, since we all know who wears the pants in that family.

"Oh no, you did not just compare yourself to President Obama, Nina. He was president of the United States, you're not even president of your HOA. You go saying something like that in front of your father and let's see what happens." Marisol laughs out loud at the thought.

"Fitzroy will have zero patience for you comparing yourself to Black royalty knowing you used to wrap a yellow bath towel around your head as a child. I never get tired of hearing him tease you about trying to have long blonde hair like Christie Brinkley." Marisol's howling. In Fitzroy Morgan's world hierarchy there's Jesus, there's Martin Luther King Jr., and right in between, there's Barack Obama.

"Gotta go search Roan's office for Red Bull and a pack of Pop Rocks to wake myself up." Bless him, I was warned when Allister and I hired Roan as our director of admissions that he had some "unconventional" practices and whispered a little too loudly at school events. But his boss—Josie Bordelon, the head of school at Fairchild Country Day in San Francisco—assured me that Roan was relocating to Pasadena for love and to settle down and that taking a chance on his audacity was worth it for his hard work and daily entertainment. It's a rare occurrence that I meet another woman in my same occupation, let alone a sister, so I knew Josie was serving me the truth. I was the final decision maker as Roan would work only one year under Allister, then his second year as director of admissions would be my first as head of school. Given Josie's recommendation and confession that she was devastated to see him go, I hired Roan without a second thought and prayed he would be more class than ass. Best executive decision ever.

"The board meeting starts soon, and I look tore up from the floor up. Thanks for absolutely nothing, Marisol. I'll remember this conversation next time you want to trade tea about Jaime, your stanky sons, or one of your waxing girls." Marisol's the founder and self-titled chief extraordinary officer of the Clean Slate, a one-stop-shop for waxing, buffing, sugaring, painting, spraying, and scrubbing any body part a person might request. BEST part, every studio has a fully stocked bar for hours of grooming with a side of day drinking. I was client zero in the basement of Marisol's house twelve years ago when she was perfecting her signature waxing technique up to my knobby knees. Now with twenty-two locations throughout Los Angeles County and clients who schedule out weeks in advance, the Clean Slate is harder to get into than most restaurants. Aside from being the only person I trust to wax my legs, Marisol's also the only one I immediately forgive for calling truth on me. We've been working out our dreams together since childhood.

"That's wax women to you, Even Obama knows *girls* is insulting. I'm just saying. Fact: you ARE the head of school. Fact: you are nursing a wounded ego."

"Heart," I correct her.

"There, case in point. Maybe you're a little touchy today. And fact: you ARE Black. Like real Black, not the diluted kind like Obama. Courtney was just honest enough to point out what everyone's talking about behind your back. You know there are parents who want to send their babies to Royal-Hawkins for 50K so they can appear woke to their neighbors and tennis partners."

"Fact: your bedside manner blows. So glad you didn't join the medical profession. I gotta go, holla later." I rush to get off the phone so I can grab ten minutes of quiet before it's time to turn on the charm. I wonder if there will ever be a day, just one day, when Marisol tells me what I want to hear, not what she wants me to know.

"*Jai*, sista."

FOUR

Walking outside, I chuck the empty Red Bull I raided from Roan's office into a recycling bin and see Winn Hawkins standing directly below the school motto engraved into a Carrara marble slab above the formal entryway.

Where every child lives in the front row.

—*Royal-Hawkins School Motto*

The school motto is Royal-Hawkins's version of a welcome mat.

Winn's wearing his Yale twenty-five-year reunion class tie. Surprisingly, a blue tie with miniature white bulldogs doesn't look completely hideous with khakis and a pink button-down, at least not on him. He may have graduated bottom of his class at Yale, but watching Winn shake the hand of every trustee that arrives for the first board meeting of the year reminds me that Winn Hawkins has charisma for days. His gravelly voice, graying temples, and subtle swagger of an athlete past his competing days but still in prime shape are definitely worth a second look from any woman, or Roan.

"My soon-to-be sister-in-law's Pilates instructor said he thinks he saw dear Winston sans wife at the Under Carriage early Sunday morning," Roan whispers in my ear, not taking his eyes off our distinguished board chair.

"So, what I'm hearing you say is that you think YOU saw him at the Under Carriage in the wee Sunday morning hours. Is that a wise place for a bride-to-be to spend his free time?" I ask, raising an eyebrow to my colleague. "And why were you there so late with work the next day?"

"My visit was work related, my life is Royal-Hawkins," Roan sing-songs back, nodding a second time toward Winn. "That man knows how to wear a pair of classic-cut flat-front khakis."

The obvious genetic trait that links multiple generations of Royal-Hawkins offspring is flawless, sun-kissed California good looks. The White kind of pretty those bland Beach Boys made a whole career singing about. The grainy black-and-white photo of founder and first Headmaster John Patrick Hawkins, known as J. P., hanging in my office leaves no room for debate. In five generations the flaxen blond hair, striking green eyes, and slender nose of the Hawkins clan have not been watered down by one drop of ugly.

J. P. Hawkins did not rush to California in 1852 for the gold; he came to capitalize on all the chumps who were heading straight to the hills to hunt gold. Whatever a fortune-seeking fool needed to survive in the Wild West, J. P. provided. Pickaxes, drills, rockers, hooch—he was front and center to sell goods to any dreamer with a buck in his pocket and no sense in his head. After establishing an empire in San Francisco, J. P. put his brother in charge of his Northern California operations and headed south to expand the Hawkins business in Los Angeles as rumors of a transcontinental railroad circled.

After the gold had run dry and the railroad was a go, J. P.'s bank account read full. To seal his legacy, he decided to start an academically rigorous boarding school in the bustling tourist town of Pasadena, just east of Los Angeles. His mission: to raise young men to be educated doctors, lawyers, and businessmen, not idiots chasing crazy fantasies in the Wild West. Given J. P.'s tremendous accomplishments, parents across the West willingly scraped together their last pennies to send their chosen sons to the Royal-Hawkins School. Up until the moment he dropped dead in what is now my office, J. P. Hawkins dedicated the last years of his life to raising a select class of well-schooled boys.

His widow, Alice Royal—who, urban folklore has it, was mute at the side of her boisterous and demanding husband—stepped right over J. P.'s cold dead body and into the role of headmistress. Because she was a woman, the community never formally acknowledged her as head of school during her five-year tenure. However, the first thing she did in her demure power grab was admit girls to Royal-Hawkins. In fact, Alice offered to pay the college tuition of any female graduate who chose to attend Radcliffe, Smith, or Wellesley rather than marry immediately following graduation. Alice did not want the girls she educated to see marriage as the only option to improve their lot in life. Perhaps marrying J. P. had been Alice's default choice.

Second, Alice amended school bylaws to reflect that when a Hawkins descendant wanted to be chair of the board of trustees, they were granted the leadership position. Not one head of school has challenged Alice's decision. Six feet underground, Alice has remained a quiet force.

The boarding component is long gone, but the tradition of challenging students with a demanding curriculum has stayed intact. The leadership bylaw Alice established legitimizes Winn's perceived influence over the direction of the school. Back from a double-decade stint living in Australia, he plucked himself a beauty of a wife right off Bondi Beach who fits in perfectly on the Hawkins family Christmas card.

Everyone wants to have a beer with Winn, be invited to his courtside seats at Lakers games, or play eighteen holes with him at the Annandale Golf Club. On the surface, I understand why. But I think if one were to scratch below the beachy smell, there's something a little off, maybe even a little rank. Or as my father would say, *I'm not sure what it is, but something's not right with that man and Jesus.* In Winn's presence, my guard goes up and I'm extra careful with what I say, though I can't pinpoint what it is, in particular, about him. Face-to-face, I find myself leaning in to take a deep whiff, wondering if his affable appeal comes with a side of Smirnoff, or if his French double-cheek kiss is a preempt to a double-butt-cheek grab.

Winn seems to want something from every person he meets. Last year when I was attending board meetings in preparation for becoming head, there were three times Winn didn't show up. No email, no text, no call. A few days later, when I finally tracked him down, he talked in circles about intermittent fasting, a funky biome, things slipping his mind, and isn't aging a bitch . . . ha, ha, ha. I wasn't laughing. I was full-on judging and wondering what angle he was playing. But then Winn would donate a half million to the financial assistance fund, call the president of Yale on behalf of two Royal-Hawkins seniors, and run a tight board meeting that concluded on time.

"Should we get started, Nina?" Winn holds one of the front doors to the school wide open with his hip and foot and gestures for me to walk in ahead of him. I glance at myself in the window to make sure my rushed makeup job is holding. The fuzzy glass masks any flaws staring back at me.

"Why thank you, Winn," Roan flirts. "I bet you get whatever you want with those chivalrous manners." Roan blocks me and gives Winn a deliberate wink. I shake my head and remain hopeful Roan's sharp sense of humor and quick compliments continue to work in Royal-Hawkins's admissions favor with prospective moms who collect witty, well-dressed gay men. I'm pretty sure he's going to make a handful of fathers, like Winn Hawkins, sweat in their socks.

"Nina, a moment?" Winn asks, clearly flustered, pulling me aside after Roan is well into the foyer. "After the meeting I need to chat with you for a few. Just something I want to tell you about, not a full board discussion yet. Let's get off campus and grab a drink." Winn gives me a smile that says, *I'm your boss and you have no other option than to join me.* I want hot tea and bed.

"You bet, Winn," I agree through a polite but tired smile.

"Great. Settled. Then let's go bang the gavel. We want to start this party on time, make sure you do it right for your inaugural meeting. All hail the queen and everything that comes after that . . . Oh look, there's Hank, I've been trying to catch up with that bastard all summer."

"Well, that's a stretch, but something to strive for, right?" I say to Winn's back as he trots over to shake hands with a fellow board of trustee bastard and yacht club member.

"Nina, you need anything?" A familiar hand touches me at the elbow as I'm making sure I have enough copies of the fiscal report before going into the conference room. I love hearing my name in Pablo's Spanish accent, it sounds so beautiful.

"No gracias, Pablo, estoy bien." I smile and put my arm around him for a warm side hug.

When I started my high school teaching career at my alma mater, Spence, my mother was full of all kinds of advice having spent her entire career as part of the invisible housekeeping staff at New York's St. Regis Hotel. Some of it I ignored and instead learned the hard way, but there's one piece of advice I've held on to tightly, and it's paid off time and again.

Celia would preach, *Nina, the most powerful people in any organization are the ones who go unnoticed and unthanked. They do the work and pay attention to the details that make all the difference.*

In schools, the support staff are the all-knowing eyes and ears of the community able to move freely among conversations, stealthily through the halls, in and out of groups without most people taking notice. They find the crib sheets of the cheaters, spy the mom drying her tears before entering the school, and hurt for the child who has spent a few too many recesses without a playmate. They are the invisible heroes that keep a schoolhouse humming, and I have never taken them for granted.

"Faculty and staff have been back in school for a bit and still no empanadas from Yolanda? *Dónde está el amor?*" All last year, Pablo Galvez, our facilities manager, would leave his wife's fresh empanadas outside my office door on Friday mornings. I know Yolanda made them for me so I would have something hot and delicious for lunch at the end of every crazy week, but the empanadas rarely made it past 9:00 a.m. I've never been good at delayed gratification.

Pablo pats his stomach. *"Sus empanadas están aquí."* We laugh, sharing a common bond of having zero discipline when it comes to Yolanda's specialties.

"You do good in there, Nina. I got you." Pablo nods his head at the door and hands me a tissue from his coveralls, an old-school gentleman. I appreciate Pablo's faith in me, that makes one of us. "You going to do a poem?"

"Always, Pablo." Recitation is my secret weapon. I start every meeting with words from a song or a poem. I have a pitch-perfect alto voice, and I use that gift to quiet a room, center my audience, and give myself a hit of joy and a boost of confidence before jumping into the evening's agenda. Tonight, I'll be sharing a couple of lines from Tupac's "Old School" to stir the pot and keep this buttoned-up crowd on their toes.

"This year we'll keep working on your Spanish," Pablo reminds me. I laugh again and head into the conference room to find my seat next to Winn.

Ding goes my pocket, loudly. I knew Marisol couldn't let the day tie up without laying down a little love. Her ability to play bad cop never lasts longer than a half hour, sixty minutes max.

It's still three months and change until my baby, Xandra, comes home from boarding school for Christmas, but I need her tech savvy now. As much as I want to check my texts, I can't be doing it in a room full of eagle-eyed, opinionated board members, particularly the ones who didn't want me to be their child's head of school in the first place. For the life of me I can't figure out how to get my phone not to ding out loud when a text comes in, and I'm too embarrassed to ask our IT guy such a rookie question. It's like an invisible dog fence; the ding always surprises me, even though it really shouldn't for the 2,838th time. Looking from me to my jacket, Winn pulls my chair out for me with practiced manners. I quickly fish the phone out of my pocket to check the text before bringing this first board meeting of my new professional life to order. If not Marisol, it might be a much-welcome hit from Leo. Yep, a text from Leo would definitely get me through the next few hours and keep me from spiraling down a "does he or doesn't he" miss me toilet bowl.

Graham 5:59 PM

Call me. It's about Xandra.

My ex never texts.

FIVE

Look at this," Roan says, shoving his phone in my face, bouncing in his spa chair like a toddler fisting a handful of Cheerios.

Once a month Marisol and I get our nails done at one of her studios. She calls our visits *quality control*, but I call them putting the fear of God in the manager's life if something is not up to Marisol's sky-high standards. Marisol's the definition of *boss bitch*. I know, I've been on the other side of a tongue lashing from her and wouldn't wish it on anyone. Once Roan got comfortable at Royal-Hawkins and got wind of our monthly treatments, he crowned himself Prince of the Pedicure and invited himself along.

Today, the afternoon light in the Colorado Boulevard Clean Slate is dull, which is fine for picking a pedicure color and nursing a happy hour cocktail, but not for reading. I need to adjust the phone to see what Roan's squawking about.

"Soooo, what do you think?" Roan asks, practically levitating in anticipation.

"Of Coachella?" I push his hand away from my face to get a better read. "I've always wanted to go. Well, I did until people started referring to it as *Oldchella*. Now, I'm out."

"You need to get yourself a pair of Eyebobs." Roan wilts a little.

"What are those?" I ask, taking the phone from Roan's hand for better inspection, my effort to meet his enthusiasm at least 10 percent.

"Fashionable readers to make vain middle-aged women feel better about losing their eyesight," he informs me. My enthusiasm drops. "The frames are oversize and thick, so they cover up the crow's-feet. Grab yourself a pair," Roan says, gesturing with his trendy cocktail.

"I told you it was poor taste to bring a child into a spa," I say to Marisol, who, against my better judgment, caved at Roan's begging and invited him on our first afternoon extracurricular activity of the new school year. Mimi is well trained never to schedule meetings for me on Fridays after 4:00 p.m. She knows my self-care time with Marisol is sacred. Former Headmaster Nevins had birding to destress, I have shellacking. "The drinking age should be raised to thirty-five."

"Don't hate, Nina. Celebrate. With me, Marisol, and alcohol," Roan declares, clinking with Marisol's champagne flute. Five minutes into their initial introduction last year, these two clicked, and since then Marisol and Roan have only had eyes for each other. Either that or Marisol wanted to add another gay friend to her beauty industry entourage and Roan wanted free waxing. It's a toss-up with these two.

"Celebrate what exactly?" I know better than to say yes to Roan about anything without full disclosure of information followed by my own research.

"Well, if you could see, you'd know I'm trying to show you the web-site for Mudchella. It's right before Thanksgiving. I'm thinking you, me, and Marisol can do it together. It'll be phase one of getting in fighting shape for my wedding. We'll tap into our inner animal instincts and sculpt our cores." Roan purrs at us, more kitten than eye of the tiger. "We can come up with a great team name, like A Babe and Two Beards or A Bride with Four Boobs."

I'll be politely declining phase one of bridal boot camp and bracing myself for phase two, the breakup. Marisol and I have a bet going that this engagement won't make it through the end of the calendar year. Though Roan swears he only has eyes for his partner, Tate, I swear I've seen his eyes everywhere *but* Tate. Personally, I don't think the engagement will make it past Veterans Day. Marisol's giving Roan until

December 30, so he can collect on holiday gifts. Knowing Roan, phase two will consist of movie marathons, boxes of tissues, and sleeves of Girl Scout Thin Mints. That's my idea of a triathlon.

"HA! Mudchella, have you met us?" Marisol says, waving her par-affined hand around indicating that we are getting clipped, filed, and painted, not scaling a wall. "Plus, that is the WHITEST race I've ever heard of. All those people out there paying all that money to run and crawl through mud, slipping and sliding, sweating hard to cross a finish line looking more brown than white." Marisol grabs Roan's phone off the side of his chair and points to the images on the home page. "Nina and I can stay brown for free from the comfort of our own couches."

"Amén, mi hermana." I fingertip high-five Marisol. "Roan, what about me screams 'I want to haul my booty up and over a two-story wall only to drop into a petri dish of dirt, sweat, and tears on the other side'? Besides, don't you have any guy friends to do that stuff with you?"

"No thanks. I choose you two. I've always been a Black woman trapped in a gay man's body." That's some spot-on self-awareness. "Okay, if not Mudchella, then for sure a bubble run. Tutus and tiaras for all, perfect for a gride like me."

"Gride?" Marisol and I ask at the same time.

"Seriously? Do you two not have any other gay friends besides me?" Roan claps back, frustrated at our failure to keep up. "Gay bride!"

"Ahhhhh . . . and on that note, I'm officially bringing my own magnum of bubbly to get me through THAT event." Marisol points to her flute and takes a big swig. The word nerd in me wants to ask, Why not a *gade*?

Roan turns his back on Marisol's negativity. "Nina, you're going to need something to distract yourself while Leo's gone. And you're really going to need something to keep yourself from face-planting in Yolanda's empanadas when you go missing him. That's right, I know your little secret with Pablo. Fried food will do you NO favors." Roan gives my belly a little pat. Caught before I'm even guilty.

"How am I supposed to distract myself when Leo sends me photos like this?" I hold up my phone so Roan can see my new home screen image, a picture of Leo on a white-sand beach in Singapore.

"If you ask me, Leo's totally selfish leaving you AND leaving me during my engagement season. He was my first pick for my Mudchella turned bubble team, then you two. A man who can bike up and over the San Gabriel Mountains is welcome to roll in the mud with me anytime." I know Roan and his fiancé, Tate, boldly asked Leo, whom they have only met two times, to officiate their wedding. Roan wants three beautiful men front and center for his ceremony, but he claims to want someone in the legal profession to make the marriage legit. When Leo told Roan that his specialty was labor, not family law, and that he was going to Singapore to open a satellite office, we got to witness Roan's first full-blown gridal panic attack.

Leo's everything I forgot to shop for when I picked Graham out for husband material at twenty-six years old. He's kind, he appears curious about me and my work, and he seems to roll with whatever is thrown his way. I promised Roan I wouldn't allow my novice long-distance relationship skills to ruin his nuptials. Here's hoping.

"The next few months you get five conversations about missing Leo." Roan holds up his newly moisturized hand, fingers outstretched. "The rest of our conversations are all about my wedding. And we can talk admissions, too, from time to time. Me, school, you," Roan says, pointing in turn as if wielding a wand. "That'll be our weekly meeting agenda. So back to me. The three of us are going to look beyond gorgeous under the chalupa. People are going to swoon. The banker, the dream maker, and the legal anchor."

"*Chalupa?*" Marisol mouths to me and shakes her head while Roan cackles at his own Mother Goose rhyme. She points to herself, then to me. I point back to her and vigorously nod my head yes; the Latina should clarify Mexican culture to the Irish marrying a Jew. This Jamaican is out.

"It's called a *chuppah*, not a *chalupa*, you lapsed Catholic. That's what you'll be standing under when you marry your Jewish bean counter from Jersey. You didn't learn this before you packed up your fabulous single-in-San-Francisco life and moved here to settle down? A *chalupa* is what you eat at the summer street fair in Santa Ana," Marisol explains with a hint of *really?* in her voice. "You know, that one day a year when rosary-wielding devout grandmas are okay selling overpriced Mexican food smothered in queso to men roaming their neighborhood hand in hand," Marisol offers for added context. "*Abuela's* rationalizing of course, not mine."

Roan tips his chin in full understanding. As director of admissions, the gatekeeper of diversity and inclusion at Royal-Hawkins, the fact that Roan has mixed up the two cultural traditions should be unnerving, but it's not. Whenever Roan shatters his cover of cultural competency, he simply chalks it up to being an equal opportunist. Jewricans, Mexipeans, Blaurvians—Roan loves them all. And he's made love to them all, as he takes every opportunity to brag. That's why Marisol and I are waiting to buy our dresses for the wedding until forty-eight hours before go time.

"Whatever it's called, we're going to slay. Everyone's going to be so jealous. I can't wait."

"Building your wedding ceremony based on best angles and a jealous audience, that touches me deeply." I tap my heart with my index and middle finger. "I'll remember to bring tissues for the Hallmark moment."

"Everyone personalizes their wedding in their own special way." Roan raises his glass for a snarky *salud*.

"Gotta down and dash." Marisol finishes her last sip. "If I don't hit the grocery store before I get home, my family will be eating meat-lover's pizza for the fourth night in a row. A vegetable has not passed a Garcia mouth in days. My thirteen-year-old is growing chest hair, and the can of Glade in the bathroom is empty. Why I didn't hire a nanny who can cook is beyond me. A decade in I can't fire Spanny, though. The boys are too attached, and she irons Jaime's boxers. They have a little thing." Roan raises his eyebrows at Marisol.

"It's okay," Marisol assures, waving off Roan's concern, "she's inching close to sixty and is as wide as she is tall. And even if they were having an affair, I'd have to turn the other cheek. I can't parent without her," Marisol admits, knowing her family train doesn't run without Super Nanny as the engine.

"Can I get a ride, Sol? Roan drove me here. My car's getting a massive tune-up so I can drive it for two more years and then pass it on to Xandra. She needs something to drive when she's home from boarding school."

"You're a head of school now, why are you still driving around in that duct-taped jalopy?" Marisol questions. "You're making bank, it's time to start treating yourself."

"I was planning to cheat on fashion with new furniture and a new car this year, but the financial aid office at Pemberley School got hip to my new salary bracket. Higher salary, no financial aid package. Between that, the nonrefundable custom-made sectional I had already ordered, and my dad staying with me since August and showing no signs of leaving, I gotta keep the jalopy in fighting shape." Since Mom died and Clive moved to London for a two-year stint for work but fell in love and stayed for a Somali PhD student at Oxford, I think my father has been lonely in Queens. Each visit to Pasadena has become longer and longer to the point now that I only buy him one-way tickets.

"Damn those FAFSA forms. Okay, hustle if you want a ride! My two gamers and their father will grow restless if I'm not home with some grub to throw in front of them." Marisol hands my nail technician my flip-flops to slip onto my feet so we can waddle out of here without jacking up our paint job.

"Nina, hope you're back to your old self soon. This whole half-healthy thing is not a good look on you. Royal-Hawkins needs you on point," Roan says as I shrug into my caramel-hue sleeveless duster that hits me perfectly midcalf; a staple piece from my closet I'll never toss out.

"Awww, thanks, Roan." Finally, someone who loves me acknowledges I haven't been feeling my best self.

"Those pants you're wearing," he says with a small shake of his head. "They scream 'I quit. Game over.'"

I'm horrified at Roan's take on my high-waisted navy harem pants. Despite boarding school's claim on my paycheck, I've been trying to up my style to match my salary bracket from what Marisol calls my "bank branch manager look." Even if I don't feel like I own the Royal-Hawkins boardroom, I need to look like I do. I paired my harem pants with gold heels, a fitted off-white silk tank top, and a chunky walnut wood bracelet. I think the ensemble is fabulous New York eighties throwback chic, minus the shoulder pads. I look to Marisol to have my fashion back.

"*Sí, mami. Basta.* That outfit is done. Never go shopping without me again. And that includes online. Leo's gone, and you've put your whole sexuality on lockdown so soon after you got it up and running again. Is that how you're going to survive not getting any?"

"Roan, you're never invited back to our sip and clip club again. Today was considered a tryout, and the committee of me has unanimously decided you failed miserably," I say, taking back the conversation. "And Marisol, you're now on club probation. One more infraction and you, too, get the boot."

"Uh, I own the spas and the alcohol you consume, so no, I'm not going anywhere. Besides, drinking alone is not a good look." Marisol turns my hands over several times, making sure Clean Slate store number eight has done an up-to-standard job, and then she gives me the *let's go* thumb. "Nor is it considered a club; it's considered a problem."

Roan leans forward enough to plant a kiss on my forehead. "Go home and rest, Nina. You've lost your sense of humor and your sense of style."

SIX

A few more days of this and I'm going to get worried," Marisol declares, circling her finger at me. "Are you sure you're starting to feel better?"

I give Marisol the universal *maybe* head bobble.

"Now that we've ditched Roan, tell me about the board meeting last night," Marisol says, starting the car. We use our Friday spa dates to catch up on school gossip, but with Roan in tow today I had to keep some semblance of professionalism.

Even though Marisol's a parent at Royal-Hawkins, she was my friend first. An only child, Marisol Santiago was raised by her Mexican grandparents in Queens one apartment building over from mine. Being from Mexico, and living in New York, she was not only a long way from home, but the Mexican community was so tiny that Marisol and her grandparents were ruefully removed from their roots. So, the day I met her I brought Marisol home, and my family welcomed her with open arms. My family wasn't much better off than hers, but my parents were just hitting their stride in the US and managed to always have enough so Marisol could be included. She came with us to church and to Jamaican festivals where she learned to love reggae more than her grandparents' preferred Tejano music. Everywhere we went, Marisol came too. In fact, Marisol spent so much time with us that my father began affectionately referring to his adopted Mexican daughter as his little Chaco Taco.

After undergrad, Marisol and I shared an apartment together in a Harlem four-story walk-up with a hot plate, while I went to Columbia's Teachers College and then returned to Spence to teach high school science. My love of teenagers had solidified tutoring young women in math and science while I was at Wellesley, and Marisol hopped around hawking nail polish to New York's high-end nail salons. Edging up on twenty-five, we were both antsy for adventure, neither of us having ever traveled west of the Mississippi. Problem was, Marisol had no money. So, the little savings I had, I offered to split with her if she promised to come with me. Between the two of us we packed three duffel bags and swore to my parents we would take care of each other no matter what. All these years later, Marisol's nickname stuck, and on campus, at the Clean Slate, really anywhere, I still have to make a conscious effort not to howl "CHACO TACO!" at the top of my lungs like my ten-year-old self when I see her. And we've kept our promise to take care of one another.

"Hank Chambers's third wife dumped him over the summer, and it looked to me like Cynthia Wright is laying down some groundwork for the coveted spot of spouse number four. Also, I'm sure I spied freshly planted hair plugs on Anders Nilsson. And when the topic of our pilot year of robotics and coding curriculum came up, all eyes swiveled to the Pacific Rim contingent. Lots of eager parents wanting to know if there are multiple AP offerings with this new curriculum and how it will read on school transcripts." I think about what other juicy tidbits I may have for Marisol. I come up empty minded. "Other than that, it was a pretty tame meeting."

"Did Winn show up for the meeting, or was he MWR like last year?"

"MWR?" There are an insane number of acronyms in education: CWP (crazy while parenting), DMW (dead man walking, aka any child being sent to my office), and my personal favorite that applies to anything and everything unexplainable—WTF.

"Missing While Rich. It's when you forget all about your responsibilities because you decide to jet off to the Seychelles last minute."

"What's got your thong in a twist this early in the school year?" I call out. Marisol's not usually the skeptical one when it comes to families at Royal-Hawkins.

"Thong? Please, I prefer to let my flower breathe. A thong is for when there's a chill in the air and I need to cover up." It's true, while Marisol dresses business chic on the outside, underneath is a nudist wanting to break free. "Did you hear that mother sitting next to me getting her nails switched out? She was screaming into her phone organizing her kid's teacher, speech therapist, friendship coach, and violin instructor to meet, and it's the very beginning of the school year. I don't know how you deal with these people. It took all my effort not to grab her phone and dunk it in the foot basin."

"Speaking of those people, Winn asked me to get a drink with him after the meeting last night. I promised him one drink and suggested we walk the few blocks to Bottle Shoppe. He was reserved at the meeting, other than calling for a few votes, but when we were walking together, he started talking all about our new sixth grade teacher, Jared Jones. How they share a love of basketball, how lucky we are to have him on faculty, how he could make a real difference in the school. Noise like that."

"Do they know each other?"

"I don't think so, unless Winn follows Ivy League basketball. Harvard, not Yale. Besides, Jared's twenty-four. Winn's obviously not, so I don't even know where their paths may have crossed." Influenced by an afternoon spent with Roan, Marisol raises her eyebrows. I know what she's thinking, and I shake my head no, I'm fairly certain Jared has an exclusively all-female five-star dating rating. "I had to remind Winn I only had one drink in me, so he'd better get down to business. I can only fake interest for so long after a fifteen-hour day. He told me he'd talk fast if I promised to keep the conversation between the two of us."

"You mean the three of us."

I throw Marisol an *obviously* glance.

"I was ready to hear something big, but the next twenty minutes were spent talking at me about the school and diversity hiring and our athletic teams and how we can't do anything to lose Jared Jones because he's such a necessary addition to the school."

"Who's this guy, the second coming?"

"To schools? Yes. He's a Black, double Harvard degree, hoops pla-yin', six-foot-four, stylin' package of cougar meat. He was out front the first day of school introducing himself to all the kids and their families. Hand to God, the receiving line to meet him was a hundred mothers deep."

"Wow, you really landed yourself a diamond. I bet there's more than a few school leaders in Southern California who are none too happy with you getting your hooks in Jared on your first cast into the hiring waters."

"No doubt. Once again, they have to explain to their parent body why they couldn't hire outside the White female teaching pool." Marisol nods. Schools are flooded with White women, particularly in Pasadena. Every spring when job openings are announced, schools practically throw down and wrestle over applications from men and people of color. If you are Black or Brown, have a college degree, and pass a background check, you're going to get an interview.

"Anyway, by the end of my cranberry juice to his two craft beers, Winn's monologue had nothing important to do with the day-to-day, or even the future of Royal-Hawkins as far as I could tell. Seems this year Winn's looking for a new buddy to go with him to Lakers games."

"Doesn't he have enough clout chasers to fill his courtside seats?" Marisol asks with a look of annoyance for ultrarich people's inconve-niences. I hold back from reminding her that her pocketbook is plenty padded these days.

"Yeah, but the street cred he gets with the players by bringing a young king who looks like Nineties Air Jordan is tough to pass up. Winn and Jared would make one fine-looking salt-and-pepper set on the jumbotron." I may be his boss, but I'm not blind. If teaching doesn't work out for Jared, I may have to do a little digging and find an alumnus of Royal-Hawkins who is a successful Hollywood agent.

"Get the Gen Z balls on this guy," I whisper, leaning in. Marisol's eyes grow huge. Once it was out of my mouth, I knew she had taken me literally. "After his new teacher orientation to Royal-Hawkins, Jared swaggered into my office and asked for three days off in November to attend a basketball camp. The first day of his first year of teaching, and he has the balls—I mean, guts—to ask for time off!"

"And?"

"And HELL NO! Spend a handful of years putting in the time and killing it teaching in my school and then maybe, MAYBE you can have a few days to go to man camp."

"I hear about employee friction 24-7 in my own company, I don't need to hear about it in yours. But I'll tell you this, I'm raising men right now. Not one of them turns out that perfect, not even in the best of circumstances. I bet Jared's got a pile of unpaid bills and empty Chinese takeout cartons under his bed stinkin' up the joint like he's buried General Tso's body under the sheets," Marisol says, growing bored. "So, come on, I'm barely keeping my eyes open here. At next month's spa date, you better bring me something juicy. This stuff is sorry. I'm going to have to start binge-watching a dark Hulu series if your life becomes as dull as mine."

"Sorry my stability has cut back on your entertainment."

"It's okay. I'll send you my streaming bill. I need to stop for gas, you okay on time?" Marisol asks as a courtesy, not waiting for an answer as she pulls into the Shell station.

I lean back against the headrest. Marisol's heavy foot at every stoplight sent waves of nausea rolling through my stomach.

I can hear Marisol struggling to get the nozzle into the gas tank. The back door of her ratty family minivan slides open, and snack carnage from her boys tumbles out. "I swear the back of my car is a biohazard. I have no idea what my boys have rubbed into the seats and floors to create all these stains."

"And smells. That's why I only mouth breathe when I'm in your minivan, self-preservation. I much prefer your drop top."

"Me, too, but my boys aren't allowed anywhere near my baby," Marisol says, ignoring my sensitive stomach. "You know this is my favorite gas station, right?"

"Didn't know you had a gas station rating system. Seems there may be better things to do with your idle mind."

"This one brings back particularly fond memories of Food Stamp Floyd." Marisol loves a good trip down the memory lane of my dating life. "You remember him when we first moved out here? How many slam poetry contests did you drag me to when you were stalking him searching for your artistic soulmate? Five? Eight? And then when he finally asked you out, he took you to that In-N-Out Burger across the street and tried to pay with his EBT card." Marisol howls as she points across the street to ground zero of bad date number 164 of my lifetime.

"I don't think I've ever laughed as much in my life as when I got your call after you ran to this exact bathroom. You hid in there until I came to get you. And you made me bring hats for both of us, so we could hide on the way out. God that story never gets old!" Marisol's doubled over, lost in the comical history of my early love life.

"Okay, if you didn't appreciate the board meeting and Jared update, then how 'bout this." I blow out a big breath of air. Back in the car, Marisol doesn't turn the ignition on. Instead she shifts in her seat, giving me her full attention. I know she's hoping for something juicier than the picture of Leo in his swimming trunks I've been showing off, but I don't have much else to share other than the text sent saying he reached the office and an accompanying image of Leo standing in front of the Smith, Bodie, and Strong sign by the elevator bank. I texted back something lame like, "Have a great day," and then our communication went dead. I'm not ready to deconstruct that abysmal first attempt at long-distance banter with anyone, even Marisol.

A car waiting for gas honks. Marisol gives the driver the middle finger in her rearview mirror without skipping a beat.

"Graham texted me last night. First time ever."

"How the hell have you been communicating about Xandra with that *cabrón* the past couple of years if you don't text?"

"We have a strict email-only relationship. You know Graham treats every communication like a business transaction."

"Old-school contentious coparenting. Totally 2000; but okay."

"More like sanity preservation." Our entire marriage Graham publicly touted my professional success while privately criticizing me for being an absentee mother and wife. Graham existed in constant judgment of how I spent more time at work than at home. His critiques became our nightly pillow talk.

Graham and I met in a coffee shop. Behind him in line, I was drawn to his lyrical accent as he ordered an oddly specific coffee drink. Feeling bold, I stepped out of line to ask if he was from Jamaica. Graham answered, *Bermuda*, to which I jokingly countered, *Close enough*. How many folks from the Caribbean Islands could there possibly be in Pasadena?

In the moment, Graham didn't appear to be entertained by my humor, but when we sat down to sip our coffees together, he did appreciate a fellow scion of the islands who had been educated in the best schools America has to offer, just as he had. I was too naive to realize that moment was the beginning of Graham ticking off the boxes on his wife-to-be prospectus.

Both West Coast transplants, in retrospect, we clung to each other, more out of familiar comfort than young lust. We gravitated toward the same foods, the same music, and the same festivals. Graham was as passionate about his work as an entrepreneur in the technology field as I was as a science teacher, and we teasingly fought over who got to read *Wired* first on Saturday mornings. Though not the steamiest relationship, it was an easy and comfortable one, and between Marisol and Graham I felt safe and loved so far away from home.

A year later, Graham's father, CEO of the Bank of N. T. Butterfield & Son in Bermuda, took a rare vacation from his work to escort Graham's mother to California to size me up. Both Clarkes, rarely out of their versions of a tan linen suit, regaled me with stories of Graham growing up with a father who held up the banking system of Bermuda while the missus held up the home front. Each of them had distinct jobs to do, and they performed them according to societal expectations. Mr. Clarke made the money, and lots of it, and Mrs. Clarke made sure all four Clarke children were accepted to Pemberley boarding school and ultimately went on to make a name for themselves in business and finance.

Within a week of the Clarkes' visit, Graham and I became engaged on the night of my twenty-sixth birthday. During our lavish engagement party hosted by the Clarkes, Graham's mother pulled me in for a hug and whispered, *You're going to find caring for your children and my son a busy and purposeful life, just as I have. You must be relieved you won't have to work anymore.* I smiled and hugged my future mother-in-law back, chalking her sentiments up to a difference in generations.

Graham and I were married six months later. While our backgrounds contained many commonalities, given our youthful inexperience, we failed to find out if we shared similar views on how we saw our futures unfolding. What I discovered all too soon after Xandra was born was that Graham envisioned a future that was an exact replica of his childhood and his parents' marriage. I imagined everything but being a replica of Mr. and Mrs. Clarke.

"What'd he want?" Marisol asks, jarring me from my memories.

"For me to call him. Something about Xandra."

Marisol's face goes from high interest to high alert.

"AND?!"

"I don't know all the details, yet. The text came right as the board meeting was starting, then I had to go have a drink with Winn. By the time I got home it was way too late in New York to dive into a long discussion, so instead I called Leo, looking to catch him at lunch. It went straight to voice mail again." I'd like to redirect Marisol from discussing Graham because I'd much rather dissect why Leo and I are having a hard time reaching each other.

"YOU DIDN'T CALL GRAHAM BACK?!" Marisol's teetering on hyperventilation. "What if something's really wrong with Xandra? Like she's in the hospital? Or missing? Oh shit, Nina, what if she got a tramp stamp of smudged Arabic letters?"

"Relax, Doomsday Debbie. If you're under eighteen, you have to have a legal guardian with you to get a tattoo. I did get in touch with Graham as I was following Winn out of Royal-Hawkins. I asked if Xandra was in one piece, breathing, and with all her blood on the inside." I will admit, I was happy when Graham took a job in New York before Xandra started at Pemberley. Not just because he's out of my hair, but also because he's only forty minutes from Xandra if something were to go wrong. Graham is the best kind of ex: far away but useful.

"But nothing was wrong. Graham said yes, Xandra's absolutely fine, no loss of blood whatsoever." Judging from her side-eye, Marisol's not convinced. "And then I said I had to go, because Winn was holding open the door for me. Graham threw out a rude one-liner, something like, 'Let me know when you can find time to talk about your daughter.'" In the past that would have agitated my working mom guilt, but now I can decipher when he's just in a picking-on-me sort of mood. "You know how he plays me, now he's just doing it from New York."

Marisol nods. Eleven years on the sidelines of our marriage and several more witnessing our divorced life, she gets it.

"And I did get in touch with Xandra. You know I don't leave anything to chance when it comes to my baby. I panic texted her when Winn was calling the board meeting to order. She let me know she's all good. Out with a group of friends getting frozen yogurt, then heading back to the dorm to study. Since it obviously wasn't an emergency, just Graham messing with me, I turned the worry down a notch." Marisol releases the breath she's been holding and signals for me to continue.

"First text Graham's ever sent me should have started with 'Xandra's fine.' Who texts a mother like that? 'It's about Xandra' *Pfft* . . . I thought my head was going to explode. He doesn't know what he's doing because he was barely around when I was raising her and trying to grow my career. He was too busy nurturing his start-up." Marisol nods again.

"I've felt so blah all day, I haven't had it in me to call Graham again and deal with his narcissism, our past, or be bothered with Graham's questioning my dedication to Xandra."

"Maybe you're on edge more than usual because Leo's gone and you're missing that double ass tap." Marisol's familiar with how to coax me out of my Graham-bashing mood. "But seriously, Nina, you're the most responsible mother I know. Not staying on the line with Graham to get all the details about Xandra is completely out of character. I'm getting you home right now so you can call Graham immediately. Xandra may have answered your text and said everything was all right, but something could still be wrong. Don't you want to know what's goin' down? I do."

"Am I a bad mom if I say I only want to know when things are going up this year? Parenting a problem from three thousand miles away is really hard." I don't know how Graham's mother did it from Bermuda when Graham's appendix burst his junior year in high school and she couldn't get to him for forty-eight hours because she was hosting a dinner party for Mr. Clarke's banking cronies. "You know me, remember last year when Xandra was a freshman? I almost got on a plane after she cried over a lost retainer, even though I had two papers to write and Back to School Night." Marisol knows. She once drove in the dark of night to Nevada to hand deliver her son Paco's lacrosse pads to a tournament.

Attempting to divert Marisol from the topic of Xandra, I say, "You know, even though my dad teases us for what he thinks is spending too much money fussing over ourselves, I think when I go to work, he Ubers to get a mani-pedi over at KayCee's Nails." I knew it was dangerous when I taught him how to use ride-sharing so he could get around town. "He's been looking way too shined up lately for a man his age."

"A man should be shined up at any age. *Claro*, Fitzroy always looks good, but doesn't he know I'd give him the family discount?" Marisol asks. "Tell him my studios do men's feet, too, but he's not getting one penny off if he goes cheating on me with another shop owner behind my back. And nope, not on topic at all"—Marisol hates conversational detours—"but I'll require more on that later."

"Fine. This is supposed to be my year as a no-drama mama. I'm not ready for whatever Graham wants to drop. Who knows how long my dad's gonna be here, I've got all eyes on me in a new job, and I'm hurtin' over Leo right now. Do you really think I can take on any more stress?" Marisol fully ignores my question.

"You can if it's about Xandra. You gotta call Graham."

SEVEN

Whack!

"What the . . . ?" A surprise attack from my father, and I'm not even three steps in the house. His smacks to the shoulder are always swift and let you know he's not messing around.

"Nina, why am I getting voice mails from Graham like we're still related? Why's he taking up my time calling me asking why you haven't rung him back about my granddaughter?" Typical Graham, pushing all the boundaries by calling my father to tattle on my mothering.

"Dad, I just walked in the door, give me a sec," I say, setting my bag down and kicking my shoes into the front closet.

"I don't think so. I already called Graham back and promised that you'd be ringing his line the minute you got home. He says he needs to talk to you about Xandra. Wouldn't tell me what it's about," Dad says, leading me into the living room. "Jeezum pees. Not telling me what's going on with my granddaughter like he forgot who paid for the wedding night that produced her."

I give a slight smile. I'm happy to know my father and I are on the same familial side on this one. "Dad, I checked in with Xandra last night, and she said she was doing well. So whatever Graham has to say, it's not an emergency, he's just trying to get under my skin like he always does. Stand down, Sarge," I joke, trying to loosen up the tense atmosphere. I need a cool beverage and a little more time before I can catch whatever Graham's about to throw my way.

I roll my neck, left then right. I locate my phone in the outside pouch of my purse and shake it in Dad's direction. Juvenile, I know, but the power balance in our living room is leaning way too far toward Jamaica.

I move at a glacial pace sitting down at the kitchen table to make the call. Dad follows, pulling out a chair to sit, folding his hands neatly on one of the brick-red place mats, and nodding at my phone. He's not stepping out of this room to allow me privacy to stall making the call. Fitzroy's awaiting evidence Graham's on the line.

"That phone isn't going to dial itself," Dad says, offering up the obvious. Who dials anymore? I huff petulantly and tap Graham's contact. Three rings pass. In my head I formulate a message to leave.

"Hey, Nina." Graham's voice traveling cross-country grates on my last nerve.

"Hello, Graham," I say with a hint of irk.

"Thanks for calling me back." His smooth, familiar accent meets my harsh one head-on, ensuring he's in the controlling position, his favorite place. You would think that after seventeen years, I'd be better at not letting Graham get to me.

"I texted with Xandra last night, and she sounded fine to me. She was out getting frozen yogurt with some friends and said she did well on a recent paper in her art history course." I rattle off facts about Xandra, needing to prove I'm a loving mother in the know. "I didn't share that you're in her business and causing me to worry unnecessarily."

"You're right, Nina, Xandra's not in any real danger. Physical danger, that is." Yeah, you know I'm right, there's nothing I don't know about my baby even if she's all the way across the country. "But I am concerned by the company Xandra's choosing to keep at Pemberley."

"What? You don't know what you're talking about. I've always made sure she has lovely friends. Running with the wrong crowd is not how

Xandra rolls," I insist. Dad shoots me a fierce look that tells me this is no time for defensive language. I can't help myself.

"I'm not so sure," Graham says. A heavy silence hangs over the line. We're each waiting for the other to speak. I stand up from the table and take the phone out to the front porch for some fresh air and distance from Dad's burning ears.

"Xandra's acting out at school, sort of trying on a new persona. I think she's being influenced by Dash."

"Please, what does Xandra have to push up against other than the occasional bad hair day 'cause no one in ten miles of that school knows how to do a tight braid." I cannot believe this is what I'm hearing. This certainly is not worth all the fuss over calling Graham back. "Her life is the dream life. All the freedom in the world at Pemberley, none of the responsibilities. Don't go creating extra issues, Graham, we've already had enough. You always were the more dramatic of the two of us."

"Maybe she's out of sorts from seeing her mama macking all over some White dude she had never met? Do you think THAT could be it?" I'm stunned speechless. "I thought we agreed we would talk to each other about any relationship we were in before introducing the person to Xandra."

My eyes are burning with instant tears. "She has met Leo," I stumble, skipping over yet another failure at our coparenting communication agreement. Section 18A—what to do when dating someone new. From what mutual friends tell me, Graham's had a not-so-secret revolving door of women since he moved to New York. I figured my first relationship since our divorce was none of his business.

"Yeah, she told me. She met Leo AFTER she saw the two of you all over each other in the driveway. After you had been together most of the summer. Seriously, Nina? Even I didn't expect that coming from you."

I close my wet eyes, dropping my head in my hands. I didn't know. Thinking back now, Xandra was a little tense when Leo came in and I introduced the two of them. She gave short answers to the questions Leo asked and was eager to get out of the house. The moment was certainly out of character the more I consider it. Xandra's usually a chatterbox. I just figured she was itching to meet up with friends for an end-of-summer hurrah before I took her back east to school. The whole encounter was five minutes, six tops, and Xandra was gone.

"If that had been me going at it with some random chick in front of Xandra, you would have ripped my head off, and you know it." Graham pauses, letting his proclamation sink in over the line.

"Leo isn't random," I utter, barely audible.

"Listen, I don't know if having a dude in your life is what's rubbing Xandra raw or if it's something else completely, who can tell with teenagers." I'm relieved that Graham has downshifted from copanicking back to coparenting as he shares a litany of additional concerns about Xandra's behavior that he gleaned from a conversation with her dorm parent.

"Just let me know if she opens up to you, okay? I got to go."

Dad bellows from the open living room window to the front porch, "Nina Morgan Clarke, what are you doing out there like someone collecting signatures. Get back in this house and tell me what's going on with Xandra." He slams the window frame shut, my signal to hustle up and spill. Walking in, I'm struggling how to tell my dad that Xandra saw me kissing a strange man—and that she's also hanging out with a friend her grandfather considered a no-good ragamuffin from the moment they met last year. I decide to tackle the easier of the two topics and leave Leo out of it.

Before I get through the front door, Fitzroy lays in, "So, what did Graham say? Is Xandra having trouble in class? You know I thought she was signed up for too many activities. She needs to focus on her studies." Dad is pacing with concern.

"That's not it, Dad." I shake my head, caught up in my own worry of how me dating Leo is affecting Xandra and irritation with Graham claiming to know more about our daughter than I do. I used to know what every sigh, nose scrunch, and nail bite meant when it comes to Xandra. Now she's keeping secrets from me, and I'm forced to rely on

Graham to interpret her actions to determine which ones are worth reporting home.

"Graham was calling about some concerns he has with Xandra's, uh, attitude in school."

"What kind of concerns could he have? Xandra hasn't given a single soul a problem one minute of her life. Morgan children do not fool around with their education." Dad dismisses such nonsense with a wave of his hand. Next to a heavenly singing voice, Fitzroy Morgan's greatest talent is short-term memory loss when it comes to any past failings of his family.

"Remember Xandra's roommate from last year?"

"Yes, I remember that roommate, Nina. I remember telling you that I did not see the kind of polish on her necessary to get along in this world." Fitzroy's rubbing his hands together, distressed.

"Yeah, well, you may not have been a huge fan, but she and Xandra became pretty tight, so they decided to room together again this year." The flare of Daddy's nostrils speaks volumes. Today's accusation is, *Oh no, you did not let that happen.* "She's fifteen, Dad, she can choose to live with whomever makes her feel happy and safe when she's so far from home."

"You know I never understood why you sent her away to school when she could easily continue on for high school at Royal-Hawkins. Jeezum pees, Nina. You run the school and could have been watching her to make sure there's not a thing shady going on." When Dad rolls out the Jamaican Patois, it means one of two things: he's reminiscing about his boyhood, or he's bracing for a verbal standoff.

"Dad, you know I sent Xandra to boarding school for that exact reason, because I'm head of school and I have my eyes and ears on absolutely everything on campus. Xandra wanted to be able to have a normal high school life without being the head's kid. Besides, Graham and all his siblings went to Pemberley, so I never stood a chance in that debate anyway," I explain for the millionth time to my father, and really to myself. In my first year of my doctorate program, I didn't have the energy to fight Clarke family tradition and Xandra's badgering to apply to Pemberley. They had me beat. But it's days like today I'm still searching for reassurance that it was the right thing to do by my baby.

Fitzroy met Xandra's roommate fall of freshman year for Grandparents Weekend. When we reached Xandra's dorm room, Dad stopped short and stared at the door. Designed on brightly colored card stock was Xandra's name, as was her dormmate's, Sha—A Green. Xandra was not in her room, but Sha-Dash-A was, and she informed Dad, with a daring look, that she preferred to be called *Dash*. Dad smiled tightly and sat balanced on the edge of Xandra's bed, not taking his eyes off Dash.

Packing up her clarinet, Dash confidently answered questions as Dad peppered them her way. He wanted to know who *her people* were, where they were from, and what they did, as if *our people* were Jamaican royalty. Proper behavior and upbringing are valued by the Morgans, and Dad was putting Dash through the paces, politely and seeming genuinely interested. I knew exactly what Fitzroy was doing, determining if Dash was *broughtupsy*, his old-school term used to describe an expectation of manners.

It was during Dad's interrogation we learned that Dash lost an older brother during a police shooting near their home in Chicago. It was an event that changed the course of life for the entire Green family. Dash informed Fitzroy that she had spent her childhood practicing her clarinet while riding the 'L' train with her parents, traveling to and from protests and rallies all over the city of Chicago. Once Dash was nearing high school and pushing back on her parents for independence, they made the decision to send her to boarding school.

After Dash left the room to meet up with her jazz trio, Dad informed me it was obvious that Dash had packed up and carried her parents' grief and anger with her to school, where it was taking up space in Xandra's dorm room. For Xandra's roommate, Dad would have preferred a nice pianist from Beverly Hills with a strong GPA, impeccable manners, and less generational trauma.

"It turns out, possibly with the support of Dash, that Xandra has become worked up and has been speaking out, I guess you could say. She claims there's a biased culture at Pemberley," I finally share, blowing out the breath I didn't realize I was holding. "Graham didn't have specific details yet, but he went to campus yesterday to take Xandra to dinner, and he overheard some of the girls in her dorm talking about Xandra and her recent rants." I could not bring myself to admit out loud that Xandra's anger may have something more to do with me than with Pemberley.

"I told you," Dad says, shaking his head. "Anybody fool enough to name their child Sha-Dash-A has no common sense. Their child probably doesn't have good common sense, and YOU don't have good common sense letting Xandra room with this girl again. When we saw her name printed on their door last year, we should have grabbed Xandra and flew out of there like a dog was chasing us."

"Dad, really, not this again," I begin, only to be cut off.

"Why any two people would name their child some ridiculous mash-up of letters and punctuation is beyond me." With Dad fussing like this, I could tiptoe out of the room without him noticing.

"I remember back in the day folks gave their children good solid Christian names like Ruth, David, or John. Ohhhhh noooo . . . now everybody's got an apostrophe, or their name is spelled backward, or there's a *La* at the beginning. I don't know why they keep bringing all these funny-sounding babies into the world." Dad's working himself up, throwing his arms in the air. "You got a name like that, you get all sorts of ridiculous ideas about how you can behave. And I tell you what, no one's gonna hire somebody named Sha-Dash-A. I don't care how smart she is, she's not running some big-time important company with that kinda name. I certainly wouldn't hire her."

"Dad!" I admonish loudly, but it doesn't matter, his soapbox is too tall for me to yank him down. I plop onto the couch and reach for the remote. This conversation has added a headache to my malaise, and I want thirty minutes to catch up on the news.

"What? You think you're going to find the answer to what to do about Xandra from Don Lemon?" Fitzroy snatches the remote out of my hand. I tip over onto the couch and cover my face with a decorative pillow.

"I'm not sure there's anything to be done right at this moment, Dad. This may be more of a wait-and-see-how-things-play-out scenario," I muffle into the pillow.

"I can't think of one thing good that's come from waiting and seeing. Can you imagine where you and Clive would be if your mother had decided to *wait and see* on your education? Not here in this beautiful house in California with the job you've wanted since you were a little girl. So, I'm gonna give you a day or two to figure this one out, and I hope your solution involves packing boxes and finding a new living situation for my granddaughter."

It's futile to tell my dad that finding Xandra a new living situation when the school year has already started is all but impossible. Instead, I choose to placate the old man in the name of dinner.

"I'll see what I can do, Dad," I say, and give my father a kiss on the cheek. "But for now, I'm going to go change. I'll get on making dinner in a minute."

—

"I just got out of a meeting and have another one in ten; just enough time to call my mother or FaceTime you." Ahhhh it sounds so good to finally hear Leo's voice before I drift off to sleep after this crappy day. My father barely spoke two words to me at dinner, but he managed to muster up a cheery attitude and forward Clive a couple of funny emails while I did the dishes. I snuggle all of my body into my comforter cocoon, making my world just me and Leo.

"Tell me all about your day and then say something sexy that'll perk me up and keep me awake through my deposition," Leo requests, breathing heavily into a jiggling phone. It's 1:00 p.m. in Singapore, so he's either racing between work commitments or hunkering down in a bathroom stall. I really hope it's the first.

"You sound winded. Are you out of breath thinking about me?"

"It's hot as hell, and I'm soaked through my shirt in this humidity. Monsoon season in Singapore is no joke." Leo didn't pick up on my fishing for a compliment. "It's easy to spot the Americans, we all look like we just got out of the shower the minute we step outside. Sloan's my saving grace, though, she keeps me in clean, pressed shirts." Who's Sloan, I want to ask, but bite down on my lip. Our long-distance journey so far has been a few scenic pictures and brief texts promising future video calls. I don't want to spend one of Leo's ten precious minutes in a huff of schoolgirl jealousy.

"Enough about me, how's the start of school?" Leo still sounds rushed, but at least his jiggling phone has settled.

"No fiascos to report yet. On the home front, though, red alert. Xandra saw us sucking face in the driveway the night you met her." Talking about Xandra is good neutral territory.

"Really? I don't remember that."

"Meeting Xandra or that toe-curling kiss?" Leo's hearty laugh relaxes us both. "It was right before you met her. You had me pushed up against the driver's side of your car, and I'm afraid she caught more than the PG moments. My skirt may have been hiked up to where no child wants to see on their mother."

"HA! Seriously? That's kind of funny, but I believe it. She's just now getting around to telling you? Why didn't she call us out on it that night?" I see a leggy young woman in a pencil skirt walk behind Leo, pausing to rest her hand on his shoulder. Is that Sloan?

I've been wondering why Xandra didn't mention the kiss since Graham brought it up, but I don't want to deconstruct my mothering angst on our first real phone call since Leo left. "Teenage girls prefer for their mothers to suffer endlessly and without a clue. Xandra didn't tell me, but she sure didn't hold back telling her father. Apparently now she's acting out at school, and I don't know if her ranting around campus is for a real reason or because she saw us and feels like she can't talk to me about it." As it's coming out of my mouth, I'm wondering if this would have been a conversation better saved for Marisol, but now I'm in it with Leo, and I hope to hell he's not going to judge me for it. So much for keeping it light and loose while he's overseas.

"I'm sure it's no big deal. She can't be surprised that her beautiful mother has a man who can't keep his hands off her." Finally the compliment, but Leo's input is a typical man-with-no-kids answer. Xandra has never seen me with a man other than her father, and ours certainly was not an amorous relationship in the final years. The more I think about it, the more I'm convinced it is a big deal. The guilt of putting Xandra through a strained divorce and now the confusion of seeing her mother with another man rouses tears all over again.

The pencil skirt is back in the screen, giving Leo his second warning it's time to go. "Crap. I have less time than I thought. Can I call you in an hour or two when I'm over my work scramble for the day?"

"Sure, can't wait," I say, forcing a smile, hoping to leave on a good note after laying the latest teen trauma on Leo's sweaty shoulders. I want to believe I'll be able to stay awake to see if Leo actually calls back, but I know I'll be fast asleep. I'm left with little comfort coming to Leo with issues about Xandra. It's not fair for me to expect sage advice from Leo, so from now on I'll be sure to keep the kid talk between me and someone who actually has them.

EIGHT

Hey, Mimi. Is Jared here yet?" The energy bar I gulped down in three bites between the library and my office hasn't kicked in. With my adrenaline running high, I'm ravenous all the time. I was hopeful my appetite would shrink by the first of October as I comfortably settled into the role of person in charge who supposedly knows what the fuck she's doing. So far, no such luck; a few weeks into school and my impostor syndrome continues to flare when I shake hands with students coming through the main gate greeting me with, "Good morning, Ms. Clarke." I smile back and wish them a beautiful day and think to myself, How did I get here and why do these families trust me with their child's future?! What awaits in my office is another aspect of my new job: supporting young teachers settling into their first teaching gig.

"He's been in your office for a handful of minutes. Not sure how he got out of his classroom and up here so fast," Mimi says, nodding at the clock hanging on the wall. October is the month students start to cross over from enthusiasm for a new school year into the grind of a month straight with no federal holidays. Jared's request to meet must be important, his lunch break started barely three minutes ago. Before I head into my office, I check my texts and voice mail. No response from Leo after sending him two texts when I woke up this morning asking him to give me a ring before he goes to bed.

I blow out a sigh of disappointment before turning on the charm. "Nice to see you, Jared. I'm glad we were able to find a time to meet so quickly," I say, seating myself across from Jared Jones, who fills out one of the oversize wingback chairs in the living room environment I've set up in my office. Jared has his phone out and his boots kicked up on my coffee table. He looks too comfortable using my office to relax and catch up on social media after teaching back-to-back periods separated from his device.

"Courtney Dunn, Benjamin's stepmother, sure has great things to say about you. Or I guess it's Benjamin who has given you the amazing review. He seems to love your history class. And he's really looking forward to basketball season." I find it's always best to start any conversation between administrator and teacher with a compliment, it can help ease the inexplicable tension that can taint the teacher-administrator relationship. I want Jared to know I'm in his corner, though first I'd like him to recognize he's in my office and get his feet off my coffee table. I don't know where those Timberlands have been.

Unable to set his phone aside, Jared pushes off with the toes of his boots and leans his chair back on the two hind legs. "Yeah, all parents have a thing for me. Particularly mothers of sons." I reach my hand over and forcefully push the arm of the chair, full of two hundred pounds of solid muscle and ego, sending it back down onto all fours. Jared looks at me, finally lowering his phone. "What can I say, every mama I know wants their son to turn out like me, a baller and a scholar." Bam, there it is. The winning smile and attitude that ensure Jared gets what he wants, including this job.

I press my hands together hard. I read in some management journal that at the moment you want to reach out and strangle an employee for lack of professional judgment, you should press your palms together, hard. Apparently, it lowers your blood pressure, cools your nerves, and keeps your employee alive. Jared's overconfidence with parents and too-casual comfort with me are fueling my residual aggravation over his personal request for three days off for a basketball camp.

"Why is it you wanted to meet with me so urgently?" I ask, deciding it's best to limit further banter and get right to the point.

"So, here's the ish. I know I was hired to teach middle school social studies and coach sixth grade basketball, but yesterday I met up with the varsity coach to shoot some hoops in the gym and get to know him." Okay, I decide, Jared's making up a little ground by being first to reach out to a fellow colleague. I'm impressed, very mature for a man in his early twenties.

"He's a nice guy, but a busted ball player. Feel me?" Jared holds his hand up waiting for a fist bump as if we know each other like that. Maturity misdiagnosed.

"And you needed to meet with me because?" I want to keep this conversation on course and continue to believe Jared's the promising hire I hope he will be.

"I can run circles around that guy, on and off the court. When he jumps you, can barely slip a credit card under his feet. Trust me, I love middle schoolers, my kids are hilarious, but I think I can serve Royal-Hawkins much better as the varsity coach rather than hanging with the younger team." Jared's on a roll, getting all worked up, believing his own hype.

"Here's the ish." I intentionally pause after throwing Jared's slang back at him, and then I give a smile that's meant to strike fear more than warmth. "At Royal-Hawkins we don't do God, we don't really do sports, but on March 14 every year we do a blowout Pi Day. It's our Super Bowl." I suspect my new humanities teacher is not following my scholastic declaration.

"Jared, Royal-Hawkins is first and foremost an institution that serves kids for whom academics are their ultimate competition. Shakespeare is sport here. This is your first year teaching in a classroom and coaching, do I have that right?"

Jared nods, and I can tell he's searching that limber brain of his for a witty retort, so I jump right back in to wind this request down quickly. "I suggest you focus on dazzling me with your teaching skills when I come in for your first official evaluation, Jared. I would think doing me and Harvard proud in the classroom would be your first and foremost priority." I hope to pacify and encourage him to do well by mentioning that I remember he's an Ivy League product. Stroking the male ego always helps. "In a couple of years, once you've nailed teaching and demonstrated some coaching chops, then we may have something further to talk about." I stand to signal his time's up. I need to take advantage of this moment to cement roles here, so I pause on my way to the door to tower over this young king.

"I got you, Nina," Jared says, nodding while heaving himself out of the cushioned comfort of my wingback chair.

"I look forward to seeing great things from you, Jared. I know I will," I say with finality, holding my doorknob. Start on a compliment, end on one too.

"I know you will too." Jared gives me a quick salute and strides off my court. I have a feeling this is not the last time we'll be facing off.

—

Xandra 12:24 PM

> I have a study group but need to talk to you tonight, my drama teacher's a real dick.

Xandra knows she's not allowed to throw around curse words with me. In our family I'm the one with the filthy mouth that Xandra's always quick to edit. I'm going to need to open a bag of corn chips to decode this text.

Nina 12:25 PM

> K. I'll call then. I'm worried. Or call me earlier if you can. Whenever. I'm available. And I LOVE YOU. Really, really love you.

I reread my text and delete up to *worried*. I can't come across too over-bearing and desperate to solve my teenage daughter's life from across the country. Marisol would be proud of me for checking myself.

Xandra 12:27 PM

Hand out of the chip bag Mom, I'm OK.

I pop a handful in my mouth and chomp down in defiance of my fif-teen-year-old know-it-all. I kick open my lower cabinet door. Turns out this is my only bag, so I need to make it last through the day. A bag used to last me a week, but I'm currently excelling at eating my job perfor-mance insecurities. Plus, I think Mimi forgot to stock my fall collection.

"Mimi," I singsong out my office door. "Do you mind hopping over to Trader Joe's when you can and picking up some more of my corn chip dippers? My summer stash is almost gone." I truly don't think I can head of school without them.

In a moment Mimi's in my doorway. "Are you sure? I restocked about ten days ago. Let me take a peek." I pull my desk chair back so Mimi can squat to inspect the bottom cabinet I just finished examining. "Wow, you're right, they're all gone. That's so strange, I know I put a couple in there, recently."

I put down the bag I'm currently devouring and dust off my hands.

"No worries, please just grab me some when you can. And on your way out, can you . . . uh . . . close my door? I have some calls to make."

"Okay." Mimi studies my face for a second before doing what I've asked. We both know I rarely shut my door, so the look of concern she aims my way is not unfounded.

My hands shake as I scroll back through my weekly calendar. Past the first day of school. Past the day Leo left. I search past my dad's arrival, all the way to the road trip Leo and I took to Yosemite at the beginning of August.

Soon after our tryst in Santa Barbara, Leo called me to reissue his camping invitation.

Rather than jumping in an SUV with a man I barely knew, I suggested we try a meal over a table rather than a campfire for our first real date. At that dinner I admitted to Leo I had never been to Yosemite. Once he recovered from his shock at that piece of Nina trivia, he cracked the competitive campsite reservation game and insisted he was the one to show me the national park wonders I had only seen in Ansel Adams's photographs.

Like many Black people living in urban areas, my family does not camp. Or hike. There were a lot of people staring at me on the trails as we explored the outdoors. I had folks passing me left and right with looks I was sure said, *First a Jamaican bobsled team, now this!* I high-fived the one brown-skinned brother I saw coming down North Dome as we headed up. He lifted his chin at me, we shared a sly grin, and, no doubt, the same thought—*We're everywhere!*—before continuing in opposite directions.

As it turns out, I like everything about hiking! The exercise, fresh coffee before starting out in the crisp morning air, watching Leo's backside flex with every step without seeming creepy. I can, however, do without sleeping on an inch-thick mattress pad and having to eat dinner with a utensil called a *spork*. I'm a grown-up, damn it.

I return to today's schedule and email Mimi on the other side of our shared wall:

Cancel my meetings for the afternoon.

~

"You're so lucky I'm at a shop being remodeled," Marisol says, laying a clean piece of plastic down on the stripped wood floor of the bathroom. We both slide down the wall and inelegantly land on the ground. "While you were in here peeing, I gave my contractor two twenties to quit early and take his guys to have a beer on the Clean Slate." I nod, thankful for Marisol's swift action.

"You didn't sit on the toilet seat when you peed on the stick, did you? The workmen have been using this bathroom for two months and still haven't cleaned the bowl. And they don't lift the seat!" Marisol cringes at the thought.

"What, you think I'm a rookie?"

"At pregnancy tests? Yes. I've been riding shotgun to your love life my whole life."

"No, nasty bathrooms. I work in a school, remember. You only learn that lesson once."

"Truth," Marisol says, nodding. "Those are some gorgeous shoes you got on. Seems you actually got it right for once shopping without me. When did you get those?" I can't tell if Marisol's paying me a sincere compliment or trying to distract me while we wait for the plus or minus on my pregnancy test to show up.

"Saks sale. This is their first day out for a spin. They're last year's Gucci, but still a big win for me." I look down at my well-clad feet, and they wave back and forth at me. Marisol elbows me twice. Time. Clenching, I unfurl my fingers from the stick and pass the test to Marisol.

"Well, I'd wear those shoes every day for the next couple of months, 'cause soon they're not gonna fit." I squeeze my eyes shut and cover my ears, hoping I heard wrong. Marisol pulls my hands away from my head, gripping them tightly in hers, trying to pass strength on to me, or to take away some of my pain.

"This . . . this . . . CANNOT be real. This cannot be my life right now, Marisol. NOPE! It really can't," I insist. "My life is too full already running a school, guiding Xandra into womanhood, and making sure my dad can travel back and forth whenever he pleases. I've been work-ing on getting me, Dad, and Xandra to this place for years." Marisol squeezes tighter, she knows. "And I'm marking off the days until Leo comes home, so he can take me to dinner, not to ultrasounds!" I'm choking on my sobs, stuttering to finish my thoughts.

"Mom died, and I finally left Graham. Graduate school, Xandra going to Pemberley, starting this huge job. It's been seven hard fucking years. I deserve some breathing room!" I'm not sure which is dripping more, the tears from my eyes or the snot from my nose. Marisol unhooks the toilet paper from its holder and hands me the whole roll.

"You still keep a paper calendar?"

"We're sitting here on your disgusting shop floor finding out I'm forty-three and pregnant, and you want details about my calendaring?" I feel the onset of a hysterical laugh-cry. "I don't know how this happened, Sol!"

"Sure, you do. Think back to the bee talk Fitzroy and Celia gave us as kids. Remember the stinger? That would be Leo." At the warning look I give, she continues, "Sorry. I say stupid things when you cry."

"My period has been all over the map the past few years. I swear last week I had a full-on hot flash sitting around scrolling Instagram," I explain, attempting to prove to Marisol and myself that I have a better chance of being perimenopausal than pregnant.

"Yeah, that was Friday, and you were wearing a wool-cashmere blend turtleneck and it was sunny and eighty outside. You were pushing sweater weather before the rest of us were ready, including Mother Nature." Marisol remembers dates and events by what outfits we wore. It's actually very effective for memory recall.

"Who would even want to do this in their midforties, Marisol? Hell, it sure never crossed my mind. When it comes to having kids, I was always one and done."

"Yeah, I tried to give you one of my kids years ago, and you wouldn't even consider it."

"There's no way I'm doing this again." Saying it out loud, even to Marisol in this stripped-down bathroom, feels like sacrilege. I have the money, I have the house, I could give a kid the best education in the world . . . but I don't want to. Besides, I can't even get my supposed boyfriend to call me back.

Marisol wraps her arms around me, holding me close like she fears someone will rip us apart. "You don't have to do this if you don't want to, Nina, you absolutely don't. I'll admit, it's not the perfect beginning to the second half of your life, but it's up to you. Your life can be whatever you want it to be." *Damn straight,* I think to myself. I've put in the work for everyone else, it's my turn.

"But, if you decide you do want to have this baby, between the two of us, we have three kids, I know we can figure out what to do with one more." I can feel the calming hum of Marisol's voice through my back, her cheek pressed hard against me, but for the first time in my life it doesn't help.

⌇

Xandra 6:18 PM

> I saw you called. Give me fifteen to finish up my chapter.

The house is semidark. I've been home for thirty minutes with the lights off, not ready to look at myself in any of the decorative mirrors down the hallway. I close my eyes, tilt my head up, and thank the lucky stars Dad's at a dominoes tournament with a few fellow retirees he met at the Pasadena YMCA. Fitzroy Morgan loves to chat while logging miles on the treadmill.

Lying corpse still on my bed, I wonder in what order I should tell my people about this pregnancy. I suppose it should be Xandra first, since I'm talking to her in a few. Or maybe Dad who, if I don't tell him first, will be able to read it all over my face in the morning. It might be best to keep it on lockdown until Leo and I talk. Leo needs to come to his own quick conclusion to what I already know: having a baby at our age and unmarried—not to mention hardly even knowing each other—is a terrible idea. Or I don't have to tell anyone at all, I can just take care of this business at a clinic right away.

Ring.

Ring.

Cursing myself for getting into this mess at my age, I set aside my thoughts and settle into a better frame of mind to talk to the baby girl I already have.

"Hi, Mama. I know you swear grandma's rum cake is by far the best dessert in the world, but Dash just got these toffee-almond cluster things in the mail from her mom, and they are off the hook! Definitely gives the cake some competition," Xandra says in between chews.

I want to reply, *Don't be disrespecting the memory of your grand-mother's baking. You know Dash's store-bought cookies couldn't touch her skills.* But I don't. I know better than to dump my personal disappointment on my daughter.

"So good to hear your voice, sweetie. Tell Dash, hey," I offer, keeping it light. Besides, it was firmly established during Xandra's freshman year that I am a subpar care package constructor. I can't help it, the educator in me takes over in a Target, and I end up sending printer paper, pens, and three-ring binders.

There's not yet been the right time to bring up Graham's conspiracy theory with Xandra, but every time she mentions Dash, I listen a little bit harder for hints of what may be going on. Peer pressure from Dash? Or just flat-out teenage-level poor decision-making on Xandra's part? And who am I to be calling out anyone's decision-making right now? I certainly can't put Dash in the "she's a bad influence" category for sharing goodies at nine at night. "How was the first drama meeting today?"

"I'm so frustrated, Mom. You know I've been thinking about trying out for a theater show for a while. Dash and I both decided to go for it. And you know what?" I bristle at her acerbic tone but wait to hear more. "The teacher's a total asshole!"

I refrain from telling Xandra to clean up her language. For her to throw around curse words twice in one day means there's a bigger issue at play than her vocabulary. I've listened partway through a half dozen podcasts from *New York Times* bestselling shrinks on the right language to use to keep communication open with your teen. Time to put my listening skills to the test and see if the professional advice works. "Really? Tell me more."

"The audition was long and kind of boring. Dash and I were just trying to entertain ourselves while all the upperclassmen were on stage doing nothing, and in the middle of it, the drama instructor turned and yelled at Dash and me to stop monkeying around in our seats. Can you believe that?!" Xandra shouts, worked up by the time she finishes her story.

"Can I believe what?" My mind's preoccupied with this afternoon's revelation, so I'm afraid I may have missed an important detail.

"That the teacher called us monkeys!" Xandra's voice teeters on total indignation. Okay, I don't like it either, but I think Xandra's missing the subtle misuse of metaphor for the bigger issue at hand, the fact the girls were playing around when they were supposed to be quiet and paying attention. I continue to tread lightly here; I can tell Xandra's feeling unfairly called out.

"It doesn't sound to me like the teacher called you a monkey, it sounds like he didn't like your joking around behavior and being disruptive. I agree with you, using *monkeying around* was probably not the best choice." I try to muster up the appropriate level of sympathy, but teenage girls are dramatic. I remember, I was one. "From what I'm hearing, I'm not sure I'd classify the teacher as a grade A, giant D, but I'm listening."

"Fine. Then how about a racist? That's what I really think. I was just being nice calling him a dick." Xandra's voice is hard. And a little angry. Without seeing her in person, I can't tell if her facial expressions and body language match up, but this is not the Xandra I'm familiar with.

"How 'bout we FaceTime to talk about this? That's a pretty big allegation to toss out there on a Tuesday night." I had been planning to bring up the Leo kiss she witnessed, but this is most definitely not the time. The butterflies already rumbling in my stomach now feel like they're breaking furniture as I realize there's more truth to Graham's phone call about Xandra a few weeks back than I was willing to believe. I definitely hate it when Graham is maybe right.

"Nah, gotta go. Dash and I have a few videos on YouTube that her cousin recommended. We want to check them out before bed." It seems Xandra has moved on to the next to-do item on her night's agenda, and I'm left holding her boarding school baggage.

"Well, okay. G'night, baby girl. I love you."

"Love you too."

My evening plans are now solidified. I'll be figuring out how I can track Xandra's search feed from the West Coast.

NINE

Hey there," I coo at Leo as his picture comes into full pixelation on my laptop. I miss my man like crazy. I'm wearing Leo's favorite pink tank top with a dab of lip gloss to match. I've added white cotton boy shorts that allow my plump butt cheeks to peek through the bottom hem just enough to make him salivate.

I have on the jade bracelet Leo sent me accompanied with a note explaining that in Chinese culture, jade symbolizes perfection, and in his mind, I am perfect. Oh, how wrong Leo is. There's nothing perfect about the predicament I'm in, nor my indecision over telling Leo about the baby, but the FaceTime show must go on. After a week of Leo setting up and canceling calls due to work conflicts, we have both miraculously carved out an hour for this video date, so I think I'll just enjoy Leo's company for tonight and save the maybe-baby news for another time when I'm firmer in my conviction on what I'm going to do.

Leo's smile stretches across the screen. I lean forward and kiss the monitor, my heartbeat picking up speed. He puts his index and middle finger to the camera on his side to receive it, fingerprints be damned. I pull back and wink, then relax into the pillows leaning against my headboard. I perch my laptop on my knees, ready to hear about Leo's most recent adventures in Asia that I'm positive pale in comparison to the tween drama I've been counseling the girls' volleyball team through.

"Have I mentioned the eighty-hour workweeks?" I flinch at the Graham déjà vu. "And if I'm not working in the office, I'm out for seven-course evenings with clients. Most of those courses being drinks, not food, mind you. And it's always all men, thank goodness I have Sloan in the mix!"

"Yes. You told me," I reply, not taking the jealousy bait from the mention of Sloan's presence. This better not be some kind of gaslighting to cover up a guilty conscience.

"Where's your dad?" Leo asks mischievously.

"He's at one of Marisol's son's football banquets. He's the fill-in grandfather."

"I wish I could fill you in, Nina, you look beautiful," Leo says as his hands head south and disappear. I can't see where they've gone, but I can make a pretty good guess. He hasn't even asked about my week.

"What's going on here?" I ask, kind of annoyed. What, he has Sloan for stimulating conversation and me for screen sex?

"Nina, can you lean in closer, I want to see more of you in that top, that, by the way, has always been a little bit see-through." On top of annoyance, I start to feel a little clammy and nauseated. I think I have a box of crackers on my dresser.

"I miss you. And there's no reason we have to go another three months without, you know, when we have modern technology at our fingertips. Come on, baby, let's give it a try. I told you we can make up our own rules to this relationship, and you got me aching over here." I can tell Leo is eager for me to play in his fantasyland, but I have no interest in video sex when I feel reflux brewing.

"I'm pregnant." In my head I can hear Fitzroy's voice saying, *Heel nevah go before toe*. Deal with important matters first, or in this case, change the subject.

"Come again?" Leo's hands magically reappear.

"Actually, that's what got us into this mess in the first place." I give a halfhearted laugh at my quick but queasy wit, hoping to crack Leo's stunned face.

"Wait, wait, wait. You're pregnant? How'd this happen?" Exactly the same thing I've asked on several occasions! See, not such a dumb question after all. I'll have to tell Marisol.

"Apparently, Yosemite's a very romantic spot, and inflatable camping pads are conducive to baby making."

"Huh."

Our first call in days, I've just revealed I'm pregnant, and *Huh* is all he can say?

"And you're sure?" Leo double-checks. I nod and we fall silent. I spy the crack of a grin growing on Leo's face, which is not exactly what I was anticipating, nor does it match how I'm feeling. Maybe it's a facial tic. I'm not prepared for what looks like growing excitement on Leo's part for a prospect I find unimaginable.

"I'm as sure as three positive home pregnancy tests in a construction zone and one OB-GYN appointment a few days later. And while you were starting to get freaky over FaceTime, all I could think about was texting my dad to bring me back some chicken tenders from the football banquet for when I wake up at two a.m. starving, so yeah, I'm pretty sure I'm pregnant."

"Wait, you went to a first doctor's appointment without me?!" Leo accuses abruptly, sounding perturbed. My man is all over the place emotionally on this phone call, and I'm the hormonal one.

"Ummm, I'm going to point out the obvious here and remind you that you're in Singapore, I'm in Pasadena. How exactly would you be going with me to my appointment when we can barely find the time to connect with one another?"

Ignoring my verbal jab, Leo picks up his laptop and shakes it so all I see is his midsection, taut but jiggling with the moving screen. "With THIS!!" he demands. I'm getting queasier.

"Well, I'm sorry, I guess. But it made no sense to hit you with a pregnancy scare unless I was sure. Who wants to know that piece of unwelcome news?"

"ME! I WANT TO KNOW! I would have liked to know immediately if I were in the dad zone," Leo insists, grasping at his chest to emphasize his presence. I have had plenty of girlfriends share their baby reveal stories from triumphant to tragic, but never have I heard one where the man was interested in being part of the "is she or isn't she" pregnancy purgatory.

"Nina, I'm having a baby with you. This is incredible, beyond, beyond I don't know what! This is more than video sex good!" Leo has broken out into a celebratory dance. "I didn't think kids were in the cards for me, then, BOOM, you, my summer surprise, deliver!" Leo mimics lighting fireworks for emphasis.

"I didn't know you wanted to have kids, we never even talked about it. I figured if you wanted to have children, you would have planted your seed in some fresh young soil."

"Well, talking about kids isn't exactly early relationship material. You have Xandra, and you're on the backside of this parenting thing." *Exactly*, I think to myself. "Truthfully, I was just focused on you and trying to get us past this period of distance when I knew I was going to be buried in work." Wow, I really didn't realize how committed Leo was to keeping our relationship alive when I was giving us a fifty-fifty chance.

"Being with you was, I mean still is, more important to me than having a baby. But if I can have both—YES, PLEASE." Leo's squeal is a bit disconcerting coming from a six-foot-two man, but it makes me giggle. I've just gotten a glimpse of what Leo must have been like as a kid on his birthday. And then it hits me, Leo believes we're having this baby for certain. More than likely, he thinks my desire to have this baby is a given. I'm a woman, I'm already a mom, and I work in a school, which must mean I love the idea of being surrounded by kids all the time. Who wouldn't presume my uterus wants to populate the planet?

Me. That's who.

Leo has no clue the kind of commitment raising a child requires. He already puts in eighty-hour workweeks, and babies need at least that much caretaking. There's not enough time left to sleep in a week with a baby, let alone jet-setting around the world launching new legal ventures. I've already raised one child as a full-time working mom with a career-obsessed partner, but I was young and at least that one was living under my roof. At forty-three, I'm definitely not up for that kind of parenting repeat. Work aside, though, there are other issues weighing equally on my mind.

"Listen, Leo, there's a lot to discuss, but I'm really tired right now. I think springing this news on you is enough for one call." I'm eager to get off this video chat before I say something Leo may not want to hear.

"Oh, okay, right, you're going to need extra rest. No skimping on sleep right now, Nina. Just one last question, and then I'll let you go," Leo says, lowering his voice. My breath hitches in my chest, and I feel his emotions despite the miles between us. The hopeful look on his face, the pleading gaze in his eyes, and lips set in a strong line hint that he may ask the one question I fear having to answer.

"We are going to do this . . . right?"

Yep. I was right.

TEN

FROM: Nina Morgan Clarke
DATE: October 29
SUBJECT: Halloween at Royal-Hawkins School
TO: parentbody@royalhawkinsschool.org

Dear Royal-Hawkins Parents,

I'm looking forward to seeing those who can attend the Royal-Hawkins Halloween parade on the grassy field tomorrow at 2:00 p.m. While we cherish creativity and self-expression at Royal-Hawkins, I must ask that before you send your child to school in their Halloween costume, you please review the following guidelines:

- If you have a younger student, make sure they are able to get their costume off in time to go to the bathroom, independently.

- If you have an older student, make sure their costume will not terrify a younger student.

- Costumes cannot interfere with the classroom or PE.

- No full-face coverings.

- No items resembling guns or weapons.

- No costumes that promote stereotypes based on race, religion, color, national origin, age, gender, disability, sexual orientation, or gender identity.

Yours in Community,

Nina Morgan Clarke

Head of School

The Royal-Hawkins School

Nina 6:18 PM

Sol, check your email and get a load of the PC BS I just sent out to Royal-Hawkins parents.

Halloween blows in the era of cancel culture. I miss last century when there were more than a dozen acceptable costumes to choose from. Can't America have a hall pass one day a year from trying to be our better selves? Isn't the point of Halloween to get dressed up, live out a fantasy, be something you cannot be the other 364 days a year, and then gorge yourself on candy until you're ill? That's living the Halloween dream.

Marisol 6:20 PM

You forgot to mention that all treats coming to school for classroom parties need to be gluten, sugar, dairy, nut, soy, and taste free. Nothing says par-tay like some squeezy applesauce.

Nina 6:21 PM

I'm leaving the food intolerance mine field to the room parents.

I'm excited to wear my Cleopatra costume on my first official holiday as head of school. Though it adheres to the Royal-Hawkins standard dress code by just a few threads, I love this formal gown. I had gold cuff hair rings added to my braids this afternoon, and I look like African royalty. Exaggerated eyeliner and boldly colored lids will highlight my dress, an off-the-rack emerald-green fitted Prada ball gown I found on a trip to the designer outlets near Palm Springs. Marisol convinced me to buy it. She swore at some point in my life there would be the perfect occasion for it. That occasion is now. Is this costume too power-wielding, over-the-top attention grabbing for a head of school? Maybe. Is there too much skin showing up top? Probably. Can I get away with it for one day in an entire school year of dressing proper verging on pious? I guess I'm going to find out. The bigger question at hand is if I can fit into said dress. The beginning of a bulge is pushing my waistline, reminding me decision time is soon.

I put the dress on to test the fit before it goes to school with me tomorrow. Though I can get it zipped up over my midsection, the dress is relocating excess flesh into my rack. I hike the neckline up with a forceful one-handed tug and push my boobs down with the other. Physics is working against me. The more I shove the girls down, the more they pop back up in a repeating game of peek-a-boob.

"Are you trying to draw people's eyes away from your belly by putting your bosom on display?" Dad asks as casually as he might wonder when I would be stopping by the dry cleaner to pick up his Sunday suit. Hiking up the dress's skirt, I pass by my father in the living room where he's reading the newspaper. I don't want to trip from shock of his mentioning my belly.

"After you slip out of that sausage case of a dress, I expect we should talk about whatever you got going on that you think I don't know about." Dad comes over to me and carefully helps unzip the back of my dress. Ah relief, I can breathe. "Nothing gets past me when it comes to my children, Nina. You think I don't see something's been weighing heavy on you? I've been an expert at reading you for forty-three years; and that was after nine months of staring at your mother's belly. Are you pregnant?"

"I don't know how this happened Dad, I really don't," I crumble. Adult or child, I still fall apart at the thought of disappointing my father. Worrying over his reaction, I've shed tears all over town the past few weeks. Heading through the Wells Fargo drive-up ATM, I whimpered entering my PIN, Xandra's birth date. Last Tuesday at the YMCA, I could feel heat rising and tears pooling in my eyes as I met with the executive director about discounted memberships for Royal-Hawkins employees. It turned out she has twin newborns. Don't even get me started on picking out melons at Pavilions market. The cantaloupes were next to the bananas. I know, juvenile, but I can't control my mind or my mood, and everything seems to set me off these days.

"I know we didn't get it all right raisin' you, but I know for sure Celia and I taught you the facts of life. And here you are at your age, pregnant, no husband." Dad squeezes his eyes shut and holds up my robe left on the back of the couch from this morning. I step out of my dress and slip my arms through the sleeves. My pre-Halloween catwalk is over. I don't respond to Dad's recitation of my predicament. My age. Pregnant. Not married. I'm all too familiar with the details.

"Nina, I need to know that you have respect for yourself and for that nice man you were seeing over the summer. You stepping out on Leo, or is this his baby?"

"Dad! Of course, it's Leo's. Do you seriously think I'm sleeping around on him?"

Fitzroy throws up his arms.

"Well, I don't know, Nina, the way I hear you and Chaco Taco talk about who's sleeping with who, who's trading boyfriends, girlfriends, husbands, wives. I don't know where your generation's sense of commitment and Christian values have gone. Thank goodness your mother is not here to hear how you two gossip."

I can't fault my dad for that judgy comment. Last time Marisol was over at the house, we were cackling like two old hens about who was getting sexy behind their spouses' backs. Sometimes people really don't want to see what's right in front of them, but Marisol and I always see it. It's a hobby we share, and a gift. I thought Dad was engrossed in his crossword puzzle that night, but turns out his ears were tuned to the kitchen.

"Does Leo know you're having his child?" Dad asks me.

"Yes, he knows I'm pregnant." That's the most I can say to my father about my indecision. Any hint that I'm considering terminating the pregnancy would be cause for Fitzroy to throw me in the car, drive me to church, and beg the pastor for a baptism redo.

"You about done playing dress-up? Because I'm going to make us some tea. I look forward to hearing how Leo received the news that he's going to be a father. I'm missing my dominoes game tonight so I can hear all about it." When Fitzroy steps foot in a kitchen you know shit is about to get real.

FROM: Courtney Dunn
DATE: October 31
SUBJECT: Halloween at Royal-Hawkins
TO: Nina Morgan Clarke

Good Morning Nina,

I can't wait for you to see my Megan Rapinoe and Giannis Antetokounmpo—minus the blackface of course, we read your all-school email. The Dunn family are professional athletes in the making! I know what you're thinking, Benjamin is taking a risk being a Milwaukee Buck in Lakers territory, but my great-grandfather landed in Wisconsin from Ecuador, and Benjamin is proud of his family lineage.

Looking forward to seeing you at school drop-off in a few, I will be out front championing the annual fund. Would love a moment of your time to talk board of trustees seats.

Trick or treat,
Courtney

Having dropped my bag in my office and finished my last bite of breakfast sandwich, I make a quick turnaround to head out to the front of the building for my favorite school drop-off of the year. Royal-Hawkins is passionate about Halloween, and as head of festivities, I take my job seriously. Today is not about learning. No way. It's about pageantry, trading turkey sandwiches for TWIX bars, and a long-standing tradition I started my first year as a science teacher: candy house building competitions. Education enthusiasts would try to kill all the fun and link the competition to curriculum by calling it design thinking, but I call it straight-up, old-school, kid-on-kid combat. Why should competitive gingerbread house decorating at Christmas get all the food fanfare?

I'm trying to decide whether I should explain to Courtney that as an immigrant, one does not *land* in a landlocked state. You pretty much arrive there by any other mode of transportation than boat. And, technically, Benjamin is no more Ecuadorian than I am Egyptian since he's her stepson and I'm just wearing a costume. My thoughts fall away once I catch a glimpse of Courtney nagging people for their loot on the Royal-Hawkins front steps in a full-on pirate costume.

"Argh . . . hand over your treasure for the Annual Fund! It's a pirate's life for me! Gold or bust!"

Courtney's getup is complete with an eye patch and a hook hand. Her costume is notably in defiance of rule six from my emailed six-point Halloween protocol—no costumes promoting stereotypes or disabilities. I bet that hook hand cost her a fortune, it looks like it's made out of pure silver. Am I going to say anything to her? Nope. That white, flouncy, ruffle blouse she's wearing is off the hook. Pun intended.

Courtney limps over to me, I suppose feigning a peg leg. "Hi, Nina. You could take that Cleopatra costume right from the school steps to the LA Philharmonic gala. Brava! You doing the best you on Halloween, I love it!" I press down the front of my dress and take a second to consider a proper response to her cryptic compliment. Instead, I let the comment roll off my back. I know there's not one other woman in this school who can pull off a Macedonian temptress quite like I can.

"Speaking of having a ball, last night Geoff and I had dinner with Winn and his wife, Gemma. We discussed all the ways I could contribute as a board member. Did Winn email you this morning?" I only shake my head no, knowing from experience that Courtney has a closing line to deliver. "What Winn and I could do together would light this school on fire!" Courtney says, pointing her sword toward the front foyer.

"Well, I would prefer to avoid a fire at all costs, you know how sensitive Californians are to the mention of hot flames, but your support for the school is noted as always, Courtney. I appreciate your dedication to Royal-Hawkins." I click my Heqa staff two times on the concrete sidewalk and stroll past Courtney to join a sea of Frodos, Harry Potters, disco queens, and mini–Wonder Women heading into school.

"When my mommy saw your costume, she said it was a good thing my daddy didn't do drop-off this morning," an adorably small lion says, slipping her hand in mine so I can walk her into school. I tighten my lips to keep from letting out a gut-busting laugh. I don't think the seams in my bodice can handle the pressure. "But I told her daddy loves princesses just like I do." *And that's exactly what Mommy is worried about,* I comment to myself. I have to remember to tell Marisol this morning's gem.

"And I love courageous lions," I say, walking my small friend to her classroom door. I've been spending so much time in the beginning of my headship focusing on the upper grades that I've missed the honesty and unconditional love from my youngest students. This little bundle of faux fur reminds me of the countless times Xandra and I have watched *The Wiz.* Before I was deemed embarrassing, we even dressed up as Dorothy and Toto one Halloween. Xandra made me be Toto, but I still loved it.

"You can have some of my courage. I have a lot and I don't mind sharing," my king of her kingdom offers and opens the door.

"Thank you, I could use some right about now." I smile and give her hand one last squeeze. Heading off to my office, I'm once again reminded that I prefer the uncomplicated company of kids.

"I think you're a bit overdressed to meet with the florist, but hey, I appreciate the effort," Roan says, giving me the once-over as he enters my office.

"Wait, what?" I have no idea what Roan's talking about. I'm in a bit of a fog having skipped my usual three cups of coffee this morning; going to the bathroom while wearing a full-length taffeta gown is a bit of a trial.

"Lunch. Then you and I are headed straight to my florist to do a fast first pass of designing a color palette and creating a floral strategy for my wedding before Mimi realizes we're gone."

"Ohhhhh. I thought you were joking while stress eating over shades of fuchsia last week. We're really going to do this seven months before the big day?"

"Well then, joke's on you, Nina. We made plans a while back to shop flowers during lunch today. Don't worry, I read online somewhere that crabby moods and an aging brain both affect your memory, so ya know, that's like two strikes for you. But here I am, your personal reminder. On my way in, Mimi told me you have a meeting with Winn in ten in that power get-up you got going on, but then we're sneaking out to go daisy picking." Roan begins to skip circles around my dress in his Bruce Wayne power suit. "And as long as we are on the topic of my wedding . . ."

"Which we actually weren't," I correct Roan. He gives me a pouty face before launching back in.

"Tate and I, okay mostly me, want to get married in the Royal-Hawkins foyer," Roan announces. I raise my eyebrows, curious that Roan is considering going so mainstream formal.

"I mean, the black-and-white ballroom dance floor has been in place for, like, a hundred years, and I figure given my stellar service to this school, the appreciative head may offer me a deep, deep discount." Roan gives me a wink and double thumbs-up. Wow. Marisol and I really thought Roan would become bored with monogamy, but turns out he's full-on fiancé fierce.

"This is more than I can handle on a day where I have to rule out liquids. Listen, Roan, please, please, please can we rain check on the florist? If you reschedule for a Saturday, I promise mani-pedis after, on me."

"Fine. But only if it's a paraffin job and you throw in the ten-minute extra shoulder massage. Then I'll reschedule."

"You got it, Princess Di." I extend my hand to shake and seal our new floral arrangement.

"I suppose if you're channeling Cleopatra, you've got to OWN being Cleopatra. Go ahead and take care of royal business, your highness." Roan bows and walks out of my office.

I'm at my standing desk like a good modern-day manager, but my feet are killing me in these gladiator sandals. A flat footbed with no arch is brutal on a woman over forty pushing a little pregnancy weight. I pore over Google, assessing the militant mom opinions versus medical research on drinking caffeine while pregnant. Truthfully, the coffee stance is the least of my worries when contemplating if I want to bring a baby into this world as a single parent who is now older, wiser, and tired as hell just thinking about chasing after a toddler. I am certain, however, that I cannot go another day without murky hot java coursing through my veins. I'll give up something else to balance out the need for coffee. Maybe sushi? Yikes! That one's tough to give up too. I pause. My spinning wheels over minor pregnancy concerns feels like a woman leaning toward having a baby. Damn if that mighty lion from this morning didn't do a number on me.

The meeting with Winn was a good distractor from the around-the-clock ticker tape running through my brain reminding me I'm unexpectedly expecting another child. We touched on a topic I have not given a great deal of thought to when it comes to the past, present, or future of the Royal-Hawkins School: the athletic program. Parents rarely seem to inquire about the sports programs or how many of our students are awarded athletic scholarships to college each year, let alone if there has ever been a Royal-Hawkins graduate who has gone on to become a professional athlete.

During the Admissions Open House Q and A, most parents play a game of academic hot potato seeing who can ask the most affected, wannabe-intellectual questions. The rule of the game is to show off how closely they follow trending child development advice. My favorite from this year was the father who quoted an article about the merits of having a cadre of on-site therapists and affinity groups for children when they feel troubled or when someone looks at them sideways. Instead of answering the parent, I looked right to Roan. He gave me a barely perceptible nod and put a check mark on his clipboard. That hand-wringing, worrywart of a dad is now red-flagged for eternity.

Frankly, I was unaware Winn had such an interest in the athletic history of Royal-Hawkins until today's meeting when he showed up in my office with a spreadsheet and a lecture. He detailed every female and male basketball season record dating back to 1984, the year he became a Royal-Hawkins alum. I gave it a cursory glance, not noticing anything obvious, but feigned interest in his concerns nonetheless. Winn specifically pointed out to me that we have only had two seasons in thirty or so years when a Royal-Hawkins basketball team has made it to any finals in the school's athletic division. I would have guessed Winn's birdie would be in a bundle for not having a golf team before he would be sweating it out over basketball stats. Shame on me for assuming.

Without being clear on his desired outcome for our meeting, Winn asked me to take some time to review the numbers and consider what kind of legacy I want to leave as Royal-Hawkins's first female head of school. I told him I was unaware I would be exiting the school anytime soon and needed to be pondering my legacy five hot minutes after I got into the head's seat. Winn chuckled but assured me I needed to seriously consider addressing Royal-Hawkins's athletics. It's just like a man to tell a woman what she needs to consider even while she's dressed as Cleopatra, one of the most intelligent and powerful female rulers.

Slightly intrigued by where Winn's going with all this talk, I decide to take a walk around campus to consider sports at Royal-Hawkins. I know for sure we can improve on the basketball uniforms, those things are fugly. Why somebody would take gangly, pimply, awkward teens and wrap them in a polyester mystery blend is lost on me.

Walking the halls of the middle school, I see an unfamiliar, towering man from the back with scuffed shoes, torn jeans, and a dirty oversize blazer with something that looks like garbage peeking out of the pocket flaps. On his head is a backward baseball cap that looks ratty and sweat-stained. I hold tight to the walkie-talkie that goes everywhere on campus with me and get ready to call for backup to escort this unfamiliar gentleman out of the school. This is my first brush with a stranger on campus, and in today's climate, school safety is every parent's, teacher's, and staff member's primary concern.

"Excuse me, sir," I say once, using my inside voice, then quickly following up, "EXCUSE ME, SIR," in my outside voice when the man doesn't immediately turn around. My feet are firmly planted on the ground, but my heart is flying fast. My index finger hovers over the red emergency button on the walkie-talkie that goes directly to the police station. The fist of my other hand is clenched and ready to throw a punch if the man attacks. Marisol took our self-defense class years ago seriously, never allowing us a single absence, and right now I'm more relieved than ever she enforced perfect attendance.

The man slowly turns around. "Oh hey, Nina. Sorry. I was engrossed reading one of my student's essays. For a thirteen-year-old, Bojing is crushing it making connections between the rise of the Weimar Republic in Germany and his thoughts on modern-day US politics. Sharp kid for sure." Jared's rubbing his lips together, bopping his head to a tune that apparently only he can hear. I blow out an audible breath. Lord have mercy, it's only Jared. Though I've barely had a sip of water all day, I think I peed my panties a little.

I can't get past the black smudges Jared has artfully placed on his cheeks. "Um, Jared, who are you supposed to be for Halloween?" I ask hesitantly, hoping this young man has a reflective side that will offer an astute explanation, but I brace myself for the musings I fear are coming my way.

"I'm a hobo," he declares, spreading his arms wide to give me the full view of his costume. "I left my bandana-stick bag in my classroom. I've got my basketball in it for after school."

Hope crushed.

"You mean a homeless person? You came to celebrate Halloween at school . . . dressed . . . as . . . a homeless person?" My emotions have swung from disbelief back to panic. Sweat's trickling down my back as I imagine the number of emails that will be coming my way from parents after Jared's students share at the family dinner table that their history teacher dressed up for Halloween as one of Los Angeles's most devastating social ills.

"Nah, not a homeless person, a hobo. Like from the Dust Bowl era a la John Steinbeck and *The Grapes of Wrath*, my favorite book. That's how my people made their way to California. My great-grandfather and his brother jumped trains all over the United States trying to get a little work here or there, sleeping under bridges, running from authorities, until they made it to the Golden State." Jared's pumped up with pride sharing the backstory of his family. It's pure sweetness wrapped neatly in a PR nightmare.

"I'm telling you, Nina, my family has stories for days that have been passed down in vivid detail about my great-grandfather and my great-uncle Otis. As a social studies teacher, my goal is to wear a Halloween costume every year that honors an era in US history. This year I'm honoring my great-grandfather and his struggle to get out of the South and become a proud Californian. He loved it here more than anything."

"Did it cross your mind that the tweens you teach, whose most pressing thoughts are what's being served for lunch today, might assume you are posing as a resident of Skid Row? That while your costume choice is obvious to you, it may not be to the rest of Royal-Hawkins? That, in fact, it had me moments away from alerting the police?" I ask, working to control my voice from betraying the anger brewing that Jared did not consider any of these ramifications on the school when he came dressed as a retro homeless person. Sorry, hobo.

"Pot calling the kettle black, don't you think?" Jared straightens up and directs his accusation right at me with no concern he's speaking to his boss.

"Excuse me?" I can't imagine what he has to say after that accusatory statement that's going to improve this interaction, but I'm curious as hell to hear.

"Parading around as Cleopatra, a narcissistic ruler, owner of domestic slaves and devourer of kingdoms. I'm sure you had fun putting together your look, but what message might your costume send to the community?" Jared lays out his argument like he already had it ready. As a science teacher, I really hate debating with history buffs.

"I'm just saying, Nina, before you throw shade on someone else's costume without knowing the context, just like I tell my students, watch your own assumptions." I feel like I've just sat in on an Ivy League philosophy class, and there's a small part of me that wonders if I deserve being schooled right now. The other part of me is amazed this young man is handing out lessons to me, while I'm dressed as one of the most powerful women in history, *and* old enough to be his mama. "People are so quick to jump on one another and assume the worst. What happened to believing in best intentions until proven otherwise? Don't you think if you had me jump through your rigorous hiring hoops, you should trust that I can make good decisions around kids? Wouldn't have expected you, of all people, to find me guilty before being proven innocent."

That last sentence stings, hard, because as a Black person, I know he's not wrong.

I allow a moment of silence to hang in the air and consider what tactical position to adopt next: boss, mentor, mother, or colleague. I clasp my hands in front of my gown to slow my blood pressure and remind myself that I'm indeed the one in charge of this interaction. This young man can hardly be considered a fully formed adult. Cusping maybe, but no adult.

"As a US history teacher, I give you props for aligning your Halloween costume to your curriculum. And it's always nice when I get the opportunity to learn about the backgrounds and family histories of the faculty and staff at school." I pause to take in another steady breath and allow the clench in Jared's jaw to ease up when he realizes my attack is on retreat. "But I also need you to see this from my perspective. Who knows, you may be a head of school one day." I hope my appeal to Jared's possible professional aspirations will end this conversation on a neutral note. "At Royal-Hawkins, we are in the customer service business. And with that perspective, we're always on high alert for what may offend, upset, or cause distress in our clients. The ones who are five, fifteen, and the ones who are fifty-five."

"So basically, I work for the Nordstrom of education. That's what you're saying," Jared says, giving a muffled chuckle.

"You got it, Jared. You can even return that costume of yours to me, and I will find it a more appropriate home. All returns accepted in my office."

"Lucky for you I have an extra college T-shirt and my basketball shorts in my desk drawer. I can go change into them if you prefer," Jared offers. Harvard types are never more than an arm's distance away from their school swag.

"That sounds great, Jared, thank you," I say with as much warmth and grace as I can muster for my Gen Z ding-a-ling of a teacher. I can't wait to tell Leo about this conversation. Making fun of Gen Zers is one of our favorite topics.

"Happy Halloween, Nina. You make a perfect Cleopatra," Jared says, and gives me a salute before strutting down the hall and leaving me to wonder, just like with Courtney, Was that a shady compliment? I do hope that when I sit in on one of Jared's classes for his first formal evaluation, his teaching is as smooth as his mouth. I fear for his tenure at Royal-Hawkins if it is not.

ELEVEN

Throughout my career, I have found that no one appreciates veterans more than educators. And not just because teachers nationwide would be white knuckling it from Labor Day clear through to Thanksgiving without a day off, but that definitely helps. I personally give veterans a big shout-out in my weekly Royal-Hawkins message from the head of school when the November 11 remembrance rolls around.

"I can't believe my baby is on the seventh grade Bar and Bat Mitzvah circuit this year." Marisol dives right into conversation, skipping the normal salutations between two friends who haven't seen each other in a handful of days. My bestie came ready to distract me since I sent her a text right before meeting at the Mar Vista Clean Slate that requested no talk of you-know-what.

"These late-night party pickups are killing me. The amount of time and money I'm spending to get the pit stains out of Diego's shirts and blazer is ridonkulous." I know this seventh grade parental complaint well. "I told him to quit dancing with all those blossoming girls or he's gonna pass out from overheating. You'd think his Mexican heritage would help him out in high-heat situations, but whenever I pick that kid up, he's dripping like a Popsicle in the desert. And then he wonders why the girls don't like him. No mystery there, buddy."

"Jaime and I were invited to a Bar Mitzvah a few weeks back by a mom who swears by my sugaring technique. I wore the vintage Chanel pantsuit I found at a Bel Air estate sale, and for sure one woman at the Bar Mitzvah was eyeing me like it used to belong to her mother-in-law. Anyway, Diego said best in show so far for the middle school religious party train. The bash was in the ballroom at the Chateau Marmont. Four open bars AND you should have seen the swag bag at this thing. Aviator Nation sweatshirts for all. So wannabe-throwback SoCal for a Jewish transplant family from Baltimore, but hey, I'm not turning down a free two-hundred-dollar sweatshirt. If I don't end up wearing it, I'll hawk it on eBay."

"Why didn't you snag me one if they were handing them out like free pound cake bites at Costco? You know I love a good gift bag."

"Wouldn't you be burned at the stake if the head of Royal-Hawkins walked around in pricy Bar Mitzvah giveaways? Isn't that the private school equivalent of an ethical violation?"

"Yeah, but I need some, shall we say, less body contouring clothing." Drew, our favorite Clean Slate bartender, has brought Marisol and me our sodas and cranberry juice, but not without shooting us a look that asks, *Who are you two and what have you done with the REAL Marisol and Nina?* Drew was on vacation when Marisol vowed to be a sober sister with me until I figured out the solution to my current state. I watch her stir her drink with a frown like she's preparing to down a gallon of saline water before a colonoscopy.

"It's only a nonalcoholic drink, not a poison chalice," I remind Marisol.

"Pretty much kissing cousins in my book." Marisol cheers with a smirk and takes a sip.

"If we can't talk about the baby SIT-U-A-TION," Marisol says, circling my stomach with her index finger. "Can we talk about the grown baby you already have?"

"Absolutely." Since Xandra's no longer at home to talk to, I relish any opportunity to talk about my girl. Even though she's in her second year at Pemberley, the house still seems unnaturally quiet. When my dad stays with me, we enjoy each other's company, but no doubt I miss Xandra every day.

"So, what does your big baby think of this maybe baby?"

"Do you need to check in on your boys?" I ask, pointing at Marisol's phone and trying to distract her from the topic of my offspring.

"Nope, Spanny's got 'em. Driving to some soccer field who knows where." Marisol waves away my concern over her boys when Super Nanny's in charge. "God did not intend for me to spend every afternoon cheering from the sidelines. I only show up for the games. Back to you, sis."

I marvel at Marisol's ability to ignore the pull of her children when she's not at work. Call it Graham or call it guilt, but if I was not at work, I was racing home to Xandra. It never crossed my mind to carve out me time, and Graham would have never paid another woman, regardless of how wonderful they were, to help raise his child when, in his mind, he had me for free.

"What happened to my no 'situation' talk request?"

"You said I could ask about Xandra," Marisol says with mock innocence. I see there's no way out of this conversation. Her Bar Mitzvah chatter was only meant to throw me off scent so Marisol could tee me up for this topic.

"Over the weekend, Xandra and I attempted to have a mature conversation about Leo, but most of the maturity was left to me. I told her that Leo and I have been in touch since he left for Singapore."

"How'd she take it?"

"With a side of silence. So, then I moved on to the topic we both have been avoiding."

"The baby?"

"NO! I told Xandra that I knew she saw me and Leo smooching in the driveway before she left for school. I apologized that she had to see that without first being properly introduced to Leo. I explained it was never supposed to happen that way and we should talk about it."

"How'd that go?"

"Xandra's contribution to this important mother-daughter exchange was, 'Yeah, okay. It's whatever, Mom. I gotta go. Dash is waiting on me.' Then *click*," I recount to Marisol. "Given the chilly reception I got and with a country between us, it was not the moment to call back and say, 'One, last thing, your old mom had sex and the result is that right about the time of your sweet sixteen, you're going to be a big sister!'"

"Yeah, keeping Xandra on hold about the maybe baby is probably a good idea. So then, four out of five of us know you're knocked up."

"I'm not quite following your math," I admit.

"So far you, Leo, Fitzroy, and me know you're hiding a baby in there," Marisol says, pointing to my waistband. "Xandra's a TBD."

"Ah, got it. Right."

"Real talk, then. Since most of the important people in your life know, I'm done tap dancing around this topic. Leo's over the moon about having a baby. You know that, ring on the finger or not, Fitzroy will love this baby like crazy. A new grandchild may even get him to move here full-time like you've been hinting at the past few years. And Xandra, well, she's our wild card, but we will take on the teenage beast when the time is right." I close my eyes; I know what Marisol is going to say. "What's holding you back from having this coffee bean you got brewing? Which, by the way, since its Leo's ain't gonna be dark roast. People may think it's my baby." Marisol laughs quickly at her ill-timed joke. I give her a courtesy hoot.

"You promise not to judge me for anything I admit to you in the next few minutes?" If I can't tell my best friend my truth, I'm screwed, because I'm about to lose it from the thoughts consuming my every waking moment.

"Girl, I'm behind you one hundred percent. Whether you choose to have this baby, which I know is a hard choice, or you decide to terminate this pregnancy, I'm not going anywhere." Marisol takes both my hands in hers. To the women attempting to spruce up our feet she asks, "Will you ladies excuse us for a moment? We're going to need an extralong foot soak." The nail technicians discreetly walk away, leaving our feet to bubble in the soapy blue water. What I'm about to say is meant for their boss's ears only.

I blow out an enormous breath before I start in on what's been holed up inside. "My entire life I've done exactly what Fitzroy and Celia expected of me, I couldn't shoulder the barrage of sacrifice stories that would rain down on me if I didn't. I worked myself to the bone in school. I sang in the church, and I sang in the school choir. Did you know that the longest I have ever been unemployed in my adult life is fifty-six hours? I even married the Black prince of Bermuda because my mom said she could hear my biological clock ticking from the outside. You know she didn't come to America to not have grandchildren. I went right from working hard to please my parents to busting ass to please my husband."

"Don't go blaming your poor choice in husbands on Celia. She didn't hold a gun to your head and make you walk down that aisle," Marisol says, jumping in to defend my mother.

"I know that, I think. But I have a lifetime of my parents' sacrifices riding on me, and every decision I have ever made starts with, Will Celia and Fitzroy be proud, or will they have to skip church? And don't tell me you've never felt it from my parents, growing up they made you show them your grades too."

"Remember that rickety piano your mom made us practice scales on for fifteen minutes every day before we were allowed to play actual songs?" Marisol reminds me. "Even then she only let us play gospel hymns. Why couldn't your parents be Rastas?"

"Yeah, my dad rescued that piano from the free pile on the street corner before it became someone's kindling. He sanded it up and stained it to make it Celia approved and living room ready. After you, me, and Clive, it was the pride of the house."

"That's what your folks did for me that my grandparents couldn't, and I will always be grateful. They shined me up and made me life ready." I can complain about anything to Marisol except for my parents.

She will always defend them because her childhood depended on them. "And remember our piano teacher, Mrs. Richards? Her apartment smelled like a litter box. She'd teach stroking one of her precious pets. We learned to move our hands along the keys quickly, or she'd send one of those furballs home with us. To this day I still hate cats."

"Yeah, Mom fought hard for concert pianists." I laugh at the memory of Mom swatting at me to sit my butt down and practice Beethoven when all I wanted to do was sing En Vogue. Celia always won. "My parents' pride in our little immigrant family was my number one priority. I never considered myself. I always considered us."

"But it worked out all right, we turned out okay," Marisol says, nudging me. "And I hate to burst your bubble, but you raise Xandra like Fitzroy and Celia raised you. High standards, little room for error." I get a gut bomb in my stomach knowing there's some kind of error going on with Xandra right now and I'm failing at figuring out exactly what it is. She's holding her feelings tight to her chest, which, unfortunately, she learned from me. "And my guess is you run Royal-Hawkins much the same way."

"You're right, and that's exactly my point. I'm full up on babies to parent and people passing judgment on how well I'm doing, or not doing, my job," I whine. "I have Xandra and fifteen years of Graham pointing out all the ways I'm failing her as a working mother. Now I have Royal-Hawkins and a whole board and parent body looking out for my every misstep, waiting to offer unsolicited advice." I haven't been able to shake Winn and his random conversations about sports at Royal-Hawkins, nor Courtney's push to join the board of trustees. "And, given Leo's new work venture he's struggling to fit giving me a call into his schedule as is. How's that all going to work out when there's a baby in the mix? Trust me, I know how this story plays out, I'll end up a work widow twice over." Marisol cannot deny I've been here before.

"I'm at capacity when it comes to taking care of people and all their expectations. What little free time I have, I'm hoping for some space to take care of myself. Hell, to be by myself." The tears are back at the idea of eighteen more years prioritizing someone else's needs, someone else's desires, over mine. Before I start back up, Marisol holds up her index finger signaling she needs a second. She grabs her cocktail napkin and dabs the cascade streaming down my cheeks.

"Don't get me wrong, I wouldn't change my life for anything, the ups, the downs, the stress, and the love, all of it. I really wouldn't. But with Graham and graduate school behind me and then this summer with Leo and starting my dream job, I was feeling like it was finally my turn to have MY LIFE." Remembering I'm in public, I take it down from a ten. "That I finally get to be number one. Spend my time the way I want to spend it. Jesus, to have free time for the first time in two decades is a luxury I want to explore. I might want to do nothing or pack my schedule with a bunch of random shit like mah-jongg or collaging." Marisol gives me a doubtful face. "I know I know, probably not going to join a quilting circle, but I know where they sell thread." I let out a defeated sigh.

"I know it sounds bad, Marisol, but I've earned my forties, and I don't want to give them away. If I do, then the next time I'll be able to get a massage or go to brunch, let alone go to the bathroom by myself, will be when I'm sixty-five. And don't get me started on my career, I just got to where I want to be." Every selfish thought I've had since finding out I'm pregnant is now out there for Marisol's review. It's the truth, good, bad, or really, really dreadful, and there's a relief to hearing the words out loud versus them bouncing around my brain.

"This is a terrible time for us not to be able to drink," Marisol says, exasperated, holding our tear-soaked hands together.

"There is one other thing,"

"*Ay Dios mío!* Seriously? I can't take another thing." Marisol leans back into her pleather chair, fanning herself with one hand.

"We would make a pretty cute baby," I whisper. Marisol looks at me to see if I'm for real. "Maybe I could do a better job this time around."

"Ohhh, Nina. You've done a wonderful job with Xandra. Don't let Graham's ridiculous ideas of your parenting get under your skin." I don't look up at my best friend. Even though I've never missed a game, a recital, or a middle-of-the-night nightmare, she knows how I've struggled under Graham's opinion that I have not balanced work life and home life very well.

"I'm assuming you probably haven't shared any of your thoughts with Leo?" Marisol asks, surely guessing the answer.

"Not yet. Nothing says get ready for a breakup like 'I'm too selfish to want your baby.'"

"Nina, let's get one thing straight, you're not selfish. You're anything but. Not only have you raised an amazing daughter, but you've been a fabulous daughter too. And to top it off you've spent your entire career helping hundreds of parents at Royal-Hawkins raise their sons and daughters."

"Then if I'm not selfish, what am I? Because from where I'm sitting, everything I just said sounded horrible to me."

"It didn't sound horrible. It sounded like life. Messy fucking life. That's what it sounded like."

TWELVE

I have a love-hate relationship with FaceTime. With Xandra so far away, any day I get to see every square inch of her is a blessing. But the fact that I have to view my middle-aged neck on screen makes it a stressor I could happily do without.

"Hey, baby girl," I say, pulling my braids over one shoulder and hoping Xandra will notice the hoop earrings I found online last weekend. Xandra knows I've been in a year-long hunt for a pair of large but tasteful closed-back hoops. I nailed it if you ask me.

"Hi, Mom. Nice earrings. Glad to see the search is over," Xandra says, leaning into her iPad to get a closer look. I'm grinning like I just won *Project Runway* because my girl approves of something I'm wearing. I spent many years where Xandra sought my approval for every goal scored and robotics competition entered, and then one day—WHAM!—the tables turned, and I'm now working hard for my daughter's endorsement.

"Thanks, you can borrow them when you come home, which, not that I'm counting, is in five weeks and two days."

"Really? I thought it was sooner." Xandra's face falls a little, and my concern rises.

"Sweetie, I'll talk to your dad and buy you a ticket home for Thanksgiving if that's what you'd rather do. I know it's your dad's turn for Turkey Day, but I'm sure it won't be a problem, promise. If you want to come home, I want you to come home." I know Graham will throw a fit since his parents are flying in, but I don't care. My heart is doing jumping jacks that Xandra wants her mom and she wants to come home. "We can go to the movies, go shopping. Whatever you want to do, we'll do."

"Mom, you're so transparent bribing me with shopping. You sound like a clingy girlfriend." I'm busted as Xandra lays her fall semester psychology elective rap on me. "Plus, Dad promised to make me pecan pie. He says he has your recipe." The other reason I hate FaceTime is you can't sport a dirty look without being caught by the other end.

"But Mom, I need to tell you something," Xandra states, setting her jaw like she's bracing herself for a stand-off. No matter, my daughter still needs me, hooray!

"Of course, you can tell me anything. No wait one second, let me get more comfortable." I pull off my heels and tuck my legs under me on my office couch, so I can fully settle in for a gab session. Or to listen. Whatever Xandra needs.

"You remember a while back when I told you about my drama teacher?"

"Remind me." I know exactly what Xandra's talking about. There was something about Xandra goofing around off stage and monkeys, and I recall I couldn't help wondering if Xandra's sense of right and wrong was too quick to judge. So textbook teenager. It's like the twelfth step of adolescence: though I've barely lived, I know everything.

"Before I tell you what happened, let me just say, it's so unfair, it's not my fault, and like I already told you, Mr. Petrov's a total racist, and this just proves it." Xandra's voice is the perfect cocktail of indignation, anger, and whine. My instincts would have me jump in and get busy fixing this problem, but instead I take a moment to remind myself that Xandra needs practice working through her own issues.

"Go on," I say with complete neutrality. I deserve a medal for my calm.

"I got a part with only two lines and maybe seven minutes on stage. Dash is about the same." Okay, small part, but good for Xandra and Dash for trying. "Mr. Petrov picked an all-White leading cast for the winter musical, *Wonderful Town*. I'm in the A-Capellettes singing club, and I barely get any lines in the school musical, how's that possible?!" Xandra's eyes go wide to emphasize shock at what she thinks is questionable casting for the school play.

"I know you're a good singer, love, but did you make any mistakes? What could have happened?" My potential sympathy has turned to confusion. Xandra is anything but lazy, particularly when it comes to singing. She's a third generation Morgan who lives to show off her vocal skills.

"I don't know. I came right back to my room after checking the cast list that was posted when I saw how far down I was on it. It was SO embarrassing, Mom; all the other kids were high-fiving, and I looked like a fool."

"So, your tryout was great, but you got a small part?" As Xandra's mother I want to believe my child's telling the truth, but all my years working with kids, with only that tidbit of the story I know something's not adding up. I've had dozens of kids sent to my office for acting out in school, ready to sell me their version of the truth. I know when there's more to a story. "Go back to the beginning. I want all the details."

"The first day I was a tiny bit late. Maybe missed the first few minutes of auditions."

"So, the reason you got a small part is because you were late?"

"Heather walked in with me and Dash. She was late, too, but she got a lead part."

"And Heather is . . ."

"White," Xandra answers; she knows the question I'm asking. That's it. I google Mr. Petrov. I need his email. He's getting an eyeful from me in his inbox. I'll have my facts together right before I go buck wild on this teacher.

"Okay, let me make sure I have all the details. You, Dash, and Heather showed up at tryouts a little bit late, and Mr. Petrov punished you and Dash by handing out ensemble roles, but Heather got a lead role. Is that what I'm hearing?" I'll need to have Marisol read my email, so I don't regret what I send.

"Silence.

"Did I get that straight, Xandra?"

"Sort of. Supposedly Mr. Petrov made all the announcements about casting before we could even get there. Somebody told me later he said only upperclassmen get the lead roles."

"And Heather is?"

"A junior."

"Why didn't you know this information if the announcements were at the beginning of tryouts?"

"He only talked about that part in the first fifteen minutes."

"You were fifteen minutes late?! That's not a 'tiny' bit late."

"Mom, it's not that bad."

"You showed up late for the audition, disrespecting this man's time. Did you talk to Mr. Petrov after to find out the information you missed and to apologize for your tardiness?"

"Well, Heather did, and she confirmed only upperclassmen get leading parts, that's how I know for sure."

"There's your reason, Xandra!" Thank goodness I got the whole story before I fired off that email. This girl would have had me cussing people out cross-country. "You should have talked to Mr. Petrov afterward like I taught you. I'm disappointed you didn't find out on your own what you missed."

"Okay, okay, Mom, you're acting like this is all my fault. Did you not hear me say there are no Black kids in the leading cast! I'm telling you the arts department is racist!"

"Xandra, please, save the dramatics for the stage. Just get your behind there on time." It's just like a teen to converge tardiness with racism.

"Dash told me this is exactly how you'd react. You've lost your edge for the struggle of our people sitting up in that fancy office of yours all day."

Direct from Pemberley my baby DID NOT just call me bougie. Damn, Graham's right. We've definitely got a situation.

FROM: Nina Morgan Clarke
DATE: November 16
SUBJECT: Xandra
TO: Graham Clarke

Graham,

Between your call in September, my conversations with Xandra lately, and her current conflict in the play, we do have a problem. I still don't have a clear picture of what's going on with her, but I know I don't like this new Xandra.

Thanksgiving is almost here, and Christmas is right around the corner. I don't want to ruin your holidays or mine, but confrontation time is coming.

Nina

‿

Leo 3:30 PM

> I know you're at work but I'm in the airport and thought I might catch you. I'm traveling through Borneo the next couple of days. It's going to be pretty remote, so we'll talk when I'm back in cell range. I miss you like crazy. I still can't believe I'm going to be a dad! When can I tell people?

Ugh, I didn't see Leo's text until close to five o'clock, and by the time I hurriedly called him back to hear his voice, if only for a minute, his phone went right to voice mail and my spirits sank. Our infrequent conversations the past few weeks have resembled more of a doctor-patient relationship than desperate lovers missing one another. Leo wants a blow-by-blow description of what I'm eating, how much sleep I'm getting, if I'm remembering to take folic acid up until my twelfth week but not a day after, and for the love of God I better be staying away from tuna. Or more vital to me, my beloved Sunday afternoon greasy tuna melts with waffle fries. I had to cut him off before a mention of future hemorrhoids surfaced. If I didn't know better, I'd think Amazon Prime delivered *What to Expect When You're Expecting* to Leo's Singapore apartment. I much prefer our brief texts when Leo professes how much he misses me.

For our last video call, I made smart use of my swelling bosom and squeezed the now C+ girls into a B cup push-up bra Xandra left behind to get an extra rise, literally, out of Leo. He looked right past the twin peaks and deep valley staring him in the face and wanted to know, in detail, what my doctor said at my first "official" appointment. He was still upset I chose not to include his mug on my phone during the visit. Before I could even decide whether or not to drag Leo down with the news that my doctor said I had a few weeks left to make my decision, Sloan's hand appeared on Leo's shoulder reminding him, as it always did, that he had to go.

Leo's ready to spread the news to family and friends, and the minute he does he will no longer be my boo, he will become the father of my child. UGH. When Leo returns from whatever remote destination he's currently trekking to, I'm either going to make his day by making him a dad or be grateful we're an ocean apart. Our honeymoon dating period will abruptly come to an end as we move from lust to life. Not over distance; not over conflicting, busy professional schedules; not over race; but over sweaty campground sex, and there will be no more of that with a baby in tow.

As I close up my office for the day, Pablo's waiting for me outside my door. He looks visibly uncomfortable, though I like his new haircut. "Nina, can I talk to you for a minute?"

"Sure, come on in, Pablo. It must be serious if you're not speaking to me in Spanish and then giving me a hard time when I answer in English," I say to remind Pablo of our ongoing joke. *"Todo bien con su familia?"*

"Ay, sí Nina, todo bien en mi casa. Gracias," Pablo says, giving me a big smile and subtle head nod. "You know I always arrive at Royal-Hawkins around six thirty in the morning, I like to make sure the school is perfect for the children and the coffee is hot for the teachers." The way Pablo's tongue enunciates *children* always gives me the warm fuzzies.

"Yep, Pablo, you're here before my feet even hit the ground in the morning. Nice haircut, by the way." Everyone likes to hear their turn at the barber went well.

"It was dark this morning when I arrived, and the fog was, was . . ." I can tell Pablo's searching for the word.

"Dense?"

"Sí, dense, *gracias.* There was a nice car blocking the driveway into the underground parking garage. I heard the electronic gate go up, so I walked over to see who was coming to school earlier than me. Usually, I'm the first one here."

"So, who was it?" I've gone from nonchalant to fretful in two seconds. I hope this story doesn't end with stolen equipment and an evening spent on the phone with multiple insurance companies.

"I saw Mr. Jared, the new teacher." Pablo raises his hand high above his head to indicate the tall guy. "He was getting into the car, and I noticed Mr. Hawkins was driving."

"Are you sure it was Jared? He's been out sick with a sub the past two days. When I checked in with Mimi this morning, she said he was out sick again, today."

"I don't know any other men who look like him who would be coming out of our garage," Pablo says, looking down. I know this is his way of saying Jared is the only Black teacher on campus, so he's absolutely sure it was him. I want to tell Pablo it's okay to name skin color as a defining characteristic, but social norms in America have instructed him otherwise.

"Did it look like either Winn or Jared had been in the school at all?" I ask, racking my brain, imagining what they were doing at school in the predawn hours. We have a board meeting tonight, so maybe Jared was bringing something out to the car that Winn needed? Or maybe Jared was dropping off lesson plans for his sub, and Winn offered him a ride home? I'm grasping for an explanation, but nothing comes to mind to explain the two men driving off into the fog of sunrise together.

"*No sé*, Nina. I just hid back by the trees. I didn't want Mr. Hawkins to think I was spying and disrespecting his school, but you know how much I care about this place." That is the one thing that bugs me about Pablo. His reference, always, to Royal-Hawkins being Winn's school. My days of trying to correct him are over. Instead, I remain grateful of Pablo's deep care and swallow my annoyance in the name of cultural differences and soldier on to resolve this bizarre mystery.

"Well thank you, Pablo, this is helpful." I'm just not sure what I'm going to do with this information other than chew on it for now. I already have my eye on Winn, and now the precarious foundation of trust and goodwill with Jared has been further shaken.

The chat I just had with Pablo is swirling in my head. It's now 5:58 p.m. and no Winn. Our board meeting starts in two minutes and neither the email, phone call nor text I sent Winn during the course of the day has been returned. My meetings start on time, and we have a packed evening. I send Pablo to the front of the school on an optimistic mission that Winn will show up in the next few minutes and need to be let through the gate.

With Winn MIA, Vice Chairwoman Kym Lee steps in to call the meeting to order. To open tonight's meeting, I share Henry Burton's poem "Striving" and get us started on the meat of the agenda.

I'm excited for our CFO to share our balance sheet. I get an overwhelming sense of smugness whenever a quarter ends and the actual Royal-Hawkins budget is well under previously projected numbers. I demurely brush off the glory bestowed upon me by the finance committee while internally giving myself a high five. Coming in under budget is a head of school's A+, and I've always been a grade grubber.

In the midst of my moment of adoration, the door to the conference room flings open and a breathless Winn Hawkins stumbles into the room. "Sorry, sorry, so sorry, Nina and everyone. Oh, hey Andrew, good to see you, missed you at men's night at the tennis club last week." Winn is quick to reach for a handshake from a fellow Royal-Hawkins alum. While he's making his round of hellos and apologies for his tardiness, I get a nose full of Winn's scent, and it's not Downy fresh. Not to mention he's styled in some dressed up, dressed down attire, a light-blue pressed button-down with purple-and-gold basketball shorts.

"Traffic from Staples Center was awful. I thought I left plenty of time to be back to Pasadena by five thirty, but no such luck," Winn says, addressing the entire board with the assumption everyone cares where he's been and why he's late.

"Were you checking out a Lakers practice?" Andrew asks, taking our night further off track.

Sitting down in his seat to my left, Winn rounds out his mystery day with an entire board share. "Nah, a few months back at a silent auction for the children's hospital, I won two entries to a three-day basketball camp with the Lakers. There was no way I wasn't going to win those tickets, and let me tell you, I paid a pretty price for them. It was worth it, though, to get to spend three days playing hoops with the boys on the team." I bite down hard on my lower lip to keep from saying out loud, *You were not playing basketball with them, Winn. They were passing the ball to you because the insane amount of money you pay for your courtside seats pays their inflated salaries.*

"I invited the new basketball coach with me for some hang time, and we had a blast. Best couple of days I've had in a long time."

Andrew and a few other men on the board vigorously nod their heads in manly agreement. I don't have time for the testosterone musings of the ultrawealthy. I'm not sure I heard a part of Winn's sports fantasy correctly.

"Excuse me, Winn. Who did you say went with you?" I ask, the muscles in the back of my neck and shoulders starting to spasm.

"Jared Jones." That's what I thought he said.

"The kid played b-ball at Harvard, started all four years. As soon as I got the tickets, I told him to mark his calendar, he had to go with me." If I weren't aware of twenty-two people staring at me waiting to bring our meeting back on track, I'd be busy picking my jaw up off the floor.

"Nina, before you keep going on the agenda, I want to throw out there that I'd like twenty minutes to share with the board my thoughts on the Royal-Hawkins athletic program."

I look right at Winn. I don't think I even blink, I'm so stunned by his bravado. First, he takes one of my teachers out of the classroom to relive their childhood aspirations, and then he wants to replay their fun back in my board room? I don't think so.

"I want to share my thoughts tonight while my thinking is still fresh after three inspirational days with the Lakers." Winn finishes his demand, smiling at me and then the rest of the board to seal the deal.

"No, Winn, you cannot." And with those four words, I've done what no Royal-Hawkins head of school has ever done before. I said *no* to a Hawkins descendant. How's that for sealing my legacy?

THIRTEEN

With Xandra in her sophomore year at Pemberley and my intense year of weekend classes at UCLA over, I have taken to staying in bed late on Saturday mornings. Under my snuggly goose down duvet, I sip coffee and catch up on nonemergency school issues that could wait until now. After five days of nonstop talking and decision-making, I cherish the quiet and comfort this new weekend routine promises me. Or I would cherish it if not for my father's meticulous morning habits set to Jimmy Cliff's "I Can See Clearly Now," the Jamaican version of reveille. My whole life, Fitzroy has been the early bird pushing his family to get out there and catch the worm.

"You know, Nina," Dad says, sidling up to my open bedroom door like a geriatric hit man, "my father used to have a saying he'd wake us kids up with on a Saturday morning, 'If you're up in my house then you're UP in my house.' And we knew that meant out of bed, wipe the crust from our eyes, and get to work." Dad's posture reads disappointment having to wait on me like a princess even though he's a guest in MY house.

"Wait a minute. Why aren't you at the Y? Shouldn't you have left an hour ago?" I ask, startled by the change in plans by a man who NEVER changes his plans. "Won't the boys send out a search party if you're not there to claim your locker?" For forty-five years my dad drove the MTA bus route from Queens to midtown Manhattan. His ten-hour shift started at 6:00 a.m., by choice. Every morning, on the way out the door, Dad would leave a handwritten list of chores on the kitchen table for Clive and me to finish before school started. He would double-check that the alarm in our shared room was set for 5:30 a.m. and then be on his way. Fitzroy believes the most important work in life is accomplished before the sun comes up.

While Mom got Clive and me off to school and herself to the St. Regis Hotel for a 9:00 a.m. start, Dad chose the early shift so he could be home to supervise us after school. Not helpful with our intense academic load, he did ensure our bottoms were planted at the kitchen table, books out, snacks ready, study on. There was no such thing as "free time" in the Morgan house. There was only chores, homework, music practice, and church attendance. Even the importance of sleep ranked low on the family to-do list because it was not considered productive. I'm still catching up on my *z*'s from childhood.

For all his efficiency, Fitzroy is no busybody, so being all up in my Saturday morning business is out of character. "This is what I do on Saturday mornings when Xandra's at school and you're at the gym, I catch up on work from the week, in bed."

"Eh, so this is what people your age call 'working from home'?" Fitzroy accuses and rubs his hands together before getting to work making my bed with me in it. "Some friends from the Y are coming over this morning. We're switching it up today. Gonna play dominoes in the morning and get our exercise in this afternoon. By the time they get here you better be up and properly dressed." I roll my lower lip out in a pout. "And swipe some lipstick on those lips. Pretend like you got a smile on your face." Since Mom died, Dad's been playing both parents for me and Clive. He was clearly paying attention to Mom for decades, because believe it or not, his beauty tips are often spot on. Or maybe he's actually been listening to Chaco Taco's self-care talk all these years.

"Oh, Dad, your buddies don't care a lick what I look like. Half of them can't even see. I'll just stay back here, and no one has to know I'm home."

"No, you will not!" Dad says sharply and swipes at me to get me out of bed so he can fold my sheets into hospital corners.

"All right, all right, I'm moving. I'll get dressed and head out to a coffee shop to work while your game's going on. You're wound tight this morning. Did you get up on the wrong side of the bed?" I accuse and head toward the bathroom.

"You'll do no such thing. I've worked hard to arrange this morning, and the good Lord willing my prayers will be heard. I know you've met Earvin and Billy, but they haven't seen you in quite some time."

When Mom died, Clive and I worried that Dad would be lonely, the two of them spent every night together their half century of marriage. And during Fitzroy's first couple of solo visits to come see me and Xandra, I thought we were going to have to entertain him every waking moment. But with his gym membership in hand, Dad's bus driver sociability kicked in as a survival skill, and now his friend group in Pasadena is bigger than mine. His effort to keep me close by is piquing my interest.

"I don't know what's gotten into you, Dad, but you're acting all kinds of crazy. Are you crushing on someone?" I tease like we're elementary school besties.

"Ah, get on out of here," Dad says. Then to the sky directs, "Celia, darling, what do you think of this nonsense your daughter's stirring up?"

"Dad, it's early in heaven too. Mom's probably still sleeping."

"Either way, Nina, if you believe in love, then you better stick around."

I follow Dad's request without further fuss and put on the robin's-egg blue dress he bought me for my fortieth birthday. Dad likes the dress because the neckline is high, and I like it because the hemline is also high. It has a kind of Black Jackie O. vibe and highlights my legs, which are the only feature of my pregnancy bod holding steady. I put on my fresh hoops to add a modern hint to the dress's vintage vibe. It actually feels good to be put together and ready to take on the day.

"Now that's what I like to see, Nina, a woman dressed as a woman should be dressed to greet gentlemen in her home. There's no need to parade around in that second skin with your business hanging out."

"For the hundredth time, Dad, they're called yoga pants." We have this conversation about once a month and always near Xandra's birthday when she wants a new pair of Lululemons.

"I've never seen you do yoga. I like this much better." Dad grabs my left shoulder and spins me around for final approval. "You look pretty, Nina. Would you mind heading into the kitchen and putting together a few snacks for the boys? Nothing fancy. Oh, I think I hear someone coming up the front steps." Couldn't Dad have asked me to do his catering when I was still in my comfy pj's? And what kind of snacks do you serve a couple of old men at nine in the morning anyway? They don't seem like a sliced fruit kind of bunch.

"Sure." I hesitate. This is the first time my dad has offered to host dominoes, so I want to help make sure it goes off without a hitch and his buddies have a good time. But when I made my coffee earlier this morning, the folding table and chairs hadn't moved from the garage, and the kitchen is still untouched. Something other than Dad's fussing is most definitely up. I take a few extra minutes in the kitchen to nose around for some clues before I throw a snack tray together.

AHA! Dad's laptop, open to Expedia, is plugged in at my kitchen desk. I look at his recent search history and see he's been on several travel websites in the past week. Is Dad going home? Is he taking a big step and finally joining an organized trip for seniors? He's always wanted to go to Italy.

"DAD, I need to talk to you for a minute. IN PRIVATE!" I holler, heading toward the living room, sans snacks, ready to snatch my dad away from his company for a round of *What the heck is going on here?*

I stop fast in my tracks. Fitzroy is standing in the middle of my living room looking terribly pleased with himself, and next to him is Leo. Touché, Dad. The opinions I thought you were holding close to your chest about the baby, you just laid them out pretty for me to see.

"I'm off to the Y, then. The boys are all in a lather wanting to know if I was able to pull this surprise off," Dad says, collecting his gym bag from where it was hidden behind the curtains. "You two have a lot to catch up on and discuss. I hope you'll be joining us for dinner, Leo, I look forward to getting to know you better. I think we need to treat you to a good ol' American cheeseburger. Nina, you up for grilling?" Dad insists in the form of a question, patting Leo confidently on the back. His cunning ways keep on coming.

"Nowhere else in the world I would be," Leo says, salivating for a burger before breakfast. Or hopefully salivating over seeing me.

"It's settled then. See you around six thirty p.m., we'll have a beer," Dad singsongs triumphantly as he heads out the door exceedingly pleased with himself. "Oh, and Nina, I'll be going home on the seven a.m. flight to New York tomorrow morning. You and Leo have some important decisions to make, and you don't need your old man hanging around while you do it."

The front door clicks closed, and I jump into Leo's arms, sending him stumbling back onto the couch. "You're here! I can't believe it, you're really here!" I realize I've been suppressing how terribly I've missed Leo in the name of surviving. It's either that or the horny pregnancy hormones kicked in seeing Leo's biceps stretch the arms in his T-shirt. I plant kisses all over his face, neck, and head, each peck affirming he's truly home. "Oh, I see how it is. I was such a great long-distance girlfriend, you couldn't stay away." Suck it, Sloan, and your sway over my boyfriend. "Did you catch me pretending to be Zen when I thought I had to make it four months without you? I was good, right? Wasn't I? I knew I was. You have to tell Marisol I killed it. She had her doubts, and I think she even bet against me with Roan." I keep pecking away at Leo like a starving bird.

"Other than your eyes bugging out every time Sloan passed by my desk, you did all right." Caught. "And since when do you use the word *Zen*?" Leo laughs.

"Oh, I've become a whole new woman since you've been gone." Leo raises his eyebrows in hungry interest. "Okay, that's not really true, but I do have a few new pairs of sneakers you've never seen. Also, Marisol and I discussed going to a pottery class but decided to try out a new Vietnamese restaurant instead. And I'm still playing it cool with Xandra and her mysterious behavior." Leo looks at me like he's not buying it.

"By playing it cool, you mean you didn't hop on the first plane to New York to explain our hot kiss to your kid?" Huh, maybe Leo does know more about the crazy things parents do on behalf of their children than I've given him credit for.

"I didn't even search for a cheap last-minute ticket," I say proudly. I've been obsessively counting the days until Xandra gets home for Christmas so I can grill her in person and get to the bottom of what's been happening with her and Dash at school.

"Wait, aren't you supposed to be in Borneo? I thought you were going to check in with me today or tomorrow."

"I'm checking on you all right." Leo slips his hand under my short hemline. He's getting right to business opening the candy shop back up, and I don't mind a bit. "Checking on you and my baby." His hand moves right past my sweetness onto my belly. "The trek was just a ruse to keep you from trying to contact me so I could pack up and fly home without blowing our surprise." Leo's stroking my belly like he's trying to coax this baby out of my bottle. I wish I had on yoga pants, I'm feeling a little exposed with my dress now hiked up over my hips and my end-of-the-week underwear on display.

"Our surprise?" I ask. Though I know the answer.

"Let's just say, among other things, I'm learning that willfulness is a Morgan family trait," Leo whispers, nuzzling my neck.

"Yeah, Fitzroy's determination is legendary," I offer, wriggling my clavicle away from Leo's lips. I'm not feeling it with the mention of my father. "When he wants something done, he gets it done. Did I tell you about the argument over my prom dress?"

Leo shakes his head no as his hands continue to wander.

"Well, that's a story for another time. Back to today."

"Hold on," Leo rolls me off him and reaches into his back pocket. Out comes a stacked bundle of paper that he carefully unfolds and presses flat on the coffee table.

"Go ahead." Leo kisses me and nods to the papers indicating he wants me to read them. The first email printout is from one Fitzroy Morgan, dated Halloween.

FROM: Fitzroy Morgan
DATE: October 31
SUBJECT: Time to come home
TO: Leo West

Dear Leo,

I dislike email so I will keep this brief. You are now going to be a father. Nina needs you here so she can see this baby is a blessing. For all of us.

Fitzroy Morgan

The man likes to make his point in as few words as possible. Next page.

FROM: Fitzroy Morgan
DATE: November 1
SUBJECT: Time to come home
TO: Leo West

Dear Leo,

I went to the offices of Smith, Bodie, and Strong and met with your boss. She's a lovely woman. After we exchanged pleasantries, she assured me that if you returned home early from your post in Singapore your job will be waiting for you.

Fitzroy Morgan

I skip over the details of the remaining brief emails and count only the pages. Twelve emails in total, at times three a day, all seemingly with the same message: Come home. You're going to be a father. Nina needs you.

I'm mortified, but also surprisingly grateful. It's not my father's job to determine what I need, but he's not wholly wrong either. I didn't know how to talk through my concerns about having a baby with the daddy half a world away. So, I didn't. But my not doing it didn't mean I didn't need to.

I can't imagine how he figured out where Leo works. Then to go to downtown LA to meet with Leo's boss on behalf of his daughter, that's channeling Mom-level madness right there.

I don't know whether to slug Leo or hug Leo. "Are you just here because my dad guilted you into it because of the baby?" I ask quietly, internally cringing over what the answer may be.

Leo wraps his right arm around me, pulling me in tight next to him. Though I'm craving his touch, I pull away so I can look him straight in the eyes and see the truth. Please God let him be here for me and not because a bossy old man bullied him.

Interpreting my body language, Leo shifts his posture, readying himself for a debate like the trained lawyer he is. "Nina, I'm here for you. I've always wanted to be here with you, we just had to get over the hump of my time in Singapore." As I'm trying to read Leo's face for a trace of falsehood, he hits me with, "What I don't know is if you're happy that I'm here."

"Of course, I am!" I can't believe Leo would think otherwise. "But that's not the point in all of this."

"Why not? I'm happy to be here with you, you're supposedly happy I'm here, we have the best surprise ever on the way, let's enjoy right now and see what develops."

Of course, as a guy, it's that simple. Why get bogged down in the dizzying logistics of what's beyond this moment? Meanwhile, even with Leo right in front of me, my estrogen-overloaded mind can't stop questioning, Do we know each other well enough to raise a child together? How is Leo on four hours of sleep? Is history repeating itself and I would yet again become a work widow? And today's most pressing issue seeing Leo face-to-face, *Hey, White baby daddy, you don't have a clue how to raise a Black child in America.*

"Why are you home now instead of Christmas or New Year? It didn't have to be a surprise. I could have planned our reunion."

"A planned reunion—that sounds sexy as hell," Leo says, irritated. "Because," he starts back in, choosing his words carefully, "Fitzroy hinted in his last few emails that you may not want to have our baby." Leo pulls a single sheet of paper out of another pocket. "When I did the math, I knew you would have to make a decision soon, and I didn't want you to make it without me, without being reminded in person how good we are together." My dad really stuck his nose in it this time. It's probably best he's going home tomorrow.

"Nina, is it true? Are you considering not having this baby?" Leo envelops my hands in his, his voice turns empathetic, and his body language invites me into his arms. I drop my head on Leo's chest, so I don't have to look at him.

"Yes," is all I can muster, barely audible.

"Yes, what?" Now Leo's the one pushing the conversation into uncomfortable territory.

"Yes, I'm conflicted. I don't know how I feel. I'm nearing the end of raising one child, I don't know if I have it in me to do it all over again. By the time this baby is grown"—I point to my belly—"I will have been a mom going on forty years. I'll be sixty-five."

"I'll be in my sixties too."

I briefly look up, sending Leo a *whatever* vibe. His sixties don't come with stretch marks.

"And we'll be old parents together, Nina. I promise you won't feel like a single parent, I will be with you every step of the way."

This is not the time to mention that Leo's enthusiasm speaks to yet another concern I have. This is his first child, and I fear he will be like all first-time parents: too excited, too cautious, too obsessed with all things baby. His first-time father fervor is sure to crawl right up under my skin and drive me nuts.

I look at my watch and realize I have a trapdoor out of this conversation. "I know we have more to talk about, but I'm supposed to meet Roan soon for flowers, french toast, and french tips." Leo looks at me, confused, and I remember that the men in my life do not always speak the same language. "Roan and I have a date to pick out flowers for his wedding. But first I have to feed him. You want to make Roan's day and come along?"

"French toast at Russell's?" Leo asks with interest.

"If that's where you want to have french toast, then you got it." I smile and squeeze Leo's hands. How quickly a man can slip out of adult discontent and back into boyhood happiness over something as simple as bread and syrup. It's a gender trait every woman exploits at moments like this one. "I better text Roan and let him know you'll be joining us."

Nina 10:48 AM

Surprise, Leo's back. We'll see you at Russell's.

—~

"That Peruvian maize has made you all kinds of Latino swarthy," Roan says, giving Leo a slow body scan. *"Ay, caliente!"*

"I was actually in Singapore, but thank you." Leo laughs and pulls Roan in for a chest bumping man hug. Roan turns the opportunity into a full-body squeeze.

"Geography aside, why are you back so soon to see us?" Roan asks as we fall into line following the hostess to our seats.

Leo pulls my chair out for me to sit. "I wanted to come back ASAP so I can be here for Nina and our baby."

Fuck me. I forgot to tell Leo to keep his mouth shut. See, too much enthusiasm.

"OH, THANK GOD!" Roan roars in relief as if he miraculously found out he doesn't have an STD. "I thought you were packing on pity pounds while Leo was off in Sweden or wherever getting ripped. Before you two showed up, I was deliberating how to suggest you order from the lite side of the menu, Nina." Apparently, my shirt-dresses have camouflaged nothing when it comes to Roan keeping tabs on my middle-age spread.

"I wonder who the baby's going to look like? I hope it gets your big brown eyes and stunning smile, Leo. And all that commanding lawyer charisma you got going on." Roan is holding up his thumbs and index fingers at Leo as if he is taking in important measurements through a lens.

"Hey, what about me? I'm the one cooking this baby." Whoa. Leo's barely back, and I'm starting to sound like I'm keeping this kid.

"Well, the dark skin of course, so that baby will never grow older than thirty-five, but a better sense of humor. Hey, I have an idea. If you guys decide you don't want the baby since you already have Xandra, can Tate and I adopt it? We both want kids, and yours will be a bona fide looker. It'll fit perfectly with our family planning."

"You don't know, it could come out looking like Elmo, all awkward red fro and freckled. It can happen, not all Black and White combos turn out like Rashida Jones. You should see my childhood friend, Malik." I debunk the common myth that all mixed-race babies are pretty. Just like any other mash-up, some come out busted.

"I think Tate and I will take our chances. We'd be happy with a Mariah Carey look-alike. Leo, any chance you have a rogue musical gene lying dormant in there?" Roan reaches across the table and pokes his index finger at the same biceps I was ogling earlier. There's no give, only muscle.

The familiar brunch-time banter with Roan at this baby's expense is making me crave a Bloody Mary. I raise my hand to signal the waitress, so I can ask her to bring me their best virgin version. I catch a glimpse of Leo not appreciating the jokes about pawning the baby off to Roan and Tate.

"Nina, do you want to have this baby with me?" Leo asks directly, unencumbered by the fact we're at a table for three in the middle of one of the busiest breakfast spots in all of Pasadena. Roan looks shocked, which is saying something for a guy I've never seen flinch.

I knew it. Newbie parents have zero sense of humor when it comes to their first offspring, but sitting here next to Leo again feels so right.

So, I might.

SECOND TRIMESTER

FOURTEEN

It's been nearly a month since Leo arrived home, and I haven't laid eyes on Marisol once. Between the exhaustion of leading Royal-Hawkins, when all I want to do is crawl under my mahogany desk and nap, and Leo tracking my every move and morsel, my BFF and I have fallen down on the job of propping each other up. Just this week, I feel like I've hit my second trimester stride and am game for an escape from the pregnancy police, but I suspect Marisol may not want to waste a family hall pass on a sober outing. I agree to sneak out of school early, and we move our December nail care date up to 3:00 p.m. at the West Hollywood shop.

Marisol 2:52 PM

Don't be late. Curious if the Moncler Mamas have been parading this season's winter wear around Royal-Hawkins like they're hoping for a freak snowstorm.

Nina 2:52 PM

I can't stand clothing with poultry for a logo. I'm not late, I'm already here.

"Nice tented cashmere blend," Marisol says, feeling up my sweater. "Hides that bump while keeping you CEO sharp for winter. Sooner or later, you're going to have to tell Winn Hawkins you have an applicant baking."

"I know, but I want to hold out until the end of January before I tell the board. I don't want all the memories of my first year as head of school to be of me pregnant. Give me six months to be *me* before *us*."

"Hey, look at it this way, you nailed your legacy just by getting busy. And now that you're for sure having this baby, I'm out," Marisol declares, raising her hand to wave the bartender over. He doesn't come immediately. He must be new, and clueless, and about to get an earful on customer service from the Clean Queen herself.

"I thought you were going to stay sober with me until this baby is born," I say, incredulous.

"Please, that was only until you got over yourself and decided to push this kid out. I was being supportive in your time of need. Your time is over, and I need a drink."

Even if Marisol's patience with me had run dry, I still needed her ear as the first week Leo was home proved tricky. Too often I felt compelled to assure Leo that his responsibility for my situation was minimal and that if what he really wanted was to sling himself back to Singapore, I totally understood, no hard feelings, we could each go our own way. Initially, he listened to my protestations and assured me he was going nowhere. Here, he claimed, was exactly where he wanted to be.

As the days wore on, his patience for my martyrdom grew thin. Walking along Santa Monica Beach, wrapped in sweaters, enjoying a chilly November sunset, I was revving up my *I can figure out what to do by myself* mantra when Leo shot me down once and for all. "Why don't you leave me with the baby, and you ride off into the sunset? Or better yet, leave me with summer Nina and spring baby, so whoever this fall woman is who won't accept I'm all in, she can take a hike." Leo does love a hike.

"You better be ready to deal with all my seasons," I insisted, knowing the discomforts that pregnancy and infancy were about to rain down on us.

When Leo was done responding to my list of concerns, I turned to complaining late at night to Marisol. I told her Leo was not taking seriously my feelings of wariness about having a baby with him when we barely knew each other. Marisol also grew tired of my hand-wringing and finally told me *don't believe everything you feel* and then called it quits on her late-night support hotline.

After the evening on the beach and Marisol's tough-love therapy, I started to notice Leo's baby fever seeping into my skin. The more time I spent with him, watching eagle-eyed for signs of I don't know what, the more I could imagine a mini-us. We'd get coffee, and I would watch Leo gaze and smile at a dad wrestling with the release button on a stroller. The dad's real struggle prompted me to imagine Leo smoothly popping the contraption open with one hand while balancing our kid and my cappuccino in the other. Evenings I would catch Leo hiding his online reading of the stages of embryo development like he was watching porn. Before I knew it, we were reading the same saccharine sites together nestled in bed with a bag of Ruffles, my chip repertoire recently expanded.

Walking Pasadena's streets as carefree as we had all summer, I reminded Leo this is what it could be like going forward without a kid begging to swing from our arms. Leo would reminisce about his storybook childhood in Omaha with his parents at his games, at his school concerts, at the helm of every large, rowdy family holiday that often started with Nerf gun wars with his sister, Julia, and cousins in the backyard. His favorite memories, though, were being with his dad when his mom traveled with her sister. His father never made the West brood shower, eat broccoli, or go to bed on time. Leo so much as insisted Marisol and I travel out of state and out of cell range at least twice a year so Leo could father wholly uninterrupted. In Leo's mind, a hovering mother was no good for anyone. The child, the father, and most certainly not the mother.

It was during the late-night pillow talk when Leo marveled at his sheer luck that the mother of his child is the queen of childhood development. When he promised he would do everything possible to support me staying in the professional world, it slowly came to me that perhaps I really wouldn't be going round two of the parenting game feeling alone like I had with Graham, who had spent Xandra's childhood raising a start-up rather than a daughter. My opposition to becoming a mom again turned to optimism when Leo claimed he would happily be the one to hold down the fort with our baby when I had evening events at school. He even suggested we have a second set of hands around to help like Marisol has, since we would be dual working parents and we also needed our own adult time together. I allowed myself to consider that perhaps this surprise baby could be a blessing after our birth control blunder.

As I began to see the bits and pieces of how the two of us could raise a baby together, it did start to sound more feasible than terrifying, especially the nights Leo would come over after I had an evening committee meeting. While sipping a robust red to my Pellegrino, Leo would cook for us from his wide Italian repertoire. No one had cooked for me since Marisol and I lived together and she would whip up late-night quesadillas after a Friday night bar crawl.

"So, what are we up to, two proposals or three?" Marisol asks before popping a second gin-and-vermouth-soaked olive in her mouth.

"No Chardonnay today?" I ask, avoiding Marisol's question.

"I'm gonna need something stronger than Chardonnay to get me through your pregnancy. And your diversions never work, Nina, my drinking habits are not the topic here. What's the latest from Leo?"

"One rushed marriage proposal, but I think Leo was delirious from seeing his baby on ultrasound. Uh . . . let's see, three conversations about living together and one request to spend New Year's in Omaha with the entire West clan. Apparently, cousin Karl is dying to meet me."

"You chose living together, right?" Marisol prides herself on knowing me well. I love it when, after a lifetime of friendship, I can still surprise her.

"I'm not ready to share my space with a new man AND a new baby. I'm going to Omaha for a few days in late December when Xandra flies out to meet Graham in Miami over New Year's."

"No shit. I can't wait to hear how Operation Mixed Baby goes over in the heartland. And I really can't wait to hear what White people do with their weird uncles at holidays." Marisol raises her glass in a gesture of good luck.

"The baby is more than enough for now. Moving in together, marriage. That's a whole other can of I don't know what that I have no intention of opening right now."

"You always put off emotional tasks, sister." We both nod in agreement knowing how true that statement is. "Speaking of tasks, tell me what's happening with sharing the joyous news with your ex and with Xandra."

"I'm telling Graham tonight and then Xandra first thing when she gets home next week for Christmas break."

"Ohhhh can we call Graham together and put him on speaker? I promise, I won't say a thing. I want to hear him squirm long distance. So fun!"

"I don't need extra mess, Sol, I'm trying to be a responsible adult here." Marisol and I erupt into giggles knowing how absurd *trying to be adult* sounds when the two of us get together about Graham. "How about if I call and give you the CliffsNotes after?" I suggest, knowing Marisol would grab the phone ready to give Graham a verbal beatdown before I could even eke out a *hello*.

"Well then, tell Graham I'm so glad New York's working out."

"I think he already knows you're thrilled he's over there hugging the Atlantic Ocean way outta your way."

"I bet that's the only thing he's hugging. I can't imagine any woman wanting those leftovers. He's not worth the calories."

⌐

"Well, this is a surprise," Graham answers, distracted. Déjà vu, I can hear his fingers banging on a keyboard, probably barking out an order over email. It's going to be a surprise all right.

"I need to tell you something, and I'm choosing to tell you before I tell Xandra next week. I'm trying to be fair to our parenting agreement." Sitting in my car, I have Graham on speaker. I'm letting my toes dry a bit more before driving home.

"Okay." The clicking stops immediately. I realize my tone leaned too far toward the dire. Graham could be imagining I've been diagnosed with the big C, since my mother was not much older than I am when she first discovered a lump. Even Graham doesn't deserve that kind of scare.

"Leo's back from Singapore, and we're making it work. I should have told you about him this summer, but I'm telling you now. We're together," I state. That was some strong adulting if you ask me.

"Oh, Nina, you really must be thirsty to go dippin' in the snow. What, you couldn't find yourself another leveled-up brotha like me?"

"Screw you and your dick measuring, Graham." A leveled-up brother would have been there for his family, not hiding out in a face-less tech park obsessed with making bank when his baby was learning to walk.

"Damn, you're touchy. I'm just messing with you, Nina."

I blurt out, "I'm also pregnant. And before you clap back with something smart, yes, it's for sure Leo's." Graham doesn't clap back with anything, the opposite of what I expect. Verbal toe to toe is what we've always done best.

"Graham?"

"Sounds to me like you're trying to replace the child we already have." Graham has nailed my greatest fear in telling Xandra. I worry terribly that not only will she feel replaced, but that she might feel so removed from our growing Pasadena three that she will attach herself to Graham's world back east and disengage from me.

"Wow, Graham, that was jacked up, even for you. You're obviously stuck in your feelings and trying to hurt me." Graham and I can too easily sink right back into the crux of our failed relationship. I thought we would operate like my parents, who shared the financial and parenting load of life, and Graham thought we would operate like his parents, who divided and conquered.

"I'm not trying to hurt you, Nina, I just know how much this is going to hurt Xandra, and she's obviously in a vulnerable place right now. What were you expecting from me, a congratulations?"

"I don't know what I was expecting."

"Well, I'll tell you what I'm expecting."

"What?" I scoff, but willing to give him about thirty more seconds of my time.

"I'm expecting you to call Xandra immediately. Or I will. I'm not driving her to the airport to fly home with your father next week holding on to this piece of information. I assume Fitzroy knows?"

"He does."

"Well, since your old man is nice enough to fly to Los Angeles with Xandra, I don't think he needs to be sitting on a plane next to his granddaughter for six hours keeping your secrets. You tell her now or I will."

FIFTEEN

I know both of you have better things to do on a Thursday night than come to a R-H high school basketball jamboree (well maybe you do Roan, Marisol I know you'll be home in sweats), but I need you to come tonight and see what's happened to my baby girl.

Roan 2:46 PM

I'll be there. I have news to share too and I need you both to be on my side. BTW there's a yummy Guyanese Indian Queen here who I'd like to make my King. If I were single of course.

Today I sent Roan, along with a handful of Royal-Hawkins teachers, to a local conference on how to attract students of color to private schools. My cynical side believes this to be a fool's errand when the high cost of living surrounding Royal-Hawkins makes attendance from other Los Angeles County neighborhoods a herculean trek. But my hopeful side and confidence in Roan plopped down close to two grand of the school's budget to find out if we can attract more depth to Royal-Hawkins. Still,

I bet he's spending the lunch on Pinterest perusing wedding tablescapes instead of networking.

Marisol 2:48 PM

Lucky for you both my favorite sweats are in the wash.
See ya there. May have a kid in tow.

Leo wanted to drive me to the airport to pick up my dad and Xandra, ready to get a jump start on ingratiating himself into the small but mighty Morgan Clarke clan. He attempted to mask his eagerness by saying he didn't trust all the drivers rushing late to the airport, that extra precautions needed to be taken now that I was *with child*. Yes, he actually used the old English, *with child*. That phrase has moved to the top of the list of irritating things New Dad Leo has said since finding out he knocked me up. I reminded him that when I was late to pick him up for his flight to Singapore, he sped to the airport like a man possessed and managed to get there safely with no pregnant women harmed in the hard scramble. Leo compromised by insisting I take his tank of a car, and I promised not to exceed the speed limit. Xandra and I needed some quality mother-daughter time first before bringing Leo and his zeal for fatherhood into Xandra's broody teenage orbit.

Before taking off from John F. Kennedy airport, Dad gave me a call. I thought he was ringing to let me know the flight was on time. If only. Fitzroy was calling to tell me to breathe deep, swallow my thoughts, and brace myself. The last thing he reminded me: "You are a lady and a mother, and Xandra is a child of God. I'll see you soon." He made it clear that the Xandra I last saw organizing her dorm room with supplies from Target was not the Xandra coming home for Christmas. All I could envision was a cheap tattoo running down her arm like Marisol predicted. It better say I LOVE MY MOM.

I knew from his tone of voice Graham was serious about his threat to tell Xandra about my pregnancy if I didn't get to it first, and in this rare instance he was right. The hard needed to happen now. After hanging up from that conversation, I called Leo to come over immediately for emotional support. With reinforcements on the way, I drove home and made myself a PB and J to carbo-load for the FaceTime with Xandra that would certainly drain both our energies.

I left Leo pacing in the living room and stepped into my bedroom to make the call. I appreciated that even in his new-dad delirium, Leo respected that I'm Xandra's mother and having this conversation was all on me. Fortunately, I caught Xandra in her room, alone. Dash was at a group session reviewing for her herstory women's studies final. Xandra claimed she was suffering from writer's block on a paper she was working on, so she was happy for the distraction. It felt good to hear Xandra sound upbeat and chatty about which of her friends was doing what over the winter break, the movies she wanted to see when she got home, and a quick mention about the gift she and Dash went in on for their faculty dorm parent. I could think of nothing more I wanted to do over the holidays than share a box of Sour Patch Kids and an hours-long shopping spree with Xandra.

I was going to mention how thrilled I was to hear her sounding so positive after a fall semester of conversations laced with accusations about Pemberley faculty, but I decided if Xandra wasn't going to go there on this call, I wasn't going to go there either. I knew in that moment a break from boarding school to rest, spend quality time with me, and get to know Leo would be what Xandra needed to head into the second half of the school year with a reset in attitude.

I told Xandra there were a few things I wanted to share with her now, and then we could talk more about them once she got home. That I was an open book.

"Is this about that pale dude you're dating?" Xandra asked out the gate while I was still stretching my brain for the right words.

"Yes. His name is Leo and he's White. Pale is not a color."

"So, what do you want to tell me about the *White* dude?" Xandra's voice was blanketed with sarcasm.

Not calling Leo by his name was pointedly disrespectful, but I gave her some room for error since this would be a difficult conversation. "When you get here, Leo's going to be spending some time with us over Christmas because recently, we've grown close." I waited for a response. Nothing came. All my years teaching high school science, dead air is a teenage tactic I know well, so I pushed on. "And we're having a baby together."

"I guess you have gotten close, huh? Sex before marriage, I thought that was a no-no in our family." I was about to explain to Xandra that she was not getting a new stepfather along with a sibling when she cut me off. "So what, time running out on your clock? When you planning on doing the pregnancy thing?" Xandra said with the impatient tone of a teen interested only in information as it affects her life.

"No, sweetheart, I'm trying to tell you I'm already pregnant," I said softly, looking directly at my girl, wanting the news to land as delicately as possible. Xandra's eyes rolled so far back that any farther and she could read her own mind.

"Wait, what? A baby? God, Mom, that's so gross! Nobody asked me!" Xandra yelled and put the phone facedown on her bed to block me out. I could still hear her screaming in the background.

Uh yeah. Nobody asked me either, but here we all are.

Dad found me first in baggage claim and reminded me, without so much as a hello, that a parent's love for their child is unconditional and can weather any storm. I wasn't sure if his cryptic message was because I was about to get Xandra's report card and her first semester grades were not up to expectations, or if she spent the whole plane ride tearing me to shreds with her grandfather. I couldn't believe Fitzroy would go soft on the grade front with his granddaughter. Growing up, my mother would put her version of love notes in Clive's and my lunch boxes on test days, notes that said things like, *Your father and I say an A today is the only way.* I'm pretty sure Fitzroy's message was to remind me I had no idea what was coming for me from my daughter, so I better focus up.

The only thing I recognized on Xandra was the navy four-wheel suitcase she was rolling, a bon voyage and birthday present I gave her when she turned fourteen, shortly before she headed to Pemberley for her freshman year. The navy suitcase was precisely chosen to send Xandra the subtle message to come home often and that young women shouldn't accessorize with black—it's depressing.

The suitcase was being pulled by a leather-clad, shaved-headed young woman with so many piercings in her ears I could have sworn I heard the wind whistling through the few holes that were not filled with mismatched studs. With her newly shorn head, I was actually grateful for the enormous size ten feet clad in heinous combat boots serving as weights to ground my lithe daughter to the earth. How was it my angel had come home looking like an angry White girl from Calabasas, sullenly posing on a street corner in Venice, opposing the patriarchy that's paying for the Benz that drove her there? All I could think was that I should have had Leo come with me so he could get a front-row seat to what it's like when your child causes your stomach to drop like the Times Square New Year's Eve ball. The hooker-red matte lipstick, that will be the first thing to go, Xandra, you can count on that. Taking it all in, I concluded that in the week since we FaceTimed my once demure, sweet Xandra looked rough. Rough and tough and tragically without her baby Afro-puffs.

I had to look away. The shock of my daughter looking more butch than baby was too much for me to linger. I pretended to fumble in my purse for something, and then I walked over to the baggage claim to help Dad pull his luggage off the conveyor belt before he gave himself a double hernia. Dad grabbed my arm to hold me back from laying into Xandra, and it felt just like my mom used to do: putting a hand on me, telling me to pump my brakes when she could sense my anger was about to let loose.

"You want a hat, so your head doesn't catch a cold when we step outside?" I ask Xandra after giving her a hug. I waited a moment, I really did.

"Nice job, Nina, took you a whole minute to get into it," Dad said, striding up to take hold of Xandra's hand and walk her toward short-term parking.

Just that quick, the two against one dynamic was in action. Did Fitzroy not spy the safety pin in one of his granddaughter's earholes?

"Hey, Jasmine," I say, giving a big hug to one of my favorite seniors before I head up the bleachers to where I see Roan and Marisol have already claimed spots. With R-H letters in kelly green and rose red adorning her cheeks, and a pile of ribbons holding her high pony, Jasmine has exuded school spirit since her first day in kindergarten. When her teacher asked her what she wanted to be when she grew up, she hopped to the center of the sharing circle, kicked her leg in the air, and roared, *A CHEERLEADER!* I never did tell her parents that their school tuition was paying for such five-year-old aspirations. Turns out, thirteen years later, Jasmine also wants to be the next RBG. "I saw your mom last week hobbling around the upper school on crutches. Is her ankle doing any better?"

"She's way better, Ms. Clarke. I'm glad, too, 'cause I'm sick of having to reach everything in the house. You know I'm not that tall." Jasmine puts a hand on her hip and gives me a pout for show. Not one member of her Filipino family stands above five-five, and Jasmine is no exception, maybe hitting five-two in her platform sneakers. "I think she's keeping those crutches around to get me to do more chores."

"Smart woman if you ask me. Enjoy the game, Jaz." I nod to the one-woman pep squad.

"I hate the Royal-Hawkins basketball shirts and shorts. I believe synthetics are killing our environment more than cows," Marisol shares in her mock activist voice. Since discovering that listening to podcasts while doing laundry makes the time fly, Marisol has become the climate change police. It's a bit hard to listen to her preach when she's picking remnants of a paper straw out of her teeth, but her intentions are good.

"Okay, here it is." Roan is waving his cell phone inches in front of his eyes trying to create enough wind to keep from crying. Oh my God, is he moving? Is Tate making him go back to New Jersey? This cannot be happening to me this year, of all years! Roan's racking up families for Royal-Hawkins like I haven't seen in a decade, and he's the one I need around to smooth out the rumors when the HOS is MIA when the B-A-B-Y arrives. He absolutely cannot leave me.

"Tate wants to elope!"

Oh, thank God, Roan's not going anywhere other than into a panic.

"Elope-elope, or more like a destination wedding?" Marisol questions before we go chasing Roan down a rabbit hole.

"ELOPE. No toasts. No first dance. No running off to our honeymoon under a canopy of sparklers."

"No gifts," I chime in.

"EXACTLY. And I want a Vitamix BAD." Roan sulks.

"You want the panini machine we got for our wedding? It's still in the box," Marisol offers, always looking for a way to clear out her cabinets.

"Dairy's my new don't." Roan pats his stomach. "I mean, look at these pictures of us in Disneyland." Roan's aggressively swiping picture after picture of Tate hugging him at the happiest place on earth. In tennis shorts, Tate's tanned and muscled legs are on display, his Mickey Mouse ears perfectly propped atop his golden crown of hair. "I want the world to see THIS is my man. At least I want my world to see it. My relatives back in Dublin don't believe I'm marrying someone who looks like he just stepped off a *Baywatch* television shoot."

"Does Tate want to elope anywhere good?" Marisol asks, hoping for a silver lining to Roan's devastating news.

"Lake Tahoe. The Nevada side." We all pucker like we've been served something sour.

"That's unfortunate," I say, unable to come up with anything better, but knowing the consoling has to start.

"I know, right?" This is exactly where Roan's demand to stand by his side comes into play. Marisol and I nod our heads vigorously in solidarity with our wounded gride.

"Why does Tate want to elope?" Marisol asks, scrunching up her nose, put off by the idea. I dig my heel in between Marisol's big and second toe so she recognizes her misstep. "I mean, does he have a fear of performing in front of crowds or something?" Marisol attempts to deflect from her rudeness.

"He's hung up on the numbers. Money and people. Tate came up with an impossibly small budget for our wedding. It's absolutely ridiculous to ask me to plan under his conditions. The budget alone won't cover my suit, the photographer, and our rented 1975 Alfa Romeo getaway car!" Roan has worked himself up into an emotional lather that I know, from experience, we need to let run its course. "So, when I told Tate he was suffocating the creative vision that will set the tone for the rest of our lives together, he suggested we elope. To Heavenly!"

"Well, that will save you money and still set a nice foundation for your marriage," I suggest, because Marisol is too busy choking down her fit of laughter.

Ignoring me, Roan continues, "So I had a thought, Nina." I'm unsure which is worse, spiraling Roan or thinking Roan. "What if we have a double spring wedding to cut down on costs?"

"With who?" I ask. Marisol lets loose howling.

"With you! The one who decided to do it dyslexic and get knocked up first."

"You two have to stop! I'm trying not to pee my pants in public," Marisol gasps out, tears running down her cheeks.

"No way. I'm not getting married anytime soon. And I'm definitely not getting married pushing nine months pregnant."

"So that's it? You're going to let me walk down the aisle, alone, surrounded by penny slots?"

"*Cha ching!*" Marisol belts out, mimicking pulling down a machine arm. Not helpful.

"What's going on down there?" Marisol nods to the bottom of the bleachers, knowing we should probably change the subject from Roan's nuptials lest he also find out Marisol and I have a bet going that he and Tate won't make it through New Year's. I assume Marisol has laid eyes on Xandra and her current goth wardrobe fit for a funeral procession. My need for consoling over my brooding daughter trumps Roan's wedding woes, and I'm instantly bumped to the front of the friendship line.

"What are Jared and Winn doing down there cuddled up on the team bench?" Roan asks, following Marisol's sight line. I'm looking around the gym for Xandra, but my eyes land on the mismatched couple hunkered over clipboards, furiously writing after a three-point shot is missed by a starting Royal-Hawkins junior.

"A high school basketball game is an odd choice for a date with your closet sugar daddy. Or I should say, not so closeted anymore," Roan states more than speculates. I wave my fingers, signaling Roan to lower his voice.

"What? I'm just serving the tea while it's hot. Jared's a first-year teacher in pricey Pasadena. You know he's living in a two-bedroom with three other people, barely making ends meet. Someone needs to take care of that Adonis, otherwise it's a waste of a flawless physique."

"Is Jared the varsity coach and Winn the helicopter parent assisting him?" Marisol asks, more interested in the ins and outs of high school sports than I ever would have given her credit for. "I know you didn't cave and give that kid the head coaching position when he whined for it earlier this fall," Marisol insists, fishing around for the chink in my leadership chain.

"Absolutely not. He's still in charge of coaching our middle schoolers. He doesn't even particularly like the varsity coach, so I have no idea why he would be down there on the bench. Or why Winn's with him."

"Weird," Roan offers as his final thought on a topic he's quickly lost interest in. He wistfully returns to the half-built wedding website on his phone. Marisol shoots *excuse me* eyes in my direction. She's the only person who knows what went down in the November board meeting when Winn showed up late from his three-day basketball playdate with Jared.

Lethargy, uncertainty, or the three slices of pizza I ate for dinner— something is keeping me from leaving my perch and marching down to find out more about the Winn-Jared bromance. The "should I stay or should I go" question clouds my brain when I hear what sounds like a pair of pointy heels climbing the bleachers heading right for me. I pull my jacket tight to hide my midsection when I see Courtney Dunn laser in on the spot next to me. Is she climbing all the way up here to have a better vantage point on the game, or on Winn Hawkins? Maybe Marisol was right and Courtney's persistence to join the board is akin to a fatal attraction plot line. Oof, our team just missed two baskets in a row. Even I know that ain't good, but why do Jared and Winn whisper to each other and scribble notes after each lost point?

"Oh, Nina, so glad we can catch up before the holidays and before I officially join the board in January." Good Lord those are some killer stiletto knee-high boots in olive suede Courtney's sporting. They even look comfortable. I elbow Marisol and give her a quick nod to take a look. Her jaw drops in jealousy.

Marisol and Roan slide over several inches to make room for Courtney in our row. "Good to see you, Courtney. Do you and the family have exciting plans for the holidays?" I ask, shifting gears into my polished head of school voice. I know the answer, of course they do. People like the Dunns are always scheduled up on school breaks, but I need a decoy conversation before we return to her assumption of being on the board come the new year.

"Oh, you know, the usual hot/cold Christmas. Punta Mita pre-Christmas and then Vail for New Year's. We always fly from sea to ski on Christmas Day to save money."

It takes every ounce of restraint I have to not remind her to pack her Moncler. "Sounds sensible," I briefly comment to keep my mouth from getting me in trouble.

"I'm so grateful to Winn for offering me a seat on the board. We will be a formidable force when it comes to moving the state of the school forward."

"Is that so?" I ask Courtney while glaring a hole into Winn's back. What are you up to, Winn Hawkins? First taking a teacher thirty years your junior under your wing for I don't know what, and now putting a clingy Royal-Hawkins mother in your pocket.

"My apologies, Courtney, I have to run. I see my daughter entering the gym. I'll let you know if your board seat is confirmed before school's back in session." Indeed, Xandra is walking the sidelines and it seems in the twelve hours since I left her at home, fast asleep, she has bleached her scalp to match Courtney's blonde lob. Where did she even get the hydrogen peroxide? Fitzroy, you better not have chaperoned my baby to CVS.

"Oh, it's confirmed, Nina."

"Thank you for sharing," I assert, my go-to statement to shut down a conversation with another adult. That one-liner has stumped many a parent in my administrative tenure. So as not to let Courtney get to me, I smile, close my eyes, and think of kids like Jasmine and her enthusiasm for Royal-Hawkins. It's always the students who remind me why I show up to school every day.

SIXTEEN

It's the last day of school before holiday break, and this afternoon Fitzroy and Leo are coming in for the Royal-Hawkins winter concert. This is Leo's first time seeing his baby mama in action at school, and based on today's, uh, early morning enthusiasm after Leo's sleepover, I would venture to say he likes a woman in charge.

The air at school the day before a break is always frenetic. The anticipation of staying up late and sleeping in for two solid weeks is almost more than the students can bear. This year, for our winter concert, I boldly went where no head of school has gone since Y2K. I told the music teacher to go for it: sing Christmas carols, Adam Sandler's Hanukkah song, anything she can find on Kwanzaa. I'm tired of every holiday having to be secular and devoid of ritual. Why can't we all celebrate each other's traditions in one big mash-up rather than pretending none of them exists with a placid (read: boring) program. "Silent Night" never killed anyone. In fact, many of these parents pray for one.

Mimi hands me an envelope as I walk into my office after observing a junior year calculus class with a brilliant teacher who, I happen to know, would rather be teaching applied mathematics PhD students at USC. We're going to have to work on his homework load come the new year, but his love of math is infectious. The kids in his class were happily puzzling over problems I couldn't begin to comprehend. "Mrs.

Dunn dropped this off for you first thing this morning. She wanted me to make sure you got it before break."

"Thanks, Mimi." I smile, grateful for an assistant who saved me from preholiday face time with Courtney. The envelope has no weight to it, and I'm wondering if Courtney mistakenly dropped it off empty.

In my office, I unbutton the back of my skirt that's being held together by a rubber band and a prayer and plop down in my chair. I'm at that pregnancy stage where I'm sure whispering about my weight gain is happening with the bony moms in the school parking lot, but I'm not ready to give in to maternity couture. The discomfort, however, is real, so tomorrow when all Royal-Hawkins families are tucking into their holiday plans, I may be hitting Mom's the Word for stretchy denim with Marisol.

I rip the envelope from the top and realize a check's inside, hence the weightlessness. I pull it out, and a quarter mil stares back at me with a lime-green Post-it note:

Designated for the Royal-Hawkins Athletics Department.
—Courtney

Apparently, I was wrong. Courtney has just had the last word from our conversation at the basketball jamboree, and now I know the end-of-year clearance cost for a board seat. I take a minute to consider, on a merry last day of school before vacation when every child is overflowing with contagious elation, Am I going to let Winn and Courtney be my holiday wet blanket? I don't think so. I write "Do Not Throw Away" in red Sharpie on the check envelope and put it in my top right-hand drawer to ensure I don't accidentally toss it in a compulsive moment of office nesting. Before leaving my office to head to the gym, I take the check out one more time to confirm I read correctly. Yep, $250,000.

"Roan, keep the mistletoe in your pocket and remember school's still in session," I warn sternly as I watch Roan peeking around the school gym hoping to spy a handsome father who has ducked out of work early to join the estrogen-heavy crowd. "And I love your Christmas plaid jacket, so preppy Grinch."

"Swing by our rancher tomorrow for some latkes, you will die when you see the Hanukkah-blue velvet blazer I found on eBay."

"Just don't bankrupt yourself dressing for eight nights."

"Already have." Roan grimaces. "Oh, there's Leo! And that gentleman with him is a better dressed, cheerier version of you! Maybe I'll take your dad on a spin around the gym to shop the local grandmothers." I give my dad a long look from afar, and I have to agree with Roan, Dad does look younger and happier than I have seen him since my mother died. I know he enjoys being in Pasadena with Xandra and me, but I think it's his friends at the Y and endless dominoes games that have given him a new lease on life. Roan waves to Leo, then grabs my wrist, and we create a wall to part the mob and head over to my two men.

"Hey, beautiful. What's the protocol for kissing the queen in her castle?" Leo whispers in my ear. Feeling frisky, I let a schoolgirl giggle escape.

I back up into Leo. "You get one quick ass grab, that's it. The head can't be caught breaking the dance code of keeping arms' distance apart."

"Ahhh, naughty headmistress, I'll play along." Leo's handful lingers, and I have to physically move his hand to my waist.

"Not in front of my father and hundreds of gossip-hungry moms, you won't!" I admonish Leo, but then I give him a quick peck on the cheek as a consolation.

"So, this is where our baby will be going to school, huh?" Leo asks, looking around the gym.

"SHHHHHH!!" I spit all over Leo's jacket lapels. I swear Maggie Tilman, mother of triplet girls in fifth grade, turned to look at us. That woman understands pregnancy surprises. "I don't want to have to discipline you for talking out of turn."

"Or maybe you can. I'll stop by the principal's office after the concert to find out my punishment."

As much as I'd love to stay by Leo's side and role play in a gym packed with folks who pay my salary, I wiggle myself loose of his hands and head to the stage to kick off our winter concert. I'm sure the first song will spark a handful of emails in my inbox by day's end.

Turns out, the majority of families know the chorus *fa la la la la la la la la* and sing carols with gusto. The crooked bow ties on the kindergarten boys make my heart melt, as do the second-grade men whose pants are more reminiscent of clam diggers than full-length slacks, the sort their parents hope will last ONE. MORE. SEASON. For thirty-two minutes time will stand still, adults of all races and religions will revel in the unjaded souls of children, and all will feel right with the world. I look over to Leo, hoping to catch his glance. I want him to see me at the top of my profession. The mistress of ceremonies at the happiest show in town.

"If you were the head of a Catholic school, do you think you would have a Black baby Jesus in the nativity scene?" Jared whispers in my ear, taking me by surprise. My bliss bubble of appreciation for our collective community has popped twelve minutes into the concert. Jared's hubris and random moment of Black solidarity simultaneously impress and irritate me.

"Why in the world would you ask me that?" I whisper through my smile as the third graders exit the stage and the fourth graders rise to shuffle up the steps. I'm trying to telepath to Frieda Solano to stop picking her nose before she hits the bright lights of public humiliation.

"Curiosity. I didn't take you for the religious type until this concert, but now I suspect you have more God than gangster in you." It occurs to me that Jared, too, was schooled in a generation that only sang audience-neutral songs like "Somewhere Over the Rainbow" and "You Are My Sunshine." I never considered he would issue my first concert complaint.

"Speaking of curiosity, I noticed you and Winn were quite chummy at the basketball game last night." I'm keeping my body loose and voice low, so I don't come across as stressed by their fraternizing.

"Yeah, Winn's a good dude. We have a lot in common."

I choke hearing that statement. Luckily, it comes out as a seasonal cough and no one notices. I let some silence hang in the air to consider my next move. I've been holding on to the fact that I know Jared lied to me and called in sick to go to man camp with Winn to use in my favor when the time is right. I'm debating if this is that time.

"Yes, it seems you two share a real affinity for basketball." I decide to leave it at that, letting Jared wonder if I know about the camp. I can use my knowledge as an uncomfortable drip over time.

"Yeah, he's trying to make me a Lakers fan, but I'm true to the Clippers through thick and thin. Can't turn on a dime." Either it's not registering that I may know about his playing hooky, or the guy really doesn't care. "We've been having a good time together checking out the public school games and the youth league season. Winn feeds me some good grub, and I find where the dopest kids comin' up are playing around LA. He's also included me in his pickup games. Those old guys are slow, but they still got it. Also, I'm killing it networking on and off the court."

While their friendship is growing more curious by the minute, Jared checking out the Greater LA youth basketball scene makes sense. Many of our teachers who coach for Royal-Hawkins also coach club sports for extra income. Jared's probably trolling for a plum coaching job with older kids to balance out the low level of play that often plagues private school teams. What's in it for Winn remains a mystery. I'm actually impressed by Jared's ingenuity and fortitude—he clearly does love the idea of coaching teenagers.

"Winn's become a mentor to me."

"What the fu . . ." I bite down hard on my last syllable. Luckily, the fourth graders are crescendoing to the end of their song, and neither Jared nor the audience members hear me almost throw out what would be, under any other circumstances, an appropriately placed f-bomb.

"I'm definitely impressed with how you're easing yourself into the Royal-Hawkins community, Jared." I need to tie up this chat and head to the stage to introduce the middle school so the sixth graders can have their chance to share their musical mediocrity.

"Yeah, the parents have been great, not what I was expecting actually." Jared gives me a wink and a light elbow nudge to my arm. I know the implication behind that wink and nudge: *Who knew rich White people could be so cool?*

"Happy holidays to you, Jared. I hope you have a nice vacation." I'm full up on Jared for this calendar year and hoping our interactions improve in the next.

"Yeah, you, too, Nina. Enjoy your break." Jared flashes his high-voltage smile that has his middle school students swooning on the daily. I notice for the first time his red corduroy pants have tiny white snowflakes on them, and he has paired them perfectly with a crisp pink button-down and fresh white leather sneakers. I recognize Jared looks sharp and has swagger in a manner only a Black man like he and Graham can pull off. I peek over at Leo in his conservative pinstripe suit. It's not that I'm embarrassed of Leo, but looking back and forth between these two men, even I would assume the Black woman in the room was paired up with Jared before I would bet on Leo. And I know I'm not alone in that assumption.

Though he can rub me wrong, I give Jared's arm a motherly pat. I do like the on-point style of this young joker, even when I suspect he ain't playin' it straight.

⌒

Dad and I are seated in front of cups of tea at the kitchen table, staring at a letter that arrived today from Pemberley. Xandra's in her room, I assume lost in a haze of YouTube videos, blissfully unaware that her elders have gathered to read her fate. Dad's sitting on his hands fighting his instinct to rip the Band-Aid and expose whatever wound lies in that letter so he can go right to fixing it. And me? The official-looking post sends a shiver through my body. I imagine what's inside is akin to a parenting report card, and I know I've failed the last pop quiz.

"Dad, you want extra hot water?" I ask, more as a stalling tactic than an offering.

"I'll take some more hot water," Dad agrees, holding up his cup, "but jeezum pees, Nina, I could be six feet under before you get to reading that letter." Fitzroy reaches to the middle of the table to nab the envelope while I'm filling his mug.

"Hey! It's a federal offense to open someone else's mail," I remind, grabbing Dad's wrist. "I should read it first."

"Read it out loud, then," Dad insists, impatient with me.

Here goes everything . . .

Dear Parents of Xandra Clarke,

Xandra is a student of great talent in the classroom and a treasured member of the Pemberley community, but so far in the drama production of *Wonderful Town*, she has been noticeably dissatisfied with the role she earned as an underclassman. She consistently shows up late to rehearsals and is struggling to memorize her lines and stage direction in preparation for opening night. In the end, I hope her performance will be of high quality, but the journey to get there has been a difficult one for the entire cast, me included.

If Xandra would like to continue in future Pemberley theater productions, this letter will need to be signed by Xandra and parents and returned to me before the start of winter term. I hope this break will provide much-needed reflection time for Xandra.

Thank you.

Dave Petrov

Theater Department Chair

Pemberley School

Neither Dad nor I speak. In this day, a written letter is sent only in dire circumstances. I rarely have to communicate beyond an email or phone call. I'm contemplating heading back to grab Xandra from her tech coma and dragging her butt out here to deal with this and explain it to her grandfather. Luckily, greater parental sense prevails.

"Sounds like Xandra's drama teacher may be Russian. And formal. Perhaps with his accent he's difficult to understand and there were some misunderstood communications with Xandra," I offer out loud, grasping for a solid excuse for my daughter though I know there isn't one.

"His name's Dave, so I'm guessing his English is just fine. And I understand Dave Petrov loud and clear. Xandra has shown her teacher all kinds of disrespect, and she has crossed his line." As an immigrant and a dedicated Christian, Fitzroy has very clear parameters on how one lives life. In Dad's mind, following the principles established by both personas was essential in his adopted country to ensure people wouldn't whisper about your comings and goings and attention wouldn't be called your way. Behave and blend in or be sorry was how we were raised.

"That's not the granddaughter I know. And I also know you didn't teach her any of those ill manners. Lord knows your mother and I never taught them to you." Dad's viewpoint on his and Celia's impeccable parenting is surfacing.

"So, Nina, what're you gonna do about this?" Dad asks, looking right at me, jaw set. Oh, this is rich. When Xandra is fit for public consumption—well dressed, well behaved, and well turned out— Fitzroy's there to lap up the credit and the compliments. But as the second generation of our immigrant family begins to stray from the prescribed code of conduct, it's all my fault and my job to get her back in line. A straight line, and quick.

"I can't believe I'm going to have to repeat myself," Dad continues. I can tell he's getting revved up and about to take this family gathering from gentle to gloves off. "Nina, I told you to move Xandra out of that living situation with Dash at the first sign of trouble this fall, and you didn't do it. So here we are sippin' on tea, fretting over Xandra and her future. A girl like Xandra doesn't turn without some wayward influence. Don't I know it, I saw it play out time and time again on our block. Those that know better don't always do better."

It's easy for Dad to lay blame on Dash, but deep down I know that I'm the one who lit Xandra's rebellious flame. I suspect Xandra's behavior has little to do with her roommate being militant or her drama teacher being racist and everything to do with her mother being with a man who's the opposite of her father. And now that man is taking her mother and creating a brand-new family that she's not sure has a place for her.

"You know what, Xandra thinks she's grown. It's time to bring her into the kitchen, let her read the letter, and explain herself." *And,* I think to myself, *force her to share her true feelings about me and Leo.*

"I'll go get her," Dad offers, and I accept, giving myself an extra minute to refine my opening line.

"What's up? I'm FaceTiming with Dash. Yesterday she was helping her mom's friend host a neighborhood watch meeting in Cabrini-Green, and right now she's on her way to a protest. Apparently, the new African savanna installation at the Field Museum was designed by an Asian architect. My life's so boring!"

"Seriously? The planet's imploding, but there's a protest over an architect that builds life-size dioramas for a living. Should the architect be African American, or does he have to be born in Africa, Black or White will do? Or real deal African with a click in his mother tongue and all?" Not the conversation opener I was planning, my emotions are already too hot and starting the conversation off with Dash at the center is making me fume.

"You should be happy you're home in Pasadena, your bed has a blanket, the light bill is paid, and the icebox has milk. If you're bored, the garage needs to be swept out, or you can put some elbow grease to those windows," Dad claps back at Xandra. Okay now, clearly we're both on board to tell Xandra what's what. Dad just took two verbal steps over his grandbaby to join my side.

"Sit down and get comfortable, because we're going to get into it, and no one is getting out of this family meeting without some clarity about what's going on with you, Xandra," I say, pausing to take a breath to let the mission of this conversation settle in with the three of us. Before I can speak, Dad, usually the reserved one with his words, pounces.

"It's time to get down to the nitty-gritty, baby girl, and we're going to start at the top. What did you do to your crown? Hair is power. Did all those nights of me lulling you to sleep with the story of Samson and Delilah go in one ear and out the other?" Dad asks, running his big bus-driving hands over Xandra's bleached skull. I can think back on a hundred times when Dad would praise me for straightening Xandra's hair, making sure it laid flat like all the other girls at Royal-Hawkins. The more Xandra and I blended in with the dominant American culture, the more it pleased Dad that we could walk through the world without inviting trouble, and he could rest easy. Dad's not resting easy now.

"And those piercings, I can't imagine what germy, dirty hands touched your ears. I'm surprised one hasn't swollen up, crusted over, and fallen off." Dad is now pulling on Xandra's right ear, inspecting it for either cleanliness or crud. At this point, I've decided to sit back and let him work over Xandra. He's killin' it.

"Dash took me to the place where her cousin got her piercings. It was in a mall, so it was cheaper than doing it at a tattoo parlor. Those places are hella expensive," Xandra informs, proud that she did her due diligence and got the equivalent of a teenage Yelp review.

"You relied on someone you don't even know to tell you where to get minor surgery on your body?" Now I'm grabbing Xandra's other ear. "Apparently four times! I know you don't have the extra money at school to get a piercing done right one time, let alone four!" I step back to examine Xandra, and I don't see my little girl anymore. I don't see the girl whose hair I braided, barretted, and bunned day after day, year after year. I see a young woman attempting to assert her independence. And based on her current lack of style, she's doing it badly.

I realize we need to get off the superficial and get into the content of Mr. Petrov's concerns. I hand Xandra the letter. "Some Christmas cheer from your drama teacher to me. Minus the cheer."

Steeled to hear Xandra's side of the story I ask, "So, what do you think?"

"In rehearsals a few of us were joking around and talking during our five-minute break," she begins, and I see my dad wince at her admission of goofing off at school. "We didn't hear Mr. Petrov call out that break was over. When we didn't stop talking, he marched over, looked right at me, not at the other girls, but at me and said, 'As long as you're part of this program, I own your time and I own your attention.'"

I look at my dad and then back at Xandra. The two of us lean in for more, but Xandra doesn't continue.

"And?"

"And, what?" Xandra asks, schlumping down in her chair, eyes fixated on the fringe of the place mat that she's been twirling. Xandra's defeated body language tells me there isn't any more to this lame story than she's claiming.

"And what else? What am I missing here? You disrespected your teacher, and he called you on it. And from what I've heard from both your father and you, this has been a pattern all fall." Disappointment is written all over my face and I don't care.

Xandra's eyes grow huge, and a sneer indicates that she thinks her mother's a complete idiot. "He said he *owns me*. Owns me, owns me, like a slave. He literally said it in front of the whole class THAT HE OWNS ME. I can't believe you didn't pick up on that. Dash went ballistic too. Couldn't believe a teacher at Pemberley would say something like that to a Black student. We've been coordinating how we're going to call attention to the lack of cultural competency among the faculty. It's offensive, and you don't even see it, probably because you've lost your Blackness since you landed yourself a White baby daddy."

I knew Leo was going to come up eventually, but not my Blackness. I'm stunned. Thankfully, Fitzroy doesn't miss a beat.

My dad starts right back in. "Baby girl, you and your generation think you're the wokest people to have lived. That you're going to reveal a truth that other generations have been too blind to see. Please, you aren't even the wokest person in this house. I haven't slept a wink since I got to the US in 1974." Dad waves his hand in front of Xandra's face like she's spewing petty nonsense. When Fitzroy launches into the topic of wokeness, I know he's channeling Celia from up above, and my job has now shifted to cleaning up the carnage he's about to make of Xandra's unearned ego.

"He's also always saying 'you people.' White people are so clueless," Xandra insists, staring right at me on that one, trying to regain some righteous footing. "Like, 'You people need to come in here ready to work hard.' Or, 'You people think this is your best effort, I don't see any effort at all.'"

"Sounds like 'you people' are teenagers and 'you people' are being lazy. I'm not paying for you to be lazy," I jump in, unable to not see dollar signs when it comes to Xandra wasting time at school. The look I get back from my bald-headed baby is cold. Ice cold.

"Maybe you people do need to work harder. Has that crossed your mind?" Dad follows the line I've laid down. I've never heard Dad go toe to toe with Xandra like this, and I love him for not leaving me alone in this fight.

"I just don't think when you spend your whole life in service of privileged White people you can understand what I'm going through. You may not want to have a backbone and acknowledge racism when it's staring you in the face, but I do." *Oh no she didn't* is all I can think. If this were a horror movie, I'd be covering my eyes.

"Xandra, you got the brittlest backbone of the three of us. One injury to your resolve, one misunderstood sentence spoken from your teacher, and you fall apart. Make sure you hear me, now. Your generation are the lucky ones. You have never been the only Black anything or received undeserved treatment at school solely based on the color of your skin. There are more Black students at your school, in your grade, than there are spots in the Pemberley show. 'THE ONLY' is a title reserved for older Black generations."

"That's not true, Grandpa, look at Mama. She had it 'easy,' too, at Spence and then at Wellesley." I cringe. Xandra put air quotes around *easy*. Air quotes are like nails on a chalkboard to my father.

Dad rises slowly from his chair, pressing his slacks with both hands. He walks to the head of the table so he's opposite Xandra, looking at her head-on. I'm so grateful to have a real coparent in this moment, even if it's a grandparent, because the things that need to be said to Xandra right now are best not said by Mom. Though I'm focused on the unified front my dad and I have formed, I can't help but wonder how Leo will be in these types of tense moments, from toddler tantrums to teenage ones. I pray he dads like Fitzroy, because I am one lucky daughter.

"Xandra, you hear me loud and you hear me clear, 'cause this is the one and only time we are going to have this conversation. YOU have had the privilege your whole life of NOT seeing hardship and struggle. Your mother has lived her whole life being the lone polka dot in a sea of white. For Nina, going to Spence was lonely. No kids of color in her class until eighth grade. The girls were interested in her hair, her speech, why she took multiple buses to school when the other children came by cab or driver, but they were not interested in her friendship. Celia and I thanked God every day for your aunt Marisol." I never knew my mom and dad realized all that and still continued to wake me up every morning and ship me off to Spence.

"There were no birthday parties. No sleepovers. And then there was that blasted outdoor program. I mean good Lord, what in the world is GORE-TEX and was there any way we could find it at Goodwill? It never crossed anyone's mind at Spence that we might have no money and no knowledge of how to dress for winter conditions coming from the Caribbean. When you're poor and Black, dressing in layers is not something you've heard of. You're happy to have one layer!"

I remember my trip to the Adirondacks in fifth grade when I slept in a cabin with Ms. Trenton. She claimed it was in case I got scared because I had never slept away from home before, but I knew it was because none of the girls wanted to share a cabin with me. They were all scared my Black might rub off on them.

"Nina's equipment was abysmal, and in those days the brand of your backpack mattered. You, Xandra? When it was time for you to go to Joshua Tree with your class, your mother made sure you were suited and styled. You came home with long underwear that still had tags on them."

I throw Xandra a side glance. Her gaze has dropped from meeting Dad's directly, to focused on her feet.

"And your mother endured all that with parents who stuck out like sore thumbs attending school events in our work uniforms because we had jobs that if you left early or missed, you were fired. You, Xandra, your mother has always been by your side meeting your every need." My daughter doesn't look like she's buying it.

"You've been given a top education and now you have a teacher pushing you, expecting you to step up and be the best you can be. Racist, you don't know racist. There's no excuse to go wasting the opportunity and privilege that you have at your fingertips. That's what Mr. Petrov is telling you; no more, no less. You think you're so woke, Xandra Clarke. Please, you're not woke, you're Sleeping Beauty." Dad shakes his head and walks out of the kitchen, marking the end of this family conversation, the scent of disappointment lingering in the air.

"But you were never replaced by a newer, shinier, WHITER model," Xandra says to me when her grandfather's left the kitchen.

I knew I was right. Down deep what's bugging Xandra is not just that she thinks her drama teacher's a racist; it's that she also thinks her mother's a sellout.

SEVENTEEN

Growing up, Christmas in Queens was a five-star affair. The rest of the year, me, Clive, Mom, and Dad lived off the clothing exchange program at church, but no expense was spared for baby Jesus's birthday. It was the one day a year where we thought we lived similarly to the way other Collegiate and Spence families did. The wings of the angel crowning our tree always brushed the ceiling. Instead of an Advent calendar with stale, flaky drugstore chocolate, Mom made fresh peppermint bark and traded some with an elderly seamstress in our building to make a unique calendar for Clive and me. Each present under the tree was fancifully wrapped and arranged in the order they were to be opened. When Mom died, Dad picked up the Christmas charge to spare no expense when it came to our present exchange. Admittedly, my history of Morgan family Christmases sets an impossibly high bar for Leo.

What's not overflowing with good cheer this Christmas is Xandra's attitude. This morning in particular I'm missing the days of rainbow footie pajamas and the two of us waking up early to check under the tree before Graham arose from his overworked slumber. We would select a gift, rearrange the others to fill the gap so it wouldn't be noticed, and sneak back into Xandra's bed to open our presents under the covers. This Christmas morning I'm greeted with my daughter grunting for coffee.

"Merry Christmas, Leo," Xandra mumbles, reaching across me for the freshly brewed pot. Leo beams like the novice parent-to-be that he is, blinded by the inch of headway he thinks he has made with Xandra and fully missing the holiday mom snub delivered to me.

"You, too, Xandra. Again, thanks so much for sharing your mom and granddad with me on Christmas."

Leo puts his hand up to land a high five with Xandra, and she leaves him hanging. I shake my head and chuckle at his resolve. Though I have warned Leo to slow his efforts to ingratiate himself to Xandra, he can't help his sweet self. Leo looks adorable in his red plaid flannel pajama pants and scruff, but the Pemberley T-shirt he ordered himself is over the top and possibly crashing headfirst down the other side. I nod at the arrangement of chocolate croissants and then at Xandra while she's pouring her coffee. Leo hops to, placing the largest one on a napkin, handing it to Xandra.

"Thanks." Xandra smiles and bites right in. Leo looks like he's going to pass out from the win.

"I went a little overboard this Christmas, hope you don't mind," Leo whispers in my ear, grabbing a growing handful of hip as he sweeps behind me heading right for the bacon frying on the stove.

"I don't mind at all," I reply, with a hint of sexy through my mouthful of pancakes. I look over to the tree, trying to make out which box might contain the coal-gray pebbled leather purse I've been visiting for months at one of those boutiques that only carries about ten items but every single one is gorgeous. The hints I've dropped about it have been endless since December 1, the official date one can start hounding for specific gifts.

"Can I get you some breakfast?" I ask, sitting down next to Xandra with my plate. The entire kitchen table is a blessing of Christmas morning riches. This is the one day a year Dad owns the kitchen with his Jamerican holiday feast, complete with fried plantains, mangos and starfruit, scrambled eggs with ham, the blueberry cornmeal pancakes I'm inhaling, and Xandra's favorite, chocolate croissants. Dad made sure to spare no sweet tooth.

"I'm not hungry," Xandra mumbles, then takes the fork I'm holding, stabs herself a chunk of pancake off my plate, and drops it in her mouth. She must not know you don't take food from a pregnant lady.

It's been a rough couple of days since the Morgan Clarke family round table, and I feel stuck in the middle. I appreciate, as an immigrant, where my dad's bias and lack of understanding of Xandra's behavior at school are coming from. Surrounded by high school students daily, I also see Xandra's perspective and why she has zero tolerance for language that may smack of bias. Fitzroy knows race and socioeconomic status determined his limited life choices, but nothing could dissuade his belief that education is the gateway to the best possible life. And with Clive off in London and me having worked my way to the tweed mountaintop, we prove Fitzroy's theory correct.

After our showdown, I tried to play the neutral party, to be the Switzerland of our family. I let Xandra know that I recognize kids her age are growing up with the freedom to oppose authority and to speak out against perceived slights. I want Xandra to have a voice, to question and push for what she believes is right and what she thinks she deserves. She's playing a young person's game of raging against the machine, thinking the machine is anyone over thirty. Problem is, when you are raised in a loving family, have a warm home, and attend the best schools in the country, the issues you feel angry about are only an inch deep, and it shows. Xandra is an amateur at hardship, and Dad and I know it.

"Load up your plates and head into the living room," Dad announces as he drops the last two plantains on Leo's plate. I can tell Leo is struggling with really wanting those fried perfections and thinking best protocol with your baby mama's father is to give them to his daughter. I really want those plantains too.

"You've made it clear this week you're no longer my baby bird, so get a plate and feed yourself," I tell Xandra, grabbing my food before she can dump her favorites onto my plate and stroll into the living room hands free. "Let's go see if Santa thinks you've been naughty or nice."

"You would love it if I was always nice, yes ma'amin' everyone, pretending I'm looking forward to having a snowflake for a stepdad." What is it with Graham and Xandra and the winter weather references when it comes to Leo? And who said anything about a stepdad?

"I don't want to hurt your feelings on Christmas, but I expect you to be nice today," I snap back. This teen tantrum is not going to kill my Christmas spirit. Leo mouths *"Good one"* to me. I internally cringe that he caught that snippy mother-daughter exchange, but I'm happy he's picking up that he shouldn't take everything that comes out of an angsty adolescent's mouth to heart. I blow him a kiss.

"Youngest goes first. Here, Xandra, I got this one for you." Dad's been out of sorts these last few days, unnerved by the cold shoulder Xandra's giving him. His attempts to get back in her good graces have been met with a lukewarm reception. I, however, am better practiced at surviving long stretches of teen banishment. One of the perks of being a highly trained high school teacher.

Dad hands Xandra a package that looks like a hefty book. Nice, Dad. I haven't seen Xandra do much with her brain since she's been home, so I'm on board with a good book to soak up some of that sulking.

"NO WAY, Grandpa!!" Xandra rips off the last of the wrapping paper and launches off the couch and into Dad's outstretched arms before I can see what she got. I know it's not *War and Peace*.

"Whaddya get, Xandra?" I ask, excited to see what has turned my sour child sweet.

"A new iPhone!" Xandra shrieks. Is this the man who ignored countless slurs slung his way while driving a New York Metro bus for four decades but folds at the first sign of Xandra being upset with him? I look over at Leo, wondering if he sees the same old man who's gone soft for his granddaughter that I do.

"I took your grandpa shopping for the phone," Leo proclaims, hoping to earn some points with Xandra too. I look at him with a face that reads, *SERIOUSLY?!* "And I thought you might want these to go with your new phone." Leo rummages around under the tree and hands Xandra a box that looks suspiciously the same size as one that would contain earrings. Xandra could use an upgrade from safety pins for her ears.

"No way, AirPods! Thank you, Leo, that's so nice of you!" Xandra beams a huge smile at Leo. He looks like he might explode with happiness. Or relief. I have to give it to Leo, nailing a present for a fifteen-year-old girl who isn't fond of you is no easy feat. I cannot wait to see what Leo picked out for me!

"Nina, how about you open my gift next?" Dad suggests, content with Xandra curled on his lap.

"Absolutely," I say, picking up the beautifully wrapped package in silver cellophane that Dad's pointing to.

"Remember Mrs. Richards, the piano teacher back home? She made it for me to give to you," Dad says, watching as I open my gift. I nod with a forced grin, acknowledging his hometown hint. Marisol would be on the floor dying if she were here. We have a mutual distaste for homemade gifts and for pickled old Mrs. Richards.

As the bow comes off and the cellophane falls open, Leo whoops, "NO WAY!" I can't believe it's a yes way. I'm staring down at a crocheted yellow baby blanket on MY Christmas. Xandra got an iPhone, and I got a blanket with holes and a faint whiff of cat litter. Oh, let me correct myself, I didn't even get a blanket, my unborn child did. I'm just the servant unwrapping it for them since they aren't out in the world yet to do their own dirty work. Does Fitzroy not know me at all?

"Do you like it?" my sweet father asks, his voice dripping with hope. Luckily, I'm saved from having to answer by Leo being bitten by the gift-giving bug.

"Okay, okay, Nina, now you have to open one of mine." Leo hands me a box that looks like the perfect size for the crossbody purse. From the look of expectation on Leo's face I can tell he's pleased with himself for getting me exactly what I want. I'm not actually sure how this crossbody bag will work with my growing belly, but I'll take it after the debacle of the baby blanket.

I tear open the box knowing it's going to be something good. I'm speechless. Leo's on his feet, bouncing on his toes like a ten-year-old boy who just opened an Xbox. Turns out my boyfriend doesn't know me at all either.

"Look, look! This is my silver rattle from when I was a baby. My mom still had it, so she sent it out from Omaha. She wanted to give it to you when we got there, but I really wanted to have it for Christmas morning. She did a great job polishing it for you, though." I'm silently faking enthusiasm following Leo's holiday tale. "See here, mine's engraved with my initials. And then here's a matching one, which took me forever to find, but after our baby's born we can put his or her initials on it. Best part is, look, they're like baby barbells!" Leo picks up the two rattles and starts pumping silver in the living room. "Our kid's going to be ripped!" My father puts his hand out for a brotherly fist bump, approving Leo's fine gifting work.

"That's pretty cute," Xandra says, putting her hand out to Leo for one of the rattles. He gladly hands it over, an olive branch in the midst of our mixed-up holiday dynamic. Does no one in this family understand that I have yet to receive a proper Christmas present?!

"Do you want to see what else I got you for the baby?" Leo asks on a roll, his new cheer squad of Xandra and Fitzroy egging him on. I wish Marisol were here so I could shoot her an expression that says, *I'm not ready for this baby to take over my Christmas let alone my life just yet, and if the attention's on me one second longer I'm gonna cry*. I look back under the tree and spy a box, wrapped in the same paper as the rattles, that looks suspiciously the size of a breast pump.

⌒

FROM: Winn Hawkins
DATE: December 29
SUBJECT: Well done
TO: Nina Morgan Clarke

Nina,

I hope you and your family had a great Christmas. I meant to email sooner, but we're in Australia with Gemma's family and I always get confused if we are

a day ahead or behind California, and then before
I knew it Christmas was over.

Anyway, I wanted to say, WELL DONE, your first
half of the school year. You came into your position
under groundbreaking circumstances, and you have
exceeded the expectations of the board of trustees
as the first female head of school.

Here's to continued improvement and success for
the Royal-Hawkins School in the New Year.

Best,
Winn

"Look at this," I say, elbowing Leo while we're killing time before our
flight to Omaha. Our departure is delayed waiting on a Dallas flight
coming in. "Totally unexpected and really nice of Winn." I hand my
phone to Leo so he can read how awesome his girlfriend is. "Check out
the line about me *exceeding expectations*." I'm leaning over Leo's shoulder, making sure he's soaking up every word. Admittedly, I'm feeling my
oats that I was able to manage a cross-country wayward child, mask a
first trimester pregnancy, weather a long-distance love life, and STILL
crush it at my job. I should add #badassbossmom to my email signature.

The reference to me being the first female head of school is a bit
underhanded, but I'm not going to let it take the shine off this email.
At least Winn didn't comment on me being a well-spoken Black person.
That backhanded compliment is decades overplayed.

"Nina, is that you?" I startle even though the voice is familiar. I hop
up out of professional instinct to always greet another person eye to eye.
"Oh, WOW . . ." I follow Courtney Dunn's eyes directly to my belly.
Turns out this was not the day to wear my new Tory Burch athleisure
wear. The one good holiday gift I got from Leo. The white Lycra crew

neck shirt has bandaged itself tightly around my belly. Leo jumps in to save me from the stunned silence between me and Courtney.

"Hi, I'm Leo, Nina's boyfriend."

"Clearly," Courtney responds, not taking her eyes off my belly.

"We're heading to Omaha to see my family. Where are you off to?" Leo puts his hand out to shake with Courtney and presumably lure her eyes off my belly bump.

"I'm Courtney. Courtney Dunn, parent and new board member at Royal-Hawkins." Oh no she did not just say that. "I just flew in from Dallas, and I'm catching a connecting flight to Denver to meet up with my family in Vail."

"I thought you mentioned at the basketball jamboree you all were flying directly from Mexico to Colorado on Christmas Day?" I'm panicking because I can see it registering on Courtney's face that she now has something to lord over me.

"Well yes, that was the plan, but I had to stop in Dallas unexpectedly to deal with a few issues with my family. Geoff, Benjamin, we have him this school break, and Daisy did fly into Vail on Christmas Day. So, you're pregnant?" Courtney draws out *pregnant* as if each syllable is its own sentence.

I take a big breath and hope that the connection of us both being female is strong and the connection of us both being mothers is stronger. "Yes. But I'm hoping to wait a few more weeks before I announce. Perhaps closer to the end of January." January 30 is not arbitrary, it happens to coincide with the six-month mark of my first contracted year as head of school.

"Is there such a thing as maternity leave for a school head? Probably why most schools prefer headmasters. How does one miss months of school?"

I hadn't thought through how maternity leave would work just yet, it's a fair question.

"I haven't worked out the details, but I'm sure when I announce, Winn and I, along with the executive committee, will figure out a plan that serves the school community well in my absence." My voice is calm and steady. I can tell Courtney is chewing on my answer. She takes in my bump again, which is protruding more than usual after three days of holiday leftovers.

"I'm sorry, Nina, but since you're brand new at your job, I think important information like this should be shared with Winn and the board immediately. Anything that threatens the long-term health and stability of the school needs to be dealt with as swiftly as possible. I guess one never knows when a surprise is lurking right around the corner."

On the heels of Winn's email this is a crushing blow. Leo picks up my hand either to support me or to keep me from throwing a punch. "I think brand new at my job is a bit of an overstatement," I challenge Courtney. I'm feeling confident in my tenure thus far given Winn's words of encouragement, but I also have a living reminder in front of me of how pissed I am at him for selling a board seat. "I'd ask that you give me the professional courtesy to tell Winn about my pregnancy on my own timeline. Not yours." Again, Courtney studies me.

"I'm having lunch with Winn on January 6. I'll expect that you will have shared with him by then so the two of us can celebrate your exciting news. Sooner rather than later is best for the school," Courtney concludes, adjusting the overnight bag digging into her shoulder. Has she been speaking to my ex, the two of them laying down ultimatums about my pregnancy reveal? "In the meantime, enjoy your New Year."

"You too." I pseudo smile and watch Courtney stride off to baggage claim or to Vail.

"Jeez." Leo blows out a whoosh of air. "I can't believe you asked that woman to be on the board."

EIGHTEEN

We're delayed for a second time on the tarmac, so I turn my phone back on to text Xandra and find out what she and Graham are up to in Miami. Since we have to stay buckled, I also need to distract myself from having to pee. Oh, and I forgot to text my father the watering schedule for my houseplants, as well as a list of leftovers I have organized by Tupperware color. Fitzroy's cholesterol is on the low end of highly unhealthy, so I cut up a vat of fresh vegetables for him. We'll see if the container's full and rotting when I get home.

It felt weird leaving my dad alone in my house while he's still visiting, but he assured me he wanted to stay in town for a New Year's dominoes tournament. I tried to keep my fussing over him to a minimum. Oh yay, there's already a text back from my girl!

Xandra 10:42 AM

Leo put this note in my suitcase. Tell him thanks for the Starbucks card, that was pretty cool of him.

Embedded in the text is a picture of Leo's handwriting:

It was nice spending time with you, your mom, and Fitzroy over Christmas, thanks for sharing. Have fun with your dad and Dash in Miami.

I look at Leo and my heart feels full. Or the baby is pushing up into my ribs and I can't get a full breath. Either way, I feel a pang in my chest. Leo nailed it over our holiday week with Xandra. He listened intently when she spoke and asked her nonjudgy questions (he left those for me). He knew the exact amount of time to hang around with us and when to beat it so we could be alone. And the crown jewel to winning over a teen—he bought her things he knew she would like and never get from me. I can't help but be pleased that in such a short time, Xandra and Leo have begun to develop their own relationship, but the question remains, why did I continue to get the lukewarm shoulder over Christmas from my usually warmhearted daughter?

I show Leo the text. "Well played, Mr. West. Turns out you know how to woo women of all ages," I say, planting a lingering kiss on Leo's cheek. He beams with pride and turns his shoulder to me so I can ceremoniously pat his back. "I think you may have misheard a conversation, though. Dash isn't in Miami."

"Sure, she is. When Xandra and I were waiting in line for popcorn at the movies and I asked her what she and Graham had planned for Miami, she told me her dad has a ton of work to do so he bought Dash a ticket to come and keep Xandra company."

Of course, he did. Graham hasn't taken a vacation from work since our honeymoon. You would think he could pull it off when he has his daughter only a few weeks a year, but yet again he's proven what's in his computer is more important than the person who is in front of his face.

"I thought the girls could use the Starbucks card to get breakfast in the morning. I'm sure there's one near the hotel. You can't walk two blocks without running into the big green in any city in America. And yes, before you even begin to make a snarky comment, even in Omaha."

I nod my head in agreement, but I'm only half listening to Leo while I'm texting Graham.

Nina 10:52 AM

> If you couldn't focus on Xandra for the week she could have stayed with her family and friends in Pasadena. Not sure Dash is the best fill-in for a father.

Okay, that last line is a little bit too ex-wife witchy, even for me. I change the whole text to . . .

> Not sure Dash is who we want Xandra spending free time with right now.

"Please turn off all electronic devices. We have been cleared for takeoff. Sit back, relax, and enjoy the flight," says our flight attendant as he begins his final walk down the aisle to make sure all passengers are in compliance. This is America, though, and half of us are not responding, as if turning off one's device is an infringement on individual liberties. As a rule-follower, I make a point of holding my phone up high for acknowledgment that I have earned a gold star flying the friendly skies.

Ding.

Damn, gotta take a quick peek.

Graham 10:54 AM

> My week, my rules. The girls are doing their own thing. Besides, aren't you off playing family with your Ken doll? I hear blond is the new Black.

How many times have I told Graham that Leo isn't blond?!

"I'm going to take you by my high school where I was the varsity quarterback. We went two seasons, no losses, with me throwing the ball." Leo drops my hand to wind up his old rubber arm in the confines of economy class. "You mind if I have a beer?" Leo asks, picking my hand back up as we reach cruising altitude.

"You drink a beer in front of me, and a football will be the only thing your hand will be cupping." Leo has proven himself a boob guy, so he knows my threat is valid. I lean over and plant a big kiss on his lips as a consolation prize.

I need to distract myself from the run-in with Courtney, so I decide to fuel Leo's excitement for heading to his homeland and ask him to repeat, one more time, all the cousins, aunts, and uncles I'll be meeting. His sister, the lone female in the family of Leo's generation, is at LEGOLAND with her husband and kid for New Year's. It blows because I actually met her in late November when she was in LA for work, and our lunch turned out to be an enjoyable three hours of good-natured Leo ribbing. I liked Julia right away, and I could tell she approved of me. If my Omaha debut nose-dived, I had hoped she would be there to vouch for me.

"My aunt Nancy and uncle Bruce are the best. Uncle Bruce has worked for Omaha Steaks for over fifty years, so be prepared to talk meat."

I give Leo a thumbs-up. "And Aunt Nancy?"

"She and my mom have been docents at a museum not far from my house since I graduated high school. And their dedication to their book club is going on forty years strong." Yikes. If there are two things I know very little about, it's steaks and fine art. But I can talk books.

"And your cousins are Karl, Steve, Jake and . . ." I knew the last one when Leo had me memorizing the West family tree the other night, but pregnancy brain is real.

"Tommy."

"A grown-ass man still goes by Tommy?"

"He's the baby of the family, three years younger than me, and he continues to milk his family position. He didn't move out of Aunt Nancy and Uncle Bruce's house until he was thirty-two!" I don't remind Leo that Fitzroy has more or less been living in my house for a handful of years. Dad leaves with just enough days to spare before he has to start paying California taxes. "And seriously, don't call him Tom or Thomas, he hates it," Leo warns. Note to self, how not to get off on the wrong foot with Tom. I mean Tommy.

"And they're all married, right?"

"Yeah, except Karl. But I think he's hiding a girlfriend or boyfriend or something from the family, trying to sniff out the right timing for a big reveal. He's been a serial bachelor his whole life. I think he's waiting to see how it all goes down with my pregnant Black beauty in the land of the bland before he makes his move."

"Let the record show that YOU called Omaha the land of the bland, not me." Seems my speculations about Omaha are not that far off the mark. "So, what kind of Black girl do you think your family's expecting? Or really your mom, if I'm being honest, because I'm sure she wasn't expecting one at all."

Leo rolls his lower lip out at my question and stares at me in contemplation. It's kind of the same face he's been giving me lately when I'm too tired for sex and he's begging me to throw a leg. I always do, because there are many, many things in life to regret, but having sex with Leo is never one of them. That said, the facial similarity is slightly disturbing since we're talking about his mom.

"Well, I think she hopes you are a woman, not a girl. She knows you run a tony private school in Pasadena. And, of course, she thinks you're smart because you chose me."

"That's it?" I doubt.

"All of that, and I've told my whole family you're a knockout. That may be the real reason all my cousins are showing up for dinner tonight." Good Lord, I adore this man; he knows exactly how to appeal to my vain side.

"I'm talking more along the lines of what *type* of Black girl do you think your mom's expecting you're bringing home. Banjee girl who's hip-hop street and always lit up at a party? Or maybe more Black power with her hair in a natural and sporting Ghanaian patterns even though she's from Glendale. She's appalled by the White centrist culture and believes every Becky with the good hair is out to steal her man."

"If we have a daughter, we can't name her Becky. That's the name of my middle school girlfriend who broke up with me in the cafeteria in seventh grade. It was brutal." Becky, was that a joke, or does Leo actually think a name like *Becky* would be in the running for my child?

"Am I going to meet her, too?" I riff back, enjoying Leo sharing imperfect nuggets of his childhood.

"Nah, she lives in Toledo. My parents have seen pictures of you, Nina. They know your hair is braided and you prefer department store to dashiki. What else you got?"

"I hope they don't think I'm Black Barbie who seamlessly blends in and works hard to shake off everything about her culture other than her color. I know, because I work at Royal-Hawkins, there are plenty of people who think I'm that type of Black woman, including my kid at this exact moment. But Black Barbie rubs me raw." From the way Leo's now looking at me, I suspect Black Barbie is not too far from the narrative he's spun to his parents. "So that leaves us with gold digger. She's working hard to get on the train of the great White way by boosting her credit score."

"Yep, definitely that one. They think you want to hitch your star to a guy with a boatload of law school loans and high auto insurance 'cause he has a lead foot." Leo laughs, mimicking flooring a gas pedal.

I shake my finger no and inform Leo, "The gold digger runs the show."

"Well, if you would agree to move in with me like I've brought up several times, you could run the show without having to be a gold digger, fine by me. But since the only thing I can get you to do is fly over the Rockies for a few days, then, verdict's still out on just what kind of Black woman you are." Leo yawns out the last sentence. "The last two nights tying up cases before vacation has me shot. Mind if I take a snooze while you get some work done?" Leo asks, closing his eyes before I can answer. Letting Leo sleep will allow me to review Royal-Hawkins's midyear financials as well as get me out of yet another conversation about cohabitation.

"Go ahead." I smile at Leo and watch him conk out in seconds with his neck cocked at that awkward airplane angle. Even asleep, his excitement at coming home with his baby in tow and with the woman attached to the embryo is palpable under the plane's recirculating air. I know he's thrilled to introduce his girlfriend to the four male cousins he's been in competition with his whole life. In fact, I'd be willing to bet they've committed to memory what I look like—statuesque, curvy in all the right places, and a stacked rack compliments of pregnancy—but I doubt one of them remembers I'm a head of school. It's all part of the never-ending male battle of *whose honey is hotter*.

Leo has convinced himself differences of race, family structure, and left coast liberal values versus heartland ideals won't register with his parents. He's claimed, more than once, that his mother is over-the-moon happy that, finally at forty-five, he's dating someone age appropriate with potential to go the distance. I don't buy it at all. Since we purchased our tickets, I've been digging at Leo to engage in deeper discussion concerning his family's speculations about me. According to Leo, simply being off your parents' auto insurance makes you eligible marriage material with the Wests.

Though Leo may not have given our relationship's impact on his family a whole lot of thought, Marisol and I gave it plenty of air time at the Clean Slate Palisades Village, deconstructing Leo's tidbit that only his father would be at the airport to pick us up. That was all I needed to hear from Leo to know his mother was skipping over the middleman and sending a clear message to me that Mother West is not putting out the efforts and charms for a woman she's hoping is a passing fetish. Marisol's take on the whole thing was maybe the woman has a life.

"Please put away all laptops and place your tray tables and seats in their upright position. We should be landing in Omaha in about twenty minutes," announces the same flight attendant who demanded we shut down our electronics for takeoff.

By the time Leo has pulled himself out of his mile-high nap, I've worked myself up into a lather that not only will I be the only Black person at the West family dinner table, but for all I know, I may be the only Black person in Nebraska.

"Leo, Leo, wake up." I'm poking my man to bring him out of hibernation under the guise of putting his seat back up. "I forgot to ask you. Do they have Black people in Nebraska?"

"No, Nina, you're the first. Tomorrow there will be a coronation on the capitol steps. I think the governor's going to give you a scepter or a key or something. I hope you brought a nice dress to wear," Leo says, stretching his arms out wide then picking my hand back up for landing.

~

"Nina, it's so good to meet you!" Leo's dad, Curtis, booms, pulling me in for a bear hug before he's finished his sentence. Leo's face reads, *I told you*. "Aren't you a lovely looking lady. Leo, how were you able to land this fine woman when you're as funny looking as me?" Mr. West keeps me tucked under one arm as he puts his other out to shake his son's hand and bring him in for an equally hearty embrace.

"Truck's parked not too far away. Got a new one, Leo. Since this is probably the last car of my life, your mom let me get that midnight-blue double cab Chevy I've always wanted. I look good in it running your mother's errands like coming here to fetch you." Two identical laughs barrel out of Leo and Mr. West.

"Dad's always the one to pick everyone up at the airport. If Mom comes, she spends the entire time complaining about how the airport gouges you at ten bucks an hour for short-term parking." Father and son nod in agreement on a lifelong quirk about the missus.

"That woman does not part with money easily, don't you know it. Let's get a move on. You two have more bags other than what you're lugging with you?" Mr. West asks, surveying our efficient rolling suitcases.

"We're good to go." I smile, reaching for my handle.

"Leo, grab Nina's suitcase and be the man I taught you to be." I'm liking Mr. West straight away. "Your mom's so happy you're home, she's been fussing around the house cooking and cleaning all day. She's making your favorite stollen cake right now. Wants me to call her when we're about ten minutes away. If our arrival home is not perfectly timed with that stollen coming out of the oven, we may have to circle the block a couple of times." Though Marisol wants running commentary on the trip, I'm not telling her she was right and Mother West not coming to the airport had nothing to do with her desire to immediately ship me back to California. When Marisol gloats, it's unbearable.

"Nina, my mom's the Fitzroy of the Midwest. Always making sure everything is as it should be and all manners are on display," Leo says, shaking me out of my thoughts on Marisol, genuinely trying to make a connection between our two families. I refrain from pointing out one difference, Fitzroy's never ridden in a double cab.

"MOM!" Leo throws open the door from the garage into the kitchen. Emily West is at the sink looking exactly the same as every picture I've ever seen of her. Dark wool pants to stave off the winter cold and a cheery-red sweater set that I bet she owns in rotating colors for changing seasons. Her bottle-blonde hair is pulled into a perfect bun that I suspect has not moved since being sprayed into place earlier this morning.

"My BOY!" Out go the arms and in goes Leo. They're hopping around in their tight embrace, a party for two leaving me feeling self-conscious if I should enter the kitchen or wait in the garage until I'm invited inside. Mr. West is busy with a chamois cloth, wiping down dirty snow crystals that have mucked up his truck from the round trip, seemingly having forgotten about me. Leaving a guest hanging would never fly in our house. Celia raised me to know you always introduce anyone new first, a proper welcome is expected, and a feeling of comfort on behalf of the guest is the number one priority. You take care of family second. I guess that's not common etiquette in corn country.

"Leo, are you going to introduce me to your friend?" I blink in surprise. I'm carrying your grandchild and your son has been begging me to live with him, and the most you consider me is a *friend*?

"Nina, this is my mom, Emily West. Mom, this is the fabulous Nina Morgan Clarke." Leo flashes a proud smile that makes me feel welcomed in his boyhood home and thaws my concerns just a bit. The tension in my neck releases slightly and my shoulders drop back into place as I put my hand out to greet the matriarch.

"Nice to meet you, Mrs. West. Leo talks about you all so much." I can hear myself slip into my practiced administrator voice. Leo looks at me, not recognizing the formal tone coming out of his *friend's* mouth.

"Oh Nina, please, call me Emily. And I hope that old fuddy duddy out in the garage invited you to call him Curtis. Sometimes he's a stickler for old-school ways."

I relax my smile a bit. "I have a father who would see eye to eye with Curtis," I offer, keeping the conversation light.

"Oh yes, does he spend too much time hunting and watching golf on TV, too?" Emily laughs as she gestures to Leo to take my jacket. *Not in a million years,* I think to myself.

"Sounds like tonight's going to be a lot of fun. Leo says things can get a little rowdy when all his cousins come around."

"Oh, they certainly can, but I think this evening everyone will be on their best behavior with you as the guest of honor. We can't remember a time since law school that Leo's brought a girl home, so I think curiosity has the best of all of us. Nancy's called me twice asking what she should wear." Emily smiles, and I can tell she thinks she's paid me a compliment, but the former science teacher in me recognizes the setup for dissecting a specimen. I'm the frog in tonight's lab.

Marisol 6:12 PM

> You landed three hours ago, no text, WTF?! I stopped by your house to check on Fitzroy. You'll be happy to know he's not pining over your absence. House was dark. Speaking of dark, how's Operation Mixed Baby going?

Nina 6:13 PM

I rode in a truck for the first time in my life. And Emily, Leo's mom, offered me one of those chunky wool sweaters that looks like there might be twigs in it. She said it was to keep me warm, but I'm thinking it's to hide my baby bump so there's no evidence Leo and I had sex out of wedlock.

Marisol 6:15 PM

Well, that's two Wests who wish you were married.

Nina 6:16 PM

Gotta go, I was just summoned for the first Nina viewing.

Marisol 6:18 PM

Leo put up with your people over Christmas. You do him right by embracing his midwestern brand of crazy. Hear me?!??!

Nina 6:19 PM

Don't want to but I hear you. You LOUD as hell.

⌁

"Let me grab that tray for you," I offer and jump up as Emily tries to balance an oversize plate of sliced flank steak in one hand and serve her nephews with the other. The cousins are occupied recounting stories of West family adventures from their shared past while keeping eyes peeled for spills as the assembled youngest generation grabs for cheese slices and baby carrots. Even Leo is lost in tales of failed childhood fort building and holiday fireworks with Karl. Apparently, it's still hilarious, thirty years later, the time they almost burned down the neighbor's house with homemade bottle rockets.

"Oh no, Nina, you sit down and relax. You're the guest of honor, and I've been feeding this family most of my life now. I can do it with my eyes closed." It's not my intention to disregard my hostess, but I am used to contributing with both hands. Besides, my movement is automatic since the scene is a familiar one. My mother prepared Jamaican dishes from scratch for every celebration, whether she was the host or not. Jerk pork, rice and peas, and oxtails were her specialties, and I was often her sous chef and junior waitress. At a later age I found myself chafing at the unfairness of the men and boys seated around a feast as the women and girls bustled around them. I hope to raise Xandra with the same interest in caring for her own family one day, minus the generational chauvinism. Back in Pasadena, Leo is a champ at busting suds when I prepare dinner.

"Leo and I can carry the rest," I insist.

"Nina, don't you let any of those boys in my kitchen, ruining my dinner. I worked all day on this. I don't need any dirty thumbs getting in my side dishes. Please, please go sit down with Leo. Enjoy yourself," Emily says with a warmth I can feel is genuine if not enhanced by a few gin and tonics and taking multiple items out of the oven.

"Okay. But let me know if you need help," I concede, turning back to the table. My mother would have had the same response to an offer of men mucking up her kitchen.

"Your hair reminds me of pipe cleaners. Does it hurt to sleep on pipe cleaners?" my five-year-old dinner companion asks, with a mouth full of mashed potatoes. I've had similar questions before about my braids. It's usually followed by asking if I got the pipe cleaners or straws or extensions from the prize box at the pediatrician's office.

Jake nervously jumps in before I can respond to his son's inquiry. "Why would you ask that? Are you trying to make silly conversation?" A parent frantically attempting to cover up an honest question coming from a curious kid is also something I'm used to. Twenty years in schools prepares you for every possible social interaction with a child and their parent. This is where I shine.

"I've never seen brown pipe cleaners. Only blue, yellow, green, and sometimes red ones." My mini-journalist is fact-checking his past life experiences against the one he's having right now. I like this line of critical thinking posed by a fair-headed boy to the most different person he's probably come across in his short life. I also notice everyone at the table leaning in a little closer.

"Ah, so you all are kind of curious to know the answer, huh?" I suggest, maybe a bit too self-assuredly. I'm relieved to have the social propriety of not talking about my Blackness broken by a kindergartener.

"What else do you all want to know?" I embrace Marisol's advice and decide to open the floor to answer any and all West family questions. I want Leo to see that if his family wants to get to know me, I'm open to sharing, but I sure hope this doesn't turn into an episode of How the Black World Turns.

"So, you grew up with your mom, dad, and brother, is that right, Nina?" Emily asks first.

"And my best friend, Marisol. She spent most of her childhood being a Morgan. Lots of big personalities in my small family, so it always felt like we had a full house. The rest of our family lives in Jamaica."

"And you have a daughter in high school too. Leo tells us she's very smart. She attends a school outside New York City if I remember correctly. That's quite a place to be." Curtis pulls on his beard, probably trying to imagine living any place other than Omaha. I slide my hand onto Leo's thigh. I'm touched he's spoken so positively about Xandra given the fact that her cold war on him only began to thaw with the peace offering of AirPods.

"Yes, Xandra's the best of me and the entire Morgan clan rolled into one. She goes to school near where her father lives, but I miss her every day. I really hope she comes back west for college."

"I know a thing or two about missing your children when they move from home. I never expected mine would end up so far away." Emily pauses for dramatic emphasis. "I will say, Omaha's a very nice place to raise a family, good public schools in our area. I've been telling Julia and her husband that for years, but they don't listen. They think Seattle's the best place on Earth."

"Mom, give it a rest. The West is a great place to raise a family," Leo counters.

Ignoring her son, Emily continues, focused on me, "Leo had a wonderful time growing up here, and I'm sure there are plenty of opportunities for a lawyer at any one of the big firms in town. Wouldn't you like to give your son or daughter the same solid, family-oriented childhood he had? There's nothing wrong with a white picket fence," Emily says, leaving me wondering if she's joking or not. While Leo claims his mother is a woman without an agenda, I knew there had to be some iron will behind that sweater set. Obviously, Emily set herself a goal since Leo announced I was pregnant. I'm getting the impression that goal does not take into consideration my job, Xandra, Fitzroy, Marisol, or the fact that California has been my home for almost two decades.

"The Freemans just put their house on the market, you remember what a huge backyard they have, don't you, Leo? They even have a pickleball court now. I bet I could get you two a tour for tomorrow." Emily gives me a cursory nod, acknowledging that I'm hothousing the baby that is slated to grow up in the Freemans' backyard. I squeeze Leo's thigh tighter, cutting off circulation. Dear God above this flyover state, Operation Mixed Baby has gone awry. Someone please change the subject off this woman thinking there's any chance in hell of raising my baby in Omaha. Or me playing pickleball.

"So, Leo, are you Nina's first taste of vanilla, or has she been to Baskin-Robbins before?" Bachelor Karl throws out for the save. Is there any chance he knows Marisol?

NINETEEN

L eo, are we ever going to talk about Karl's question from dinner the other night? You know, the one that almost sent your aunt Nancy into a seizure." In exchange for a quickie in his childhood bedroom that now doubles as Emily's crafting studio, Leo has agreed to fifteen minutes of postcoital pillow talk about how the trip has gone before Curtis takes us to the airport. In a twin the only way for us to talk face-to-face is with me sitting on top of Leo, but the girls are proving distracting. I reach over to grab my sweatshirt off the floor, but the baby that is now the size of a basketball stops me short from being able to reach the carpet. Leo sighs in disappointment that the peep show is over and hands me the sweatshirt.

"Come on, Aunt Nancy barely flinched. You can't spend forty-five-plus years at a dinner table of mostly boys and be that soft. Or sensitive. Actually, what you saw as a seizure was probably shock that for the first time in forever the conversation avoided all matters of bathroom humor. A universally favored topic of males everywhere." Leo speaks as authoritatively on male eating rituals as he does about the legality of various tax loopholes.

"You're the one being ultrasensitive because you've spent most of your life at a table of strong women. You're not trained up to dine with men. And don't tell me I don't know what I'm talking about. I've been at your table, and I'm here to tell you your dinner topics don't land in the gutter like ours do. Do you know how many times I've had to excuse myself to go to the bathroom and let one out not to offend your family? Growing up we would just lift a cheek, let it rip, and devolve into hysterics before asking for seconds."

"I doubt that. Remember, I've now met your mother. I don't believe for a second Emily would put up with that shit." I giggle at how easy it is to slip into potty humor.

"She had no choice! She was always outnumbered. If we have a boy, your dinner table conversation will be forever changed." Doesn't matter what flavor kid we have, I know there will be no foul talk at my table when Fitzroy's around.

"How about your mom's quick pivot to asking me if I go to church. You don't think that was a cover-up for the bomb Karl dropped at the table?"

"That wasn't a bomb dropped at the dinner table, Nina. Karl was saving you by joking with me, distastefully I'll admit. But that's what we do, we heckle each other. Giving each other a hard time is a West family sport. But yes, I think my mom saw Karl's off-color ice cream question as an opportunity to find out if her sweet son is fucking a church girl."

"I can't believe I lied and told her I did."

"I think that was a wise move."

"But she knows you don't go, right?"

"Not exactly."

"So, your mom thinks my brown baby is going to grow up Episcopalian? And apparently behind a white picket fence." I roll off Leo, pull on my leggings, and toss Leo his jeans before our lying asses get walked in on. Emily is downstairs packing us enough snacks for our flight to feed the whole plane, but she may be up here any minute to tie them up in a hand-stitched baggie.

"*Our* baby, Nina, it's not just your baby. And I don't know what religion it will grow up in, if one at all, we haven't talked about it. But I'm not going to lie and say that a childhood in Nebraska wouldn't benefit our kid. I had it good here." With the words *our kid* and *Nebraska* uttered in the same sentence I'm officially done with this conversation, but there's about five more minutes of our agreed fifteen minutes of pillow talk that Leo is now fully engaged in even though I now want out.

"I want a neighborhood gang for our kid to ride bikes with after school. I want our kid to go to the drugstore and buy candy that turns his tongue purple even when we tell him not to. And I want him to play baseball in a park where I don't have to worry about him being mugged. Doesn't that sound good to you?"

"That sounds like the suburbs to me."

"What's wrong with that? You live in Pasadena, the gold standard of suburbs."

"Yeah, but my suburb is thirty minutes from LA. Besides, that's not how I grew up in Queens as a Morgan."

"But this baby's also a West." The first brown-skinned West. Is Leo really sure his family is ready for that?

"Fine. Whatever." I grab my mules and head out of the trophy-laden Leo shrine to shower and finish packing. And to keep Leo from seeing me cry. Adding a baby to my relationship with Leo has been something I have slowly become used to with the support of my small but mighty tribe of Fitzroy, Roan, and Marisol. Xandra's coming around, but at this point I wouldn't yet call her return to using smiling emojis when she texts encouragement. What's getting under my skin is the cavalry of cornfed people and their opinions riding into my life and setting up camp. I've been here before, same feeling I had with the Clarkes, different family with the Wests.

After I'm showered, packed, and dressed, Emily stops me as I struggle to roll my suitcase down the carpeted hallway. "Nina, there's something I want to show you before you go." I quickly wipe my eyes on my sweater to make sure I've left no traces of frustrated tears.

"Leave your bag there, Curtis will get it for you." Emily places her hand on the back of my shoulder and steers me to the opposite end of the hallway where the master bedroom is. I really don't want to see where Curtis and Emily sleep, that's oversharing even for people who birthed the man I'm fuming over right now.

As I'm about to protest, Emily opens a door to the right of her room. "This is the room Curtis and I set up as a nursery when Sadie was born. Even though she lives in Seattle, we want her to always know she has a home in Omaha." I look around the room, there's a sweet bed decorated in hues of purple with an enormous stuffed giraffe leaning against the wall. A beautiful white wicker bassinet cradling a big bear sits opposite the giraffe.

"Was this Sadie's bassinet?" I stumble over my words taking in the setting. "It's lovely. I bet she was a gorgeous baby, I saw those soft auburn curls on Julia's phone when we had lunch in Pasadena."

"She was a beautiful baby, but I suppose all babies are beautiful to their families. But now this bassinet is for your baby. We always hoped there would be another grandchild coming along. And maybe one day Xandra would like to visit, too, she can have Sadie's bed." I'm touched by Emily's interest in meeting Xandra.

"I noticed this for the first time in our grocery store," Emily says, steering me to the changing table. "There are special sections in the beauty aisles for Black skin and hair. What products do you think I should get for the baby? I'd like to keep them right here." Emily opens a drawer that's currently empty.

A collection of books on the shelf above the changing table catches my eye. Among the classics like *Goodnight Moon* and *Mother Goose's Nursery Rhymes* is *Whistle for Willie* by Ezra Jack Keats. I recognize the books as beginning efforts to prepare for their next grandchild who will be different from their first. But I'm also cautious that no matter how much Curtis and Emily may want to know me and to love on their grandbaby, the Wests have no idea how to be with a Black child, let alone be a part of raising one. And, as painful as it is to admit, neither does Leo.

"Nina, I don't mean to pry, but I have to say, I really don't like it when I see um, African American baby girls, newborns really, with pierced ears. Seems so unnecessary to inflict pain on someone so innocent." Emily lowers her voice as if there is someone eavesdropping on the two of us, "You agree with me, right? You wouldn't do that if you have a girl?"

"I had my ears pierced before my first birthday," I respond. *And I turned out pretty damn good*, I think to myself defensively. Emily seems taken aback by my answer so I assuage her fears for now. "Let's just focus on having a healthy baby, we can talk accessories later."

~

It's my turn to sleep the whole way home on the plane. Four solid days of being "on," I need to turn myself off for a bit. Or pretend to. Life stresses that took a back seat to ringing in the New Year with the West clan are now vying for real estate in my brain. I have five days to tell Winn, before Courtney does, that as board chair his legacy will include crafting the first Royal-Hawkins head of school maternity policy. I need to check in with Graham to make sure Xandra is heading back to school with her mind set right. And my first performance review with beloved wonder teacher, Jared Jones, is coming up fast. Amid my growing anxiety for what awaits me back in California, I steal angsty glimpses of Leo, nose buried in a thriller, the fine hairs on his arms looking fairer than I've ever noticed before.

When we were parking the car for lunch yesterday, out the driver's side window there were two young Black men being questioned by mall security. It didn't seem like the altercation caught Leo's attention, getting to "the world's best chili" was his focus. I saw it immediately and couldn't shake the scene. How the two of us were in the same environment in Omaha but seeing different views out the window made me wonder if this happens with us at home, as well, and I just haven't noticed.

I can no longer minimize that raising a Black child will be a challenge for the West family and for Leo, no matter how smart and caring they are. The way Leo will see his son is not the way the rest of the world will see his son. If the two of them are in a store together, people will assume Leo's watching a friend's kid. If they are eating in a restaurant, the waiter will assume Leo's kid is in the bathroom and our son is the best friend tagging along. The two of them being related will always be the second guess.

"Other than Karl's tasteless humor"—Leo looks at me, sensing I can't sleep, eager for an invitation out of the doghouse—"I would say our trip was a success. I've landed myself a woman worthy of my cousins' jealousies. Aunt Nancy clearly told Uncle Bruce to keep his rants about juicing Californians ruining the beef industry to himself. And I can tell my parents really like you." Leo puts his hands on my belly, looking pensive. A few moments pass before he lifts his eyes, looking right into mine. "I love you, Nina."

"You do?" I ask suspiciously, wondering if Leo's riding high from four days straight with his fan club, immune to the trepidation I'm feeling.

"I do. I really, really do." Leo takes his hands off our baby and reaches into the chest pocket of his vest. "Nina, will you marry me?" This time the marriage proposal feels real, feels weighty, and it's presented with a ring. All I can do is stare.

"Are you sure you love me, not just your baby who happens to be attached to me?" I know this is not what Leo wants to hear in aisle 12 seats C and D, but it's what falls out of my mouth while my eyes are glued to the ring.

"I love you both. Do you have anything else to say to me?" Leo asks, eyes pleading.

"I love you both too." At least I think I do. I can't shake feeling unsettled even though Operation Mixed Baby went fairly smoothly up until this morning. I pick up the hand not holding the ring and put it back on my belly. I blink slowly and put my hand over Leo's, both of us radiating love and body heat to our baby. Though my mind's spinning, I'm grounded enough to know I'm satisfied being in a cramped space with only Leo. Is that enough to want to marry the guy?

Leo fakes a smile, unsatisfied with my answer. "Nina, if I promise you will never have to live in Omaha, will you marry me?" I feel like Becky from seventh grade breaking Leo's heart all over again.

~

"Ouch. So, you said no? Was there a ring?" Marisol responds, feeling the pain of my airline proposal fiasco. We're sitting in my driveway after dropping a silent Leo off at his house, which, other than a rushed thirty-minute pack job for Omaha, he hadn't been in since before Christmas when he settled into my house for the week to participate in all the Morgan Clarke holiday cheer.

"There was a ring," I admit. "Leo pulled a solitaire diamond on a thin platinum band out of his pocket." I glance at Marisol. The purse of her lips tells me she's picking up what I'm putting down. "So, help me, this wonderful man proposes marriage to me and the first thing that came to mind was: 'I know he is not giving me a first wife's ring! Do I look like I'm twenty-four?'"

"*Ooooo.* Rookie mistake," Marisol says, eyes filled with sympathy.

"One look at the ring and I knew he hadn't talked to you."

"Men are so dumb," Marisol says, playing with the stack of precious gems on her ring finger. Not one of those were purchased by Jaime without me right by his side. "But real talk Nina, it's not really the ring, and we both know it. What'd you say to Leo? I know it wasn't good, because that man was hangdogging in my back seat."

"I didn't so much say 'no' as I said 'I don't know,' and then I made a stupid joke about how altitude was making him all kinds of crazy." I wince recalling my immature response.

"Terrible ring choice aside, I watched that kind, loving man get out of the car and walk through his front door crushed to the core, Nina. What's your holdup? Take a leap of faith off the platform of your perfectly planned life for God's sake. Xandra's heading back to school, hopefully with a much-improved attitude, Fitzroy's healthy and happy to spend half his time with you and the other half in Queens when he's tired of you. You got plenty of dough, and, news flash, you do love this man you're about to have a baby with. I know you do. So, what's your problem?"

I shrug.

"Then put the man out of his misery. If you aren't going to marry him, for the love of my personal time and growing boredom over this topic, move in with him."

"Okay, here it is, Marisol. How's a White man going to raise a Black son?"

"Do you know you're having a boy?!" Marisol lights up.

"Hypothetically speaking."

"He's going to learn on the job. Same as a Black man, or any other man for that matter."

"So, what? I'm finally gaining personal confidence again after dealing with Graham, and building a strong foundation on my own two feet, and now I'm supposed to abandon myself and commit to Leo?"

"Yes, that's generally how it works when two high-functioning adults fall in love. Jesus, if Roan and Tate can do it and make it last way longer than either of us gave them credit for, then I'm willing to bet you and Leo can hold strong too. Unless your hesitation has nothing to do with the baby or your sense of independence and everything to do with how you feel about Leo," Marisol challenges. I fall silent.

"Nina, please say that is not what it is." Marisol turns my shoulders and keeps hold so we are looking each other squarely in the eye. "Are you hearin' me, girlfriend? I want it understood, right now in this driveway, that I cannot go another five years back in the dating pool with you. This is it for us, Nina. Leo's our guy. I know it, so don't blow it."

"I know we're best friends, didn't know we are sister-wives too. And no, my feelings for Leo as a man haven't changed. It's my feelings about us together as parents and how complicated our lives have become with a baby on the way that are tying me up. With this baby, Leo also comes with a family who has loads of child-rearing opinions and zero experience with my culture." Marisol is genuinely listening to what I have to say, soaking it in, not perched waiting for me to shut up so she can offer her solution, per usual.

"So did Leo's family say something out of pocket while you were there?" Marisol digs, ready for some drama.

"No, but you know how it is as the only melanated person around. Being on constant guard includes seeing those things that go unsaid."

"Don't tell me they had a lawn jockey in the front yard." Marisol grimaces.

"Dolls," I deadpan.

"They had dolls in the front yard? That's weird!" Marisol shudders.

"No, you nut. I saw two blonde-haired, blue-eyed dolls in the nursery when Mrs. West gave me a tour."

"Come on, her granddaughter probably just left them there," Marisol suggests.

"Nope. They were still in the box," I correct. "One soft hairbrush plus one Black children's book does not equal multiculturalism."

"Look at you with the mathing." Marisol elbows me to lighten the mood. I'm too deep in my emotions to turn off my thoughts now.

"You know how it is. It's not just the dolls, though they were creepy, but at work I'm immersed in a predominantly White universe all day long, always putting a positive spin on everything, making it look easy, making it look like I don't mind spending my days smoothing an already level path for White folks. That's all okay, at least for me, because when I come home to my dad and Xandra, I can be the real me no one else sees. And Leo can join if he wants to, but either way for a few hours a day I can truly be me." I stop, but Marisol waves me on, uninterested in my dramatic pause. "On top of work, I'm going to have to join THEM. The fairest family in America. I can't even wrap my head around the amount of sunscreen that family must go through after long Nebraska winters." Marisol stays quiet, she knows there's a punch line to my predicament.

"If I move in with Leo, my world gets Whiter. If I marry Leo, my life is White. Every holiday spent with the Wests will be me Blacksplaining our Jamaican family recipes at Christmas as well as what it means to be ashy and why shea butter is the cure. And you know I will be constantly encouraging Emily not to use *please* on the end of every sentence when asking my child to do something; just tell the kid to do it. Twenty years in schools, and I still don't get why White parents think every interaction with their child is a teachable moment followed by endless explanation."

"You just went allllllll the way off into left field. When are you going to stop looking at what's wrong with Leo and start seeing what's right? Please tell me you did not lug all this emotional baggage with you to Omaha?" Marisol demands. "'Cause that kind of load needs a mule to carry it."

"Not all of it. Some of it I picked up as a souvenir after four days in Nebraska," I answer, rubbing my palms against my forehead, warding off a headache.

"Well, we're not going to solve centuries of interracial procreating in your driveway tonight, so I'm kicking you to the curb. Work tomorrow for both of us."

Marisol's right, we both need to be getting to bed, so I feel around on the floor of the car for my purse and open the door. Marisol grabs my arm. I knew her last words were coming. "I'm not going to say there aren't some complications here, Nina, there are. But come on, you're way overthinking this thing. I'm here to tell you that you and Leo are not that unusual. You two had the hots for each other, you made each other laugh, you started dating, you knocked boots, and now you have a kid on the way. This ain't nothing special in the grand evolution of humankind. Spoiler alert, it's been going on for centuries."

"Then if what Leo and I have is nothing special, maybe we aren't meant to be together."

"You're nothing special to the rest of the world, but you two are special to each other, and that's what counts above all else. Besides, how many women can tolerate kissing a man who eats as much cilantro as Leo does. Gross." Marisol scrunches her face up tight. "Trust, he's meant to be yours."

TWENTY

"NINA!!" I hear Roan roar, charging toward my office. I fumble for my phone to text Marisol for reinforcements but remember she's on a seventh grade field trip to the Getty Museum. Said she didn't trust her son, Diego, to keep his hands off the art. Apparently, he's behind the rule "you break, you buy." I bet Roan's rushing to tell me he and Tate broke it off over the extended Martin Luther King Jr. weekend. Not timing I would have suspected as January can be a long and lonely month, but love is fickle. I move my box of tissues to the edge of my desk.

Weird. Roan's translucent Irish skin's aflame, and he looks more angry than sad when he blows through my office door.

"Congrats on crossing the application finish line," I offer, allowing Roan a moment to compose himself and decide if humility or hysteria will be his tactic when recounting his three-day weekend breakup. Friday at 4:59 p.m. was the last possible moment a parent could slip a Royal-Hawkins application in for fall. At 5:00 p.m. sharp, the WeeScholars submissions link went dark, and every director of admissions at private schools across California released a collective sigh of relief. I have to give Tate credit for holding off on breaking up with Roan until after he cleared his professional Mount Rushmore.

"Six years, Nina," he begins with a flat tone. Familiar with Roan's extraness when it comes to relationship stats, I stop myself from pointing out that I'm not sure he had even dated Tate for six months before they became engaged, let alone six years. If Marisol were here, she would jump right to, What the hell happened? I'm more of a dance-around-the-perimeter-of-a-personal-problem kind of woman.

"I was promised, when I took this job, that you would LET ME DO MY JOB."

I open my mouth to engage in the conversation, but Roan shuts me right back down.

"What happened to your claim at the first faculty and staff meeting that you 'believe in transparent leadership, empowering your people'? Or my personal favorite, 'I trust you as director of admissions, Roan.'" Roan is spinning around my furniture, not sure where to land his amped energy. Time for me to step in and cool this diatribe down.

"So, this outburst you've brought to me before I even get a chance to eat my second breakfast has nothing to do with Tate?"

"NO! Wait, why do you ask, have you talked to Tate? Is something wrong?"

"No, no I haven't talked to Tate. We're not phone friends." I cautiously walk over to Roan like I'm approaching a rabid Maltipoo and put a hand on his back to steer him to my wingback chairs. Steps away from plopping him down Roan pivots left to my desktop, and I almost topple over.

"Good. We had a nasty fight over going to Acapulco for our honeymoon. I told him that's an Acanono." Okay, that's progress. A middling joke tells me Roan is slowing his synapses.

"Then what are you talking about, Roan? I promise you I haven't turned into a tyrant since I left you on Friday. Last we spoke you were waiting to finalize our application numbers. The only thing I've done is get a full set of gel nails and send Leo out for bagels Sunday morning." I wave ten fingers in a perfect shade of firehouse red.

"Friday at lunch when you gave me the names of the two families you want to make sure we give extra consideration to this admissions season . . ." I try to jump in because I know where Roan's going with this, but he shuts me down with a finger inches from my lips and shakes his head no. "And when you promised me there would be no more than two on your list this year, were you telling me the truth? The absolute truth, swear on that little one's life?" Roan points to my belly.

"First of all, I'm not swearing one thing on this baby's life that doesn't save mine. Second, you know I think you've been crushing it running admissions. The way you assist parents in parting with their young students the first week of school is already legendary in the lower grades. Passing out waterproof mascara to the kindergarten moms on day one was brilliant."

"That was a stroke of brilliance, huh? Pun intended," Roans says, self-satisfied.

"Can we get to the point, Roan?" The ego-stroking portion of our impromptu meeting is over, I actually have a job to do other than hand-holding Roan through minifits.

"Well, if everything you've said is true, then explain these two partially completed high school applications that, I have no idea how, came through WeeScholars to my inbox this morning. You mind if I log in to my account so we can look at them on your big screen?" I motion Roan to go right ahead as I take a seat in my desk chair. "Actually, I'm going to print them out so we can both look at them."

I read the names at the top of the two applications, Dontrelle and Marcus Burns. Twins I assume, currently in eighth grade at a public middle school in Crenshaw, a neighborhood in South LA.

"Before you get locked in to reading, let me share that I have reviewed every electronic sign-in sheet for the twelve fall school tours, and there is not one adult who attended on behalf of these applicants. There are no SSAT scores, grades, or teacher recommendations. So, somehow an administrator at WeeScholars was persuaded to push the applications through without them being complete." Roan's in business mode, which is good, because even though the Burns boys are only applying for high school admissions, not college, in Los Angeles County it's a blood-sucking sport. If there's even a sniff of foul play at

Royal-Hawkins on the application front, I'm going to be accused of a white-collar crime, and jumpsuits are not my best look. I'm not quite tall enough to pull them off.

"So, if there's no visit, scores, grades, or recs, what is there?" Trying to answer my own question, I flip through the thin pile of papers that Roan has printed out for me.

"All the general information is complete, full name, birthday, address, etc. . . . and the essays. Also, the tuition assistance pages have been completed, but incorrectly, almost like it was done in a hurry and without reading the directions."

"Okay, well, Crenshaw's a long way for the boys to travel for school, so I can't imagine the consideration for attending is very high. Let's start by assuming best intentions, there could be an obvious explanation we're missing." After taking in the general information on the boys I turn to the parent essay, which is always written with tedious perfection. Dontrelle, I assume, is Black, and from the address provided, he's coming up in a hard part of town with his brother, Marcus.

What are your child's strengths?
Dontrelle has been dedicated to the game of basketball since his father took him to Jim Gilliam Park near our house when he was three and big enough to carry his own ball. He has consistently played up in rank in several youth leagues with boys older than him because his level of play has always been advanced for his age. Whether it's on his school team or club teams, Dontrelle averages about 25 points a game and is often awarded MVP status in regional and state basketball tournaments. In high school Dontrelle and his brother Marcus will most definitely work tirelessly to bring a league championship to their school.

I turn to look at Marcus's essay about his strengths. His is the exact same answer as Dontrelle's, only his name has been swapped out with his brother's. These essays were clearly banged out in about five minutes.

"And you double-checked, no SSAT scores, grades, or teacher rec-ommendations? Maybe they're still pending?" I thumb through the incomplete applications a second time.

"Nope, nothing. I don't know any more about this applicant family than, I'm relieved to find out, you do." Roan's shoulders finally drop from his ears for the first time since he entered my office. "Well, I'll refund their application fees and email the parents to let them know that we can't consider the boys for admissions due to partial and late application packages. I seriously want to know how these two even made it through the system; WeeScholars will be getting a call from me. Two decisions down, five hundred more to go." Roan smacks the applications he's holding on his right thigh, signaling he's ready to leave.

"Hold up on emailing the parents and calling WeeScholars until you hear from me. I need to think on how to best handle this. I might call the principal of the boys' middle school, see what they may know about this." There's something about the Burns boys and their scram-bling to apply to Royal-Hawkins at the last minute that's piquing my interest. For this family to consider traveling from Crenshaw to Pasadena every day makes no sense, particularly when there are plenty of private schools closer by.

Even from the slim information in front of me, there is something about this family that reminds me of mine. Celia paid no mind the hour-plus travel time each way for Clive and me to attend top schools. Sure, there were others near our home, but Celia had a list of successful alumni who went to Collegiate and Spence, and she wanted our names added. I never saw what my mother submitted on our behalf with her limited knowledge of American culture and private school admissions. For all I know they may have sounded a lot like this one. What I do know is that Celia and Fitzroy would want me to dig a little deeper on behalf of these boys, and that's what I'm going to do.

"Okay, so you'll get back to me by . . ." Roan trails off, waiting for me to offer a time frame. I understand anytime you can move some-thing off your to-do list and onto the done pile, a director of admissions is eager to make that move, but right now I'm in charge of this ship, and it sails on my schedule.

"You'll know as soon as I let you know, Roan, but for now give me a few weeks. I'll get back to you by then about the Burns family."

"Suit yourself," Roan concedes. "But please do it in something other than that midwinter muumuu you have on. You may think it hides the"—Roan puts his hands several inches out from his belly—"but it's doing nothing for you. Truth is, it looks like Xandra's crawled back in there with the two of you."

"I'd belt it if I could," I say, sadly agreeing with Roan's fashion assessment.

"Belt it? Burn it. Later, lady," Roan chirps as he swipes the half-eaten bag of corn dippers off my desk and heads out my office door.

Winn seemed nonplussed when I called him our first day back in school after New Year's and blurted out my baby news ahead of Royal-Hawkins's self-appointed snitch, Courtney Dunn, and before I got cold feet. I told him we needed to get together to cover a couple of topics prior to the next board meeting, most pressing being Courtney's board seat. Winn's priority was what was on tap for happy hour, judging by the fact that he dropped my call and didn't call back. I would agree hammering out a maternity leave package from a sports bar is probably not the responsible thing to do, but being snubbed for potato skins was a bit harsh.

It's been two weeks and I have yet to reconnect with Winn, but his best bud, Jared, and I are meeting in his classroom the last period of the day for his midyear performance review.

As if on cue, this morning I got another email from a father singing Jared's praises as a teacher, or as a coach, I'm unclear which because the email included a litany of sports metaphors that apparently Jared uses to hook this dad's daughter on history. Since the success of *Hamilton*, the pressure to create histortainment to get kids excited about social studies is high, so I can't fault Jared for using what he's got to draw in middle schoolers who are prone to spacing out.

"Oh, sorry, Pablo, I nearly ran you over," I stutter as Pablo catches me in both arms before I collide right into his chest.

"*Más despacio*, Nina," Pablo laughs, familiar with the only two speeds I run on around this place: pants on fire late for a meeting or snail's pace leisurely enjoying my time with students in the hallways.

"What are you doing over here in the west wing, Pablo? Isn't this usually when you take a break before putting this place back together after the students destroy it?"

"*Sí, sí*, but Jared grabbed me as I was passing by. Asked me to watch his kids in class while he stepped out for an important call."

"An important phone call during fifth period?" I wonder to myself as much as to Pablo.

"Nina, while I was in there, I heard a few students say Mr. Jones doesn't give much homework," Pablo whispers to me since Jared's on the other side of the door. "They like him best because they think his class is easy. I told them maybe they're not working hard enough."

"I'm glad you set those students straight. You got your ear hustle down."

"What's ear hustle?"

"Means you're excellent at finding out useful information on the down-low. I appreciate you being the eyes and the ears of the school."

"And hands." Pablo shows me both calloused palms. "Ear hustle. I like that one, Nina, I'm going to tell it to Yolanda. I think her three sisters have too much ear hustle." I chuckle, Pablo nailed it.

Armed with enlightening information about Jared's teaching philosophy before his review has even started, I'm happy to see that Jared's classroom is tidy and devoid of clutter. *Clean space, clean mind* is a Fitzroy mantra as he reminds me to remove my plate seconds after I've laid down my fork. I do notice Jared's walls are fairly bare where highlighting student work, hanging a laminated poster of the Bill of Rights, or having guidelines for civic engagement in a Socratic seminar might be helpful, if not inspirational. As a rabid alumnus, of course there's a Harvard pennant hanging above the SMART Board.

"Hey, Nina, don't sit there. Last period's seventh graders who squatted at that table were nasty with colds. I need to disinfect that side of the room," Jared says, pulling out a chair closer to the windows overlooking the courtyard and gesturing for me to take a seat near him. I can tell by the way Jared's watching me cross his room that I'm moving too slowly and he's willing me, *hurry up, I gotta get to practice!*

"Thanks for observing my morning class today and reacquainting yourself with Mesopotamia and the Fertile Crescent. That stuff will put you to sleep, but I think the sixth graders are gettin' through it a'right. Everyone needs to know where the wheel comes from." I had no idea the wheel came from modern-day Kuwait.

I spent my lunch hour in my office, which I rarely do. I like to be out catching up with kids on how the debate team is doing and hearing about science experiments gone awry. I also enjoy very slowly heating up water in the faculty kitchen so I can stay on top of what the latest gripes are among my staff. I know my presence is not always welcome during faculty downtime, but I do it infrequently enough that I don't think I totally cramp their style.

But today, I needed a solid hour to figure out how I was going to present Jared's midyear review. Last year, I botched an end-of-year conversation with a young fifth grade teacher that resulted in her ghosting a month before the start of school to move to Mexico and apprentice with a shamanic guru she read about on BuzzFeed. The egos of the young and newly employed, I have learned, do not respond well to my direct feedback and aggressive timeline by when I need to see said improvements. This is a generation raised in therapy, and they want their reviews equal parts feelings, culture of safety, and recognition for their individuality. I want their reviews to lead to exceptional teaching.

With Jared, he's the only Black faculty member I have, and as witnessed by this morning's email, parents adore him. Ms. Bertrand, our controller, rounds out our Black employee count to a whopping three at the school, but Royal-Hawkins families don't ever see Ms. Bertrand buried in the business office, so I don't count her. Jared is it for a familiar face for Black students to casually connect with on a daily basis. I only wish I could sing his praises.

Leaning into Jared's classroom, Lamont Stennis calls out loudly, "Hey yo, Mr. Jones!" above the din of students filing out of school at the end of the day. His noggin has grown faster than his body, and all I see is a tween bobblehead.

"Hey, what up, L. Good to see you lil' man! I'm talking to Ms. Clarke here, but I'll catch up with you in the gym," Jared calls across the classroom. "Lemme finish up here and I betcha I'll still beat ya."

I know Jared is only making quick chitchat with an enthusiastic member of his team, but his flippant declaration that what we have to talk about will only take a minute sets the start of our review off at a deficit.

"How do you think things are going for you so far this year?" I ask. I like to begin reviews listening to teachers consider, in person, what they wrote to me in their reflections prior to our meeting. Given Jared's reflection, he believes he's still a number one round draft pick. I, too, can do sports metaphors.

"You know I really like it here. The community has been welcoming, and I feel like I'm connecting with my kids." *Yeah, connecting over your class being easy street,* I think to myself. "I mean, I don't want to take them home with me at night, that's not going to get me far with the ladies, but I love 'em when I'm here." I have to let out a snicker on that one, it's a fact we can both agree on for a young single guy.

"I'm curious, Jared, why'd you choose Royal-Hawkins? A guy as accomplished as you could teach anywhere you want."

Now Jared's the one taking his time, rubbing his hands together and smoothing out the tops of his jeans before placing his elbows on his thighs. "You know, I've been asked that question plenty of times already? Mostly . . . no wait, ONLY by other Black folks. I gotta assume brothers and sisters ask you the same question."

"Yes, they have, but when I tell them I went to private school my whole life, that seems to make enough sense for them. But I'm interested in your answer."

"Simple. These kids need me."

"What was that?" I ask, hearing a distinct familiarity in Jared's response.

"Royal-Hawkins students need me. I mean come on, look around," Jared sweeps his hand by the window and the controlled chaos of privilege hopped up in the courtyard. "Most of these kids living in Pasadena don't see men who look like me in their everyday lives. They might run into a brother at a barber shop or working a car wash, but they rarely if ever see teachers, administrators"—Jared pauses to include me—"friends of their parents who look like me. Who look like you." I'm enjoying this reflective side of Jared. He sounds as optimistic as I was as a new teacher who, too, felt compelled to be that positive model.

"I want these kids to get used to seeing a Black man in a position of authority, demanding their best, setting high standards for them to achieve. My goal is when my students grow up, they will be completely comfortable with anyone they have to answer to regardless of race." I appreciate the social justice sentiment, but I have to bite my tongue from offering that Jared could use some guidance of his own when it comes to having a boss. He's busy teaching lessons he hasn't yet fully learned.

"Jared, you do light up a room wherever you go, and you also command respect. Role-modeling that type of positive energy in the world is important for kids to see. You definitely bring a cheerful vibe into school every day."

"I get that from my mama," Jared admits, willing to share some of his credit.

"I'd love to meet her someday," I say, smiling and pulling my chair in a little closer. "I'm happy you're comfortable sharing why it's important for you to have strong relationships with this community." I pause and give time for my last compliment to sink in, because the time has come to get real about his teaching.

"Aside from your role-modeling and rapport with the community, let's talk about your actual classroom performance. How do you think your lesson planning and project design are going? The first year of teaching is extremely challenging, even for a smart young man such as yourself." I'm dragging my toes along the edge of what I suspect is going to be unfriendly waters.

"Like I wrote in my reflection, I've got it all under control. Nothing for you to worry about." Jared gives me a dismissive wave, checks the classroom clock above his head, and starts drumming his fingers on his thighs. "The kids are happy in my class, and they're having a good time. So, there you go, the proof is in the pudding."

"Uh-huh. But see, the thing is, the proof is actually not in the pudding. The proof is in the put-in." Jared's posture changes in reaction to my voice. He knows I'm not playing. "The sweat and soul you put into your work. The relationships you get out of it. You're only going to become a great teacher if you put serious effort in to developing your teaching skills. From what I've observed this year, I'd say you're putting a lot into making sure the parents like you, and for sure a lot into coaching basketball. I'm just not seeing you put in that same level of effort and commitment in your classroom. That's what I've got to see if you want a future here."

Earlier in the year, after a handful of observations, I tried to help Jared course correct before things got too dire, but he blew off our follow-up conversations. I'm not seeing an ambitious professional, hungry to improve his craft, challenge his students, and impress his boss. I'm only hearing about a pied piper who wants to lead children to an athletic promised land. It's my job to convince Jared there's more to it. "What I've witnessed this year are a whole lot of lengthy stand-and-deliver lectures to twelve-year-olds with three-minute attention spans."

Jared looks at me, surprised by the divergence from the *Jared is the man* narrative. I can't entirely blame him, because that's the message he's been getting from the Royal-Hawkins community. But they don't determine his future employment. I have to turn his classroom game around now because I fear if I'm forced to fire him, I'll be vilified by the whole community.

"Jared, I have all the faith in the world that you have the potential to be an exceptional teacher, but it's not going to be without effort. You are in the early stages of your career, and becoming a seasoned teacher who has impact on his students is a craft that takes time to hone. I'm up for working with you if you are," I share, trying to sell our journey to Jared's betterment as an energizing joint venture.

"Have you talked to Winn about me?" Jared asks, straight up. Given that I just delivered a barely passing grade on the first six months of his career, I'm unclear why a conversation with Winn would play into Jared's professional review.

"Faculty performance is not a part of the school that the board of trustees oversees. That falls squarely under me."

"Hmm. I'm just sayin', you may want to talk to Winn before you come up with additional plans for me outside the classroom based on your opinion of my teaching. An opinion, I might add, that doesn't align with what I'm hearing from parents. We almost done here, Nina? Winn's meeting me at practice today."

Holding your boss's boss over your boss is a boss move.

TWENTY-ONE

"I know you are not tryin' to break up with me before Valentine's Day, Leo!"

"I'm not breaking up with you, exactly, and it's only January 31," Leo semi-assures me, reminding me not to get ahead of myself on the holiday fanfare. Whew. Since the botched marriage proposal on the plane that resulted in the engagement ring being returned to Leo's pocket, we have more or less returned to our normal rhythm of life. Wednesday and Thursday nights are spent at my house since I like to be at work by 7:30 a.m. at the latest, and weekends are at Leo's, so we can more easily take in all LA has to offer. Mondays and Tuesdays we catch up on our individual lives. Though I have noticed Leo's been spending more time riding his bike after work and showing up later and later at my house, while I've been parked alone on my couch massaging my own swollen feet.

"You've shut down the idea of us being a family several times, and a man can only take so much rejection before he knows to stop asking. So, now I need some space to consider *where* I fit into your picture of life with our baby. Right now, you have me feeling like I don't fit in at all."

"Please, Leo. That's not true!" I say, waving my wrist to brush off the ridiculousness of his assertions. "Come on. Dinner's almost ready, and I'm eating for two." Why's he messing with my feeding schedule?

"Oh, no? You've made it clear that the vision I have for the three of us moving forward as a family is not your vision. You say you want me in your life, but only on your terms. And that's not okay with me. We're supposed to be partners, Nina." Leo looks more pained and tired than usual, and now I know why he's been biking so much. Our life and our future as a family are weighing heavy on him.

"Leo, you know my concerns have nothing to do with you. I have a full plate raising Xandra, running a school, watching after my father, and now having this baby. I'm tired, and being pregnant at forty-three is not what I had planned."

"Hey, it's not what I had planned either, but I'm one hundred percent here for all three of us and . . ."

"And truthfully, on top of all of this"—I'm circling my stomach with my index finger—"race is complicating our situation. I've been dealing with it my whole life. You're facing this issue for the first time, and I don't have the energy to be educating you and your family on race in America." Maybe that was a little abrupt mentioning my concerns, but there they are.

"I don't remember anyone asking you for a lesson. Since Omaha, you've made assumptions about my family without even getting to know them other than our one quick trip. We're good people, Nina. No one in my family wants anything more than to love you, love me, love this baby. But you have us falling down on the job of raising this kid before he even gets here. Why you would choose less love for a baby instead of more is beyond me."

"Listen, Leo, if we have a boy, the experiences your son will have and what he'll need to learn from you is so drastically different from how you grew up, you have no idea." I'm finally letting out the worries I've been holding inside about raising a child with Leo. I don't want to hurt him, but this is my truth.

"You don't see me telling you that you can't parent this child because you're a girl and the baby may be a boy," Leo counters. Okay, maybe that argument has a tiny bit of weight, but every child needs their mother.

"I'll admit that when I met you, you checked all my boxes, but race wasn't part of my list. I was looking for a woman who is smart, ambitious, loves her family, and doesn't take herself and the world too seriously. You being sexy as hell didn't hurt either." Leo's list should sound like a compliment, but his voice is getting heated. "I thought you had it all, but you let people get in your head, and it's keeping you from being with me."

When a man talks this much about his emotions, I know he's serious, and Leo's still talking.

"I just think we need time to focus on the baby, because focusing on us as a couple doesn't seem to be working. I've done what I can, and I can't seem to convince you to build a life with me. So going forward, I'll go with you to all your appointments, and we can grab dinner after. Other than that, right now, I need some space." Leo punctuates the word *space* with a vigorous head shake. I've known Leo for eight months now, and I always thought he was the softy between the two of us. He practically came undone when he ripped open the Jamaica flag T-shirt and matching onesie for the baby my dad gave him at Christmas. I couldn't bear to tell him that wearing matching outfits with your child is at the top of the Nina Morgan Clarke no-no handbook. But now here we are, and he's drawn a hard line in the relationship sand.

"Leo, real talk here. Are we broken up, or are you just hangry from working out?"

"I don't know what we are now, Nina. Other than about to be parents." Hearing my dad's footsteps coming down the hall, Leo picks up my hands and places my palms on his cheeks, giving each of my wrists a kiss that feels a bit too much like goodbye.

"Hey, Mr. Morgan, I was just about to leave. Hope you weren't hiding out in your room on our account." Leo stands up, awkwardly offering a handshake to my dad. We look at Leo funny. Since the two of us started dating, Leo's always called my father Fitzroy.

"You two all right in here?" my dad asks cautiously, looking at me. "Haven't seen you around here as much, Leo."

"Yep, yep, all good. I'm buried under a stack of cases that I'm still catching up on after our trip to Omaha, so I need to head back to the office."

I haven't taken a breath since my dad stepped into the living room, and my heart starts palpitating. Leo's really leaving.

"Well, hold up, Nina has some coconut drops for you if you're working late these nights. You sure everything's all right?" Again, with a question for Leo, but a beatdown stare for me.

"Oh, I'm fine. Along with all this work I've been training for a multi-day race that's coming up at the beginning of April. Been riding pretty intensely with my bike club, so I'll eat whatever you're willing to give me," Leo assures, following Fitzroy into the kitchen and leaving me more alone than I've felt in five years.

What just happened didn't really happen, did it? Leo's gone from wanting to marry me, to wanting time away from me, and it's all my doing.

"I'm perfectly oversnacked now, but I'll miss your dinners, Nina," Leo whispers, grabbing his jacket off the back of the banister, careful not to crumble the dessert.

"You don't need to miss my dinners, Leo, you really don't." My voice cracks, panic charging the air. "Let me walk you to the door," I say, moving to get up, hoping between the couch and the door I can miraculously come up with something to say that will undo what Leo's obviously been pondering all month in the bike saddle.

Leo leans over and gives me a real goodbye kiss this time. "No, you stay, Nina. Staying put seems to be your comfort zone."

⌒

"Hey, Nina," Winn calls, skipping, two at a time, up the front steps of Royal-Hawkins on an unusually cold February morning. The last of Winn's tan from a Christmas spent at the Great Barrier Reef is still noticeable against his white collared shirt. "I can't believe we haven't seen each other since December." It takes every ounce of restraint not to ask him if he's been hiding from me following his Courtney Dunn board decision. I would be hiding from me.

"Who . . . are you . . . heading into school to see today?" I ask in fragments, my attention focused on shaking hands and offering *good mornings* to all the students brushing by me on Monday's rush.

"I'm coming to see you. Did you not get my email last night?" Winn asks, a bit taken aback, which is fair. I have a pretty consistent track record of checking work email every Sunday evening so there are no surprises waiting for me when I get to school on Monday. Turns out what I needed to watch out for was Leo's Sunday night surprise. I slept with a cold washcloth across my face hoping for an eight-hour miracle cure for swollen eyes and a raging headache.

Usually, I have a text from Leo by 8:00 a.m. on Mondays reminding me not to take an obstinate child hostage or steal anyone's fifteen-dollar acai bowl from their lunch box, but today, nothing. I tap over to emails, yep, there it is. An email from Winn at 6:42 p.m. yesterday. Right around the time Prince Charming ran out of charm. Or maybe I'm the one who ran out of charm, so Leo just ran out.

"Oh, yes, here it is."

FROM: Winn Hawkins
DATE: January 31
SUBJECT: Quick chat post drop-off tomorrow morning
TO: Nina Morgan Clarke

Nina,

I'm on drop-off duty tomorrow, Gemma's at a fasting retreat in Napa. You would not believe how much it costs for Gemma to not eat for a week holed up in a remote resort. We have some board business to discuss prior to Tuesday night's meeting so I'll swing by your office around 8:00.

Best,
Winn

"Okay, let's head in, and I'll ask Mimi to push back anything I have for the next forty-five minutes. Would you like some coffee and a pastry?"

"Thanks for the offer, but no thanks. I've been eating double the past few days since Gemma's off eating nothing."

"You and me both," I say, rubbing my belly. Winn smiles but then quickly averts his eyes as if looking at a woman's pregnant belly is grounds for litigious action. "I'm going to make some tea, so make yourself comfortable in my office. I'll be back in a minute." I don't really drink much tea, but I need a moment to figure out if it's worth it to confront Winn on the topic of Courtney Dunn. I'm tired to the bone today.

"Nina, Winn in there with you yet?" Jared yells as he hustles by me on his way to class. He pivots and jogs backward down the hall to catch my answer.

"How do you know Winn's meeting me this morning?" I ask, now more interested in the conversation I have coming up than I was a minute ago.

"Winn's my man," Jared lobs back, giving me a salute before continuing on his way. I'm puzzled by Jared's commentary, so it'll be interesting to hear what Winn has to say.

"I just saw Jared in the hall, he seemed to know you're here," I say, taking a seat opposite Winn.

"I love that dude. We see eye to eye on a lot of things."

There should be a cut off age for using the word *dude*.

I take a slow sip of my tea. "What can I do for you, Winn? Tomorrow night's agenda seems more or less straightforward; nothing too urgent. Since you're here, though, I would like to talk to you about board composition." In my sixty-second strategy session with myself and the teapot, I decided it would be best for me to bring up the subject of selling board seats before any other topic comes to pass.

"Yep. Good place to start." Winn scoots himself forward in his chair, eager to dig in to this contentious topic. His enthusiasm for this discussion was not part of my bad boss game plan, so I'm a little thrown.

"Help me understand why, without discussing it with me, you invited Courtney to join the board," I say, direct and to the point.

"During my time in high school at Royal-Hawkins, our soccer and baseball teams were all right, nothing special. Never made it out of our division into any sort of regional playoff." This jaunt down Winn's high school memory lane is super boring and taking this discussion I don't know the hell where. "And when your daughter was here, what's her name again?"

"Xandra."

"Yes, Xandra. Were the sports teams she was on very good?"

"I don't remember, and it was elementary and middle school. As you know, Royal-Hawkins has a no-cut policy, so she played soccer and everyone made the team."

"You've worked at Royal-Hawkins for fifteen years, and you've also been a parent here, and you have zero recollection of anything memorable about sports at Royal-Hawkins? What about basketball?"

"No, I don't, Winn, but I also have never considered myself a big fan of any sports team, high school, college, or professional." *I mean really, I went to Wellesley for God's sake,* I think to myself. "Royal-Hawkins is an academically focused school, not a sports-driven one." I'm getting irritated at the local sports trivia, my raw emotions from last night not helping the situation. "What's your point?"

"For decades Royal-Hawkins has sucked at sports. Meaning, I can't remember a time we were any good. It's embarrassing, and it needs to change for the future health of the school. It's no longer enough to be a strong academic institution, Nina. In fact, I would argue, looking at our competition in Los Angeles, it hasn't been enough for quite some time. We have to perform on the field, on the track, on the court, in addition to in the classroom if we truly want to be one of the best day schools in the country."

"So, you want to abandon our areas of growth laid out in the strategic plan and build an athletic pipeline to D-1 schools?"

"Ah, so you do follow collegiate sports." Winn winks at me, thinking he's found an entrée to budging my leadership needle. "No, I don't want to change the strategic plan, Nina, you and the rest of the board can continue to focus on it as it stands. Courtney and I have improvements to the athletic program at Royal-Hawkins covered."

My moment of illumination is here. I open my desk drawer and pull out the envelope with Courtney Dunn's quarter mil check still in it. It's been in there over a month as I considered whether to march it over to the finance office for deposit or return it with a *thanks, but no thanks* Post-it. "I take it you are leading the sports improvement campaign, and the Dunn family is funding it?"

"I'll be putting up matching funds, and I have a few alumni on the hook for sizable contributions up to a million dollars. A lot of money can be raised on a golf course. Sports begets sports," Winn brags. This is not my time to debate if golf is truly a sport. Doesn't sweat need to be involved to call something a sport? Hey, look at me, I do have an opinion on athletics!

"A million is a lot to put toward bleacher upgrades and new uniforms."

"There's facilities and uniforms, yes, but that's the low-hanging fruit, Nina. Courtney and I have a plan and an aggressive timeline to turn the Royal-Hawkins athletic program around. We're thinking bigger. We can sort details out later, just leave it to me to get the ball rolling. Courtney is on board as my number two," Winn says confidently, reaching over to pat my shoulder for assurance and for acting as his assist. It gives me the creeps like most interactions with him do. There's no way I am trusting anything related to Royal-Hawkins to someone I don't trust.

TWENTY-TWO

For the love of keeping your job, put that finger away," I say, swiftly grabbing Roan's pointer finger and giving it a twist. My reflexes are lightning fast despite my vigilant focus on the road in front of me. "I don't need you AND Google Maps telling me where to go."

"What you need is for me to drive; you missed our turn." Roan raises his spare pointer finger and signals me to flip a U-turn. I shut up and do as I'm told. We only have a few hours to get to the bottom of the Burns boys' application mystery before I have to return to school for an investment committee meeting, and Roan has to be at his weekly Core and More cardio class. Roan and I have been tied to each other's lives long enough now that I know not to ask what the *more* stands for.

"You don't think the boys are home, do you? That'd be super awkward if they are." I can tell Roan is attempting to mask his discomfort of driving through Crenshaw with chitchat over what a couple of fourteen-year-old boys will think of us while they're grabbing an after-school snack.

"I bet they're at practice somewhere. They both play on three different teams," I offer to calm Roan's nerves. It's a guess dressed as fact since it's winter and these are teenage boys.

"Yeah, you're probably right," Roan agrees, distracted. I can tell he's looking around for my car's automatic lock button.

"You've never been to Crenshaw, huh?" I ask, figuring if I provoke Roan, it'll distract him from his concern.

"Please. When was the last time you traveled south of your sleepovers in Silver Lake? Oh, maybe never? That's what I thought. You're traveling through foreign country as much as I am, you just blend in better. And I'm not talking about that contour you use."

Roan's blathering is interrupting my developing plan to play on our joint sistahood for the meet and greet with Carmel Burns, mother of the basketball prodigies. I let the car crawl down two blocks, finally locating the address we're looking for, and find a parking spot a half block farther down near the park I suspect was mentioned in the twins' application essays. After we've stopped, I wrestle my blazer off, tossing it in Roan's lap. I undo one more button of my blouse and shake my shoulders to give my top half a bit more of a casual look. I don't want to come across too uptight. I'd even take off these pantyhose if I could, but I have Roan and a bulging belly in the car with me today, so I don't see it happening.

"What, are you planning to seduce Carmel Burns or something?" Roan accuses as I apply a coat of lipstick. I shove my oversize handbag under my front seat. I don't want to appear like an insurance sales team and have the door slammed in our faces before introductions are made. I give my purse a final swift kick to be sure it's well hidden, because I also don't want to return to find my driver's side window and two weeks' salary gone.

"You're out of your mind to leave your purse here. You wouldn't do that in Malibu, why the hell are you doing it here?" Roan admonishes like I've lost my mind.

"I don't know what kind of mother we're going to meet, and I most certainly do not want to come across as extra bougie out of the gate. Trust me, this is how Black women size each other up. It's all about being relatable."

"Then why am I here? I'm wearing emerald-green suede loafers like some sort of Keebler elf."

"I need a witness should things go sideways with Carmel. Besides, drama makes you giddy. Consider this field trip a wedding present."

"Nope. Doesn't count." Roan's injured finger rings the bell. "Let's do this."

The door swings open just enough for me to see a woman who's wearing my hairdo better than I am looking back at me with a hint of suspicion. "Can I help you?"

I do my best to give enough of a smile to convey warmth, but not too over-the-top by showing all my teeth. "Carmel Burns?"

"That's me. Who's asking?" This is when I know it's good I've come empty handed, not burdened by a designer handbag and a load of bullshit.

"My name's Nina Clarke. I'm the head of school at Royal-Hawkins in Pasadena where you've applied your sons, Dontrelle and Marcus. This is my colleague Roan Dawson. How are you doing today?" I don't put my hand out to shake because Carmel still has the security screen shut tight.

"Oh, okay!" Carmel's tone turns from guarded to flustered. "I'm doing well, thank you. They told me Royal-Hawkins had a Black principal, but I don't remember them also saying a woman. Come in. Come in."

Who's the *they* Carmel's talking about? Looking at Roan's head tilt, I suspect he's wondering the same thing.

Entering the living room, I spy an ebony cherub waddling across the carpet, double fisting LEGO bricks, diaper drawers dragging.

"This is my youngest son, Anton. A surprise blessing when the twins were twelve and I thought I was on the backside of parenting. Looks like you might be having yourself one of those blessings too." Carmel looks from my belly back to my face, surely guessing that at my age there was nothing planned about my pregnancy.

"Nina already kicked her other kid across the country to New York when this happened," Roan fills in, hitching a thumb in my direction, excited to dish at my expense. "When this one pops, the other one will be getting her driver's license!"

"A life sentence, that's for sure," Carmel cackles, and Roan joins her, enjoying this all too much. I let them have their moment and bend down to pick up a dropped royal-blue LEGO brick that may be pivotal to Anton's toddler creation.

"Please, have a seat, thank you for coming all this way. Between you two and the other men that stopped by a few weeks ago, you sure are making me, Dontrelle, and Marcus feel special."

If we were on my couch watching reality TV my jaw would have dropped to the floor, but this is real life, so instead I clench down hard and smile.

"You know things have been so busy at school since the New Year, and, well, you know how pregnancy brain is. That baby fog can get in the way of clear thinking." I'm met with a nod of understanding from Carmel and a raised eyebrow from Roan. "I'm sure somewhere in the back of my head I can remember who I sent over here to visit with you, but right this second, I can't recall. Can you help me out?"

"*Oooo*, Nina, you don't have to tell me! I could barely remember my own name by the time Anton came around. And you're running a school too?! Believe me; I know how it is." At this moment Carmel is my favorite person in the whole world. She gets the precarious balance of my overflowing plate, and it makes me want to hug her, and then have her repeat exactly what she said to Leo.

"Let me see, there was a White guy, Winn something, probably late fifties. My twins are so competitive they loved his name." Carmel lowers her voice to a husky whisper. "A little more uptight than I'm used to, but he sure was good looking. And there was a fine young brother with him. I remember his name was Jared Jones. My boys were all up in his business. I thought those two men were a strange match, but I recognized them from a few of the boys' basketball games. When they showed up and wanted to talk to me about my sons' talent on the court, I felt okay about it. They both work for you, right?"

Roan turns to me, eager to hear my answer.

"Yes, they do," I respond, with maybe a little too much attitude.

Carmel picks up Anton and places him on her lap. He drops a LEGO and fights to get down to retrieve it, but she keeps a firm hold on him. I can't take my eyes off what is going to be my future in a few short months. While I'm finally comfortable talking about having a baby, this is the first tiny person I've been around in years.

"Sorry, can you repeat that, Carmel? Did you say it was Jared Jones and Winn Hawkins who came by your house?" Roan jumps in to keep putting the pieces of our mission together without causing our hostess alarm.

"Ohhh does that man own the school?!" I want to tell Carmel that Winn Hawkins doesn't own shit, but I don't want to squash Carmel's semicelebrity excitement. "Can't believe I didn't put that together until now." Roan and Carmel share a laugh while I come to grips with the fact that Winn, Jared, and Courtney are plotting to strong-arm the future of Royal-Hawkins by going around me.

"Well, it's a compliment that Winn and Jared have been at some of your sons' games; they must be very talented. Did they share any particular reasons, other than their general interest in youth league basketball?" I'm working double time to keep the disbelief out of my voice. I know in order for Carmel to trust me with the details of her interaction with Winn and Jared, she has to believe there's no issue at play and that she's not ratting anyone out.

"I have to admit, at first I thought it was suspect that they were hanging around the gyms doing who knows what. You never know with people these days." Roan and I nod our heads in agreement. "But when they stopped by and said that they have been scouting the county to find the best middle school players to recruit for Royal-Hawkins's high school basketball team, it all made sense. Turns out they know more about Dontrelle and Marcus's stats than I do. When the boys found out their coach would be Jared, they were ready to sign on right there. Did that brotha really go to Harvard?"

"He really did," I assure Carmel.

"Wow, that's what's up. My boys have never been ones for studying, right now they only dream of going pro. Maybe at your school they could have a chance at going to college." Finally, someone recognizes Royal-Hawkins is my school.

"When Winn and Jared were here visiting, they encouraged you to apply to Royal-Hawkins. Is that where you all left the meeting?" Roan pipes back in.

"Oh no, they made it much easier than that, which I appreciate 'cause I don't know how this whole fancy private school thing works. Uh sorry, I shouldn't have said that."

I smile. "No, you're right. The place is pretty fancy." I want Carmel to feel like she has some knowledge about what's happening to her family, that she's not just being led into the unknown by a couple of overgrown knuckleheads.

"Anyway, I have my hands full with Anton, my job, and my husband, who works round the clock. They said they would do the application for us and cover some fee. I was concerned I wasn't more involved in the application, but Winn . . . er, Mr. Hawkins promised I had nothing to worry about." This visit was well worth the afternoon away from campus. After one joyride I'm getting the answers to six months of the Winn, Jared, Courtney triangle.

"It's not easy raising three boys in this neighborhood, but they're good kids and they deserve a chance. At Royal-Hawkins my sons can have a fresh start in high school with teachers who can help them with their schoolwork, and they'll meet a new crowd to run with. They need positive influences in their lives, influences like Jared Jones."

At this point I'm so heated I'm not sure I want Jared Jones having an influence over any kids at my school, but on the outside I remain cool.

The living room settles into silence as Carmel ties up the end of this fascinating tale, and a look of gratitude settles across her face. My mother carried that same expression when my brother and I were on the private school track. A different life for her boys has seemingly fallen like a gift from the sky and landed in a pretty package in her lap. No mother can resist the chance of having better for her children.

"Well, I think we've taken up enough of your time this afternoon, Carmel," I say, and motion for Roan to stand so we can start making our way to the door. "Plus, I bet this chunk of love is getting hungry for a snack." I reach over and give Anton's tummy a quick tickle. "Anything else about the visit from Winn and Jared you want to share? I apologize my schedule has been so packed I haven't had the chance to catch up with either of them to hear the full story."

Carmel shifts uncomfortably, and I give a quick side-eye at Roan.

"Roan, can you keep an eye on Anton for a moment while Carmel and I step out onto the front porch?"

"I'll do better than that, I'll keep both eyes on this little guy," Roan jokes, reaching out for Anton's hand. Walking out to the porch behind Carmel, I see Roan settle onto the carpet with Anton. Looks like I may have a future babysitter in Roan.

"Listen, Nina, I'm embarrassed to admit it, but I almost cried in front of those two men. I thanked them for the offer to get my boys into Royal-Hawkins, but I told them that it would be impossible for me to get them to and from Pasadena every day. I don't have a car. Anywhere we gotta go, we gotta go by bus. On a good day, it would take my boys at least ninety minutes each way on public transportation." Carmel's no longer meeting my eyes as she reveals her personal circumstances, a recognition that this is where our life experiences diverge.

I gently touch Carmel's forearm and assure her, "You don't ever have to be embarrassed talking with me."

"Winn offered if I send my boys to Royal-Hawkins to play ball, he would figure out a way I could have a car."

I have heard a lot of tales of rich people's shenanigans, but this one tops the list.

"Well, I promise, going forward, I'll be the one in touch with you. Us mothers have to help each other, right?"

"True. My favorite poet, Tupac, said it best in 'Keep Ya Head Up.'"

I give Carmel a knowing smile and say, "I thank the Lord for my kid too."

"You know it," she responds, enveloping me in a goodbye hug. Leaning back from the embrace Carmel adds, "If you help my boys, I'd be so thankful, sis."

"I'll try my best, Carmel, I will," I say, though I'm uncertain how my best will play out.

TWENTY-THREE

"You want to stop and grab whatever women in your condition binge-eat while freaking out?" Roan asks with a rare touch of trepidation, my silence no doubt tough to read.

"If by *women in my condition* you mean irate, then yes, I'm starving. A banh mi sandwich or poutine would be good. You decide," I suggest, distracted. "Or both."

"That's a random combo only to be found in the great American strip mall. Lucky for you they are a staple of Southern California," Roan says, craning his head left and right as he maneuvers through traffic. After visiting with Carmel, I was in stunned disbelief. To avoid a collision to top off this dreadful afternoon, Roan decided it would be best if he drove us safely to Pasadena.

Back home, having finished off my sandwich and my investment committee meeting, the shock of my visit with Carmel Burns had dwindled. I gave in to the fact that men do stupid things when it comes to playing with balls. The question that looms large is, Why would Courtney want to buy herself a third-wheel spot on this shady recruitment train with a $250,000 donation to the athletic department? I can deal with Winn and Jared. Their motive is simple: they want to be big swinging dicks winning basketball championships, even if they have to import the talent. But Courtney's personal investment, I don't yet know. I want to call and ask her if this is her tactic for paying her four foot, ten inch stepson's way onto the varsity basketball team even though he's far better suited to be the team manager. Perhaps, as Marisol predicted, this is a lusty fatal attraction scenario at play. Both answers though are too tidy, too simple. I'm going to need to consider how to deal with Courtney with cunning and without Roan.

Being head of school can be a lonely job, and this pay-to-play development is exactly why. I can't out Royal-Hawkins among its competition by bringing this ethical predicament to my heads' support group, and even Marisol's mouth is a gossip risk on this one. The danger of this backdoor deal being put on front street, by anyone, is too great. I don't want to hear Courtney's voice right now for fear of what I might say, so instead I bang out an email from my phone that will allow me some time to think about how best to deal with her.

FROM: Nina Morgan Clarke
DATE: February 4
SUBJECT: Welcome to Royal-Hawkins Board of Trustees
TO: Courtney Dunn

Dear Courtney,

It was wonderful to have you attend our February meeting. The board valued your input and abundance of advice.

Thank you in advance for your generous service.

Yours in community,
Nina Morgan Clarke
Head of School
Royal-Hawkins School

"NINAAAAA," Fitzroy sings from my backyard. "Come on out here and give me a hand collecting all these weeds I've pulled out of the garden." Dad decided to fly back to Queens right after New Year's for the month of January. I invited him to stay longer, but he brushed me off with a claim of house business to attend to. I couldn't imagine what that would be for the twelve-hundred-square-foot apartment he's been living in for fifty years, but I also didn't have the energy to get into it.

We actually bumped into my dad at LAX as Leo and I were walking out to find Marisol, and Dad was heading in to catch his flight to New York. I was startled to see him. I didn't really think he'd leave until after I got home, and we caught up on my trip. My real shock, however, was catching him heading to a midday flight, not one first thing in the morning. Was Fitzroy's New Year's resolution to ease up on a lifetime practice of *up and at 'em*? I couldn't imagine, but I also didn't want to discourage the welcomed change. We hugged and wished each other a Happy New Year, and Dad promised he'd return just around Valentine's Day to get started on my garden, a late-in-life interest he'd come to enjoy in mild Southern California winters.

When Roan dropped me at school after our Crenshaw investigation, I tasked him with figuring out how to get ahold of Marcus's and Dontrelle's academic transcripts and some type of teacher recommendation. Roan reminded me, for the fiftieth time since fighting through traffic to Pasadena, that this is not how the other five hundred applicants had applied. On time. Paperwork complete. And on their own is how everyone else, as far as we knew at least, had done it. I assured Roan I understood, but we are in uncharted admissions territory here, and as much as we make individual concessions from time to time for children of alumni or the occasional tycoon, we may have to bend some rules to get to the bottom of the Burnses' story, both academic and athletic.

Staring at the thirty emails I missed being out of the office for an afternoon, I'm unable to open even one with Dontrelle and Marcus parked in my brain. Hearing Dad's call, I close my laptop and heave myself off the couch to shuffle outside to help him, and to avoid my waiting messages.

"Dad, can I run something by you while you're out here working?"

"I'd love the company, but I'm going to need you to talk and hold the compost for me."

"I can do that." I grab the bin and tip it over slightly. Dad reaches up and pushes the bin down a little lower, making it more difficult for me to talk and hold with the baby pushing up against my diaphragm, but easier for him to shovel and listen.

"What's on your mind, Nina? Been a while since we've both sat still long enough to talk." Under normal circumstances I would tease my dad about him heading out the door to the Y before I get up in the morning and then being out playing dominoes long after I go to bed, but not tonight. My wit is weighed down by real issues. I haven't thought through how to unravel the Burns saga to Fitzroy, I only know I want him to hear the long, convoluted story and have him shrink it down to size in the way only my dad can.

"So today, Roan and I went over to Crenshaw. It's a neighborhood about an hour or so southwest of here. Kind of reminds me of our neighborhood in Queens." Dad nods his head, understanding without me having to explain who lives there or what the streets look like.

"What were you doing all the way over there in the middle of the day?" Dad probes while doing battle with a rogue root situation.

"I went to meet this woman, Carmel, who believes her twin boys will be attending Royal-Hawkins for high school this fall." Dad looks up from the dirt, signaling I've piqued his interest. It didn't take Fitzroy but a minute to figure out Crenshaw to Pasadena is a common commute for no one.

"Go on," he urges me.

"Seems Winn Hawkins and Jared Jones, the Black teacher I've been telling you about, recruited the boys to play basketball for Royal-Hawkins."

"For high school? Why would they want to do something like that? Royal-Hawkins is across the city and doesn't have much to offer in the way of sports. My guess is these boys grew up hustlin' ball in the parks."

I startle hearing my dad follows Royal-Hawkins sports. "You're not wrong, Dad, but I'm surprised to hear you know anything about sports at school."

"I don't, but I saw the level of play at Collegiate and Spence when you and Clive were coming up. And I watched enough of Xandra's middle school soccer games that I'd say private schools are rarely athletic powerhouses. Academics are your game." It's true, neither Clive nor I have any athletic laurels to rest on, but Xandra did get Graham's fast footwork. It was the other girls on the soccer team that ran faster for the postgame snacks than they ever did on the field.

"Seems Winn promised Dontrelle and Marcus entry into Royal-Hawkins so they can start as freshmen on the varsity basketball team, win us some championships, and in turn overhaul our athletic image, all the while, raising millions for the school. Winn's determined to scout out the next Black Mamba."

Dad chuckles. He loves a good Kobe Bryant reference. "How do the boys look on paper? Can they keep up with the schoolwork? If they can, other than a long commute, I don't see a problem. But, no point discussing it if they can't play in the classroom as well as they can on the court." I've always been jealous of how clear life is through Fitzroy Morgan's lens. You're qualified for a school, for a job, for a team—or you're not. If you play by the rules of a fair society, you'll be rewarded. Coloring outside the lines is not something Fitzroy has ever done, even when others were busy scribbling away.

Unsure if it's worth my effort to explain the predicament Winn and Jared have unwittingly put me in and why it's more complicated than what the boys look like on paper, I forge ahead because I need to get someone's take, other than Roan's, so here goes.

"They don't look like much on paper, though I can't even say there's much of a paper trail by which to judge. Winn wrote the essays and half assed the financial aid forms. And then, I don't know how, he got the application pushed through the WeeScholars software after the deadline. No grades, no teacher recommendations, no test scores."

"The mother didn't do the work to apply her sons to school? She let someone else do it for her and do it poorly at that. Is that what you're telling me?" Dad asks, getting his facts straight before dispensing his opinion.

"Yes, but Winn's very persuasive, so I'm not sure how much say she had in the matter. Anyway, I called the boys' middle school principal after Roan dropped me back at school. To say he was shocked by my news of Dontrelle and Marcus applying to Royal-Hawkins would be an understatement. I think his exact words were, 'Those boys have tried to crack many a backboard, but as far as I know they've never tried to crack a book.'"

"He sounds like a man who doesn't care a lick about the kids in his charge. Maybe he's lost his way when it comes to motivating young ones to do right by their education." Dad digs his shovel into the garden bed with force. He has no tolerance for adults who don't believe in the academic potential of every child. I like to believe I share the same conviction, but faced with this dilemma, my resolve is being challenged.

"I don't know about that, but I do know his account of the boys' efforts in the classroom aligns with what Carmel said during our meeting." I let out an enormous exhale. Carmel did not hold back on the truth of her boys' school experience. From what she said, it sounds like some of their teachers let them skip class to shoot hoops in the school gym. "She said the boys tolerate school so they can play ball, but she hopes Royal-Hawkins can flip that dynamic. She's a smart woman. She knows the odds of her boys ever playing professional ball are slim, so if they can go to a school where their chances of going on to college are far improved, well, she's going to grab that opportunity and not let go."

"Uh-huh. Uh-huh." Fitzroy is digging and thinking awfully hard.

"I'm not that different than Carmel. If Xandra were struggling in her current school, I'd be looking around for a better solution." Truth is, Xandra is struggling in her school right now. Her struggles may not be academic, but they're struggles, nonetheless. Should I be talking to Graham about alternative choices for her?

"This mom sounds like she's trying her best in a difficult situation," Dad concludes.

"I think so, too, but when I asked her if Dontrelle and Marcus took the SSAT test, which is a required piece of the application package, she looked at me like I was speaking in tongues at Sunday service."

Dad gives me a chin raise. His childhood Christianity was peppered with hints of the devout, and he remembers what it looks like when people catch the spirit. "Do Winn and Jared know that you know about their plan?"

"Not yet. I've got a little time to figure out what I'm going to do with those two." No need to bury Fitzroy under the absurd added layer of Courtney Dunn. There are only so many outrageous work antics I can lay on him at one time.

"Meanwhile, what are you going to do about these boys, boss lady?"

My heart gives my chest a fist bump. Leo calls me boss lady. Or he used too.

"I was hoping you would jump at the chance to tell me what to do when it comes to this mother and her boys. She's doing her best with not a lot of resources and wants to do right by her family, just like you and Mom did by us."

Dad takes off his gardening gloves and wipes his sweaty hands on his pants. He rolls off his knees with an exaggerated breath to set himself down on the ground and then pats the space next to him for me to sit. This is no small feat for a seventy-year-old man and his seven-months-pregnant daughter. "The seed of something better has been planted. We both know the current school situation is no longer going to satisfy this mother."

"I know, Dad. So, what do I do now?" I ask, elbowing my dad to spit out his honest thoughts. Given our history of heart-to-hearts,

I know Fitzroy's patience for this topic is going to time out in about three minutes.

"Carmel's situation is not so different than when your mother met that young man from Princeton in church all those years ago. He put a sweet taste in her mouth that she went chasing after for you and your brother. Carmel's now expecting better for her boys, and she thinks, because of what this Winn character promised her, you're going to deliver." Dad nailed it. Time to reveal the final absurd fact to this convoluted story.

"Winn also promised to buy Carmel a car so she can drive the boys to and from school and make it to the Royal-Hawkins basketball games. And then there's a toddler brother who'll be entering kindergarten when the boys are seniors, given our sibling policy. I'm already wondering if Winn's committed to pay for tuition and transportation for the next fifteen years on behalf of the Burns family." I watch as Dad's eyeballs blow out his eyelids.

"Good Lord, that man is playing games with this family."

"For sure. So, can you please tell me what to do? You love telling me what to do, and right now I need you to point me in the right direction."

"I do not love telling you what to do." Fitzroy frowns, crossing his arms in disagreement.

"Really? Do we need to relive your strong-arming Leo to come home so you'd be assured another grandbaby?"

"That wasn't me telling you what to do, that was me telling Leo what to do." Dad winks and looks down at my stomach, his newest grandkid packed tight inside. "All I can say is yes, every parent wants the best education they can get for their child. But a parent should also want their child's honors to be earned fair and square. If a parent is agreeable to gaming the system because they know their child can't compete, then you don't want that parent or their child in your school." I nod along to what Dad has to say, but after meeting with Carmel, I don't think she has a clue she's gaming the system. "Your mother and I wanted you and Clive to be admitted based on the exact same criteria as all the other children. It was not the color of your skin, your athletic ability, or anything else that got you into those schools. You were as competitive, on all the measurements, as the other students applying. That's how your mother and I did it with you and Clive, that's how you played it with Xandra. And that's how I think you should insist this mother plays it with her boys."

Bless Fitzroy. His belief in Clive and me never wavers. Fact is, private schools have always needed the likes of a few Black children like me and Clive as much as we needed them. Being first-generation students offered a level of certainty to our respective schools that we would perform academically under the pressure from home to not squander the sacrifices of our immigrant parents. We were low-risk kids.

"But Dad, as chair of the board of trustees, Winn's my boss. Not to mention he's a massive financial contributor and a founding family member. He's the keeper of my contract."

"Winn going behind your back and misbehaving does not give you permission to act poorly as well. If you don't uphold the standards of the school, then how can you expect anyone else to? Act like the leader you were chosen to be." There's the brutal truth I thought I wanted to hear.

"Dad, this is an easy choice for you, you've always followed your conscience."

"That may be, Nina, but since when is doing what's right easy? The simple truth is, the most difficult path is usually the right path." And that right there is a Fitzroy Morgan mic drop.

"Shoot, these boys know what a better life looks like, they see it in magazines, on TV, in those blasted phones they stare at all day long. Royal-Hawkins has some smart kids, Nina; and I'm not sayin' Dontrelle and Marcus aren't smart, but Royal-Hawkins kids are academically competitive and treat the classroom like it's their basketball court. They're playing to win. Dropping those Burns twins into that kind of environment if they're not well equipped is like building a house without a foundation. It sure might look pretty at first, but it won't stay standing long enough to live in. And *that* is a mess you surely don't want to have to clean up."

I hear Dad's point. Not accepting the Burns boys into Royal-Hawkins will be painful among the small subset of folks who know about this admissions misstep, namely Winn, Jared, Roan, Carmel, and me. But accepting Marcus and Dontrelle and then potentially having the community judge the boys' worth in an academically competitive freshman class would be a navigation nightmare.

"Thanks, Dad, I appreciate you speaking your mind." The issue of merit is more clear-cut for my dad as an immigrant, but having been raised in this country, I understand being Black is more complicated and that excellence is not the only factor at play. "But now I've got to figure out how to get up off this grass like the lady you raised me to be."

"How about being the lady you want to be?" That lady wants teriyaki and a simple answer, even though I know my dad's right. "I'm not quite done speaking my mind, Nina."

"Let's talk more about it at dinner, I need to go deal with email."

"I'm done talking about other people's children for today. I want to talk about my child. You think I haven't noticed you've been spending more nights home than not recently? I've watched you walk around here for a couple of weeks wearing a brave face, but the minute the room clears, your face cracks, I know it does."

Leo has stayed true to his word and his need for space. Being an, uh, older pregnant mother almost in her third trimester, I now have weekly medical appointments scheduled at the end of my doctor's day, and Leo has worked his meetings and court hearings so he can come to every single one. We go out for an early dinner afterward. He does all the right things to prove he's a doting soon-to-be father. However, when he high-fives me at our healthy ultrasounds or buys me a snack as we walk to dinner, there's an emotional gulf between us that no one can see, but I feel.

Leo sits across from me at dinner, not next to me so we can be shoulder to shoulder, touching, like we used to do. Our meals are full of baby business and gender guessing, our conviction to not find out the sex a shared one. We bat around names, easily adding to our growing list, neither committing to nor rejecting the other's suggestions. And the expensive crib I'd been coveting? Leo ordered without balking at the price, but UPS rather than baby daddy delivered it to my door.

After every dinner I ask Leo if he wants to stay over, and his answer is always the same, well rehearsed. *Better not. The baby needs a good night's sleep.* If not a sleepover, I ask if he wants to come in and say hi to my dad, maybe stay and watch a show with us before he heads home, but the polite refusals continue. I can tell from his downward gaze that he misses our old way of being, but Leo's a man of principle, and he is sticking to his word. Until I can commit to fully engaging in a life with him, he's not interested in compromising beyond what's best for the baby. Like clockwork Leo gives me a kiss good night, lingering an extra moment, giving me hope that this is the night that will be different, then he pushes the front door open to send me inside. Alone.

"Dad, I can't talk about my relationship tonight. I've got too much to do." I sigh, knowing my need to escape this conversation has nothing to do with my professional dilemma and everything to do with what I must face personally.

"Can't or won't?" Dad accuses. I shrug.

"Dad, I've been down this road before, and I've tried to talk to Leo about the hard parts of marriage and raising a baby, but he wants no part of it, his head is so stuck in the clouds."

"Nina, what's wrong with a man wanting to be with you? Life's too short to waste the gift of love."

Mom was the mushy one. Where's all this emotional stuff coming from? I wonder to myself.

"I can't explain what's holding me back, Dad, but I don't have the energy to figure it out right now."

"Nina, ambivalence about your future gets you nowhere other than exactly where you are."

THIRD TRIMESTER

TWENTY-FOUR

FROM: Nina Morgan Clarke
DATE: March 2
SUBJECT: Xandra's debut
TO: Graham Clarke

Graham,

I'm arriving in New York around two the day of the performance, will rent a car and meet you outside the theater at 6:30. Please bring flowers for Xandra, she's worked hard to be a Tony-worthy inanimate object.

Nina

I continue to keep Graham's and my parenting relationship strictly on email, but since Graham broke the communication seal last fall, he's embraced bugging me over text.

Graham 2:42 PM

> I happen to know Xandra would prefer a VISA gift card for her efforts. Is Brad coming to hold your purse?

As long as it's not a gift card for more piercing, I'm going to let this one go. Flowers die, but plastic cash is always the right color, always the right fit. It's so like Graham to forget Leo's name.

Nina 2:43 PM

> His name's not Brad. It's Leo.

Graham 2:43 PM

> I know that, but your Uncle Sam sounds like a Brad to me.

It never crossed my mind to ask Leo if he wants to come to New York with me. I'm pretty sure if he won't come inside my house, he most certainly won't come with me across the country. But now that Graham's trying to goad me into a verbal battle, my brain shuts off and my fingers fly.

Nina 2:45 PM

> Of course, he's coming.

Whoosh . . .

Nina 2:47 PM

> Mayday, Mayday, Sol! I just texted Graham that Leo's coming with me to see Xandra's play!

Marisol 2:48 PM

> In New York? Did I miss a major development between last month's heel scrub and today's SOS? BTW what do you think about a new Cocktails and Colonics offering? I think it would be a perfect complement to the Clean Slate's list of services. You can get cleaned up inside AND out. Yes? No?

Damn if that wouldn't elevate her brand, but right now, we're talking about my shitstorm.

Nina 2:51 PM

> I've literally never thought about colonics. On brand, but not on topic. What do I do here Sol, I fly out in three days.

Minutes tick by without a response from Marisol. I turn my phone off and back on, my only known high-tech hack. Still nothing from Marisol, but Roan pokes his head into my office at that moment.

"Are you heading over in a few to watch the middle school basketball game?" Roan asks, I assume hoping I won't make him go.

"I'm considering it. Do you think Courtney's going to be there?" I've been hustling around campus to avoid Courtney at drop-off, pickup, and parent council meetings. *Hustle* may be a strong word for a woman pushing forty pregnancy pounds, but I get the job done. Our next face-to-face will be the April 2 board meeting, and I prefer to wait until then.

Ding.

I hold my index finger up before Roan can start making excuses.

Marisol 3:08 PM

> Marry the guy.

Nina 3:08 PM

By Saturday?!

Marisol 3:09 PM

Not my fault you waited until the last minute.

"Let's go," I say to Roan. Even though he's pissed at Jared for being an accomplice to an admissions heist, I know he still likes to gawk.

We arrive at the game already underway and find a spot up the bleachers from the home-team bench.

At halftime Jared jogs over to us. "That shot by number twelve was impressive," Roan tosses out like he didn't spend the entire first half of the game with his head buried in his gift registry tabulating what's been purchased and what big ticket items remain. Number twelve is Benjamin Dunn. Who knew that puny kid could shoot?

Roan's not wrong, the first half of the game was impressive. Jared has the boys running circles around the other team, passing effortlessly back and forth. Royal-Hawkins is ahead by twenty-eight points, a high-scoring game for middle school.

"I can see the basketball court is second nature to you, Jared. And now you're making it second nature to your boys." I gesture down to Jared's gaggle who can't stop wrestling each other to the ground even when they're supposed to be resting up for the second half. I know this compliment is going to land right.

Jared runs his hand over his tightly trimmed head and beams with pride. "Yeah, they were a little motley back in January, but you do the drills you get the skills. These boys have never worked so hard in their lives, but look how happy they are." It's true, the whole squad is bouncing on their toes, their enthusiasm to get back on the court about to blow out their ears. I smile wide at the unadulterated joy of kids who smell a win. It's pure and natural and stirs up my own competitive nature. I, too, believe that with hard work and smart strategy, a win tastes good.

I look around the gym. Courtney must be here witnessing this.

"I told you, Nina, I'm your dream maker. In the classroom and on the floor. Gotta go bring this game home." Jared pounds his chest over his heart and winks. Maybe at me, maybe at Roan. "See ya, Roan." Jared glides back down the bleachers to rejoin his team. A couple of moms gaze in rapture. So does Roan.

Returning to the pots and pans on his phone, Roan admits, "I bet these would be lining my cupboards by now if Tate and I were having a big wedding."

"Hey, chin up. Bright side, you can flirt with Jared all you want. It's not cheating when a guy's straight, right?" I'm not up to speed on gay monogamy, but I'm pretty sure ogling a hetero hunk is meaningless.

"It may not be cheating on the home front, but I'm pretty sure it's foul play according to the Royal-Hawkins employee handbook. Have you read that tome, Headmistress Clarke? It'll put you right to sleep." I bite my tongue. With Roan, I sometimes forget we're at school. "But you'll let me flirt with Leo whenever I want, right? You know, just to keep my skills sharp?"

"If he sticks around, he's all yours."

—

"I was craving burritos." I hold the bag up next to my head, smile, and wonder if I'm as transparent as I feel. "I got your favorite, carne asada." My gut's hoping the thirty-minute drive and impromptu meal offering will be well received. Dinner will be served with a side of begging Leo to come to New York with me.

"Did we have an appointment today and I missed it?" Leo asks, flustered, searching for his phone to check his calendar. I stand frozen on the front landing like a delivery boy waiting for his tip.

"No appointment. It's just no fun eating a burrito alone. You have to have someone to complain to when you're stuffed after polishing off a pound of meat, cheese, and rice."

"Did you remember extra cilantro? I have to have extra cilantro."

"I did," I offer, hopeful to be let inside.

Leo opens his door wide enough for me to walk through. "Get in here then." I duck under his arm into a living room I haven't seen in far too long. Maybe the past couple of weeks I should have been inviting myself to Leo's home instead of him into mine to keep our relationship on the rails.

Leaning back into the couch, Leo stretches his arms above his head, full after his final bite. In truth, I was the one who polished off my burrito, then asked if I could have the last quarter he left sitting on the coffee table.

"Why'd you come all the way over here tonight, Nina? I know something's up."

Really? He does? I thought my stream of extraneous chatter through dinner was endearing, but I guess it was a dead giveaway. I shift to get more comfortable on the couch for the big ask. Leo pats his lap, signaling me to kick up my feet. OH MY GOD, his thumb bearing down into my arch is a third trimester orgasm. I look around the room, trying to gather the right words to ask Leo to come with me to Xandra's play and maybe if I can spend the night. On the seat of the chair to my right I spy an open binder with a couple of loose-leaf papers resting on top, Leo's handwriting scrawled across them. I can tell these aren't legal briefs, they look more like a question-and-answer type situation. I shift onto my side to get a better look and see my name in the righthand corner of one of the pages.

"What's this, Leo?" I roll off the couch and crawl over to the chair, reaching for the paperwork. Leo swigs his last sip of beer.

"That's the coursework for a parenting class I've been taking. Careful, your burrito fingers are greasing up my notes."

"You're taking a birthing class at the hospital, alone?" I had assured Leo over the holidays that after fifty-six hours laboring with Xandra, I was a pro. The tips and tricks haven't changed that much, and we didn't need to go to the multi-evening class full of first-time parents asking novice questions. Yes, it really is exhausting, and yes, it really feels like being turned inside out, and no, there's no app to make it go faster or hurt less. What else do people need to know?

"It's not a birthing class. Don't go looking to spoil my fun."

Refusing to register for a hospital birthing class was one of many times in the past few months I now realize I crushed Leo's new dad spirit as the seasoned know-it-all. The fact Leo is now taking a birthing class solo kills me. I didn't understand it was so important to him. Or maybe I did, but what I wanted, which was nights at home, was more important to me. I would do anything to take back my dismissal of Leo's interest in learning how to be a good partner in the delivery room. I can feel Marisol's disappointment in me, again, without her even knowing this latest infraction.

I put the paper I'm holding down, vigorously wipe my fingers on my dress, and pick it back up. In six steps, complete with pictures, are directions on how to create playground-perfect ponytails. No graphic pictures of an alien pushing out a vagina, just a Black dad smiling at me as he deftly brushes, twists, and clips a perfect hairdo. At the bottom, in Leo's lawyer scrawl, he's written, "How do I brush my child's hair without hurting them?"

I pick up a stapled stack of papers titled, "What You Need to Know Today Before Bringing a Black Child into the World Tomorrow." Leo has notes written all along the margins, top and bottom. Highlights and arrows direct the eye to different bullet points. In someone else's scrawl it says, "Don't ask your kid if they want watermelon. JK!"

I flip the binder on its edge so I can read the spine. In a big, bold font is the acronym BTBP, and in longhand, Black to Basics Parenting. I put the binder and papers back down on the chair and keep my back to Leo, I don't want him to see the mix of nosiness and sorrow on my face. Xandra's first three years of life, I begged Graham to sign up for a parenting group with me so we could meet other couples with newborns. When he scoffed at the idea, I signed up anyway and made excuses for Graham's absence over cheese and crackers and sharing teething nightmares. Now I've done to Leo exactly what Graham did to me.

"If this isn't a birthing class, what type of class is it?"

"Well, under normal circumstances we would have known each other for a lot longer, gotten to know each other's families better before having a child."

I drop my head; this is where Leo finally comes down to earth and admits he's overwhelmed by the responsibility of me, the baby, his skyrocketing career.

"Nina, turn around." I don't. "I'm not continuing until you turn around, this isn't high school. We're adults here, and there's no ignoring that we have a baby coming soon." Calling out adolescent behavior on an educator is a nervy move. I turn around. "But that's not how we did it. And so, what? We did it our way, and I couldn't be happier I get to be a dad, something I didn't think was in the cards for me. We're just doing it at super speed."

"If we're using school analogies, we skipped a couple of grades."

"Yes, we have. And all my buddies who are dads, their kids are already well into school. They've lost their excitement over babies, kind of like you have, because it's been ten years since they were in my shoes."

"I haven't . . ."

"Let me finish. I don't have anyone in your family or my friends to help me out on the baby front, so I had to figure out a way to educate myself."

"But why this class?" I hold up the binder and read out loud, "Black to Basics Parenting."

"I'm not clueless, Nina, though sometimes I get the feeling you think I am. I know our situation is less than typical. I know my baby's not going to look exactly like me. I know people will assume it's not mine, and there's more that I don't know at this point than I do, but all that means is I have double the learning to do."

Has Leo had more of a clue than I have given him credit for all these months?

"And you, I hate to tell you"—Leo points right at me—"but you are not the only book nerd. I kill it in the classroom too. Summa cum laude at Pomona. Stanford Law Review. And, yes, you should be impressed." Leo grins and writes a big A+ with his finger in the air. "And I plan on graduating top of this parenting class too."

"Why didn't you want me to take this class with you?" I ask, though my gut knows the answer. Leo doesn't even entertain my question.

"I need to learn how to take care of a baby, and I'm the lucky dad with the added bonus of learning how to do it for my Black child. So, I looked for a class that was geared toward parents of Black children."

I'm quickly filing through my brain trying to figure out a proper response. Nothing but surprise comes to mind.

"I went to one class I found through a community center, but all the moms in the group were too bossy. They never let any of us dads talk or ask questions." Another time I will have to educate Leo on the truth that there's nothing bossier than a Black mother. If only Celia were here, she could have given Leo an immersion course.

"So, then I found another parenting class not too far from my house for Black fathers."

I raise my eyebrows at Leo. No need to state the obvious.

"I showed up early the first night and explained my situation to the group leader. Surprise baby, stubborn mother, he got the picture real quick and had me wait outside while he checked with the other dads."

I'm taken aback by Leo's appreciation of the need for Black spaces. And who knew a story about a parenting class would have such a cliffhanger? I wave both hands encouraging Leo to go on.

"The group said yes, and the past few months the guys have been super supportive, and I've made some new friends. They're just a bunch of first-time dads like me with all the same questions, and none of them think my enthusiasm is silly. Plus, they bring beer. The other class with the moms, no beer. Speaking of, I need another one." Leo pops up and grabs the last one out of his fridge.

"Also, one dad named T. J. is a big rider too. We've been shooting emails back and forth about kid bike trailers, and we're building killer baby playlists. One for tummy time, one for car rides, and one to get the kid to sleep." Leo saying *tummy time* may be the sexiest thing I've ever heard.

"So yeah, that's my binder from class, and T. J.'s offered himself up as my resident expert for all things if we have a boy. He knows he's having a boy, and he and his wife have decided to name him Ace. I think he's secretly hoping we have a son too. Uhhhh, so that's pretty much it." Leo shrugs and drums his fingers on the neck of his beer bottle. Story time's over.

I love this man, I love this man, I love this man.

I have no idea how I get from sitting on his living room floor, eight feet apart, back to where we once were. Particularly when I have to go to New York first. "I know we are on a kind of . . ." On a break? Sabbatical? Waiting period? The lack of clarity is killing me. Leo doesn't jump in to fill in the blank.

"But on Saturday morning I fly to New York for the opening night of Xandra's play. I can't even tell you how much I'm looking forward to seeing her, plus, I want to meet this drama teacher she's been spending far too much time complaining about. And, before you ask, yes, I can still fly."

"Yeah, I know. The guys and I were talking on Tuesday about how thirty-six weeks is the travel cutoff. A couple of them are planning baby-moons." Ohhh maybe I could sell a trip to New York as a doubleheader, visiting Xandra and a mini-babymoon to get our groove back on track. "I'm having good luck flowers delivered to Xandra on Saturday morning. An extra big bunch so Dash can enjoy them too."

"Wait, what?! How'd you know Xandra and Dash's play is coming up?"

"Xandra sent me a picture of her and Dash from dress rehearsal, and I follow her on Instagram. And I do keep up with everything you tell me about your family. They're part of my life, too, you know."

So, while I've continued to keep Leo and his family at arm's distance, Leo has been actively figuring out ways to embrace mine.

"You and Xandra text?"

"Yeah. Not often, but I gave her my number at Christmas in case she ever needed anything. Like a ride home from a late-night party over the holidays when she may not want to call her bossy mother," Leo confesses, with a touch of bragging. "One of the guys in my class is a stepdad, and he's been giving me solid advice on how to build a relationship with Xandra without her calling foul on my overeager efforts." I need to send that guy a thank-you note.

"Anyway, I was a champion at sneaking out when I was a kid, but I almost got caught one too many times because I didn't have a ride home," Leo reminisces.

"Did Emily know about your creeping ways?" I ask, imagining the sweater set blowing out her bun if Leo went missing at bed check.

"Still to this day, oblivious. But there were some close calls. I didn't always account for my mom being an early riser."

"Good to know stealth will be part of our child's genetic makeup. Maybe I should keep him or her in here through puberty." We laugh together and it feels natural, for the first time in weeks, to be in sync.

"Anyway, about a month ago Xandra was working through an ethics paper and needed some help, so she reached out."

"And you helped her?" Not only does Leo care about the baby that's his, but he's making over-the-top efforts with my baby as well.

"Of course I did, Nina, you have a great kid. Xandra and I are going to be in each other's lives from here on out, so I want us to have a relationship beyond holidays and special occasions. She's got a busy mom, and I want Xandra to know I'm here for her, and that you and I are a parenting team."

A few quiet tears slide down my face. Any woman would have held a man like Leo close. I've done the opposite and pushed him away. All my reasons for not wanting to marry this man no longer make sense.

"Nina, why are you really here? Don't get me wrong, it's been nice having dinner with you, but I don't really buy the burrito delivery bullshit."

"Leo, will you come to New York with me?"

TWENTY-FIVE

And then what'd he say?!" If Marisol had her hand jammed into a tub of buttered popcorn rather than soaking her cuticles, you'd think we were at the movies.

"'I can't join you in New York when you won't commit to joining me in life.'"

"How many times have I told you to marry that man." Marisol cringes with her whole body. "Damn. Nina."

"Damn awful is what it was." Marisol's looking right at me trying real hard not to give me some version of *you so stupid.*

"Is Fitzroy going with you?"

"No, if you can believe it. Dad's gotten real comfortable bedding down in my house when I'm out of town. First over New Year's and then now. He better not be drinking my booze, throwing senior ragers."

"Someone should be drinking your booze." Marisol gives me a *salud* with her double martini. Five weeks and counting until I can pump and dump.

"So, you'll be facing Graham on your own in New York?"

"Yeah, but at least there will be a baby belly between us."

"You really think Graham's going to ease up on you when you're carrying another man's baby? Please. Vulnerable is right where he likes you."

"He called Leo 'Brad.'"

Marisol lets out a hoot, startling the other customers.

"He did not. That shit's funny. Brad is seriously the worst White guy name ever."

"Exactly." I giggle too. Graham's always been good with the veiled insults.

"OMG there you two are!! Do you know how many Clean Slate receptionists I've harassed in the last hour trying to find out which shop is plucking out your errant hairs? The least you could do, Nina, is list your location in your calendar," Roan gasps, fanning his face to cool his internal thermometer.

"How'd you see my calendar? Mimi's the only one who has access to it."

"Turns out Mimi needs a date to her cousin's fiftieth birthday in Temecula. I promised to be her escort if she let me see your calendar. Desperate times."

"What's got you all stirred up, Roan? I thought you were cutting out of work early today to head to Palm Springs with Tate for a romantic weekend." The horror of my life just turned into Roan's drama. Marisol's practically levitating in her spa chair, she couldn't have conjured up a more perfect Friday afternoon for herself if she tried. Dramedy's her drug of choice.

"I thought we were, too, but WE turned into THREE."

"Tate invited a friend along for your road trip? I don't get it," I say, waving Roan over to sit down in the chair beside me. He plops down hard.

"I do, I do!" Marisol chirps, bouncing, hand raised, but not waiting to be called on. "Tate wants to have a throuple!"

"You have a threesome. You *are* a throuple," Roan corrects her, shaking his head, disappointed by our subpar sexual referencing. "But you're right."

"Really, I am?" Marisol asks, shimmying in her chair. She lives to be right.

"Wait, you just told us you can't have a throuple?" I'm totally confused.

"You can when your fiancé has been grooming a third wheel behind your back for months waiting for the perfect time to introduce him into your couplehood. Or coupledom. Or coupleness, or whatever the hell you call a normal couple. Like I'd ever get involved with a dental hygienist," Roan asserts at a volume that ensures the whole spa is in on his relationship status. "Hold on, Tate's ringtone is chiming in my pocket."

While Roan's on the phone, Marisol pokes me hard. "Man, I really called that one wrong. My bet would have been on Roan to push for a throuple, not his straight-arrow accountant. Would you have guessed Tate had it in him?" Marisol wiggles her eyebrows at me. "Kinda makes me like him more."

Jeez, I can't settle on one guy, but Tate's settled on two. "What do you think Roan's going to do?" I whisper to Marisol.

"Well, Roan's here with us and not with Tate, so my guess is . . ."

"I'm out. O-U-T out." Marisol and I whip our heads Roan's way as he's manically stuffing his phone back in his pocket. "What? You two think I can't hear you? Being faithful to one man has been hard enough, but I was willing to give it a try because I love Tate, and any man willing to put up with me until death do us part has to be a keeper. But I'm an only child, and I don't like to share. That's asking the impossible."

"Awww Roan, who would have taken you for the old-fashioned type when it comes to relationships," I coo, trying to get him to crack a smile.

"I'm not old-fashioned, I just want what I want, and what I wanted was Tate," Roan's quick to correct, banging his head back against the massage chair. It starts to vibrate. So does Roan's voice. "I will not join a throuple now, nor will I ever in the future. Hand to God." The stare down Marisol and I are getting tells us we need to nod our heads to confirm we've heard Roan's monogamous confession. "And now I'm not even one half of a couple, which I had my doubts I could pull off.

Honest talk, though, I kind of liked being one of two. But now after a move, a new job, and an engagement, here I am, officially single, again."

I reach my hand over to Roan's and give it a big squeeze. I want him to understand it's okay to be sad. I'm all too familiar with broken hearts. I know it takes a good deal of time to heal, and Marisol and I will be here for Roan every step of the way. "You'll be all right, Roan. There will be tears, there will be ice cream binges and perhaps some light Tate stalking, but you will be. Promise."

Roan rolls his head left and looks at me like a sad little boy who's just lost his favorite toy. "You sure Jared's straight?" Roan asks with a heavy sigh. "'Cause I have an extra ticket to Paris now."

~

"I give you serious points traveling across the country for Xandra's seven minutes on stage," Graham says to me as we stand in the foyer of the Pemberley theater waiting on Xandra and Dash to change. Graham and I are taking the girls out for a late celebratory dinner at an Italian bistro nearby. "And they weren't even a good seven minutes."

"They really weren't, were they?" I deadpan. We both double over in hysterics. Graham has always had a contagious laugh, and once we get started, it's hard for us to stop. "Let's keep pushing soccer."

"Deal," Graham agrees, getting control of his breath, wiping the sides of his eyes. "No Leo, huh?"

"He ended up having a case out of town," I lie.

"That's too bad," Graham says, matching a lie with a lie.

"Yeah. You're really broken up about it," I shoot back.

"Well, no. I'm not broken up about it. No dude wants to meet his replacement. But I am curious to meet the guy who will be in my daughter's life. And in yours." Where are Xandra and Dash? Graham suddenly caring about my welfare is making me uncomfortable.

"What, no smart comeback?" Graham eggs me on, elbowing my side. "The Nina I know would have a line ready about how Leo is every bit the partner I wasn't. I bet Fitzroy even loves him."

That's a bet he would win. Graham is acutely aware of Fitzroy's fathering philosophy: any fool can plant his seed, but a dad is someone who provides for *and* is present for his wife and child.

"Fitzroy does love him," I profess, looking Graham squarely in the eye, "but I don't think we're together anymore. Well, we're 'together' for the baby, but not really for us." That's the best way I can explain it.

"Ah. I'd think you'd want to do it differently a second time around. Not all by yourself."

I'm stunned by Graham's reflection. Or confession. In Xandra's lifetime Graham's never once acknowledged that I carried the bulk of the parenting on top of my professional load. It was how he expected it to be. Graham would occasionally wash the dishes and then pout around the house until I praised him for his contribution. A call to pick up eggs and dry cleaning on his way home inevitably resulted in a rant during dinner about how our lives would be so much easier if I would just stay home with Xandra and take care of our family. Knowing I would never give up my career, after a few years the beatdown from asking for support wasn't worth the meager help. It was less exhausting to just shut up and parent on my own rather than drag along an unsatisfied partner.

"Let's just hope you have a girl. No White dude can raise a Black son in America."

I nod along with Graham, but for the first time I'm not sure I agree. Raising a child in this country takes more than food and a roof, something Graham never understood. Leo's working hard to grasp what it takes to partner and parent earnestly if not perfectly. Xandra and I are the strong, principled women we are today in spite of Graham, not because of him. I'm starting to believe that my second child will be who they are because of me but also because of their father.

Oh good, here are the girls.

"You sure you girls want Italian? We can go anywhere you want after that Oscar-worthy performance," Graham says, catching my eye in the front seat. We both stifle a giggle.

"Nah. Italian's good, Mr. Clarke. Thanks for inviting me, I'm starving." Dash's manners are spot on. I'll have to remember to tell my father. I turn around to the back seat.

Being a longtime educator, I know my opinion of their performance is less important than hearing from the girls how they feel about their brief time on stage. As Graham's hunting for a parking spot, I find my best casual voice, so the girls don't pick up my "teachable moment" tone. "Dash, this was your first play at Pemberley, too, wasn't it?"

"Yep, Ms. Clarke. Xandra talked me into it. I wasn't too sure about the whole theater crowd at first, you know, if they were my people, but it was actually kind of fun." I catch Xandra giving Dash the side-eye on the word *fun*. "Ummm, not sure I'd do another play, though."

In the dark of night, this car ride is providing clarity. I'm now thinking it wasn't Dash leading Xandra down a contentious road last fall. "What about you, Xandra? How do you think the play went? Or I guess, really, what'd you think of your performance?" Dash and Xandra look at each other knowingly. Busted.

"Dash and I killed it." This time I shoot Graham a surprised look. "But I don't think I'll be doing another play either. You saw it with your own eyes, Mom, it was all White kids up front. Like I told you, Mr. Petrov's a total racist. Dash and I are just able to see what others can't." Not this again. Xandra's selective memory is choosing not to remember that only upperclassmen get lead roles. Information she would have embraced from the get-go if she had shown up at auditions on time and heard the full story directly from Mr. Petrov's mouth. I don't want my child latching on to the convenience of playing victim to any circumstance.

"So, no. I don't think Dash and I will be doing another play." Dash and Xandra fingertip high-five each other, absolute in their assessment of the theater faculty at Pemberley. It's like watching a replay of Marisol and myself twenty-five years ago. Hard-core TLC fans, Marisol assured me we looked good running around Queens, me dressed like a Jamaican T-Boz to Marisol's Lisa "Left Eye" Lopes. It was years before I realized Marisol let us spend far too much time in sports bras baring our bellies. I don't like Xandra dragging Dash into her obstinate thinking.

"This Mr. Petrov accusation, is this something widely known on campus, or is this something only the two of you believe?" I dig, looking directly at Xandra.

"I believe I'm hungry," Dash declares, opening the car door. In addition to the baked ziti I smell, I also smell fierce allegiance to a friend mixed with waning personal conviction.

"Let's hustle, ladies, I'm starving too. We can rake Mr. Petrov's White privilege over the coals once we dig in to our lasagna." Graham hops out of the car. "I'll meet you all in there," he says over his shoulder, jogging to the door of the restaurant to beat out the two other groups heading that way.

"I know you don't believe me, Mom, but I heard what I heard in that class. And what I heard is Mr. Petrov does not like people of color." Xandra huffs as she exits the car.

I wind my way around the few parties that are separating me and the girls from Graham. I want to find out how long the wait is to be seated. Typical Graham, he's already chatting up a couple who seem to be waiting for a table as well. The din of the restaurant is loud, so Graham's leaning over to catch what an attractive petite woman is saying. She looks South Asian, her skin almost as dark as mine. I would have guessed Graham is hitting on her, but then I see the woman's holding hands with a man I think I know but can't quite place. His back's slightly turned to me, so I don't have a full view. A bored looking boy about eight or nine is wedged between them. I can't help but stare at the child. In a month's time, my baby could come out a similar hue.

"There you are, Graham." I pull gently on his jacket sleeve. Even though we've been divorced for years, I can still read all Graham's faces. The look he's wearing screams, *Get a load of this!*

"Nina, this is Dave Petrov, Xandra's theater arts teacher. I was just saying how much we enjoyed tonight's performance." Graham rolls his lips together, indicating he's waiting for me to make the next conversational move.

That's where I know him from: the stage forty-five minutes ago. I size him up and down. He's an inch shorter than me, and I'm in a low wedge. His hair's graying at the temples, and his wireless glasses could use a serious clean. Nothing about this dad dressed in Gap gives off a racist vibe. "Nice to meet you, Dave. Well done this evening." I give Dave a strong handshake to ensure my compliment is sincere. It's not his fault my daughter has no theater chops nor regard for time.

"Thank y—"

"Mom. Mom," Xandra calls.

I release Dave's hand and wave Xandra and Dash over. I'm looking forward to us all being in one big uncomfortable cluster.

"Hello, girls. Glad to see you out celebrating your first Pemberley performance."

"Hi, Mr. Petrov," Dash and Xandra mumble in unison, barely making eye contact.

Mr. Petrov continues addressing the group. "The three of us had a rocky start establishing a mutual understanding of rules and protocols for the theater, but I think we eventually got there. I hope to see you two again for the spring one-acts. Each grade has their own act, so you two have a real shot at a lead role. Quick turnaround, though, auditions are the end of next week." Wow, that's extremely generous of Dave given the performance Xandra put out there.

"That's encouraging, isn't it, girls?" I say, squeezing Xandra tight to my side.

"Sorry, so rude of me, let me introduce you to my family. This is my wife, Rashmi, and our son, Shan. This is Rashmi's third time seeing *Wonderful Town*, but she keeps showing up." Dave puts his pale arm around his brown-skinned wife's waist. I smile.

"Should we all sit down together?" Rashmi offers.

Xandra's flair for the dramatic finally kicks in. "Thank you for the offer, but my mom's really been wanting quality time with me. She hasn't seen me since Christmas." I squeeze Xandra's arms tighter. I sure do want some quality one-on-one time. To the outside world my side-arm squeeze reads profound pride, but between me and my daughter it reads *you better be seeing what I'm seeing.*

"All right then, have a nice evening," Dave says, followed by a warm smile from Rashmi. Shan's been waiting patiently to be released from this grown-up prison so he can have his noodles with butter.

I turn slowly, placing my face inches away from Xandra's. "THAT'S Pemberley's resident racist?" And before Xandra or Dash can defend themselves, Graham and I are chuckling again, at their expense. "Now I know what ears you were using when you heard what you heard, the kind that assumes the worst in White people."

"Fine, but look who's talking," Xandra snaps back just loud enough for me to hear. Wait, what did I do? "Maybe my ears heard wrong, but my eyes are working just fine, and I've been watching you assume the exact same thing of Leo. Give the guy a break already."

TWENTY-SIX

"Nina, you're here late," Pablo says to me, cranking his head far left to look over his shoulder.

"Sure am. I have a long to-do list to get through before I go on maternity leave in three weeks." And work keeps my mind off my analysis paralysis of how I'm going to win Leo back, but I know that's more detail than Pablo's fishing for.

"Aye, family is such a blessing," Pablo gushes, searching to see if my left hand has a ring on it yet. "Are you going to see Mr. Hawkins?"

"Not tonight, Pablo. Our final board meeting before I'm gone is next week," I say, by way of explanation. Pablo looks at me funny. "I'm heading to the gym right now to see if the new audio system is finally installed correctly and working for tomorrow's all-school meeting. An afternoon's task has become a monthlong ordeal. Sometimes the simplest things become the biggest headaches."

"Sí, sí," Pablo agrees. "But Mr. Hawkins and Mr. Jones are in the gym playing basketball with a couple of students. I didn't see them come in, but I could hear them when I was in the locker room cleaning up. I went out through the hallway. I didn't want to interrupt their game."

I play with my watch, hoping to catch the time without seeming rude. 7:40 p.m. There's nothing appropriate about a board member and teacher alone, at night, playing ball with a couple of students. I pray the students' parents are there as referees. I have no time for a scandal.

"Let me get the door for you, Nina." Pablo hurries out in front of me to open the left side of the gym doors. While Pablo throws it open, I'm quick to grab the door from the inside to shut it quietly. I'm accosted by DMX's "X Gon' Give It to Ya" pumping through the gym. Apparently, the new audio system is working just fine. My typical self would start singing along, *first we gonna rock, then we gonna roll,* unencumbered by anyone who might see or hear me, but tonight I don't want my presence noticed right away.

I'm slightly relieved I don't recognize the two boys playing ball with Winn and Jared. By second grade I know every child by name, so I know these teens aren't Royal-Hawkins students. They must be younger brothers or nephews of Jared. While I often refer to Royal-Hawkins as the "second home" of faculty and staff and encourage their families to be part of our collective community, comfortable on campus, late-night basketball might be pushing the family atmosphere I preach too far. Winn should know he's risking our insurance deductible.

Ever since Roan and I went to the middle school basketball game and I complimented Jared's coaching, our relationship, which was cool at best after his lukewarm performance review, has slowly warmed back up. Introducing myself to his family will keep our positive momentum going, so I watch from the boundary lines waiting for a break in play. A quick hello, a little polite conversation, and then I'll be on to the next task on my list.

The two boys running circles around Winn look nothing like Jared. They, in fact, look exactly like each other. I clear my throat loudly, twice. Jared startles seeing me and looks right to Winn for direction. The two young men don't notice play has stopped and take advantage of an easy dunk.

"Nina, good to see you," Winn bellows, jogging over to me slowly, presumably giving himself time to think of what to say.

"What are the four of you doing here?" I inquire, struggling to keep my anger at bay.

"Boys, come on over and meet your new head of school," Winn shouts, ignoring my question. He waves at the two boys whose extreme height is waiting for their weight to catch up. This is exactly as bad as I thought it was.

"Dontrelle and Marcus Burns, meet Ms. Clarke, head of Royal-Hawkins. The school my family built," Winn offers by way of introduction, sending a clear message of who, truly, is in charge here.

"Hey, Ms. Clarke, nice to meet you," the twins say almost in perfect unison, shoulders stooped trying to make their towering frames smaller in my presence. They timidly put their hands out for me to shake. I grab the first one I see and say, "Nice to meet you, too," but I don't address either of them by name because I'm not sure who's who. These boys are identical right down to the peach fuzz sprouting above their crooked smiles.

"Winn and Jared, why don't you get these boys packed up and headed home, it's close to eight." Dontrelle and Marcus look to Winn for a signal to stay or to go.

Ignoring my request, Winn barrels forward. "The boys have applied for high school next year. Just today I sent Roan a personal letter in support of the Burns family. They will be a wonderful addition to the incoming class."

"Jared. The boys." My tone purposely takes on one of a fed-up mother. I know he won't doubt I mean business.

"Winn, you good?" Jared asks, like he's wondering if Winn needs protection from a pissed-off Black woman. He might.

"Sure, sure. I'll catch up with you three in the parking garage."

"And I'll catch up with you tomorrow, Jared," I promise, letting him know tonight my attention may be on Winn, but tomorrow it will be on him.

"Later, Nina." Jared nods. "Guys, grab your gear." Jared points to the boys' bags, reminding the fourteen-year-olds to keep track of their stuff.

"Dontrelle and Marcus, it was lovely to meet you. Please, tell your mother I said hello, and give that gorgeous baby Anton a squeeze."

Winn's head snaps to look at me, his body tensing. That's right, Winn. You may think my mind is elsewhere with a baby on the way, but my mind and my eyes are also on this baby, Royal-Hawkins. I knew it would take time and it would take patience, but I couldn't have orchestrated a better moment to mic drop that I know all about what Winn and Jared have been cooking up, and it smells foul.

~

FROM: Courtney Dunn
DATE: March 26
SUBJECT: check
TO: Nina Morgan Clarke

Dear Nina,

Don't mean to bother you so close to your leaving, you must have a million things to tie up, but I too am running around like crazy before we head to Belize for spring break. Ben will be with his mother, so Daisy and I are headed off for a girls' trip.

I spoke to my accountant yesterday, and he told me the check I wrote for Royal-Hawkins still hasn't been cashed. It needs to be cashed ASAP, unless, of course, you're holding out for more. Name the amount.

Jai,
Courtney

First of all, I'm not leaving, Courtney. I'm going on maternity leave, not fleeing the country. Second, did she just offer me a blank check? Winn must have called her after our run-in last night so now she's on my back to get a check cashed to ensure spots for the twins.

Since ticking things off my to-do list is my immediate priority, avoiding Courtney is no longer an option.

FROM: Nina Morgan Clarke
DATE: March 26
SUBJECT: check
TO: Courtney Dunn

Courtney,

Your offer is overwhelming, but I would like to hear from you, specifically, how you imagine your contribution will be best used. Since time is of the essence, how about we sit down after the board meeting next week and we can discuss?

Yours in Community,
Nina Morgan Clarke
Head of School
Royal-Hawkins School

I don't like to end my workdays on a down note, so I text Marisol for a quick check-in while tidying up my desk. Fitzroy invited Marisol over for dinner, and she jumped on the invitation, that's one less lacrosse game she has to watch. He sold the dinner as his "last hurrah" with his two grown daughters before Xandra's home for spring break, the baby's born, and all talk and attention turn to feeding schedules, diaper changes, and sleep deprivation.

Nina 5:48 PM

Pack snacks in your purse. Other than Christmas Fitzroy's skills in the kitchen have not improved.

Marisol 5:49 PM

I just had a burger. It's my standard backup plan when Fitzroy's cooking. See you in 20.

Sometimes I forget Marisol's known my father almost as long as I have.

I arrive home well before dinner with Dad and Marisol and settle on my bed to book Xandra's plane ticket for spring break. I really want some fizzy water from the fridge, but I'm not ready to witness the mess I'll be cleaning up after Fitzroy's attempt at Celia's pot roast. He should have laid that recipe to rest along with my mother. Instead, our delicious Sunday night childhood memory of meat falling off the bone will be charred, literally. On my nightstand is a lukewarm half glass of water from last night. It'll have to do. I chug it and return to my laptop.

Ring.

It's Roan. In his hierarchy of communication, first comes text, next comes another text with exclamation points, then an email, and then a call as a last resort. Roan's phone phobia is real.

"Well, this is a surprise."

"Hello to you, too, lady. Check your email."

Click.

The subject reads, *Yeah, no.*

Roan has begged, cajoled, and I don't really want to know what else to get the twins' current school to release their full transcripts and state-mandated test scores. Now Roan has released them to me. I read through every page once, twice, a third time not to miss one word, number, or grade. I toggle over to their online applications to reread the essays Winn surely wrote for them. I don't know if I was expecting to see something vastly different from the school than what Carmel had prepped me for, or I was hoping Winn's essays had miraculously changed for the better, but the expected truth of Dontrelle's and Marcus's qualifications for Royal-Hawkins still crushes me. I blow out a large breath, which for me only goes about boob deep, stopped short by the baby's feet tap dancing on my rib cage. I pick up my phone to text Roan.

Nina 6:12 PM

Yeah, no.

Roan 6:12 PM

I know.

At the dinner table, Marisol's done an excellent job pushing her mushy carrots and undercooked potatoes around her plate to look like she's enjoyed much of Fitzroy's meal while fueled by her burger appetizer. I'm still starving and wishing it were Christmas morning, the only meal Dad can handle.

"I have something I'd like to share with you girls," Fitzroy starts in, palms firmly planted on the table. Marisol kicks me. We haven't been *girls* in a quarter century.

"You going to shake things up a bit and go on a singles cruise? *Papi*, you've been taking good care of yourself. You shouldn't keep all that on lockdown," Marisol launches in, circling her finger at my dad.

Please, my dad on a singles cruise? I can hear my mother laughing in heaven.

"Sit on those lips, Chaco Taco, you talk too much." I giggle like the girl Dad claims I am. "I invited you here tonight because I want you, too, to hear what I'm about to tell Nina. She may need your support." Marisol's face drops, and we look right to each other with the same thought, *cancer*.

"You two know it was tough on me when Celia died." My father takes a linen handkerchief that used to be my mother's out of his pocket and dabs at the corners of his eyes. Mine well up, too, seeing her initials embroidered in blue. "But the past year I've really been enjoying my time in Pasadena, set up a nice routine for myself here."

"It shows, Fitzroy. Happiness is the best treatment money can't buy," Marisol chimes in on a subject she knows best, looking your best. It only took her thirty seconds to break my father's gag order.

"Says the person hawking expensive treatments and potions to women all over Los Angeles," Dad jokes back, placing one hand on top of Marisol's and squeezing.

"Though I want to, I'm going to avoid responding to that comment for the bigger picture here. What gives, Fitzroy? What's got you all high on life?"

Dad straightens up in his seat. One of his favorite childhood stories was when he crushed the competition in the eight-hundred-meter race at the all-island high school track championships. Maybe Dad's been doing more than walking on a treadmill and waxing philosophical with his friends at the Y. Maybe he's been training with a master's track team and has his first competition coming up. Oh, I hope it's over Xandra's spring break, it would be so fun if we could all go together. I'm definitely getting shirts made. FITZROY'S FEET FLEET.

"I'm moving to Pasadena. My things will be arriving here in a few weeks," Dad announces.

Whoa, whoa, whoa! In my mind I just committed to an afternoon at the track cheering on my father, not seventy years of life arriving at my front doorstep the same time as a baby. I've meant it every time I've invited my father to move out here, but he's picked a hell of a time to finally agree. I know I'm not ready to have a newborn, Xandra, AND my dad all in my house. Four people under my roof and I'm still the only one who cooks. Or cooks well.

"And I'm getting married."

"*AY, DIOS MÍO!!*" Marisol shouts.

"TO WHO?!" I yelp in shock. The man eats my food, works in the garden, goes to the Y, and plays endless dominoes. I've never once seen him with a woman outside the family since Mom died. This makes no sense.

"Sex!" Marisol snaps her fingers. "That's why you look so good. I knew it! I didn't want to say it out loud, but I knew it!"

I cover my eyes. I would have preferred to start with, oh I don't know, maybe the name of my new mom.

I gather up my head of school voice to gain control of this meeting and launch into a fact-finding mission about my dad's, uh, love life. "Before we get to who this woman is, can we start with when you've been going on dates? I've never once seen you on your way out to dinner."

"Nina, before this past year, have you ever once heard of me playing dominoes?"

I quickly scan my memory.

"Ummm, noooo. I guess I just assumed dominoes is the bingo equivalent for Black men of a certain age."

"Have you ever seen me play dominoes at home, or any other game for that matter?"

I'm stunned into momentary silence by the scheming of the most honest man I know.

"No." Dad never even liked playing Monopoly with me and Clive when we were kids, so his recent devotion to dominoes should have caught my attention.

"You dirty dog, Fitzroy, you've been using outings with the boys to front your romantic life! Nina, you getting all this?" Marisol pushes, making sure we're both following along word for word.

"Okay, so you're not actually an old-school gamer. Anything else you've been holding out on me? Like, oh, I don't know, you've never stepped foot on a treadmill, and I've been paying your Y membership for no good reason?" I demand, though I'm afraid of the answer.

"The Y is what got me in shape and feeling confident to start dating. I promise, your old man getting remarried is all I have for one evening.

Well, that and I've invited my fiancée over for coffee and dessert. She'll be here in about ten minutes."

"This night just keeps getting better and better," Marisol gushes. "What's her name, Fitzroy? And do we have time to do a quick Google search?" Marisol checks her watch.

This woman's stepping foot in my house now?

"Her name's KayCee Lang, and she owns a nail salon not too far from here."

"HA! So, you have been cheating on me with another salon owner. Nina called it back in the fall, but I didn't believe you would ever do me like that," Marisol accuses, getting up to envelop Fitzroy in a giant hug. "But I'll let it pass this time. Congrats, *papi*, I couldn't be happier for you."

I want to be happy for my dad, too, I do, but first I need to wipe off the shock and swipe on some lipstick before the second love of my dad's life comes walking through my front door.

~

There were many things I may have expected when my father introduced me and Marisol to his fiancée, but KayCee being Asian and twenty years his junior were not two of them. Church going, of course. Age appropriate, I would assume. Black, no doubt in my mind. Turns out Dad really enjoys the pastor at KayCee's church, but I misread the rest.

With Marisol on her way home to relieve Spanny and wrangle her boys into bed, Dad and I have been doing dishes in silence. It's been a newsworthy evening, and we both need a moment to process. Or I need the moment.

"I want you to know, I've had a lot of late-night conversations with your mother about me, ummm, moving on."

"You have, huh? I imagine it's pretty easy to convince a dead woman to see your side of things." Dad grins knowingly at my assessment of his talks with Mom.

"You know, when KayCee came to visit me in Queens, the pilot light on the stove went out for the first time in decades. I think it was your mother's way of saying she was fine with me being with a new lady friend, just not in her house. That's when I realized it was time for me to move."

"Obviously. Mom's not letting another woman walk her worn path." The groove in the floorboards between the kitchen sink and the stove hold most of my childhood memories.

"I found it hard to convince myself that it was okay to see someone else. I finally realized that marrying KayCee doesn't mean I love your mother any less." Dad gives me an approving nod at how I'm stacking the plates into the dishwasher. We both believe a loading strategy is the key to domestic bliss.

"I'm working on being happy for you, Dad, I promise I am, it's just KayCee isn't exactly your type." Truthfully, I had never considered what my dad's type may be, but I couldn't imagine it would veer far from Jamaican.

"My type? How do you figure what my type is?"

"You know, Mom and Angela Bassett." My mom knew Fitzroy Morgan would be loyal to her until the end of time, unless, of course, Angela Bassett called. Then, bye-bye.

"Ah, you mean Black."

I nod yes.

Dad wipes his hands on the last clean kitchen towel and leans against the refrigerator. "Is that what you think? That I should only be attracted to a Black woman, want to marry a Black woman?" I shudder inside my cardigan at my father's mention of sexual attraction. "Is that what you think I expect of you, too? Or more importantly, is that what you expect of yourself?"

"Certainly, makes life a lot easier."

"Perhaps. Though you have personal experience that tells us otherwise."

"DAD!" I don't need this conversation about his love life shining a spotlight on mine.

"Okay, okay, but if your mother and I failed at expressing to you and your brother that we will embrace whoever you choose to love if they choose to love and respect you back, then we failed as parents."

"Dad, please, you didn't fail us as parents," I say, grabbing the towel from my father to dry my own hands.

"Well, maybe not, but it sounds like we should have been more plainspoken on our thoughts about love. I suppose, if you grow up with parents of the same race who mostly socialized with Black folks and attended an all-Black church, you're going to assume some things about what we expect of you as an adult. But that's not the truth, Nina. Not at all. Is that why you're not tight with Leo anymore, because he's not Black?"

I can feel my dad hurting at the idea that his lack of parental guidance has resulted in my lack of a partner. Far from it, but he has hit on a big piece of what's held me back. "It's a bit more complicated than that. But yeah, there's some truth there."

"So uncomplicate it for me." Like always, nothing's convoluted in Fitzroy's world.

"It's one thing to date, or I guess in your case, marry a person from another race, but raising a baby with them, particularly when that baby is going to be Black, that's a whole other challenge. Growing up in Omaha, living in Silver Lake, working at a corporate law firm, not only is Leo White, his entire life is White. ALL White, all the time."

"Except when he's with you. With us."

And his new parenting buddies, I have to admit to myself. Leo's put in the effort to diversify his world without direction from me.

Here it is. "I'm struggling to see how a White man can successfully raise a Black child." That's as plainly as I can put it for Fitzroy.

"He's going to raise that child like all parents do, with lots of love, lots of mistakes, and help from friends and family. What a child needs most from a parent is nurturing, not matching skin color." An easy claim from a man whose children happen to be his spitting image. "This is a lot for you to be carrying. Is that all or do you have more, Nina?"

"You ever wonder if being with KayCee, going to her church, being around her friends and family will . . ." I don't want to be the wet blanket on Dad's second chance at love.

"Go on," Fitzroy pushes, not letting me off the hook.

Here goes. "You think marrying KayCee will make you less Black?" There it is. Under it all, living in Pasadena, fighting to be the head of Royal-Hawkins, sending Xandra to boarding school, choosing to have a mixed-race baby, being with Leo, becoming part of his family, this is the question that's been haunting me, and I can't find any peace with it.

"Ah, you're afraid of losing your own Blackness. Is that it?"

Fitzroy has boiled my greatest fear down to one simple sentence. "That's it," I admit.

"Nina, baby, how Black you are, whatever that even means, is determined solely by the confidence you carry in your head and in your heart. How I think about being Black as a Jamaican immigrant in this country is very different from how you think about it as a first-generation American, and certainly miles away from how Xandra thinks about being Black. We are all Black in our own distinct ways.

"Your Blackness is not determined by where you work, the profession you choose, or who you love. The only person who can take away any feeling of who you are is you." Fitzroy wraps me in a big hug. "Did you hear me? Only you. And if anyone tries, you tell them to come talk to me."

"Uh-huh. I will, Dad, thanks." My father always knows how to make me feel like his little girl. I reach over to shut the dishwasher, marking the end of our conversation. I'm not sure I'm buying Fitzroy's argument, which conveniently justifies his late-in-life romance, but I love that he still wants to protect me.

"Don't 'uh-huh' me. Believe me. And don't go laying this burden on Leo, Nina. This is not about him. This is about you," Dad lectures, following behind me as I turn off the kitchen lights. "Is feeling more Black worth feeling less happy?"

TWENTY-SEVEN

Marisol 5:02 PM

Did you find it?

Nina 5:03 PM

Leo's in the shower, I'm looking right now. I want it bad
Marisol.

Marisol 5:03 PM

I know, I know sis, but don't get caught--that
would be so cringe. Besides, what are you going to do if you find it?

Nina 5:04 PM

I don't know I hadn't thought that far but stop texting
me you're making me nervous and I'm on a mission.

"What are you doing?" Shit. Leo showered too fast. My hands are deep
into his desk drawers.

"Looking for a pen. I have a thought I need to jot down before I
lose it," I stammer. It's as good an excuse as I can come up with. How

many places can a man stash a rejected engagement ring? As a species they aren't that clever. I WANT MY RING BACK.

"Here's a pen and Post-it." Leo hands the items to me from his open work bag on the bed. Crap, now I have to pretend to write something down.

Sourdough bread

Sharp cheddar

Salted butter

I want a grilled cheese sandwich.

"Thanks for agreeing to go on the hospital tour with me. Don't want to be pegged as the perverted single guy with a fetish for pregnant women." Leo holds up a pink button-down shirt followed by a blue pullover. Then the pink again. "Which shirt do you think the maternity nurses will like better?" Leo asks, a little flirty. He sounds like a woman heading out to meet a promising first date. I point to the pullover, the blue pairs nicely with his dark hair. The more we are in the good graces of the nurses, the more quickly I'll get ice chips when I'm in the throes of hell known as the wonder of childbirth.

"How is it you're able to make this tour? Legal hours don't bill themselves."

"For twenty years my life has been dictated by billable hours, and now I'm cutting back. Now I'm ready for it to be run by that little dictator," Leo says excitedly, circling his index finger at my stomach.

It hits me that Xandra called it. While she spent this year hearing Mr. Petrov with biased ears, I, too, may have had selective hearing when it comes to Leo and his commitment to this baby. The nursery in Omaha, coming to every doctor's appointment with me, the Black to Basics parenting class, and now this; Leo's been all in on being a parenting team from the get-go, and I'm the one who's been pushing him and his family out.

"Let's see, I have the map of the hospital pulled up on my phone. Turns out there's a north and south emergency room entrance. Who knew? I've got a water bottle. I'm still a little dehydrated from my ride with T. J. this afternoon, and I've got my baby mama too." Stifling a laugh, I look at Leo. "It's okay. The guys in my parenting group said I can say 'baby mama.' Apparently, it's pretty universal now, so I'm not culturally appropriating anything." I let out a howl. Leo's enthusiasm for our labor day dry run is contagious. Given Marisol's unsolicited opinions on my stupidity and Leo's commitment, I'm now feeling ready to stand next to him as a parental unit. I don't yet have the right words to articulate my erratic behavior and debilitating doubts the past couple of months, but manic ring hunting aside, I know I owe Leo an explanation. Calming down, I recognize tonight isn't about me; it's dedicated to the anticipation of our baby's birth day, and I don't want to steal the spotlight.

"So, I've got something big for you," I tease, wondering if the ring is under the mattress I'm sitting on, or maybe in one of the shoeboxes I spy at the top of Leo's closet. Leo raises his eyebrows at me over the slug of water he's pulling from his bottle. It's hard to imagine anything bigger than my belly.

"Fitzroy's getting married."

"*Pffft!*" Leo spits water all over his rug.

"My reaction exactly. Turns out he's been cheating on Marisol with KayCee Lang from KayCee's Nails down the street from my house."

"How's Marisol taking the news?"

"Let's just say she won't be giving Fitzroy any more free manicures, but she's been thinking he's market ready for quite some time. We had dessert with KayCee, and Marisol gave her the double thumbs-up. I was the odd one out who thought my dad had shut down that business for good."

"You okay with it?" Leo asks with concern, bending into his closet to hunt for shoes with just the right tread for hospital-grade linoleum.

"Not going to lie, it was a shock. I always thought my mom would be his one and only. But turns out all this time when I thought he was playing dominoes, he was playing house." I pause to check in with myself. Am I really okay with my father remarrying, or am I programmed to spew a neutral party line? "But yeah, I think I'm happy for him. She keeps him active. The more active he is, the less time he's riding my couch."

"He got himself a live wire?"

"He got himself a trophy wife. She's closer to my age than his."

"Go, Fitzroy. Glad someone gets to play house." I hear Leo mumble into his closet, unsure if that dig was meant for my ears.

I choose to ignore the comment to keep our date on an upbeat trajectory. Look at me, I'm acting more like an evolved one half of a couple. I know tonight marks a shift in our relationship, even if Leo's not in on the good news yet.

The bathroom, I bet the ring's in a drawer in the bathroom! Was it in a navy or dark-green velvet box? Maybe black. I can't remember. We're on the verge of running late, so I'm not going to be able to get in there and hunt around, plus Leo's already turned out the light and shut the door.

"Last chance to bail, Nina. I know you've already done this, and honestly, I'm pretty comfortable going alone," Leo says, grabbing his jacket and heading out of his bedroom.

"I'm not bailing this time, Leo. Promise."

⌒

My final board meeting of my first year as the first Black female head of school at Royal-Hawkins is in thirty minutes, and my baby has decided to head bump my bladder to celebrate. Or maybe that's my kidneys, I don't know, but the pulled pork sandwich I ate has this kid worked up.

Nina 5:30 pm

Can't wait to spend the week with you! Come straight out door 18 at United baggage claim and I'll be waiting. I have loads of grandma's jerk chicken ready.

After the board meeting, I have a quick one-on-one planned with Courtney, and then I'm driving to LAX to pick Xandra up for her spring break. The timing couldn't be better. This baby's packed tight as a drum for three more weeks, so I can focus all my attention on Xandra while she's home. She said she wanted to be here for the birth, but given the number of changes she's been subjected to on the home front and the growing pains she's had at school this year, I think some time to focus on just Xandra before the baby comes will be best. While I'm at work, Xandra's offered to help Fitzroy shop for a wedding suit and a storage unit. Afternoons and evenings will be for the two of us. Once the baby comes, our little family dynamic of two will shift forever, and that scares the hell out of me. I want Xandra to go back to school knowing her mother loves her completely and that will never change. My guess is that can be achieved with home-cooked meals, sleeping in, full ownership over the remote, and shopping for clothes I hate.

My communications with Winn since our evening of discovery in the gym have been met with cagey one-word responses. I'm not sure he'll even show tonight. I called board vice chairwoman Kym Lee this afternoon to give her a heads-up that she may be asked to facilitate the meeting in case of Winn's absence. We have a long agenda to get through, and I can't waste a moment on heads swiveling around the room searching for our frivolous board chair.

A ripple waves across my low belly. This baby really doesn't like BBQ sauce.

With Xandra good on directions, my fingers are perched over my keyboard but are resistant to move. My brain doesn't know what it wants my fingers to type, given this is the hardest email I have ever had to write. How will I be able to express myself gracefully and with certainty? I have no doubt Marcus and Dontrelle Burns are aspiring young men with a great talent for basketball, but I cannot, in good conscience, accept them into Royal-Hawkins based on standards that vary drastically from the ones five hundred other students have been judged by. If a White student struggles in school, empathy abounds and the community rallies around them with additional services. If a Black student struggles, complaints about diversity recruitment and drained financial resources tend to emerge. It's an invisible double standard that I see all too often and planned to address as I gain my footing as head of school. I just didn't expect to wage that war in my first year, and I will not put the Burns twins in this predicament knowing the full scope of their academic and application history. And I will not contend with defending the academic standards of Royal-Hawkins as the population of our school grows more and more diverse.

FROM: Nina Morgan Clarke
DATE: April 2
SUBJECT: Admission to Royal-Hawkins School
TO: Carmel Burns

Dear Carmel,

I hope you and the family are doing well. Tonight, admission decisions for the Royal-Hawkins School will be released via an email from WeeScholars. Roan and I enjoyed our time in your home, and I don't know if the boys shared with you, but I got to meet Dontrelle and Marcus the other night in the Royal-Hawkins gym. I can tell you have done a wonderful job raising them.

This year we had a record number of applications for the freshman class. As much as I wish there were a spot at Royal-Hawkins for every deserving child and family, we do have to make difficult decisions based on academic readiness and class composition to balance out gender, race, religion, family structure, and personalities. At this moment in time, we believe Dontrelle and Marcus would not be best served by Royal-Hawkins.

There are many good schools in Los Angeles County, and I know with your strong hand Dontrelle and Marcus will thrive wherever they attend.

Best wishes to you all,
Nina Morgan Clarke
Head of School
Royal-Hawkins School

Right decisions are often the hardest decisions. Fitzroy's voice rings through my head as I agonize over every single word of the email. I still remember the elation on my mother's face when she opened Clive's acceptance letter to Collegiate and later mine to Spence. In her mind, she had manifested the best possible future for her children, one she never could have imagined for herself or for my father. Decades later, I don't want to imagine the disappointment on Carmel's face when she clicks open this email from me.

I've never written an admissions email, that's Roan's job. But I feel like I owe one to Carmel on behalf of the two Royal-Hawkins buffoons who inserted themselves in her family's future. As head of school, I have to take the hit for their unethical behavior. I reread and tweak the email once, twice, five times, and then I put it in my draft box. I'll let it sit and give it one more read after the board meeting. Then I'll click "Send."

I apply my Night on Fire lipstick and clip my braids together behind my neck. I smooth my arms and hands with shea butter and make sure my B girls turned DD ladies are immovable in my dress. I squeeze my feet back into my heeled booties, barely getting the zipper up and over my swollen ankles. For comfort, flats would be preferable, but tonight I need to leave the board with the indelible memory of a highly capable woman in command of Royal-Hawkins before I waddle out the door for four months of family leave.

"Nina, Mr. Hawkins is already in there," Pablo informs me under his breath, tilting his head east. First surprise of the evening, and I've barely reached the conference room. I peek through the small window in the door and then take a few steps back. Winn's talking on the phone, dressed in a charcoal-gray suit. Seems he got the power dress memo too. I clear a tickle of self-doubt in my throat.

"Would you like some water?"

"Thank you, Pablo, but it looks like Mimi has a couple of pitchers and plenty of glasses out on the tables. I'll grab one when I go in."

"You got a good poem or something?" Pablo asks, though he knows the answer.

"We have a lot to accomplish tonight, so I'm going with a favorite quote." I've been holding on to this one since I was appointed Royal-Hawkins's fourteenth head of school. I knew a meeting toward the end of my first year would be the appropriate time to share. I hope Maya Angelou and my mother are up there listening. Together.

"Pablo my man, how you doing?" Jared blows into our conversation, a muscular hurricane, and offers Pablo a friendly fist bump. "Hey, Nina. Winn invited me to check out my first board meeting tonight." While Winn's been a champion at avoiding me, Jared read the tense gym atmosphere right last week. And it got him scared. This week he's been full of talk about teaching primary source writing with his sixth graders, and he even extended an invitation to me to visit his classroom and serve as the judge for his eighth grade mock debate.

"When your kid's old enough, I'll teach it to play hoops," Jared offers, shooting an imaginary basket toward the end of the hallway.

I wince. Oof, another kick. "Or you know, history," Jared quickly amends, thinking my wince was directed at his talk of basketball.

"Nina, you're looking well," Courtney offers in a nervous twitter, walking up to me as Pablo and Jared have moved on to discuss what Pablo refers to as "real *fútbol.*" Why is pregnancy an invitation to anyone and everyone to comment on your fitness for public viewing? I'm about to repay Courtney the shallow compliment but stop short. She does not look well at all, particularly for a woman with unlimited means for personal upkeep. Courtney's hair is revealing more gray than blonde at the roots. Bloodshot eyes hide below puffy, purplish lids, and despite the venti coffee she's toting, Courtney's grayish skin hints at an exhausted woman. Even her shirt is misbuttoned, the expensive collar sagging left.

I gently grab Courtney by the elbow and steer her away from the stream of board members sauntering into the conference room. I'm pretty sure no life coach wants to be viewed as unhinged. "Are you okay?" I ask quietly, tucking my head close to her ear.

"Of course, I am," Courtney insists, shaking her head like she's waking herself up out of a haze. "A poor night's sleep is all. Where will you and Winn be sitting for tonight's meeting?" Courtney inquires, smoothing her bangs to the side of her forehead.

"Same as always, in front of the SMART Board."

"Wonderful. I'll seat myself directly across from you two," Courtney says, removing my concerned hand from her elbow and joining the side of Anders Nilsson heading into the meeting. I'm left standing alone, utterly confused, wondering, Am I walking into a firing squad?

Seated, I close my eyes, putting my hand over my racing heart. One, two, three full breaths. I open my eyes. I look to my left and Winn gives me a tight grin, but none of the charming chatter he's famous for.

"Nice to see you, Winn," I say, my head of school tone spot-on.

Ignoring my acknowledgment, Winn cocks his head to his left. "Nice to see Jared take an interest in the future of the school, don't you think?"

Hmm, is it nice? Curious for sure. And a little concerning since he happens to be here at Winn's invitation on the one meeting a year when we talk about admissions. But nice, no.

Winn here early and dressed to intimidate, Jared joining the meeting, and Courtney eyeing the three of us from across the table like a hawk hunting prey, is unnerving. Something's up. Or more accurately, something's teed up to take me by surprise, I can feel it.

Marisol's the keynote speaker at a spa directors conference in Phoenix, otherwise I'd text her for backup support. Instead, I'm going to have to muster every ounce of conviction necessary all on my own. God, I think I need to pee again.

"What's nice is seeing Jared refocused on his classroom given the end of basketball season. That's definitely nice," I respond self-assuredly, holding Winn's gaze. I will not be the first to look away.

I run my hands over my belly, willing this baby not to give me a solid corner kick to the lower abdomen during my recitation. I clear my throat, stand, and stare out over a conference room full of people who look eager to get going on the agenda and then get on with their dinner plans. I drop into my lowest vocal register to deliver Dr. Angelou's words.

> "We delight in the beauty
> of the butterfly . . ."

"Nina, we have a packed agenda, and I for one want to get to the meat of the evening. How about we just get a move on," Winn interrupts me.

I press my palms together to keep myself from slapping him silly. *As a Black, first-generation female, I've gone through a lot to get myself here, Winn Hawkins. I've worked twice as hard as most to prove, at every juncture of my journey, I have at least half a reason to be in a room filled with the likes of people like you. You WILL NOT dismiss my moment.* I can't say out loud what I'm thinking, so instead I start again from the top.

"We delight in the beauty
of the butterfly, but rarely
admit the changes it has
gone through to achieve
that beauty."

Without looking, I know Winn's leg's rapidly jiggling, the energy radiating off him tense.

As I finish the quote, I turn to Winn with a smile dripping with sincerity that reads, *no one, not even you, interrupts me*, and then I introduce our guest presenter for the evening, Director of Admissions Roan Dawson.

Tonight, Roan will be offering a PowerPoint deck analyzing admissions numbers over the past five years and growth projection for the next three. This dog and pony show is shared with the board of trustees every April. Roan's been agitating over his presentation ensemble for weeks. He's hoping a glam slam will deflect from his fear of public speaking.

I move to sit back down and wince as a jolt of pain hits my pelvis. I clench down hard on my teeth. Roan's eyes register that something more than a baby with a distaste for pulled pork is going on and opens his mouth to speak. I ever so perceptibly shake my head no. With concern, Roan makes his way to the front of the room, and I'm given ten to fifteen minutes to contemplate how I'm going to make it through the rest of this meeting.

Roan's first slide goes up on the SMART Board. "I'm happy to report we're continuing our three-year upward trend of about two percent increase in completed application submissions year over year." As Roan continues on with statistics I've already committed to memory, I slide my phone off the table into my lap. With Marisol out of town and Fitzroy without a car, I text my next *in case of emergency* as coolly as I can, not wanting to sound any alarm bells quite yet.

Nina 6:48 PM

Hey Leo, I'm tied up at a board meeting and Marisol's OOT. A little desperate here, any chance you can pick Xandra up at the airport for me? Her flight lands at 8:00 p.m.

Leo 6:48 PM

Sure. You okay?

"Of the five hundred and two total applicants this year, Nina and I are excited to share with you that thirty-six percent identify as persons of color, up from thirty-two percent last year," Roan continues, glancing over at me every third second. I lie and give him an okay with my left hand, my right cradling my belly. Winn sits tall in his chair. I know he's thinking his recruits are certainly part of these improved numbers.

My breath grows shallow. Why didn't I revisit the birthing classes with Leo when he asked? Maybe I don't actually remember how this goes after all these years.

Nina 6:50 PM

All good, just miscalculated timing of things tonight. Text me when you have my girl.

No need to send Leo into any type of new dad frenzy until I know my first baby's taken care of. I put my phone back onto the table and pour myself some more water. Roan is killing it at his presentation, and I thank the Lord that all eyes are on his slides.

Winn raises his hand, index finger up, but doesn't wait to be called on. "Roan, let's move to the details of next year's acceptances. I'm assuming Dontrelle and Marcus Burns are members of the incoming freshman class?"

Jared snaps his attention to Roan, interested in the meeting for the first time since I called it to order.

TWENTY-EIGHT

Save me! pleads Roan's face. Damn, I have to haul myself up out of this chair and once and for all set Winn and Jared straight, publicly. I have limited time left to leave a lasting leadership impression, so it's now or never. My water didn't break with Xandra, so I cross my legs and hope this baby is not planning a slip-and-slide entrance into the world. I hold my breath during a contraction and slowly rise.

"The specifics of acceptances are confidential until each family has been informed of their status. Emails will be released to all families directly following this meeting." I sweep my eyes around the room to make sure every board member is picking up what I'm putting down: the policy is acceptances to Royal-Hawkins are none of the trustees' business. "And even after that, it's up to each family to share their outcome or not. Roan and I do not share this information," I conclude, forcing eye contact with Winn, then Jared, and lastly catching Courtney's darting eyes. Her skin's gone from a gray pallor to ghostly white and shiny with sweat. Is she sensing what's going on with me and sympathy stressing, or is she losing it over not getting her way with the Royal-Hawkins athletics department?

"I only want to know about two students who will make a significant impact on the school. I don't think that's asking too much," Winn insists, his strained calm giving way to heightened irritation.

"And what impact might that be, Winn?" I ask point-blank. I want to force Winn's ego to reveal to the entire board what he's been up to the past couple of months.

"Nina, it's no skin off your back to admit these boys into the school for a couple of years, particularly at my asking. As well, I don't think anyone here needs a reminder that I'm the only Hawkins in the room. There would be no school, there would be no you," Winn growls at me, "without me and my family." In mansplaining the school history that I'm intimately familiar with, Winn has managed to evade my question. "At the end of junior year, if Dontrelle and Marcus aren't cutting it in school, we'll send them back to their local high school, so their GPAs don't ruin the class average, nor does their academic performance screw with our top-tier college acceptances. With my plan, for the first time ever, Royal-Hawkins will become an athletic powerhouse with zero impact on our excellent college acceptance rate."

I don't acknowledge Winn Hawkins's unimaginable words of Olympic-level privilege. While Winn's leaning back in his chair, wholly satisfied with his strategy to turn Royal-Hawkins into a sports mecca and trash Dontrelle's and Marcus's lives, I lean forward to grab Jared's attention. As the only two Black people in the room, I know his blood's boiling as furiously as mine. I also know there's no way Jared knew this was Winn's plan for the twins and went along with it. This is where, our history aside, the brotha and sista in the room will come out swinging. I arch my right eyebrow at Jared to say, *Are you taking down this clown, or am I?* Jared points at himself to signal he's got this.

I lob Jared an easy question so he can engage his Harvard-educated smooth-talking skills and put Winn in his place. "Jared, what do you think of Winn's plan for Dontrelle and Marcus Burns?" I barely get *Burns* out before another contraction wallops me. I grip the edge of the table and slow moan with my lips sealed shut to not give myself away. To my best guess the contractions are now about eight minutes apart, but they're growing longer and harder to mask. I have about two more contractions in me, three max, before I'm going to be doubled over in pain.

"Winn's plan is how I got to Harvard. I gave him the idea," Jared shares with the room, rubbing his hands together and revving up to tell a riveting tale.

I'm sure I heard Jared wrong, as his answer came in the middle of a contraction. Active listening and unimaginable pain do not go hand in hand.

"Can you repeat that, Jared?" I'm back to a clear head and slower breathing so I can concentrate on his every word.

"The plan for Dontrelle and Marcus was mine. It worked for me exactly ten years ago."

WOW. So, I did hear correctly.

"A kid in my youth basketball league, his parents applied him to Chester Hill Academy. I had never heard of it, but his dad was an alumnus of the school, a huge donor, still is in fact, and he wanted me to come coach there when I graduated from Harvard. I knew I wanted to be here, though," Jared reassures, so his board and his boss don't think he's defecting.

"Anyway, this kid's dad told the Chester Hill basketball coach about me, and BOOM I was in." Jared has the rapt attention of every Royal-Hawkins board member, including me. "Of course, I went. My local high school was rough, and my parents wanted me out by any means possible." All parental heads around the room bob up and down in agreement.

"At Chester Hill, I had to study HARD to even hang in the lower middle of the class, but people helped me out because I was bringing in the wins on the basketball court. Eventually, I learned how to study right and began to take pride in myself as a student."

I think about my email to Carmel in my draft box. Is Jared's story rocking my conviction?

"Chester Hill prided itself on being an Ivy feeder school. When the boys in my class talked about college, they might as well have been speaking another language. I had never heard of most of the schools. But I had heard of Harvard, and after three years of seeing how the boys in my class lived, Harvard was where I knew I wanted to go. It was clear there was no way I could compete with the two dozen or so in my class who would be applying there. The school knew it, too, and they didn't want to mess with their acceptance stats, so at the end of my junior year they kicked me out on some sort of trumped-up academic explanation, and I went back to my local high school."

I can't believe that during Jared's interview process, and through his first year of teaching, I never heard this story. "You must have been devastated, Jared. Your parents, too," I react. This kind of heartbreak is exactly what I do not want our school to be responsible for heaping on the Burns family doorstep in three years. I notice Courtney perched on the edge of her chair, staring wildly at Winn, veins popping out of her neck. From the looks of her, I suspect this plan wasn't shared before she made her sizable contribution. Now, more than ever, I'm pleased I was judicious and did not cash in on Courtney's generosity.

"Nah, I wasn't devastated. Since I couldn't compete with the kids at Chester to get into Harvard, I figured I might have a shot from my local high school. Before me no one had gone to Harvard from there, ever. In my neighborhood school, I was an exceptional student and had no competition. Elite colleges love plucking kids of color out of what they think are 'difficult situations.' They think they have discovered diamonds in the rough. Only thing is, the joke was on Harvard—I didn't have a difficult situation. I had a great family, grew up in a neighborhood I loved, got a topnotch education for three years at Chester Hill, and won a string of basketball championships. The math program at Chester Hill taught me how to play the numbers game, and that's exactly what I did to get myself into Harvard. Graduating from my local high school was the right gamble, one that clearly paid off because it all worked out for me in the end. I'm living proof it could work out the same for Dontrelle and Marcus." Jared bangs the table with his fists, marking the end of his education journey. Winn gives Jared a hearty man slap to his back in joint victory.

"So, from what I just heard, Winn, this is the year you've success-fully screwed over not one family but two? And in my case I mean it literally!" Courtney erupts, her shrill scream reaching every corner of the conference room, if not the school. Jaws drop and ears are covered, but no one looks more stunned by Courtney's accusation than Winn Hawkins. He's vigorously shaking his head *NO, NO, NO* at Courtney. Courtney meets his every head shake with an aggressive *YES, YES, YES*.

"What's wrong, Winn? Did you really think I wouldn't find out about you and Geoff? You think you're that smart? That sneaky? The only reason I've feigned interest in your ridiculous sports charade is so I could sniff out what I suspected was your ongoing foul behavior as chair of the board. I always knew you were a slimy cheat, Winn, I did. I could smell it a mile away. I just never in a million years would have guessed my husband was a cheat too. Or had such poor taste."

I don't know which I'm more surprised by, the revelation unwind-ing in my conference room or the fact that Courtney and I actually have something in common—we have both always thought something was rank about Winn Hawkins.

"I knew I saw Winn at the Under Carriage, I knew it!" Roan explodes, dropping his laser pointer, thrilled to be in the know. "Remember, Nina, back in September, I told you I saw him there!" Roan smacks his hands together, giving himself his own congratulatory high five.

To hide the look of shock on my face, I reach over to pick up the dropped laser pointer, and another contraction hits. I keep my head between my knees and start to pant quickly and shallowly. The contrac-tions are definitely closer and more intense. I need to get to the hospital fast but without anyone suspecting what's going on. I have no idea how I'm going to pull that off without adding to the chaos unfolding in this meeting.

Roan squats down to my eye level. "Nina, what's going on?" I put my hand on his shoulder and squeeze hard, I can't talk. Roan takes my inflicting hurt on him like a man who cries at a hangnail. "Ouch, Nina, please get your fingernails out of my clavicle, no need for both of us to be in pain," Roan whimpers, more than whispers. "What should I do? What do you want me to do?"

My breathing slows down as Roan begins to panic. "Give me five minutes to land this plane, then get me to the hospital."

"Nina, you picked the worst time to have a baby. After a month of wallowing in my broken engagement, today is day two of Roan Redux. I walked to school today, got in seven thousand, four hundred steps by eight a.m." Roan peels back his shirt cuff to show me his Fitbit. "I met a cute guy at the corner of Lake and Del Mar." I give Roan as loving of an *I DON'T CARE* look as I can muster. "I'm going to let that snarl go since you're in labor. But under normal circumstances, not a pretty look. Anyway, what I'm saying is I don't have a car. Do you want me to call an Uber?"

"I don't want to go to the hospital in an UBER!" I bark too loudly. I can feel forty-four eyes bore into my back at my admission of a woman about to have a baby on the heels of Courtney's scathing accusation.

I sit up, then stand, handing Roan his laser pointer. I give my dress a little tug down on the side and compose myself for my last words of my first year as head of school.

"Jared, you're most definitely proof that the gamble that Chester Hill and your family made on your future resulted in a positive outcome. As the appointed leader of the Royal-Hawkins School, I am not as comfortable carelessly playing with the lives of promising young men and women. If Marcus and Dontrelle Burns prove themselves to be as hardworking students as they are basketball players their freshman year in high school, then they are absolutely encouraged to reapply, in the fall, following the school's guidelines." I move two steps closer to Winn to emphasize the word *guidelines*. It's an old teacher trick. Move close to a student when you want them to know that a general statement made to all is directed right at them.

"As for the personal developments between the Dunn and Hawkins families, well, ummm, I'm sure Courtney and Winn would like to continue the conversation, umm in private," I conclude, uncertain what the proper next steps are for outing a cheat.

"Oh, I'm done having conversations with Winn Hawkins. I only endured talking to him this year to get to the bottom of what I had been suspecting for quite some time!"

"Still, I don't think a board meeting is the right time to air personal mat . . . OH MOTHER FUCKER!!" The pain is unbearable. I think this baby is trying to walk out of my womb and down the hall to kindergarten. I'm done. Done with this school year. Done with trying to be an infallible head of school. Done with being pregnant. "Can someone please drive me to the hospital? Now!"

"I will, I will!" Courtney demands with no room for argument, grabbing her purse while all the men in the room remain stunned still. Whether their frozen expressions are a result of Courtney's accusations or the theatrics I'm in the middle of is unclear. Either way, if I were Courtney, I'd want an excuse to flee this conference room too.

"Come with me," I beg Roan and then lower my voice. "Don't leave me alone with Courtney."

"But don't you want me to release the admissions emails to all the families? It has to be done tonight."

"Right." I drop my head and think about the email sitting in my draft box clear across campus.

TWENTY-NINE

*D*ing.

I'm trying to heave my body up into the front seat of Courtney's Range Rover and get the door closed before another contraction kicks in and the serene neighborhood surrounding Royal-Hawkins is assaulted with guttural moans I can no longer control.

> **Leo** 7:48 PM
>
> I'm at the airport a bit early to pick up Xandra. Didn't want to take a chance being late with traffic. Should I bring her straight home?

What should I tell him? I wonder, stretching my thumbs prepping to write Leo the text that says his life is about to change forever. Tonight's events are the polar opposite of the birth plan I had for myself. This week and next I was supposed to be tying up my year at school and having a last hurrah with Xandra, just the two of us. Then with Xandra tucked back in boarding school, I had planned to get my box braids freshened up, purchase a few pairs of postbaby jeans, and make things right with Leo. Oh, and a facial to be picture ready when Leo and I stroll into the maternity ward, calm, prepared, and back together, on my due date.

Nina 7:49 PM

Check with Xandra where she would rather go—home or to the hospital. That's my casual attempt at telling you we're having a baby, tonight. Did it work?

Leo 7:49 PM

NO, NOT AT ALL! Okay, okay, meet you there in an hour. The baby won't come within the hour will it? Tell it not to come. Wait how are you getting there? And why are we texting?

Ring.

"Don't have this baby without me, Nina. Please don't!" Leo pleads over the phone.

Ohhh he sounds so desperate. I squeeze my legs together tight with his request. I feel badly I sent him to go get Xandra, but I didn't have any other option.

"Really don't. Xandra and I can't miss it."

My heart melts at his anticipation and his inclusion of Xandra in our growing family. My heart should have been melting six months ago, but here we are and it's time for me to make my move before the next contraction comes and I can't eek out anything other than profanity.

"Leo, I want my ring back," I say, covering my mouth over the phone, hoping Courtney can't hear me. I was going to text it to Leo that now that I'm in labor the prospect of being an unwed mother is much less appealing. I thought I had weeks to create the ultimate venue to profess my idiocy and my love. Instead, right now will have to do.

"What'd you say? Arrrgggghhhh I can't hear you, too many people are honking at me to move, but I'm staying here until I see Xandra. They can honk all they want."

"I want the ring back," I say louder, relinquishing my privacy in an effort to fight the sounds of airport traffic for my future. Courtney's been pretending to mind her own business and drive, but I can see the mention of a ring in front of a slighted wife hits hard. Her knuckles turn white on the steering wheel.

"Yes, when I have your daughter, I'll ring you back. Damn, gotta go, airport security is making me move."

Click.

I don't have time to process the miscommunication with Leo before animal instinct takes over and I grab Courtney's forearm and bear down. *"AAAAAAAAAHHHHHHHHH."* Without flinching Courtney drives on, her hands steady at ten and two.

"There should be a bottle of water under your seat. You don't want to get dehydrated before the main event starts." Courtney smiles at me as I grunt and sweat in her front seat. "This is an exciting end to my very shitty night." In my moment of agony, I had forgotten that the pixie of a woman chauffeuring my ass to the ER just exposed the hottest Royal-Hawkins gossip in well over a decade. Even at the center of it, she had let it rip. I have about four minutes to get to the bottom of the Winn-Geoff affair before I reenter my pain cave.

"About that check," Courtney throws out, turning left. Aha, I should have known. There really is no such thing as a free ride. So, what, Courtney wants to swing by Wells Fargo before this baby crowns? "I need to explain something, especially given my outburst at the board meeting. I swear that wasn't planned, but it's been a difficult couple of months coming to grips with Geoff's affair."

"How long have you known? And, so you know, I often feel like I want to punch Winn Hawkins in the face too," I offer, establishing a common connection.

"HA! Thanks for that, Nina." Admitting my feelings about Winn to another board member is probably the least professional thing I've ever done, but I like that I was able to make another woman laugh in the midst of her personal hell. "Well, Gemma and I have been friends since she and Winn moved back from Australia. I confided in her late last spring that I suspected Geoff was having an affair. She's a great friend and a smart woman, and she suggested I plan an extended family trip over the summer to put some distance between Geoff and his lover."

I choke a little. Everyone has a word or two that gives them the heebie-jeebies. Mine's *lover*.

"That's why we went to Costa Rica for July and August under the guise of Daisy being a budding conservationist. Please, that child spent the whole trip whining for takeout and begging to drive an ATV." I'm about to jump in and tell Courtney there's still hope for Daisy to save the Amazon rainforest, but she looks at me wistfully, tears pooling. "We had a great time as a family. Geoff was totally present. I started to believe that maybe I had been making the whole affair up in my head, reading too much into Geoff's previous elusive behavior."

"Female instinct is as reliable as hard evidence," I say to validate Courtney's line of thinking, and I believe it. Or at least I did until my intuition about spending my life with Leo betrayed me and I'm now exactly where I didn't want to be again, a single mother.

"Yeah, a woman's gut is always right, because by the start of school my suspicions were back on high alert. Then one night in October the four of us were out together, and Geoff and Winn went outside to have a cigar after dinner. A loooong cigar. At the table Gemma broke down that she suspected Winn was stepping out on her. She pulled herself together in time for our two men to reappear at dinner flushed and rumpled. That's when I started to think more creatively about my suspicions." Courtney pauses.

"Wow, all that time I was weirded out that Winn was ogling me or maybe some of the moms at school, but he was horny for the husbands."

"My husband to be exact," Courtney corrects me.

Right. That was a little insensitive of me. I place my hand on her forearm and give it a rub. This woman has been hit hard on the home front, and I want her to know I feel for her.

"So, what're you going to do? I hope you know the school is here to support you and Daisy any way we can. It's what we do." I'm riding right into the maternity ward wearing my head of school hat.

"That's where the check comes in, Nina. Once I suspected Geoff was having an affair, though I never imagined it was with a man, I began distributing his money to charities and organizations all over Southern California. Every time Geoff told me he'd 'be at work late' or had a 'work trip,' I turned around and wrote a check. I know our divorce will be brutal, and he'll fight to the bitter end to make sure I walk away with as close to nothing as possible. That's how he played it with the first Mrs. Dunn. So, I figured if I can't have it, others who actually need it can. There are loads of people all over Los Angeles County super happy with me right now. Geoff's not one of them."

"Damn, Courtney Dunn, I underestimated you and misjudged your intentions. You are fierce!" I say, shocked but profoundly impressed. This is a woman Marisol and I could be friends with.

"Thanks for that, Nina." Courtney rolls her shoulders back in the driver's seat. "Once I started to suspect Geoff's affair was not with a Winifred, but with a Winn, that's when I decided to get a little closer to Winn and figure out for myself what was going on. I did it for me and for Gemma. Do you really think I care about high school basketball?"

"Well, anything's possible," I remind Courtney.

"Don't I know it!" We both laugh, in on the joke that truth is far stranger than fiction. "My push for you to cash the check was for purely selfish motivations. I've been trying to spend Geoff's money as fast as possible. I believe I wrote you that check when Geoff left for a 'work retreat' in Cabo and missed the kids' holiday concert. I spent the entire afternoon craning my neck around the gym trying to find Winn. Instead, I found Gemma there, also alone."

"Hold on, Courtney." I want to hear the end of this private school parable I could have never conjured up if I tried, but my insides are about to tear apart. "GOOOOOOOODDDDDD LOOOOORRRRDDDDD are we almost there?!" I scream between the twisting of my insides.

"Hold on. Two, three minutes tops, I promise," Courtney assures, flooring it through a yellow light. "Anyway, this is enough of my family drama for one night, I just want to let you know I didn't plan to blow up at the board meeting tonight. I really didn't. My plan was to tell you about the affair and why I needed the check cashed ASAP in our one-on-one after the meeting. But then Winn, with Jared as his pawn, shared their plan for those young Burns boys, and I completely lost it."

Lost it is right, I agree in my head.

"Please believe me, Nina, I did not take part in any of their illicit recruitment. I would never falsely prop up another family's hopes and dreams like that. I know the pain of that crash all too well. I wouldn't do that to another mother." I can see Courtney desperately needs me to believe her intentions were not dishonorable. "Is there any way I can help clean up this admissions scandal? And if I can stick it to Winn at the same time, that would be an added bonus."

"I still haven't cashed your check. How about you void the check to the athletics department and start a Dunn family scholarship to support students applying to Royal-Hawkins from more financially challenged households, like first-generation students, single-parent households, underrepresented students, that sort of thing?" Given Courtney's offer, I'm rounding all the bases and taking this headship across home plate.

"How about a half mil?"

"That's GRRRREEEEEAAAATTTT!!" I roar, this contraction coming on top of the last. Courtney pulls in hot to the emergency room entrance and flies out the driver's side to get someone to help me because I'm gripped, unable to move.

Ding.

Leo 8:18 PM

> I got Xandra. We're on our way to the hospital. Tell the baby to Just. Hold. On. Daddy's coming. I love you, Nina.

I love you, too, Leo, I say to myself and know for sure that it's true. My door flies open, and Courtney's there with a wheelchair. "Can I offer you another ride?"

THIRTY

GET YOUR HANDS OFF MY NEPHEW!" Chaco Taco flies into my hospital room fresh off the plane from Phoenix and tosses her carry-on to Leo to catch. After a clean wax, babies are Marisol's weakness. She leans over to give Xandra a kiss on the top of her head, then turns to lift Morgan West out of my arms. I look at Leo. Beaming with new dad pride, he nods his head yes, and I hand over our nine-pound son. He looks just like me, and Leo couldn't be more thrilled.

"I can't believe you went and had this baby without me. We do everything together," Marisol accuses, the rosy blush on her beautiful brown skin streaked through with tears of joy.

Squeezing onto the vinyl loveseat with Xandra, Marisol asks the question I haven't been able to, "What do you think of this guy, Xandra?" There hasn't been a moment alone to talk with Xandra about this new bundle ruining her spring break, let alone her only-child status. Leo refuses to leave our side for a minute, and I must admit I'm reveling in our new family of four.

"I know he won't be borrowing my clothes," Xandra jokes, brushing Morgan's curls across his forehead with her thumb. I swear I hear him gurgle at his sister.

"Where's Fitzroy?" Marisol asks, looking around my already packed room. She knows he can't be far from his family.

Leo jumps on it, saying, "He stepped out to call Celia's sisters in Kingston, he'll be back in a—"

"Chaco Taco, what do you think of my grandson?" Dad booms, entering the room radiating joy that his mark on the world has expanded by one.

"I swear, Fitzroy, between a new woman and a new grandchild, you're growing younger and younger by the day," Marisol says, aiming right for his pride.

"Don't you know it," Fitzroy laughs, flexing his biceps for all to see, then puts his arms out for his grandson. Marisol aggressively shakes her head *NO WAY*. A compliment is all my father's getting from her.

A nurse walks in with the form we have to fill out to receive a legal birth certificate for Morgan. Since Leo and I aren't married, along with the birth worksheet is a paternity affidavit to legally establish that Leo is Morgan's father. I watch Leo stare down at the tiled floor drawing small circles with his left toe as the nurse explains to the whole room why we have to fill out paternity papers even though this man was on board to be Morgan's father long before I was on board to be his mother. In the middle of our bliss, the scene is crushing. Holding the pen, my hands are shaking as the innocent nurse keeps referring to protecting Leo's rights as a father. She rounds out her speech stating she will stay to witness the paperwork being filled out as an authorized notary. Okay, I guess I'm doing this with a full audience.

I heave myself upright in my hospital bed. "Leo, I want my ring back," I state. Simple. Direct. I've learned from my father. I don't want there to be any more misunderstandings. "I love you and I want to marry you." Leo's gaze snaps up from the floor.

"Here, take him." Marisol hands Morgan to Xandra so she can fully witness what's about to go down. I barely get my ring request out before the waterworks go hormonal. Marisol comes over to hold my hand.

"What I really want is the last six months back, Leo. I acted so stupid about you, about us," I choke out between gasps.

"She really did. So stupid," Marisol adds for emphasis and in case Leo didn't hear me. My dad and Xandra confirm with a round of "yeses" and "uh-huhs," giving me a moment to wipe my nose on the sheets.

"I thought by being with you, I would end up being less me. Given our differences, I decided that you wouldn't know how to be the father our child would need; that you couldn't be the partner I need." I reach my hand out for Leo to grab hold. He doesn't move, leaving my arm hanging. That's okay, I wouldn't forgive so easily either.

"But there are some people in this room who are much smarter than me." I look around to my father, Xandra, and Marisol. "They helped me understand that your love and desire to be part of my life and Morgan's life will not hold me back nor diminish our culture, but that you will be our greatest champion to celebrate exactly who we are. Are we going to have miscommunications given our racial differences? Of course. But Graham and I were much more similar than different, or so I thought, and in the end, it was not enough to keep us together."

"Jaime and I can get fired up as two hotheaded Mexicans. He's from a village one over from where I was born, and we are as oil and water as it gets, but you just never know," Marisol announces as a last bit of evidence to my mounting argument that I am a dumbass, and if Leo will have me back, I want in now.

"I want us to be a family. An under the same roof family. Yes, I want my ring back, but if you're unsure about getting married given my crazy behavior, I completely understand. I'm happy to take it slow. We can date. We can live together. We can do it however you want to do it. Please, please, let's do it. Let's do us, our way." My lower lip's quivering, my body trembling with nerves. Leo hasn't moved a muscle since I started my plea.

"If I could just get you to take a look at these papers." Hunched over to sneak around my dad, the nurse scooches them back in front of me, her discomfort obvious.

Leo swiftly grabs the papers, rolls them up, and shoves them in his back pocket. "This doesn't need to be done now. If you could go check on some other patients and come back in a few, that would be great," Leo insists to the nurse, letting her know he's not asking for permission but telling her how it will be.

"I'll be back in thirty to collect those papers," the nurse huffs, then turns and heads out the door. I desperately want to ask her to bring me more ice chips but know this is not the time. I have a negotiation to tie up.

"So, you want to date me and my son?" Leo questions, taking two steps closer to my hospital bed.

"I've already met your son, and he's a stunner, so the hardest part of dating a single dad is already over." My internal shaking subsides with a hint of Leo's humor.

"Yes, well, my son isn't even a day old, and I've already had a major parenting fail, introducing him to my girlfriend too soon."

"But I think he likes me, so that's a good sign." I put my hand back out to pull Leo right up next to my bed. "I hope his dad likes me too."

"His dad does like you, but . . ." Leo pauses. A woman knows a *but* followed by a pause is never good. I close my eyes, steadying myself for heartbreak.

"But what he really is is knock-over, put a fork in him he's done, in love with you. Has been since the moment you had no interest in talking to him at that bar in Santa Barbara. Men love women who play hard to get, and you, Nina Morgan Clarke, have been the hardest one of all to get."

I pull the bed blanket over my head, feigning embarrassment at what a fool I've been. Under the cover I'm bursting with relief that Leo and I may be okay. That we all may be okay. I roll down the blanket to give Leo the toothiest grin I got.

Down on one knee, Leo's holding the velvet box I had been desperately hunting for in his bedroom. Did he actually hear me on the phone last night and swing by his house to pick it up before coming to the hospital? Did he suspect I was nosing through his drawers looking for it? Oh, who cares, the ring's here. It's actually here.

I pluck the box out of Leo's palm. "Can I open it?"

"Please do."

Pop.

"WHAT?!" Shining back at me are four equal-size diamonds lined up along a gold band. This is not the solitaire that was presented to me at ten thousand feet somewhere over Nebraska.

"Whose ring is this?" I ask Leo, beyond confused.

"Yours. One diamond for Morgan, one for Xandra, one for you, and one for me," Leo says, pulling the ring from the box and picking up my left hand. My fingers are swollen, but Leo fights to get the ring on me just like he's been fighting for us all along.

"Wait. How? The other ring? I love it. I mean you." I can't compose a complete thought let alone a sentence.

Leo nods to Marisol. "She had faith you'd come around."

"And when you did, I didn't want you in some twenty-year-old's ring. You need something, shall we say, age appropriate." Marisol picks up my hand to inspect her good work. "Well done, Leo," Marisol says, giving Leo her sisterly approval.

"With you and T. J. on my team, I just may have a fighting chance at being a good father and a good husband."

I look at Marisol and raise my right eyebrow, reminding her, cradle to crypt, she is first and foremost on my team. She squeezes my hand to let me know she hears me. She always hears me.

"Mom, are you going to say yes? This baby's getting heavy," Xandra asks, having reached her teenage limit holding a newborn.

"I'd like to hear your answer as well, Nina. Contrary to what Marisol says, I'm not actually getting any younger," Fitzroy chimes in, having spent the last several minutes as the patriarch of our family quietly observing his daughter's future unfold.

"I haven't been asked anything yet," I say, looking to Leo expectantly. Leo lets out the easy, warm laugh I've missed.

"Nina Morgan Clarke, will you marry me?"

"Yes," I declare, falling back into my hospital pillows, breathless from fatigue and happiness.

"I can't wait to invite the world to our wedding, I love a good party!" Leo does a jig right there in our cramped room. Soooo first marriage of him.

"You can invite anyone you want, baby," I assure Leo. "Except your Singapore Sloan. That chick is not coming to our wedding."

NEW TRIMESTER

THIRTY-ONE

Marisol 8:22 AM

> How'd you do leaving Morgan with your Spanny this morning?

I look down at the two-tone gray car seat covered in a green gauze swaddle blanket. I rock it gently back and forth with the big toe of my Gucci-clad foot. I don't want Marisol to hear Morgan cry over text.

Nina 8:22 AM

> Fine.

Marisol 8:23 AM

> He's at school with you, isn't he?

Nina 8:23 AM

> He's very advanced.

Ring.

"Where's the nanny?" Marisol demands.

"I gave her the day off."

"She must be something special if she got her first day of work off." I can feel Marisol crossing her arms in judgment on the other end. "We talked about this, Nina. And did a dry run last week to get you ready for your return to school."

"I know we did, but . . ."

"But what? No one else can take care of Morgan as well as you can?" Since Morgan came home from the hospital, Marisol's been worried about me going back to work the first of August. I'd always considered myself more of a TGIM than TGIF type of mom, but turns out birthing a body and adjusting to life on baby lockdown did not go as smoothly as I expected.

Surprising to no one but me, sixteen years later I didn't remember the ins and outs of infancy nor the hallucinations that come with week after week of no sleep. More than once, I wondered if I had made a drastic mistake trading my life in for a new one, but then moments before a meltdown (mine, not Morgan's) Leo would sweep in with his Black to Basics parenting tidbits and take over while I took myself to the shower. Turns out not only is Leo a master at diaper changing, bottle feeding, and laundry, but he's already introduced Morgan to his Marisol. T. J.'s son, Ace, was born a few days after Morgan. Now the four of them hit the playground to check out the older kids' sandbox skills and Little League.

While I thought I would be clamoring to head back to work, my four-month maternity leave has gone quicker than I expected, and I'm not sure I'm ready to return. In the last month, we have hit our stride at home, and now I'm risking toppling our tenuous microcosm by heading back to work. But I guess today is as good as any to mark my first day as Royal-Hawkins's quadfecta. A first-generation Black female mother-of-two head of school.

"I can't believe I was able to leave Xandra at daycare when she was barely six months old. That was some stone-cold parenting when I was young. I've grown mushy as an old mom."

"You're not an old mom. You're the mother of a newborn in an old bod," Marisol says, getting my facts correct. "Xandra turned out just fine, and so will Morgan. But I get it"—Marisol's tone softens—"I wouldn't even leave my boys alone with Jaime their first few months, but I eventually gave in and hired Spanny when I realized spas are not conducive to sleep schedules. Besides, Morgan won't be with a total stranger, he will be with KayCee's niece."

I peel back the gauzy coverlet and peek in at the oversize chunk consumed with the wonder of his tiny fingers. Every time I take Morgan to the pediatrician to be measured and weighed, she comments that given his size I may have a budding basketball player on my hands. I haven't told Jared the good news yet.

"How lucky are you that you can now afford to step out AND staff up. Spanny coming to work for my family was the best thing that ever happened to my career—professional and parental. And it will be for you, too, because while you love being a mother, you also love being a head of school."

"Maybe tomorrow I'll be able to do it," I offer as a possible sign of progress. The beginning of August is fairly quiet on all school campuses, but particularly this week at Royal-Hawkins with Roan on his long-awaited trip to Paris. He desperately wanted to stroll the Seine for his honeymoon, and a broken engagement didn't stop him. Roan's feeding his Francophile alter ego with twice-daily croissants and bottles of Bordeaux with his past head of school and good friend Josie Bordelon. His last text to me simply read, Tate who? So, I have a couple of weeks to settle back in and redefine my leadership style now that I'm a working mother of two.

Once I'm off the phone with Marisol, I've got to go find Pablo, who, Mimi informed me, has been champing at the bit to meet Morgan. Between Chaco Taco and Pablo, I plan on having a bilingual baby. Hopefully, he'll have a better ear for language than his mother.

"Do you remember what you were doing just over a year ago?" Marisol asks mischievously. Thinking, thinking. My mind draws a blank.

"I don't even remember anything I did last week other than walk Morgan endlessly around the neighborhood, so he'd fall asleep. Last year feels like a lifetime ago."

"You were doing the walk of shame back to our hotel room," Marisol hoots, the memory surely clear as yesterday in her mind. My love life continues to be her favorite form of entertainment.

"Best walk of my life," I reminisce, remembering me in my turquoise wrap dress, stench of marathon sex and zero guilt. "And to think I had declared this last year to one as a no-drama mama."

"*Dios mío*, we read those tea leaves wrong. But I wouldn't change a thing, would you?" Marisol loves to ask questions she knows the answers to. Makes her feel smart. "Yikes, I gotta go, drama mama. Diego and Paco are barking down my back for pancakes before lacrosse camp. Later, lady. *Besos!*"

I look around what used to be an office for one but is currently home to the two of us. At least for today. I get up to close my door in case Mimi shows up with an extra latte and catches me midpump. I plug in, strap up, and crank some Diana Ross circa Motown to drown out the *whoosh swoosh whoosh* of my breast pump that has become the soundtrack of my life. I open up my inbox and see an email from Carmel Burns at the top of a four-month heap.

FROM: Carmel Burns
DATE: August 1
SUBJECT: Jared Jones
TO: Nina Morgan Clarke

Dear Nina,

Hope you and that baby of yours are doing good. I'm not sure if you're back at work or not but I wanted to say thank you for hooking Dontrelle and Marcus up to work with Jared over the summer. To have an accomplished young Black man show my boys that they can be students and athletes, that the choice is not one or the other, has been life changing for our family. Last night instead of playing video games Dontrelle was reading a book Jared gave him. I almost fainted washing the dinner dishes!

Also, it was so nice of Roan to send me the Royal-Hawkins application steps and deadlines for next year. I don't think we'll apply since it's so far away by bus, but knowing you, Roan, and Jared believe in my boys makes me think looking at private schools closer to home could be a possibility. Or maybe they'll stand out as freshmen with all the tutoring from Jared and they'll want to stay at our local school. Whatever happens, it's nice to know my boys have options.

Best to you and your family,
Carmel Burns

Roan, that softie! In our own ways, none of us could let the Burns twins fall through the cracks after Winn's spring power play with Dontrelle's and Marcus's lives.

Morgan and I were released from the hospital on a Sunday afternoon. Given his concern about driving us home in traffic, a lazy Sunday was the best day for Leo's maiden voyage transporting his son. Once we had gone a few blocks from the hospital and Leo was gaining confidence, I asked if we could make a stop before we made it home. Leo looked at me like I had two heads and one was spouting nonsense, but he relented seeing as I had just delivered him an heir.

I couldn't get past the fact that I hadn't been able to send Carmel Burns my email ahead of the Royal-Hawkins admissions decisions going out to families. I knew my laptop was sitting on my desk, email open, one draft waiting to be sent. I only needed five minutes in my office to tidy up my old life before I could fully invest in my new one.

Although Leo was initially terrified to be left alone with Morgan, I promised him our son would not combust without his mother. Leo had me check that my phone was on and charged just in case he spotted flames. My office was as I had left it. A cold half cup of coffee and an empty sandwich wrapper had been keeping each other company on my desk. The throw pillows on my couch were stacked to one side, exposing the catnap I had had to take before the board meeting four short days ago. My laptop was on my desk, but the top was closed instead of open. On it was a neon pink Post-it.

Email sent. You're welcome. Now stop worrying about work.
XO Roan

Roan Dawson, for the game-day save.

I still had four more minutes before Leo would strong-arm the police into putting out a missing mother's report. I opened my laptop and let my fingers fly before my brain caught up to consider if what I was about to send was a good idea or not.

> **FROM:** Nina Morgan Clarke
> **DATE:** April 6
> **SUBJECT:** Burns Twins
> **TO:** Courtney Dunn
>
> Dear Courtney,
>
> Thanks again for the hospital transport. Not that I deserve any more favors, you've done more than your fair share for me, but if you're still trying to Robin Hood Geoff's money, I have an idea that I think will help remedy the disaster that was Winn's

meddling. Would you be willing to sponsor Jared Jones mentoring Marcus and Dontrelle Burns over the summer?

Thank you for considering.

Yours in community,
Nina Morgan Clarke
Head of School
Royal-Hawkins School

Before I could close my laptop, Courtney was in my inbox.

FROM: Courtney Dunn
DATE: April 6
SUBJECT: Burns Twins
TO: Nina Morgan Clarke

Done and Dunn!

Jai,
Courtney

Victory is right. Turns out Courtney Dunn is more of a strategic thinker than I had given her credit for, and my school will be a better place because of it. Winn's motives were way off, but I'm willing to give credit where credit's due. He did all right strong-arming Courtney onto the board of trustees.

Nina 2:46 PM

I promise the baby won't break. Xandra's still intact as evidence. I need ten more minutes.

Leo 2:47 PM

> Morgan started to cry so I took him out of the
> car seat, reclined my seat back and put him on
> my chest. He stopped crying! But now we can't
> move so take your time.

I opened the cabinet behind my desk, and a lonely bag of corn dippers was waiting for me, knowing I'd be back. I pulled them out and ripped 'em open. The taste of the familiar, in familiar surroundings, when so much had changed so quickly was grounding. Before I left my castle to become an indentured servant to my new little king, I knew I had one last email to send out as queen.

FROM: Nina Morgan Clarke
DATE: April 6
SUBJECT: Your service
TO: Winn Hawkins

Dear Winn,

Thank you for your service as the Board Chair of the Royal-Hawkins School. Your tenure has not benefited the school in ways befitting a respectable leader. Effective immediately, you have been removed from the board of trustees. Courtney Dunn will be stepping into the chair leadership position when the board resumes meeting on August 1.

Nina Morgan Clarke
Head of School
Royal-Hawkins School

My apologies, Alice Royal-Hawkins. I closed my laptop and hoped Courtney would agree to chair since vice chair Kym Lee was moving to Baltimore, but I had already asked one favor of her today, so this one would have to wait for another day. It was time for me to go home and be with my family for the next four months.

"Look who I found in the hallway, Nina." Jared completely fills out my doorway with my sixteen-year-old daughter tucked under his arm. Xandra looks like she just discovered that heaven comes in a six-foot-four frame. I hop up, almost tripping over Morgan's baby bucket, to dislodge Xandra from her never-going-to-happen fantasy.

"I didn't know you had a daughter," Jared says, suggesting we are friends and I've withheld important information from him, rather than a boss and a young man teetering close to the edge of unemployment.

"She was at boarding school last year, but now she's back for summer. Actually, back for good." I give Xandra a squeeze around the waist that says *I'm glad you're back* and *I've got my eye on you.*

"So, you're going to go to school with your mom?" Jared chuckles. "That's a trip."

"No, she'll be a JUNIOR," I emphasize, "at one of the local high schools. She decided to return home after the Royal-Hawkins application deadline. Rules are rules." A hint of passive aggression can go a long way to remind a person of former mistakes.

It turned out Morgan's birth colliding with Xandra's spring break was good timing. Sitting side by side on the couch bingeing Netflix, me breastfeeding Morgan and Xandra trying, unsuccessfully, not to be grossed out, incited an unexpected waterfall of teenage confession. Surprise, surprise (but not to me) Mr. Petrov wasn't a racist, but a teacher with a thing for punctuality and a deep respect for the arts. And, in fact, after Xandra's many attempts to scrub the image of her mother being groped in the driveway coupled with time getting to know Leo over the holidays, my bougie ways were also not the problem. The real problem Xandra didn't know how to articulate to me or to Graham, was that she didn't want to be at Pemberley. Instead, she fell into the predictable teenage trap of being an asshole. She never wanted to attend Pemberley. And now that she had a sibling, she wanted to stay. At home. With me. And Morgan and Leo. It took every ounce of my self-control to not break out in a Rose Bowl touchdown dance.

Xandra confessed she only agreed to go to Pemberley because Graham was moving to New York, and she was worried he was going to be lonely and the idea of her going to Pemberley made him so happy. I didn't mean to make Xandra's declaration about me, but I had to know why she was more worried about Graham being alone in New York than she was about me being alone in Pasadena. Xandra had laughed out loud at my turn playing the asshole and pointed out that I had Marisol and her family, Fitzroy for much of the year, and an entire school to keep me company.

Xandra shared that Graham was now successfully navigating several dating websites, which made sense when I thought back to how upbeat and playful he had been at Xandra's play. The loneliness Xandra claimed consumed Graham after our divorce had given way to excitement for a new start-up venture he was exploring. In Xandra's assessment, Graham was solid so now she could return home—where she always wanted to be.

In rushed moments during Morgan's catnaps, we strategized how to approach Graham with Xandra's desire to leave Pemberley. Ultimately, I assured Xandra that her father would understand. Down deep I knew I might have to do some tough behind-the-scenes work to get Graham on board, but Xandra carrying the burden of her parents' happiness had to stop immediately. Xandra needed to focus on Xandra.

"What are you doing on campus?" I ask Jared, thinking he must have somewhere better to be on a summer morning.

"Just stopped by to borrow a couple of copies of *The Grapes of Wrath* to give Dontrelle and Marcus. They've been getting into reading this summer, and it's one of my favorite books, so I wanted to share."

"I remember," I say. Jared looks at me quizzically. "Halloween."

"That's right," Jared replies, scratching the back of his head with a sheepish grin. "You remember everything." Not on four hours of sleep, but I try.

"Yes, I do, Jared." Better for Jared to believe I have a steel-trap mind than a sieve. Hopefully this misnomer will incentivize him to have a better second year teaching at Royal-Hawkins than his first.

"Since you hooked me up with the summer gig with the twins, is it okay if I borrow the books?" Jared asks, looking for permission after his plan had been hatched. "Promise I'll have them back on my shelf before school starts." I nod *of course*. Even late, remembering to ask my permission is definitely a show of maturity. I still believe Jared Jones is a worthy educator in progress. I look down at Morgan in his car seat. *Men are a lot of work*, I think to myself, *but cross fingers worth the effort.*

"Catch you ladies later." Jared beams. Even his goodbyes light up a room. Tongue-tied Xandra can only wave.

"I look forward to seeing you at the end of August, Jared. It's going to be a great school year," I assure, putting a hand on Jared's back and walking him out the door. And I believe it.

I have a summer breakfast board meeting in fifteen minutes and need to gather my thoughts before the first public viewing of postpregnancy Nina. Since she passed her driver's test last week, I give Xandra the keys to the car, but not the baby. He's staying with me. I remind Xandra that Leo and I are going house hunting this afternoon, and I expect her home by three to babysit. There's a house right around the corner from Fitzroy and KayCee that I think will go fast, so I want to get in there before a bidding war starts. Consumed by the power of the car keys, I'm fairly certain Xandra heard none of my fourteen-point driving safety speech before skipping off to freedom. It's okay, my first baby's back.

Leo 8:46 AM

What are you wearing?

How sweet. Leo's checking in to make sure I didn't head back to work in sweats and a milk-stained shirt.

Nina 8:47 AM

Red flowy sundress and pink sweater in case the conference room air conditioning is on blast.

I'm so damn happy my feet fit back in my Gucci shoes; they pair perfectly with the summer sophisticate image I'm going for.

Leo 8:47 AM

Perfect outfit for house hunting.

Nina 8:48 AM

Why?

Leo 8:48 AM

Easy access.

Nina 8:49 AM

OH . . .

Leo 8:50 AM

This is our first date off the couch and out of the house since Morgan was born. We need to make sure the closets are big enough for a quickie.

Sophisticate turns tramp real fast.

Nina 8:51 AM

You're naughty Leo West.

Leo 8:51 AM

I'm not naughty, I'm in love.

"You ready to do this?" Courtney sticks her head in my office, catching me midblush. Dressed in a yellow pencil skirt and crisp white blouse, she looks like a woman who has shed some deadweight. I couldn't TOTALLY disassociate myself from school during my maternity leave. Courtney came by a few afternoons bearing gifts of Chinese food and lemonade and to fill me in on school news since my memorable exit. The day after school was out, so was Gemma. She packed up the kids and left for Sydney, and Winn followed shortly after. Polite rumor has it he went to be near his kids, but others speculate it was to flee his inflated sense of self-importance that everyone would still care about his affair once summer hit. Geoff chased after Winn, and last Courtney knew via a postcard to Daisy, he was traveling through the outback. Unclear if he was alone or Winn was in tow.

Meanwhile, with Geoff out of the picture and Courtney devastated at the prospect of Benjamin no longer being in her life, she struck up an unexpected friendship with the first Mrs. Dunn. According to Courtney, cutting out the middleman and sharing kids with a sister-wife is hands down the best way to parent.

Courtney carefully picks Morgan up out of his car seat while I strap myself into my frontloading baby carrier. I snuggle Morgan down in there, his legs spread wide, our heartbeats pressed against one another. Courtney inconspicuously tucks a spit-up cloth into the left hip strap just in case. I tilt my chin down, kiss the top of Morgan's head, and whisper, "Be good for mama, this is a big day for us."

Standing in front of my twenty-two trustees, I rock side to side, lulling Morgan to sleep and soothing my nerves. Courtney gives me the thumbs-up that it's time to get started. I clear my throat and hum to find the right key to belt out Alicia Keys's "Girl on Fire."

Nah, I wouldn't do that, that's something a twenty-four-year-old would do. At forty-four, I am woman on fire.

319

ACKNOWLEDGMENTS

We have an uncanny propensity for writing topical books that coincide with social and cultural shifts in the United States. Our first book, *Tiny Imperfections*, about gaming the private school admissions season, was copyedited mere months before Varsity Blues seized every news outlet in America. *Never Meant to Meet You*, our second book about Black Baptist and White Jewish neighbors, was written during the vacuum of the pandemic and launched just as one of the ugliest waves of antisemitism in American history crashed onto our country's shores.

The last *i* was dotted and the final *t* was crossed on *The Better Half* as hints that *Roe v. Wade* might be overturned began to appear. We started chapter one when all American women had reproductive rights protected by law, and our book highlights that security for women of all ages. Never did we consider that our lead character, Nina Morgan Clarke, as well as our sisters, daughters, friends, and even ourselves, would lose autonomy over our bodies at the same time we were finishing this book. There is no truer and—in this era of dismantling women's rights—more painful statement than "truth is stranger than fiction."

We are thrilled that Mindy Kaling, Carmen Johnson, and the team at Mindy's Book Studio fell in love with Nina Morgan Clarke and her family as well as the topical challenges the characters in the book face regarding the immigrant experience in the United States, late-in-life pregnancy, racial identity and tension, privilege, and education. That Mindy's Book Studio trusted in our ability to address these sensitive topics with humor and joy was a bonus. We would like to thank everyone on Mindy's Book Studio team for their trust in us and for giving Nina Morgan Clarke a voice in the world.

We have said it before and we will say it again and again: Liza Fleissig, there ain't no other agent than you who can do it better. We wish every writer could have such a caring and loyal professional to count on to step up and support exceptional storytelling. Alison Dasho, our acquisitions editor at Amazon Publishing, the joy is all ours every time you email, call, or we hop on a Chime. You are the third lioness in our Triple A pack, and we recognize how scrappy you are when you fight for us. Tegan Tigani, development editor extraordinaire, you deliver editorial feedback with smiles and sunshine, making us believe that all the work we need to do is not only possible but necessary because we know that you know a good story.

With every book we write our gratitude grows for our parents, husbands, and children, who allow us to continue the emotional roller coaster that is birthing books into the world, as does our appreciation for each other. Writing is an extremely intimate act, one that most writers do solo. When writing happens between two highly opinionated women (one Black, one White) and encompasses the tricky topics of race, religion, privilege, and love, some might imagine it an impossible creative feat. But we have managed to get better and better—together. Our writing, balancing our working relationship, and our shared dissection of heart-wrenching topics hasn't gotten easier, but our commitment to valuing each other's ideas with care and attention has. We wouldn't have it any other way.

ABOUT THE AUTHORS

Photo © 2018 J Garner Photography

Alli Frank has worked in education for more than twenty years, from boisterous public high schools to small, progressive private schools. A graduate of Cornell and Stanford University, Alli lives in the Pacific Northwest with her husband and two daughters. With Asha Youmans, she is the coauthor of *Tiny Imperfections* and *Never Meant to Meet You* and is a contributing essayist in the anthology *Moms Don't Have Time To: A Quarantine Anthology*.

Asha Youmans spent two decades teaching elementary school students. A graduate of the University of California, Berkeley, Asha lives in the Pacific Northwest with her husband and two sons. With Alli Frank, she is the coauthor of *Tiny Imperfections* and *Never Meant to Meet You*.

For more information visit the authors at www.alliandasha.com or @alliandasha.